Storm Testament VII
WALKARA

Storm Testament VII
WALKARA

LEE NELSON

Council Press

Council Press
P.O. Box 531
Springville, Utah 84663
ISBN 0-936860-27-8

Printed in the United States of America

Fifth Printing, September 1996

To Bobby,
whose determination and
spirit sometimes reminds
me of a great war chief.

Prologue

by Dan Storm

I have seen some remarkable sights in my day—like ten thousand buffalo stampeding across the prairie, riverboats exploding on the icy waters of the upper Missouri River, even an enraged grizzly bear roaring at me less than ten feet away. But without a doubt the most majestic sight I ever saw was on a clear May morning in 1840 when I witnessed a young Ute chief named Walkara galloping at the head of 3,000 stampeding horses towards the Provo River, where nearly 50 bands of Utes were camped for their annual fish festival. This was seven years before white settlers came to the area.

I was with my friend Neuwafe and the Paw-gwan-nuance band of Utes, or the Lake Shore People. Several weeks earlier we had moved our camp onto one of the sprawling meadows near the mouth of the Provo River. The squawfish and speckled trout had begun to spawn. The Utes called the squawfish pahgar, and the trout mpahgar. The shallow waters along the edge of the lake as well as the river were now swarming with fish so eager to mate that they seemed to have lost most of their fear of men with poles and spears.

As millions of fish swarmed up the Provo River to spawn, many of the family clans known as Utes or Yutahs, some from hundreds of miles away, swarmed towards the Provo River to feast on the now easy-to-catch fish at the annual fish festival.

In addition to gorging on fish, this was the Indians' time for trading, renewing old friendships, horse racing, gambling, even courting.

If any man could be considered chief over all the Utes it was Sowiette, Walkara's older brother. He and his band had arrived at the fish festival several days earlier.

I was walking along a rocky ridge, gathering firewood, when I saw Walkara and his herd of horses. The first thing I noticed was the dust, a huge brownish cloud that appeared to be blowing out of the mouth of Spanish Fork Canyon to the southwest. At first I thought it was a storm cloud, or smoke from a brushfire.

Then I saw the horses, at first just a few, running down a sagebrush ridge. Sometimes I had seen as many as forty or fifty animals in a herd belonging to a band of Utes. Most of the time the herds were smaller. At first I thought a new band was arriving, the Indians pushing their horses ahead of them. But the herd became larger. Soon the whole hillside was covered with running horses, with the end not yet in sight.

I had been with the Utes long enough to appreciate what I was seeing. To the American Indian tribes of the mid 1800's the horse was king. Tribes with horses were vastly superior to those without. In battle the mounted warrior had advantage over the one on foot. Upon finding a herd of buffalo, a man on a fast horse in one afternoon could kill enough meat to feed his family for nearly a year, provided his squaws were proficient at making jerky or pemican. With plenty of food put away there was time for traveling, trading, exploring, crafts, even religion. And, of course, with horses, men could engage in the favorite pastime of all, stealing more horses.

Prologue

The four items of greatest worth to a Ute warrior were horses, guns, women and firewater, not necessarily in that order, but with the horse usually first. With enough horses a man could buy guns, whiskey and even another squaw. Seldom was more than one or two horses paid for a woman. A man with two horses was looked on as well equipped. A man with five horses was prosperous, and a man with ten or more horses was wealthy.

The problem with having a lot of horses was hanging onto them. The more horses one had, the easier it was for his enemies to steal them. It wasn't uncommon for a man with a fortune in horses one day not to have any the next.

These were some of the thoughts going through my mind as I saw, not hundreds, but thousands of horses galloping out of the mouth of Spanish Fork Canyon that spring day. Several hundred men were driving the herd, mostly Indians, but also some white trappers.

I had learned earlier that Walkara and his men had gone to the land the Spanish called California earlier that spring to steal horses from the huge Spanish ranches located in the land bordering the Pacific Ocean. Apparently they had been successful. I found myself wishing I could have gone with Walkara on such a great adventure.

I had been with the Utes long enough to want to be a horse thief too. Among Indians stealing horses was an honorable thing to do, along with taking scalps and chasing buffalo. While one did not take horses from relatives and neighbors, there was nothing wrong with taking all you could get from an enemy band, the white trappers, or the Spanish in California or Mexico.

As the huge herd reached the encampment I couldn't help but notice the two riders in front. One was a muscular, bare-chested Indian over six feet tall. His

3

long black hair was not braided, but hung loose about his powerful shoulders, blowing recklessly in the spring wind. His facial features were strong, his eyes intense.

He was riding a tall, powerful, roan mare with a silver-studded Spanish saddle and bridle. He wore buckskin leggings and cowhide boots with large Spanish spurs. He rode straight in the saddle, tall and strong, like a king or a general. He and the powerful horse were one, the animal responding to every leg movement of the rider. I was impressed, even awed, at this first glimpse of Walkara, the greatest horse thief in the world.

Riding beside him, on a magnificent black stallion, was a grinning, bare-headed white trapper. His head was bald on top, a horseshoe of wind-twisted red hair above his ears and around the back.

Though I had not met the man, I recognized the trapper as the one the Utes called Wa-he-to-co, which meant wooden leg. The white men called him Peg Leg Smith. Walkara's sister had become one of his wives. The Utes said Peg Leg was the bravest of all the white men they had known.

Later that evening I met Peg Leg. He was seated on the ground beside a cook fire, and one of his young wives had just brought him a fillet of roasted trout. I introduced myself to him. He wanted to know how a white boy of only 16 years had come to live with the Utes.

After telling him my story, I asked how he had come to live with the Utes. Stretching back on a blanket, looking up at the stars, his hands behind his head, he told me his story.

His real name was Thomas L. Smith, and he was raised on a 33-acre farm on Dick's River between Crab Orchard and Lancaster, Kentucky. At an early age he had traveled with his father among the local Indian tribes, selling illegal firewater. He hated school and the brutal beatings of a drunken father, so at age 15 he ran away from home.

After spending the winter in Natchez, Mississippi he joined a band of friendly Osages, where he promptly followed his father's example and began a profitable but illegal whiskey business. He moved into his own tepee with an Osage squaw who by summer was pregnant. He found he had a talent for learning languages, not only that of the Osages, but those of the Cherokee, Choctaw and Chickasaw as well.

Then one day he was gone, heading up the Mississippi River with a French trapper named Antoine Robidoux to get a real taste of western trapping in Illinois where he mastered the languages of the Saux Fox and Potowatomie tribes.

During the winter of his 21st birthday Smith contracted malaria. In his delirium he cried out for home. His faithful Indian friends wrapped him in blankets and, by canoe and travois, moved him to Boone's Lick, Missouri, where his older sister lived. There he recuperated.

Smith rejoined Robidoux, who was then at St. Joseph. They wintered in 1822-23 in Nebraska. After a successful season of trapping, Smith went to St. Louis for supplies. After getting involved in a drunken brawl, he ended up in jail.

One day he was served lunch wrapped in a greasy newspaper. Beginning to read the newspaper, he noticed an advertisement for men to join the William Ashley-Andrew Henry expedition to explore and trap the upper Yellowstone. James Clyman, a friend of Smith's, was listed as the recruiter. Smith got word to Clyman, who bailed him out of jail and offered him a job as interpreter and trapper for the expedition. After completing his responsibilities to Robidoux, Smith departed with Ashley for the Yellowstone on March 11, 1823. He was 22 years old.

Two months later he was involved in his first Indian battle, with the Arikaras near present-day Pierre, South Dakota. When he exposed himself to enemy fire to rescue a wounded companion, he established himself as a leader among the trappers. His bravery was seldom challenged after that. By September the party had turned south into the lands of the Shoshones and Utes.

Smith had his first encounter with Utes later that year. He was trapping along the Green River with two white men, Marlow and Hooper, and three Mexicans. Suddenly the Utes attacked, killing one of the Mexicans instantly, and as the trappers scampered for cover, the Utes drove off the mules loaded with supplies and furs.

The remaining two Mexicans headed for Mexico, never to be seen again, but Smith led Marlow and Hooper in pursuit of the Utes. Two days later he caught up with them, marching boldly into their camp, shouting at them that they had made a big mistake, and if they didn't return his mules and supplies immediately, they would be very sorry.

In their astonishment the Utes returned the belongings to the white men. Never had they seen white men as brave as Smith and his companions. The three remained with the Utes, using the Indian camp as their base of operations while trapping that winter.

A few years later, Smith was again working for William Ashley and Andrew Henry near the headwaters of the South Platte River when his party was attacked by Crow Indians. In an attempt to rescue a wounded companion, in apparent disregard for Indian marksmanship, Smith was shot in the left ankle at close range, the impact of the bullet taking his foot out from under him. When he attempted to step forward, he looked down at jagged bones. The battle raged on for another hour, Smith cursing loudly the entire time.

When the dust settled, nine Indians and three trappers lay dead. Pratt, the leader of the expedition, had been scalped. The men carried Smith a mile or so to a safer location and gave him a shot of whiskey to kill the pain, but made no further effort to care for the wound. They guessed he was dying.

Delirious and angry, Smith leveled his rifle at the cook, Joseph Bejux, and ordered him to sterilize a butcher knife with which Smith began his own amputation. As he did so he cursed his companions for their cowardice.

Between periods of nausea and fainting Smith managed to cut away all the shattered bone and flesh except the Achilles tendon before passing out completely. Milton Sublette finished the job, smoothing the jagged edges as best he could.

Sublette was about to apply a hot iron to the stub to cauterize it when Smith regained consciousness. He refused to have the wound seared, saying that if he was going to die he would and didn't want to be reminded ahead of time what hell would be like.

In the days to come he raved feverishly, but refused to die. With the bloody stub wrapped in a soiled shirt and tied with leather thongs, Smith bounced along behind his companions on a crude travois they had fashioned for him.

After traveling 150 miles, Smith was still alive. Smith knew he was dying, but asked no favors, and received none, except from Sublette, who tried to get the wounded man to eat and drink.

After about two weeks the party came upon the same band of Utes that Smith had wintered with earlier. Smith was unconscious when they turned him over to the Indians, asking if he could remain with them until he died. By now his leg was as big as his waist, and full of gangrene and infection. Blood poisoning was inching upward towards his heart. Smith's white companions figured it was only a matter of a few hours before he would die.

As Smith's companions rode away, the squaws tore away his rotten shirt, cleaned the wound, and smothered it in roots, tobacco juice, and horse manure. Within 24 hours, Smith regained consciousness. The temperature began to drop. He began recognizing those around him. Once the leg healed, Smith fashioned himself an oak leg, which he fastened to his real leg with rawhide lashings.

It was late when Peg Leg finished telling me his story. I felt flattered that he would spend so much time sharing his history with me, especially after just returning from a long journey.

His wives and children were hungry for his attention. As Peg Leg told me his story they were continually bringing us things to eat and drink.

After he finished showing me how he removed and secured his wooden leg, I asked him to tell me more about Walkara.

"Not tonight, my boy," he responded, yawning. I got up to leave.

"The Walkara story cannot be told in a few minutes."

"Why's that?" I asked.

"He is a great man."

I had never heard anyone say something like that about an Indian before. I waited for him to continue.

"His share of the herd you saw today makes him the wealthiest Indian in America. He's probably the greatest horse thief in the world. He speaks six languages—English, Spanish, Ute, Shoshone, Navajo, and Goshute. He is a leader of hundreds of men, a fearless fighter, and immune to the hardships of the trail. He can ride.from here to San Bernardino in less than two weeks without a murmur, then turn around and ride back again. Yet, as tough as he is, his heart aches near breaking for a woman he can't have. Come back tomorrow and I'll tell you his story."

I promised Peg Leg I'd be back. As I turned to leave, two of his young squaws, each taking one of his hands, pulled the grinning trapper to his feet and escorted him to his lodge.

I came back the next day, and the next after that, listening eagerly to Peg Leg's seemingly endless stories about Walkara. I was even invited to ride out with Peg Leg and Walkara as they oversaw the dividing up of the huge horse herd among the 200 Indians who rode with them to California.

From that time forward I was a serious student of Walkara, up until the day he died in 1855. Even after that I would hear an occasional story about something he had done or said. In the end, I had to agree with Peg Leg, that Walkara was indeed a great man, and probably the greatest horse thief in the history of the world. Following is his story.

Some may object to the savage and brutal side of this story, but I don't know how else to tell it. Walkara lived in a savage and brutal world.

Chapter 1

Walkara was only in his sixteenth year, but he had no trouble keeping up with his older brothers as they scooped out a sizeable hole on the red shale sidehill just south of where the Pequi-nary-no-quint (Spanish Fork River) enters the sprawling grassland valley of the Utes. From where the boys worked they could see the sky blue waters of Yutah Lake and the snow-covered peaks of Mt. Timpanogos. The lush green grasslands to the north and west were just beginning to turn gold under the warm summer sun.

But the Ute boys, their backs glistening with sweat in the warm sun, did not notice the breathtaking scenery as they continued to throw chunks of red shale out of the growing pit. The usual laughter and teasing of boys engaged in tedious work was absent too.

Walkara and his older brothers—Sowiette, San Pitch, Grosspeen and Arrapeen—were digging their father's grave.

Below them in the oak brush they could hear the wailing of the women and the regular swishing throb beats of gravel-filled gourds.

Sowiette, the oldest of the five brothers, would frequently stop working, his alert black eyes scanning the familiar grasslands to the north. He didn't think the Timpany Utes would attack again soon, especially now they had all the good horses, but one could never be sure of what Pahrant, the Timpany Ute head man, would do.

With Moonch now dead, the leadership of the small family clan rested upon Sowiette, the oldest son—at least until someone else challenged. Sowiette was in his twenty-fifth year.

The Timpany Utes had attacked early the previous morning, driving off twelve of the band's thirteen horses and killing Moonch. Sowiette, Walkara and Arrapeen had been away fishing at the time.

Pahrant and Moonch had always been on more or less friendly terms, even though the Timpany Utes far outnumbered Moonch's little family clan. But in the past year Pahrant had formed an alliance with the Shoshones to the north, in exchange for horses, and had become increasingly hostile towards Moonch.

The Shoshones were traditional enemies of the Ute tribe, consisting of about 50 clans. Through intermarriages and newly developed trading alliances, the Timpany Utes had developed growing ties with the Shoshones while pulling further and further away from their traditional bonding with their fellow Utes. The attack on Moonch's band was the final move. The Timpany Utes were now Shoshones, at least as far as Moonch's tiny band was concerned.

A month earlier, while Moonch and his band were camped on the Timpanogos River, later called the Provo River, a messenger from the Timpany camp had entered the village announcing that Pahrant would come the next day to receive a gift of five horses. With the band's entire horse herd numbering only thirteen, there was no way Moonch would give even a single horse to his neighbor.

Pahrant's demand for five horses was not so much an action to get horses as it was a challenge to fight. Rather than battle his former friends, Moonch had ordered his clan to pack their things and move to the south end of the valley to Pequi-nary-no-quint, thinking peace could be maintained if more distance were put between his little band and the Timpany Utes.

He was wrong. In the early morning attack the previous morning, an arrow from Pahrant's bow had entered Moonch's body below the left arm, piercing both lungs. He had lived only several minutes longer, blood gushing from his nose and mouth.

"It is deep enough," Sowiette said, after carefully examining the pit he and his brothers had been working all morning to create. The brothers stopped, except Walkara, who continued picking up pieces of broken rock and heaving them over the edge of the pit.

Though Walkara was the youngest of the brothers digging the pit, he was the tallest, with broad shoulders and muscular arms. He had a strong, square chin, and a large nose curving out and down like the beak of an eagle.

Though his body was fully developed like that of a man, he still had the heart of a 16-year-old boy who had just lost his father. He continued digging the pit because he didn't want the next part of the burial ceremony to begin.

"It is deep enough," Sowiette repeated. Slowly, Walkara threw one more rock out of the hole, then straightened to face his older brother, who was already climbing out of the pit.

A minute later Sowiette led the clan's last horse, an old bay mare, to the edge of the hole. The mare stopped, not wanting to follow Sowiette into the pit, as if she had some kind of premonition of what was to come. But the old mare was no match for the insistent young men. With Sowiette pulling at her head, and Arrapeen and Grosspeen pushing from behind, she reluctantly scrambled into the hole. The rest of the clan, including Walkara, had gathered around the pit to watch.

The women were wailing, and the children crying,

as Sowiette plunged his knife into the mare's side, behind the left shoulder. In a sudden burst of energy, the mare reared back on her hind legs, pawing the air with her front feet. Standing to one side, still holding the lead rope, Sowiette jerked hard. The mare fell on her side, struggled briefly to regain her footing, then was still.

Walkara regretted that his brother didn't have a fine stallion to kill. The old mare wasn't much of a mount for a great chief to ride into the world of spirits. But one old mare was better than no horse at all.

Everyone's attention was suddenly diverted from the dying horse. Quinker, Moonch's brown and white dog, had begun yelping on the hill just below the pit, struggling desperately to get away from San Pitch, who had just struck the dog on the side of the head with a rock. The blow had not been hard enough to kill the animal which was now determined to get away. But San Pitch held on tightly, the second blow finally silencing the terrified dog. The limp body of Quinker was laid on the rocky floor of the pit beside the dead mare.

Next, the partially stiffened body of Moonch was carried by his four oldest sons into the pit. Moonch was dressed in his finest white buckskin leggings, shirt and moccasins—decorated with elaborate bead and quill designs. His long black hair was neatly combed and braided.

The body was rolled in a dark brown buffalo robe and placed beside the dead horse and dog. An obsidian-tipped spear, a chokecherry bow, and a quiver full of arrows was laid beside the chief's body, along with a drinking cup, a bow drill, a stone axe, and several other tools for Moonch to use on his journey to the world of spirits.

As Sowiette arranged the bow and arrows beside the body of his father, the wailing of the women increas-

13

ed. Sowiette took more time than necessary, apparently in an effort to delay the inevitable.

Moving slowly, like an old man, Sowiette got back on his feet and turned to face his father's four sobbing wives, two of whom had been selected to accompany their husband to the world of spirits.

Without any expression on his face, Sowiette climbed out of the pit. Taking the two youngest wives by the hand, he led them down into the hole. The two older wives, the mothers of the four oldest sons, would be allowed to stay behind and take care of the family. The younger, prettier wives, whom Moonch favored, would go with him. All the women were crying.

Walkara watched Sowiette lead the two women into the pit, then turned away as Sowiette drew his knife. The women continued to cry, and most of the children too, especially the little ones belonging to the two women about to die.

Walkara waited for what seemed a long time for the anticipated death screams, but all he heard was the continued crying. Finally, he looked back into the pit to see what was happening.

Sowiette, the knife still in his hand, stood facing the two wailing but unresisting women. His fist was clenched tightly around the knife handle. His mouth was twisted tight in determination to do what must be done, that which had always been done before. But somehow he couldn't raise the knife to do its work. He could not move it towards the women he knew so well, the wives of his father, the companions of his mother.

Walkara continued to watch, relieved the women still lived, wondering what would happen now. Would Sowiette muster the strength to do what must be done? Or would someone else do it? If so, who? Or would the women be allowed to live?

It was the impulsive Arrapeen who finally jumped into the pit, grabbed the knife from his brother's hand,

and plunged it into the heart of the nearest woman. Even before she had fallen to the ground, Arrapeen jerked the knife free and plunged it into the second woman. Arrapeen had acted so quickly that Walkara had not looked away. Now there was no need.

Arrapeen and Sowiette arranged the limp bodies of the two women beside their husband, then covered the three bodies with a second buffalo robe.

As Arrapeen and Sowiette crawled out of the hole, the entire clan began pushing loose rocks and dirt over their father, the two women, the horse and the dog. The living women and children continued to cry.

But the funeral ceremony was not finished. Once the grave was covered with a huge mound of rocks and dirt, Walkara, Sowiette and Grosspeen proceeded to build a small rock enclosure directly on top of the grave. While they worked, Arrapeen disappeared into the oak brush below the grave.

When Arrapeen returned, he was leading a six-year-old Piede slave boy. A strip of rawhide was attached securely to the boy's neck, like a leash on a dog. The slave boy wasn't crying. It wasn't a matter of bravery, or being resolved to his fate. Being mostly unfamiliar with Ute customs the boy didn't know why he was being led to the newly fashioned stone house on top of the burial mound.

It wasn't until the boy was placed inside the stone enclosure that he began to cry. He still didn't know what exactly was happening, or why. But as the Ute boys began closing off the top of the stone enclosure with sticks and rocks, the little slave boy sensed the inevitable doom that threatened his short life. His growing sobs were met with approving glances on the part of his captors, who believed the cries of a dying child would keep evil spirits away from the burial scene while the spirits of the dead prepared for their journey to the world of spirits. It was hoped the slave boy would cry for several days, ensuring the safe departure of the spirits from the grave.

Leaving the sobbing slave boy to his lonely fate, the Utes left the grave site, returning to their camp of brush and skin huts in the oak brush below the grave. It was bad medicine to mourn the dead too long. There was much work to do. Sowiette had given orders to break camp and move south. The little band could not stand up to the Timpany Utes who might strike again without warning. The little band would find a new land, a new home, far from their enemies, where they could live in peace, possibly in one of the high mountain valleys to the south and west.

"Who will avenge the death of our father?" Arrapeen shouted as the women bundled up their cooking pots and other meager belongings. They appeared to ignore the arrogant youth. A small family clan could not do battle with the Timpany Utes. The men and boys ignored Arrapeen's question too, as they gathered up their weapons and digging tools. Even Sowiette, the new leader, did not respond to Arrapeen's demand.

"Pahrant killed our father. He must pay," Arrapeen shouted. His comments fell on deaf ears.

It wasn't until he shouted "I will kill Pahrant," that some of the people looked at him with quizzical expressions on their faces, as if asking, "Who does this boy think he is, that he can go against Pahrant, chief of the Timpany Yutas?"

"Who will come with me?" Arrapeen persisted, undaunted by the reluctance of others to follow. "You are old women," he shouted at his brothers. "You run like dogs with tails between their legs." Still no one responded to the young brave's challenge.

"Am I the only one who loved our father?" he demanded.

"I loved my father," Walkara said, standing up to face his brother. Walkara had been helping his mother

16

roll up a large buffalo robe. "I loved my father," he repeated.

"Then you will come with me to avenge our father's death?"

"I will come." Walkara turned back towards his mother, who was beginning to lash the buffalo robe to a travois one of the dogs would drag as the clan began its journey.

"It is good for a son to avenge his father's death," she said. Her name was Tishum Igh. Even with the strong chin and long nose inherited by her son, she was a pretty woman, looking much younger than all the other women her age. She was a Paiute by birth and had spent much of her youth with the black robes or priests in their stone tepees near the Sierra Nevada Mountains to the west. In her mid teens she met Moonch, who had come to the mission to trade. Against the advice of the big hats she had left with Moonch to become his bride. She spoke Spanish and had taught some of it to Walkara.

"It is good for a son to avenge his father's death," she repeated, "if the son doesn't die doing it. Wouldn't it be better to wait until you are older, more cunning, more experienced in warfare?"

"I will be careful," Walkara answered, slipping his quiver full of arrows over his shoulder.

"Pahrant will kill you," she said.

"I will be careful."

"Driving off his horses would be enough for now. Kill him later when you are older."

"I will go with Arrapeen," Walkara said, putting his hand on Tishum Igh's shoulder, squeezing briefly before picking up his chokecherry bow and turning to join his brother. A minute later the two brothers disappeared into the oak brush.

Chapter 2

It was almost dark when Arrapeen and Walkara reached the camp of the Timpany Utes. On their hands and knees, the brothers crawled to a well-concealed spot in a thick clump of sagebrush below the crest of a hill overlooking the camp.

The camp consisted of 19 lodges, some of skin, the rest of brush and grass. They were located at the west end of a large meadow, cut in half by the clear waters of a small stream winding its way towards the blue lake. At the upper end of the meadow, nearer the spot where Walkara and his brother were hiding, fifty two horses grazed peacefully on the lush grass.

The brothers had been in the camp of the Timpany Utes many times, when the two clans had been on friendlier terms. The brothers knew which lodge belonged to Pahrant—the one with a blue buffalo on it, located nearest the horses.

A group of naked children played by the stream. Five or six women sat in a circle around a staked-out elk hide. Two were scraping unwanted flesh from the hide, while the others were just sitting and talking. Three of the older boys were riding through the grazing horses towards the camp.

None of the men could be seen. Walkara and Arrapeen guessed they were probably in one of the lodges, making plans for another raid, or just smoking and swapping stories. From the large number of horses in the meadow the brothers concluded the men were not away from camp.

As the sun began to set in the western sky, casting long shadows over the meadow, there was little conversation passed between Arrapeen and Walkara. It wasn't so much a matter of their plan already being set as it was a gradual awareness on the part of both young men of the immensity of their undertaking. How could two boys on foot dare attack the largest and strongest tribe in their part of the world? Pahrant was a powerful chief and a great warrior, who had proven his cunning and strength in battle many times. Arrapeen and Walkara were just two boys who wanted to avenge their father's death.

As darkness covered the meadow, the two brothers rolled over on their backs and looked up at the sky. Finally they began to talk, in whispers.

"Do you still want to do it?" Walkara asked.

"It would be much easier to steal two or three horses and disappear into the desert."

"Yes."

"But we came to avenge our father's death."

"How shall we do it?"

"We could walk up to the front of Pahrant's lodge, call his name, and when he steps out shoot him full of arrows, then run like frightened antelope."

"When he hears strange voices call his name, he may come out armed, ready to shoot back at us," Walkara said, thoughtfully. "What if he calls to warriors in nearby lodges before he comes out to meet us? What if, upon hearing our strange voices, he crawls out under the back flap of his lodge instead of coming out the front?"

"Is my brother's heart afraid?" Arrapeen asked.

"I don't want to die."

"Do you want to leave this place without killing Pahrant?"

"No," Walkara answered, after some thought. "I just think there might be a better way to do it."

"How?"

"I don't know."

The two brothers continued to whisper for several hours, finally deciding on a plan they both agreed had a better chance to send Pahrant to the world of spirits, while allowing the two brothers to remain in the flesh. By now their eyes were adjusted to the dark, and even though there was no moon, the stars provided sufficient light for them to find their way down the hill to the meadow. While Arrapeen began sneaking towards the grazing horses, Walkara stalked towards the sleeping village.

The plan was daring, but simple. Arrapeen, the more experienced rider, was to catch two of the horses while Walkara, the better shot with bow and arrow, positioned himself in a small clump of brush not 30 feet in front of Pahrant's door.

At first light Arrapeen would climb on one of the horses, and while leading the second horse, would drive the entire herd towards the camp, shouting and making a lot of noise. Undoubtedly Pahrant would rush out of his tepee to see what was the matter. That's when Walkara would shoot him, all the while trying to remain concealed in the brush.

As the horses stampeded through the village, Arrapeen would lead the spare horse to Walkara's hiding place. Walkara would leap upon the horse and the two brothers would race after the stampeding herd. If they could drive off all the horses, their enemies would not be able to follow.

Both boys knew a lot of things could go wrong.

Maybe Arrapeen couldn't catch the horses. Maybe Walkara's hiding place would be discovered before Pahrant came out of his lodge. Maybe Arrapeen wouldn't be able to reach Walkara's hiding place. Still the boys decided to go ahead with their plan. The father who had taught them to ride, to hunt, and to be men, had been killed. They would do their best to avenge his death. From the world of spirits their father would look down and be proud of his sons.

As Walkara drew nearer to the village, he became more cautious, slowing his pace. His biggest worry was dogs. If they began to bark at him, he would have little hope of hiding.

Continuing to creep forward, he untied and opened a small pouch that had been secured to his belt. It contained smoked fish his mother had given him. By opening it and letting the aroma fill the air ahead of him, he hoped any dog in his path would be more eager to eat than to bark. Cautiously, he inched his way forward.

For the most part the village was quiet and dark. Several of the tepees still glowed with orange light from dying fires. The rest were dark. The sound of muffled conversation came from one of the lodges, the crying of a tired child from another.

No guards or dogs were moving about, as far as Walkara could tell. It was well past midnight. Because there was no moon, Walkara and Arrapeen had decided to launch their attack at first light.

Walkara made his way to the brush opposite Pahrant's dark doorway, then seated himself for partial concealment. He was facing north with his left shoulder closest to the darkened doorway just west of his hiding place. From this position he could shoot his short, powerful bow without standing up. He drew three arrows from the quiver and waited nervously for the dawn, wondering what he would do if Arrapeen was not successful in catching two horses.

21

The time passed slowly. Walkara thought much of his father, a powerful warrior who had spent many hours teaching his sons to ride, shoot, hunt and fight. Moonch had moved away from the Timpanogos River in an effort to maintain peace with the Timpany Utes, but Pahrant had killed him anyway. Pahrant deserved to die. Moonch would be proud of his two sons who had the courage to avenge a father's death. Walkara wondered who might avenge his death, should he fail. Probably no one.

The night seemed endless, but eventually the stars began to fade. The sky turned from black to gray. Walkara notched an arrow on the string, and quietly tested the strength of his bow. He was ready. He felt a hard lump in his stomach, though he hadn't eaten a meal since the previous afternoon and had only picked at the smoked fish. He listened intently for the sound of stampeding horses. All was quiet, not even a breath of wind. In the distance he could barely hear the quiet splashing of the stream as it pushed gently towards the lake.

The time was perfect. It was light enough to see. The entire village was still asleep. Arrapeen should make his move now, before the squaws began coming out of their lodges to light the cook fires. During the warmer months most of the cooking was done over large outside fires rather than around the small fire pits inside the tepees.

To the east, Walkara could see some of the horses, still grazing. There was no sign of Arrapeen. Walkara guessed something was wrong. There was no reason for Arrapeen to be waiting. Had he been able to catch two of the horses, he would now be driving the herd towards the village. What could have gone wrong?

Walkara was looking towards the meadow when he became aware of nearby movement. While his body remained perfectly still to avoid detection, his eyes darted towards the movement. A man was emerging from the nearest tepee, from Pahrant's tepee.

There was enough light now for Walkara to identify the man as Pahrant. There was no doubt. The Timpany chief was dressed only in a loincloth. Looking towards the sky, the great warrior flexed the muscles in his arms and back in a mighty arching motion. His mouth opened wide as he yawned.

For a second Walkara thought he could hear the thundering of the stampeding horses, but realized it was his own heart racing with excitement. He glanced towards the meadow. Still no sign of Arrapeen. Should he wait for Arrapeen, or go ahead and shoot the Timpany chief?

Walkara realized he might wait an entire lifetime and never get a better opportunity than he had right now to avenge his father's death. Maybe Arrapeen had lost heart and left. Walkara found that hard to believe, but still he couldn't figure out why Arrapeen was not coming.

Finished with his stretching, Pahrant pushed his loincloth aside and began urinating on the dew-covered grass. In the brisk morning air a small puff of steam began gathering around the growing yellow pool.

As the chief watched his new creation, Walkara decided he could wait for Arrapeen no longer. He simply could not let a moment like this pass without taking advantage of it. He drew back the powerful bow and let the first arrow fly. Less than 30 feet away, Pahrant was an easy target. With a slapping sound the arrow sank deep into the left breast. Before the chief could sound the alarm, a second arrow entered the right breast. Gasping for breath, the startled warrior sank to his knees. With his lungs filling with blood he was unable to shout the alarm.

The bow still in his hand, Walkara leaped from his

hiding place. He knew he should be racing for cover, but his work was not yet finished.

Rushing towards his father's killer, Walkara pushed the dying man on his face. Taking a handful of long hair he jerked the chief's head back. Walkara ran the razor edge of his knife along the skin in front of the hairline, then sliced back towards the rear of the skull, at the same time jerking furiously at the long hair.

In seconds he had his first scalp. He hadn't done a very neat job of cutting, but considering the circumstances he didn't think anyone would judge him harshly. Tucking the knife and scalp in his belt, Walkara grabbed his bow and started racing towards the rugged foothills.

Walkara would have remained silent, but a dog began to bark. Now that the alarm was sounded there was no need to remain silent.

"My father's death is avenged," he cried as he raced past the last tepee. Shouting people began emerging from the lodges. Walkara ran harder.

He didn't stop to catch his breath and look back until he reached the top of the nearest hill, the same one from which he and Arrapeen had been studying the camp the previous evening. Five men, two with bows and three with spears, had taken up the chase. Further away, other men from the village were running towards the horse herd to catch their animals so they could ride after Walkara.

Suddenly the horses were stampeding towards the village. A lone rider was galloping after the running horses. Arrapeen had finally made his move. Why he had taken so long Walkara did not know. He did know that the horses were finally headed his way, and if he could stay ahead of the five runners long enough, his brother might bring him a horse that would allow him to safely outdistance his pursuers.

Walkara turned and ran down the hill. He could

feel the strength surging through his strong young body, hard and lean from the active outdoor life and the rigors of the trail. None of the boys and few of the men in his own small band could outrun him. Hopefully none of the Timpany Utes chasing him were any faster than his own clan members.

He stretched out his legs in long, swift strides, taking care where he placed his feet to avoid tripping on brush or rocks or stepping into rabbit or badger holes. He still had his bow in his hand, and the quiver half full of arrows on his back.

Walkara ran nearly half a mile before he looked over his shoulder again. His followers were no longer in a bunch, but stretched out, single file. Four were several hundred yards back, but one of the men carrying a spear was less than a hundred yards away and gaining quickly. There was no sign of Arrapeen. The village was out of sight beyond the hill.

Walkara tried to run faster. Still, the man with the spear was gaining on him. Every few steps now, Walkara was glancing over his shoulder.

Walkara realized he was not going to outrun his nearest pursuer. The man was going to catch up with him before Arrapeen did. Deciding he would prefer to stand and fight rather than get a spear in the back, Walkara suddenly stopped, spun around, whipped an arrow from the quiver and notched it on the bowstring. Because of his hard breathing, he knew his accuracy wouldn't be as good as it usually was. But he wouldn't have to take a long shot.

By the time he drew the arrow back, his pursuer had stopped too. He was a tall, young Ute, his black hair in two long braids. He was breathing hard too, drops of sweat running down his neck and chest. His right arm was cocked back, ready to launch the obsidian-tipped spear. Armed with only one spear the brave knew he was at a definite disadvantage, there being about 40 feet separating the two. That was a long throw. If he missed, Walkara would have all the advantage.

Walkara drew the arrow back to his chin and let it fly. There was a loud twang as the arrow left the string. Walkara's aim had been good. The arrow flew straight for the young runner's chest, but at the last split second the young man twisted to one side, allowing the arrow to fly harmlessly past.

Walkara drew a second arrow and let it fly. Again, his opponent stepped to one side and let the arrow go harmlessly by. The tall young man, knowing he would only get one chance with his spear, made no attempt to throw it. Nor did he make any attempt to get closer to Walkara. At closer range the arrows would be more difficult to dodge.

Walkara suddenly realized he was being held at bay by the tall warrior, who would soon be joined by the four other runners. Outnumbered five to one, Walkara would be easy prey. Walkara turned and resumed running with all his might. He had to keep ahead of the other runners, all the time knowing he could not outrun the tall young man who was already too close.

As Walkara ran he proceeded to notch a third arrow on the bowstring. The tall runner had not thrown the spear at 40 feet, but when he got within ten or twenty feet he probably would. At such a short distance, Walkara's back would make an easy target.

Walkara glanced over his shoulder. The tall warrior was still gaining on him, now only about 25 feet back. Soon the spear would be coming. Walkara tried to run faster, but the tall Indian continued to gain on him.

Walkara's legs were beginning to feel weak and unsteady. His lungs were screaming for more air. Without warning, Walkara suddenly stopped, dropped to one knee, drew back his bow and fired. The heavy spear hissed past Walkara's ear, burying itself harmlessly in an anthill.

This time the tall warrior was too close to dodge Walkara's speeding arrow, which caught him just below the right collarbone. As the warrior spun around and began bending over, Walkara's second arrow caught him in the side, penetrating both lungs. With blood gushing from his nose and mouth, the tall runner fell face forward to the ground.

Walkara was about to turn and resume the desperate foot race when he saw the herd of horses stampeding over the crest of the hill. Arrapeen was riding with them, whooping and shaking his bow.

Realizing Arrapeen and the horses would reach him before the other runners, Walkara decided there was no more need to run. Drawing his knife he rushed forward to take his second scalp.

Chapter 3

Walkara and Arrapeen found their people traveling southward across the highland flats west of Mt. Pack-arr-at, later called Nebo by the white men. No one was happier to see Walkara than his mother, Tishum Igh. During the long hours of walking she had come to the conclusion that not only had she lost a husband, but a son too. Walkara and his half brother would be no match for the Timpany Utes, she had concluded, and would be killed.

Then suddenly her son was galloping towards the camp, he and Arrapeen driving many horses ahead of them. It was a glorious sight. Now the camp would have horses to carry the heavy burdens. Now the men would have horses to take them to the best hunting places and to help defend the clan. She would have a son to provide for her and protect her. Tishum Igh dropped her heavy pack and ran to meet her son.

That night the clan celebrated the great victory. Walkara hung his two scalps on a pole outside his mother's lodge, where most of the dancing and feasting took place. Arrapeen told the story a dozen times, how his brother had single-handedly killed the great Timpany chief, then scalped the man right in the middle of the village while everyone slept. Too much could not be said for Walkara's cunning and bravery.

As the people danced, keeping time with gourd

rattles as Arrapeen bragged of their exploits again and again, Walkara enjoyed himself. He loved the new respect he saw in the eyes of his people, the old as well as the young. To everyone Walkara was no longer a boy, but a great warrior who had proven himself in battle. The older men wanted to talk to him. The young men and boys followed him about the camp, as if hoping some of his valor would rub off on them.

But it was the young women who showed the greatest increase in attention. They didn't follow him like the young men did, but Walkara definitely noticed the stares, the giggling, the increased teasing. Two days earlier, to them Walkara was the youngest brother, just a boy, still not a man. Now he was the most esteemed warrior in the village, and with sixteen horses, the richest, along with Arrapeen, who already had a squaw.

Walkara relished the attention. He had never been happier in his life. What more could a warrior ask for? He found out the next morning.

Walkara was awakened from a deep sleep by shouting. It was Sowiette, mounted on a bay horse Walkara had loaned him until he could get one of his own. It wasn't even light yet, and the stars were just begining to fade. In his concern for possible retaliation by the Timpany Utes Sowiette wanted to get an early start. His intention was to get his people far into the mountains of the west desert, so far away the Timpany Utes would never find them.

Walkara didn't share Sowiette's concern. Killing Pahrant had not been that difficult. The tall runner with the spear had been more of a challenge. Still, Walkara had come out victorious. He was no longer afraid of the Timpany Utes. If they came against his people, he and his brothers would do battle with them and take more scalps. He didn't want any part of this business of running like frightened rabbits to the remote corners of the desert. He expressed these feelings to his mother,

29

rolled over, and went back to sleep. His courageous exploits had made him very tired.

Tishum Igh crawled out of the lodge and informed Sowiette that her son intended to sleep a while longer, and that if Sowiette wanted to leave without Walkara, he should leave Walkara's horse behind.

Sowiette hadn't expected his leadership of the clan to be challenged so soon, especially not by a little brother. His first reaction was to rush into the lodge and beat his younger brother. But Sowiette hesitated. Reason prevailed. Though younger, Walkara was bigger and more athletic. In a hand-to-hand confrontation Walkara could very well come out the winner, causing Sowiette to lose even more face.

Sowiette decided to let Walkara sleep. He returned to his lodge to finish loading his things. Uneasily, he noticed that Tishum Igh was circulating among the other families, apparently telling them of Walkara's intention to remain camped a while longer.

An hour later, when Sowiette and his family began their westward journey, the rest of the clan remained behind with the sleeping Walkara, the young warrior who had become chief without even getting out of bed.

The sun was just peeking over the majestic reaches of Mt. Nebo when Walkara finally emerged from the lodge, feeling rested and strong. He stretched like a young lion, noticing with pride the two scalps gently swaying in the morning breeze.

He stepped over to the cook fire where Tishum Igh was occupied with a side of venison ribs she had already roasted to a golden brown. Walkara grunted approvingly as she sliced off a generous portion for her son.

As he ate he looked out over the meadow where his and Arrapeen's horses were peacefully grazing. He decided that from now on he would keep one of the horses tethered near his lodge at night, so he would have something to ride in the event the free-roaming animals ran off for one reason or another. His father had always done that.

He noticed that the bay he had loaned to Sowiette had not been returned to the herd. Walkara was not angry his oldest brother had taken the animal without permission. After all, they were brothers. Someday the debt would be repaid. Sowiette could be trusted.

Tishum Igh explained to Walkara what had happened earlier that morning, how most of the clan had decided to remain with Walkara when she told them he was not leaving with Sowiette. Few words were spoken when Sowiette finally departed with his small and lonely following.

Before Walkara had finished his breakfast the men of the clan began gathering around. It was time to start packing up for the journey, and they wanted to know what arrangements could be made to use Walkara's and Arrapeen's horses. Those with sufficient possessions to make trades were interested in outright purchases, the others in borrowing.

The first trade Walkara made was with Mo-ap, his father's younger brother. In coming to Walkara's fire, Mo-ap had led his oldest daughter, Tah-mun, one of the girls whose giggles and stares had not escaped Walkara's attention the night before. Tah-mun was in her fifteenth year.

Walkara had grown up with Tah-mun, but it wasn't until recent months he had found her attractive. She was a strong, healthy girl, a fast runner. She was not fat, nor was she skinny, just right to make a good squaw, and just the right age for marriage.

While Tah-mun raced back to her mother's tepee to fetch her things, Walkara and Mo-ap walked out on the flat to catch two of Walkara's finest horses. There was little talk. This was the way things like this happened. Mo-op was obviously pleased he was receiving two horses for his daughter. Most fathers would be more than lucky to get one horse for a daughter.

But Walkara was glad to pay two horses, though he knew he could have gotten the girl for one. It wasn't that he was in love. He had known Tah-mun for years, and knew she would make a good squaw. In fact, he guessed she was the best available woman in the clan at the time. At 16 years the physical passions were burning in his bones. He figured the pleasure Tah-mun would give him would be well worth the price of two horses, so that was the price he agreed to pay.

Dividing up the rest of his herd was not so easy. Some of the other fathers, seeing Mo-ap receive two horses for his daughter, wanted to trade their daughters to Walkara too. While polygamy was common among the Utes, Walkara figured he had better learn what it was like living with one squaw before he took on two or three. Besides, to have too many mouths to feed could take much of the fun out of hunting, and he still had his mother to take care of.

In leasing out the remainder of his horses Walkara received a wide assortment of goods—horse blankets, cooking pots, arrows, a spear and a looking glass. He didn't need everything he traded for, but with enough horses to carry many belongings, he didn't see any problem taking on unnecessary baggage.

It was early afternoon when the village was finally ready to resume the exodus away from its homeland. Walkara led the way, mounted on a fine roan stallion, his new bride riding behind him, her slim brown arms wrapped firmly around his waist. Tishum Igh followed close behind on foot, leading a horse-drawn travois stacked high with the family belongings.

Most of the men were riding their newly rented horses while their women struggled on foot with heavy burdens. No one complained or thought it should be different, not even the women. Men brought home meat, fought battles and made weapons. Women did the domestic work. That was the way things were, always had been, and always would be. No one thought to change or suggest a different way of doing things.

Because of the late start, very few miles were covered before it was time to make camp again, this time near the base of the tall mountain, near some clear, running springs. With meat supplies getting low, Walkara announced that in the morning he was going deer hunting, and those who wished to come along were welcome to do so. While some questioned the wisdom in staying so close to the Timpany Utes, none challenged the bold young chief.

An hour before daylight Walkara and all the young men in the clan were mounted and heading up the winding trails leading to the higher elevations of the mountain. In the brisk morning air the horses were puffing and sweating from the steep ascent. At this time of year the bucks were high where the air stayed cool and the grass green.

Walkara and his men began to spread out. The bigger bucks were usually by themselves with their new antlers just beginning to grow. Sometimes they were in small groups, seldom with does, maintaining relative seclusion and privacy. The does, with their new fawns, remained mostly at the lower elevations. Today the Ute braves were after the big-bodied bucks.

Armed with only bows and arrows, the strategy was simple. Spot the bucks at first light, their favorite feeding time. This was not a time for stalking and shooting, just watching from a distance. When the late morning sun finally flooded the high basins, the bucks, their stomachs full, would seek out their shady beds, where they would sleep and rest through the middle part of the day.

The strategy of the red men was simple. Watch the bucks until they bedded down, then sneak up on the beds, getting as close as possible before opening fire. Some of the men preferred to hunt alone, some in pairs. Never more than three were involved in stalking a single animal.

It was essential that the stalk be made from downwind so the deer could not smell the approaching hunter. Absolute silence had to be maintained too, especially during the last hundred yards. The alert bucks could hear the slightest rustle of grass, or the snapping of even the smallest twig. Sometimes, to ensure maximum silence a brave would remove his moccasins during the final hundred yards, which would be covered an inch at a time in total silence. The successful stalker had patience as endless as the west desert.

Walkara and Arrapeen paired off for the morning hunt. Together, they had been on the mountain many times, and frequently their patience and teamwork had resulted in nice bucks. Upon reaching their favorite basin, they tied their horses in a secluded aspen grove. While horses were useful in carrying one to a hunting area and in bringing home the meat, they were to be kept out of sight and hearing during the hunt, with an occasional exception, like during the winter when the deer came out of the mountains onto the desert and could be chased and shot from horseback like buffalo.

There was plenty of daylight, but still no sun, as the two brothers climbed to the top of a nearby ridge. Inching forward on their bellies, under the protective branches of a ridge-top juniper, they began scanning the basin beyond the ridge for deer.

At the distances involved, motionless deer were nearly impossible to find. The young men were scanning the partially wooded hillsides for movement, any kind of movement that might give away the presence of a deer. In the fall and winter they looked for gray bodies. This time of year, they were looking for brownish-tan bodies.

At first they didn't see anything, but with patience they knew they would. They had always seen deer in this basin this time of year. They waited and watched. The morning air was cool and still.

With time they began to see brown bodies, not many, but three or four. Two seemed large, and had the beginnings of what would probably be large antlers. These were the kind of deer the young men were looking for. The does, with the nursing and caring for new fawns this time of year, were usually thin and stringy. On the other hand, the mature bucks were usually fat and lazy and very good to eat, having been on green grass for several months.

Arrapeen and Walkara watched carefully, knowing that once the bucks crawled into their beds they would probably be impossible to see. It was imperative the boys see them enter their beds, so they would know the exact locations upon which to focus their stalks. Once the deer bedded, they might not be seen again until they jumped up in front of the ready archers, which might be hours later.

The two bucks were grazing randomly across the upper third of the basin, alternately grazing on the green grass and browsing on oak and mahogany leaves. The boys did not take their eyes away, knowing the deer could bed down at any time now. The sun was beginning to shine on the far side of the basin.

Though Walkara didn't take his eyes off the two deer, his mind was elsewhere, remembering his new bride and the first night they had spent together. Tahmun had been a willing, almost eager, bride. The lovemaking had been enjoyable, even with Walkara's mother sharing their honeymoon lodge with them. Tishum Igh had pretended to sleep as the couple became amorous.

Walkara had been surprised and pleased when Tahmun arose with him in the pre-dawn darkness to prepare a quick breakfast of seed gruel before he departed on the morning hunt. Walkara hoped he and Arrapeen could get a deer quickly so he could return to his new bride.

The deer were still moving across the hillside when Walkara and Arrapeen heard a distinct popping sound, almost like the snapping of a twig, but it came from far away. Without taking their eyes off the deer the boys speculated on what the sound might be. Had it been fall, they would have been sure the sound came from mountain sheep or elk banging their horns or antlers together. But in early summer elk and sheep didn't fight.

They heard it again, and this time there were two popping noises close together. Arrapeen wondered if the sound could have been made by one of the fire sticks the white trappers called rifles. But that wouldn't explain why they had heard two pops close together. It took a minute or two for the trappers to reload their fire sticks after a shot had been fired. Maybe several fire sticks had been fired. In addition to the white men, Arrapeen had heard that the Shoshones now had the fire sticks that enabled them to kill deer and men at long distances.

Walkara looked away from the deer towards the camp. Though their position on the ridge prevented them from seeing the lodges, he and his brother could see part of the meadow where the horses had been grazing the previous evening. There were billows of gray smoke moving across the meadow, too much smoke to be coming from morning cook fires. Forgetting the deer, Walkara and Arrapeen scooted out from under the tree and raced for the horses.

Walkara had a sick feeling in his stomach, like somehow what was happening was his fault. He had not been careful enough, and now he was too far away to defend his people when they needed him.

The horses didn't need any coaxing to hurry down the mountain. While the trail was too steep for outright

36

running, the horses trotted, slid and stumbled down the steep slopes, quickly eating up the miles.

The other hunters had heard the rifle shots and seen the smoke too, and joined Walkara and Arrapeen in their mad stampede down the mountain. The horses sensed the urgency of the riders and maintained a frightening pace over the ledges and steep places.

When one of the horses stumbled, throwing its rider to the ground ahead of it, then stepping on the man's ankle, the other riders did not stop to help. They knew that at this very moment their wives and children were possibly the victims of some horrible slaughter at the cruel whims of an unknown enemy, possibly the Timpany Utes or Shoshones.

After reaching the flat, it was only a short run to the village. Several of the lodges were on fire. Walkara noticed that the horses not taken on the morning hunt were gone. There were no longer any doubts that a raid had taken place. Crossing a swell the riders could finally see the morning's work. Every lodge was either torn down, burned or still burning.

Walkara led the galloping hunters into the camp. Some of the children and women were sitting on the ground wailing. Others were caring for the dead and wounded. Tishum Igh was the first to run up to Walkara, telling him his bride Tah-mun had been carried off, probably by Shoshones, possibly with some Timpany Utes riding with them.

The young warrior who had carried off Tah-mun was not a Timpany Ute. He was a stranger. Tishum Igh had never seen him before. He rode a spotted stallion—white with black spots.

Four captives, three women and a child, had been taken by the raiders, whose numbers Tishum Igh guessed to be about 15 men and boys. Calling for his hunting companions to follow, Walkara galloped north, following the trail of the recently departed raiders.

Chapter 4

Walkara first saw the spotted stallion near the headwaters of the Tim-pan-odze-pah, later known as the upper Provo River. There was no excitement or exhilaration in finally locating the horse he had been following relentlessly for four days, only a grim, seething determination to kill its rider.

Earlier in the day Walkara had found the lifeless body of Tah-mun, his bride of only one night. He couldn't tell how she had died, only that she had been treated roughly and cruelly by her captors. There were bruises and cuts on her naked body, and her scalp was gone.

Walkara guessed she would not have been killed had she not resisted the advances of her captors. He honored her bravery, and as he placed her lifeless body gently on the ground at the bottom of a sandy bank and began covering her with sand, he vowed a doubly cruel vengeance on her captors.

He found the spotted stallion grazing in an open meadow with about a dozen other horses. Some of the animals, including the stallion, were tethered to picket pins with rawhide ropes. Each rope was tied to the horse's front foot just above the hoof to reduce the chances of the animal getting tangled as it moved about. The rest of the horses were roaming free.

Beyond the grazing horses, inside a wide bend of

the river near a huge pile of cottonwood logs that had been heaped high during the spring runoff, about a dozen Shoshones were seated around a cook fire. Walkara had no doubt these were the men who had attacked his camp. The spotted horse looked exactly as his mother had described it. The trail they had been following led to this meadow.

Finally, he had caught up with the enemy. Walkara and his companions had tied their exhausted horses in a cottonwood grove about a quarter of a mile downstream.

The young Utes huddled in a dry wash to discuss their strategy. Since they did not outnumber the enemy, they felt it necessary to come up with some plan that would give them a surprise advantage. While Walkara and his companions whispered back and forth, discussing possible ideas on how they might defeat the enemy, Grosspeen waited on the bank of the wash, where he could keep a constant eye on the Shoshones and their horses.

Walkara and his companions had just decided to work their way up the river, using the protection of the bank to enable them to launch a close range attack, when Grosspeen waved excitedly to his companions to come to the top of the bank to see what was happening at the enemy camp.

Four of the Shoshone warriors, bridles in hand, were walking into the meadow to catch their horses. The tallest of the warriors bridled the spotted stallion. After catching their horses, the four warriors returned to their companions at the cook fire and picked up their weapons. After a brief conversation which Walkara and his companions could not hear, the four mounted warriors, two of them carrying rifles, galloped upstream in a northeasterly direction. The rest of the Indians remained around the fire. Behind them, next to the stump of a large tree, huddled two women and a child, apparently the Ute captives.

Figuring the advantage was definitely on their side now, the Ute braves proceeded with their plan, working their way up the river bottom in an effort to get as close as possible before launching an attack. By the time the fighting began they figured the four riders would be far enough away so as not to hear the noise, which would undoubtedly bring them back.

A half hour later Walkara and his companions fired a bevy of arrows into their unsuspecting enemies, still huddled around their fire. As soon as the arrows were released from their bows, the Utes charged, continuing to fire as they charged over the edge of the bank. In less than half a minute the enemy was surrounded. Those who had been shot with arrows were cowering in pain. The rest were standing, unarmed, sick with the realization the worst part was still to come.

While his companions tied the hands of the defeated Shoshones behind their backs, Walkara released the two women and child. They were bruised from rough treatment, and hungry, but otherwise all right, and very glad to see the Ute rescue party.

In a hurry to catch the tall Indian on the spotted stallion, Walkara didn't want to waste any time torturing and abusing the prisoners. He and Arrapeen began herding them to the top of the huge pile of cottonwood logs beside the stream. Walkara's plan was simple. Once all the Shoshones were perched on top of the log pile, he would set the logs on fire.

Walkara didn't discuss the plan with his companions. He just started herding the prisoners onto the cottonwood logs, and Arrapeen joined in.

Keeping the prisoners on top of the log pile turned out to be more difficult than expected, even with their hands tied behind their backs. Once the prisoners saw Arrapeen beginning to light the fire they began scrambling down off the logs in all directions. Facing the threat of Ute arrows wasn't nearly as frightening as death by fire.

Walkara ordered their feet be tied, but there were not enough rawhide lashings to do this. Grosspeen suggested they just kill the prisoners and take their scalps. Still determined to see the prisoners suffer the more horrible death by fire, Walkara whipped out his knife and sliced through both Achilles tendons of the nearest prisoner. Arrapeen and several companions quickly did the same to the remaining seven prisoners. Now that the Shoshones were crippled, the Utes were finally able to keep them on top of the log pile while Arrapeen got the fire going by carrying coals from the other fire where the Shoshones had been cooking their midday meal.

No sooner had Arrapeen gotten the fire going than Grosspeen walked over and stomped it out. Everyone was surprised, including the doomed prisoners. Walkara was annoyed. Precious time was being lost.

Grosspeen explained in his slow, deliberate manner that if the prisoners were burned to death, their scalps would be burned too. On the other hand, if the prisoners were killed by shooting or stabbing, everyone would have a scalp to take home to prove they were great warriors.

Walkara was furious. Not only was time being wasted, but his authority as chief was being challenged. Though Grosspeen was his older brother, he didn't pose a threat to take over leadership of the band. Grosspeen was overweight and slow, both in mind and body. He just wasn't about to let his younger brother destroy the scalp he felt he had earned.

Whipping his knife from his belt once again, Walkara charged to the top of the log pile, grabbing the closest prisoner by the hair. He jerked the man's head back, and with a wide slashing motion of the knife quickly removed the scalp. He then threw the bloody prize at Grosspeen while ordering Arrapeen to get the fire going again.

Several of the other Ute warriors, following Walkara's example, climbed to the top of the log pile and quietly scalped the remaining prisoners, all of whom remained silent while the hair and skin on top of their heads was removed.

The prisoners knew the Utes would take delight in their cries of pain and agony, so they remained silent, refusing to give that satisfaction to their captors. The Shoshone braves, their heads bare and bloody, appeared calm and disinterested as the sweet cottonwood smoke enveloped them.

Only one of the younger prisoners tried to climb down from the heap of burning logs. The Utes forced him back to the center of the pile, pushing him with long, pointed poles.

The Utes watched as the smoke and flames gradually engulfed the stoic prisoners. The flames continued to get hotter and hotter, reaching higher and higher. The heat was so intense around the blazing heap that those watching had to get further and further away while billows of greasy smoke churned skyward. Eventually Walkara and his companions turned and made their way back to their horses, but not before gathering up the Shoshone horses that would no longer be needed by their former owners.

Though everyone was very tired from the forced march of recent days, spirits were high. They would be bringing home new horses and fresh scalps.

Walkara was the only one not thinking of home. To him the revenge ride had been only partially successful, and was not yet over. The Indian on the spotted stallion was still free, and not very far away. With a little luck his camp could be found during the coming night.

As they mounted their horses, Walkara expressed

his intention to try to find the camp of the four Shoshones during the night. Grosspeen was the first to offer an objection. He said he had decided to accompany the two women and child back to the home camp. Arrapeen followed by saying the families needed to be moved to a safer place as soon as possible, and that he intended to accompany Grosspeen. All the others said they were going too.

When Walkara called his brothers and companions cowards and accused them of being afraid of the warrior on the spotted stallion, their only response was to get on their horses and head for home, leaving Walkara with the realization that he was no longer their chief. In fact, he wasn't sure he had ever really been their chief, at least not in the sense that demanded total obedience.

At first Walkara was angry, as he began following them down the canyon. But gradually the anger faded as he realized there was wisdom in the men's desire to move their families to a safer place as soon as possible. He also realized that the Shoshone raid that had resulted in the death of his new bride had been his own fault. He had been careless. He could not blame his brothers and the other men for not wanting to follow someone so young, so reckless, and foolish enough to let his band be so vulnerable to enemy attack. He was not ready to be a chief. He was not worthy to be a chief.

But neither did Walkara want to return to the people he had failed. He pulled the bay mare he was riding to a halt. None of his companions noticed, or even looked back, as they continued their journey down the canyon.

When the mare resisted turning around, wanting to continue with the other horses, Walkara broke a green limb from the nearest aspen tree and gave her a firm thrashing, forcing her to turn around and head back upstream. Walkara didn't look back to see if his companions had noticed his departure. He told himself he didn't care, not anymore. The only thing that mattered now was catching the warrior on the spotted stallion.

Chapter 5

Following the trail of the spotted stallion during the night was not easy, even with a quarter moon in a cloudless sky. More than once Walkara had to drop to his knees and feel the direction of the tracks on the rocky ground. Most of the time he was leading the bay mare, it being easier to follow the trail while walking than while riding. More than once, when he felt too tired to continue, he would drop to the ground, curl up like a weary pup, and sleep. The cold night air and the impatient pawing of the mare would soon awaken him, and he would doggedly continue his journey.

Daybreak found Walkara trailing an easy-to-follow spur through a loam and moss bed in a thick stand of black pines. He was just coming out of the pines, looking down at the tracks, leading the mare, thinking about lying down on the soft ground for another nap, when he heard the whinny of a horse ahead of him.

Looking up, Walkara saw the spotted stallion. It had been grazing in a small clearing less than a hundred yards in front of him. Walkara realized he had made a careless mistake in allowing the stallion to see him first. It was looking straight at him. It whinnied again.

Walkara glanced around the meadow, but could see no sign of men. Quickly he ducked behind a tree. He could hide himself, but not the bay mare. He knew the Indians wouldn't be far from their horses. The noise from the stallion would have alerted them. They would be looking around. What should he do now?

Almost before Walkara realized what was happening his mare stretched out, raised her tail, and began to urinate on the soft ground. At first he thought she just had to relieve herself, but when she remained stretched out, her tail high, he realized she was at the time of the female cycle when a mare wants to be with a stallion. The presence of the stallion had triggered the response in her, and she wanted to be with him.

Walkara knew that if he didn't get her nose in his hands, quickly, she would answer the stallion. He began pulling her head towards his hiding place behind the tree, trying to avoid any sudden movement. He was too late. The mare whinnied loud and clear in answer to the stallion, who was now fighting his tether rope to get to the mare.

Walkara knew the Shoshones would be looking in his direction. He guessed they outnumbered him at least four to one, and if they saw him before he saw them, they would have an even greater advantage. He was about to leap upon the mare and retreat when another possibility entered his mind.

He was fairly certain the Shoshones hadn't seen him yet. Maybe he could trick them. Quickly he slipped the bridle from the mare's head. She was now free to run to the stallion, which she did.

Walkara hoped the Shoshones would think their stallion had been discovered by a stray mare that wanted to be bred. The Indians would be eager to catch the mare. While they were doing so Walkara would be able to determine where they were camped, exactly how many of them there were, possibly even pick up and hide their weapons while they were occupied with the mare. The element of surprise would again be on his side, possibly giving him an opportunity to get the revenge he craved. From his hiding place he watched the meadow, and waited.

When the mare reached the stallion she stopped. The two horses snorted and pawed at each other for a moment. The mare began to urinate again, her tail high, her hind legs outstretched. She was within reach of the stallion's tether rope, allowing him to get behind her and begin to mount.

As he did so four Indians emerged from the trees, running to catch the mare. Two of them carried fire sticks, two carried bows and arrows. In the less than ten seconds it took the stallion to finish his job, the Indians had reached the horses and had a rope around the mare's neck.

Walkara was disappointed that the Indians had carried their weapons with them, eliminating any chance of him getting them. The Indians kept looking nervously in the direction from which the mare had come. They didn't seem to be accepting the idea that the mare was merely a stray that had wandered into their camp. Walkara guessed they were probably thinking the mare had gotten away and run ahead of a Ute raiding party. At least they thought it was a raiding party, not a single warrior. Without returning to their camp, the anxious Shoshones climbed upon their horses and galloped northward, away from Walkara, taking his bay mare with them.

Walkara knew it would be useless to follow them on foot. Believing they were possibly being followed by Utes the Shoshones would push their horses hard, making it impossible for a man on foot to keep up with them, let alone catch them.

Walkara walked to the thickest part of the pine forest and sat down, his back against the mossy side of a big fir tree, wondering what he should do now. He had eaten very little in the four days of the chase, and should be hungry. But he was not. Perhaps he should sleep.

With only a few short naps during the night, he should be very sleepy. But he was not. He thought about retracing his trail, trying to catch up with Arrapeen and Grosspeen and the rest of the Utes returning home. But he was no longer their chief. He didn't want to be with them anymore, at least not now.

He thought about his new bride and her miserable death. He remembered the stoic faces of the scalped Shoshones as they burned on the pile of logs. It had been a terrible sight. But what they had done to Tahmun was worse. The Shoshones had deserved to die a horrible death.

Walkara wondered why he felt so bad, so unsettled, so restless, so unhappy. For the first time in his short life he didn't care if he lived or died. Life that had seemed so wonderful to him a short time earlier, didn't seem that way at all now. He couldn't help but wonder if there was some purpose, some master plan, behind what was happening to him and around him.

Towats the Great Spirit would know. But Walkara didn't know Towats, the same Great Spirit who had appeared to some of the elders in medicine dreams. He wondered if the great Towats had a message for Walkara. Was there purpose in all the heartache and meanness he had seen in his short life? Could there be a mission for a young warrior who had failed his people as chief?

Walkara decided to seek out Towats. If there was ever a young man who needed a medicine dream it was Walkara. If there was ever a right time for such a dream, it was now. Perhaps Towats would answer some of his questions. Perhaps Towats would appear to him and tell him what to do and where to go. Walkara didn't know, but he decided to find out.

"Towats, do you hear my words?" he cried, looking up through the thick branches of the pines toward the blue sky. He listened for a long time. There was no answer. Walkara stood up and called out again.

"Towats, can you hear my words?"

Again he listened. Again there was no answer.

Remembering that the elders usually had their medicine dreams on top of high mountains, Walkara began walking towards the towering snow-capped peaks of the mountains later known as the Uintas.

As the excitement of the close encounter with the Shoshones wore away, his hunger returned. But he remembered the admonition of the elders that one's chances of receiving a strong medicine dream were increased by fasting. Walkara resisted the urge to nibble on the remaining two pieces of deer jerky in the pouch on his belt.

He walked all day. He didn't hurry, still tired from the forced march after the Shoshones. He had much to think about, much to ponder. The hunger pains came and went, severe at times when he thought about food, but usually absent when his thoughts were elsewhere. He tried not to think about food as he continued his lonely stroll towards the snow-capped peaks.

When night came he continued walking. When he became sleepy, he would do as he had done the night before: curl up like a dog in the trail and sleep until the cold, or the hunger, or both, awakened him. Then he would stand up and continue his journey.

By noon the next day he was walking across crusty drifts of old snow stubbornly resisting the warmth of the summer sun. It was a land of little dirt, few trees, big rocks and cold breezes.

It was late in the day when Walkara reached the top of his mountain. Having no blanket to keep him warm against the cold night air, he hacked a hole in the east side of a soil-stained snowdrift.

The task should have been an easy one, but by now his once powerful arms had lost their strength. Every movement required hard mental effort. His arms and legs just didn't want to move anymore. But he continued hacking and scooping until he had created a large enough cavity to crawl inside, away from the cold night air. He made a mattress of pine boughs. At first the cavity felt cold, but gradually his body heat warmed it up until he felt reasonably comfortable. His face was near the opening, allowing him to look up at the stars as they began appearing in the night sky. Ignoring his weariness he began to feel excited. Tonight he would talk with Towats.

"Towats, hear my words," he began, this time his voice softer, more confident, less awkward than before. After all he had gone through to get to the top of the mountain, fasting and all, he figured if there was ever a time when Towats would speak to a man, it would be now.

Walkara wondered what message Towats would have for him. Should Walkara lead his people against the Timpany Utes and recapture their homeland? Should he organize an even greater army and push the Shoshones north of the great river that curved like a snake? Would Towats tell Walkara how to get the fire sticks for his people, or how to become rich in horses?

"Towats, speak to me."

Walkara was ready for his vision or medicine dream to begin. He listened, and watched and waited. When nothing happened, he dozed in weary, restless sleep. When he awakened, looking up into a sky bright with stars, he prayed again.

He began to wonder why Towats wouldn't answer him. Was he doing something wrong? Was he not worthy? He began to wonder if perhaps there was no Towats at all. Maybe the elders had not told him the truth. Maybe the elders did not know the truth.

Walkara began to feel hungry. He remembered the last two pieces of deer jerky in his pouch. His formerly dry mouth began to water. His body craved the strength the meat would give him. He reached into the leather pouch and pulled out both pieces of jerky. He rubbed the smooth, firm meat with his fingers. He knew how it would taste. He knew how it would give strength to his body.

He raised the meat to his mouth, but stopped short of taking a bite. The thought occurred to him that if he broke his fast, gave up in his quest to speak with Towats, he would always wonder if Towats really existed. He realized that if there really was a Towats, the time to find out was now. He began to feel angry at his own weakness. He had come so close to giving up. With all his might, he threw the jerky into the night air. He would not be tempted to eat again. There was no more food in the pouch.

Again he called on Towats. Again there was no answer. Walkara continued to pray, eventually falling into a troubled, restless sleep full of dreams and nightmares, but there was nothing in all this that could be taken as communication with the supernatural.

By the time morning came Walkara was sick. The muscles in his stomach and legs were cramping. He was retching in continuous attempts to throw up food that was not there. He felt hot and dizzy. He made no attempt to get out of the snow cave. He could feel his body getting weaker and weaker. He doubted that he could stand up, even if he tried. The sickness continued. Still no answer from Towats.

Walkara's bed of snow began to rock and swirl. His world was in constant motion now, and he doubted that he would be able to stand up even if he had the strength. He thought about trying to crawl out of his hole and look for the two pieces of jerky, but that would require too much energy.

It occurred to him that Towats might be testing him

to see how determined he was. That thought made him angry. Gods should not tease helpless humans. Walkara was in a standoff with Towats, and was determined not to give up. He would speak with Towats, or he would die trying. He would show the gods how strong a man could be. He would not give up, not ever. The sickness and dizziness continued.

As the day progressed, Walkara found he could no longer focus his eyes or his mind. He felt himself drifting into a gray wasteland somewhere between consciousness and sleep. The gray became thick and heavy. He felt himself drowning, but was helpless to do anything about it. He forgot about Towats and his fasting. All he knew was that the gray fog was drowning him, and he was helpless to stop it.

Then suddenly the gray was gone. The sickness was gone. His body was strong again. He was alert, his eyes sharply focused. He crawled out of the cave and jumped to his feet. Walkara had never felt so strong and alert in all his life. He felt like he could run all the way home without stopping, like there was nothing he could not do. He had never felt better and stronger. He felt like he could literally fly like the birds, if he had a mind to do it.

He knew something was wrong, or different, when he looked back into the snow cave where he had spent the day and the previous night. He had been alone in the cave, but as he looked in now, someone was lying there. It was a man, a young man—very still, like he was dead.

Walkara suddenly realized the young man he saw was himself. Somehow he had left his body and was looking back at it. It was as if he had two bodies now, the one he was in that felt so good and strong, and the sick one in the snow cave.

Then he realized he was not standing on the ground, but in the air, a foot or so off the ground. Merely by willing it, he could move forward, backward, up or down. Somehow his mind controlled the direction his body moved.

Slowly at first, then faster, he began drifting away from the body in the snow cave, higher and higher. He began to spin. He found himself in a long, dark valley or tunnel, spinning, turning, drifting through the darkness. He began to feel uncertain and afraid, not knowing what was happening.

Walkara noticed a light at the far end of the valley. It was a warm, golden, inviting light. He felt himself drawn towards it. The light grew brighter and brighter. The nearer he got to it the better he felt.

Emerging from the end of the tunnel he found himself in the most beautiful place he had ever seen. It was a lush, green valley bathed in the same golden light he had seen at the end of the tunnel. Horses grazed in the meadows, the most beautiful horses he had ever seen, taller and stronger than the horses he had known.

There were people too, but instead of being dressed in buckskins they wore white, flowing robes. The people were moving about, apparently busy with various tasks. Though Walkara didn't know any of them he still felt comfortable, like he belonged. In fact he had never felt better in his entire life. There was a feeling of peace and contentment like he had never known before. He didn't want to leave.

"Pan-a-Karry Quinker," a voice called from somewhere behind him. It was a beautiful, penetrating voice. He had never heard anything more beautiful. The words meant twister of iron.

"Pan-a-Karry Quinker," the voice repeated. Walkara wondered if it was speaking to him, and if so, why it wasn't calling him Walkara. He turned around, discovering the source of the voice.

Walkara stood face to face with a glorious man in a white robe. There was no doubt in Walkara's mind that he was standing before Towats, the Great Spirit. Walkara dropped to the ground.

"Stand," the Great Spirit commanded, in the same wonderful voice. Walkara stood and faced the glowing personage.

"What do you want?" Towats asked.

"Only to stay here with you," Walkara responded, surprised at his answer.

"You must go back," Towats said.

"And do what?"

"A tribe of white men will come to live in Yuta lands. You are not to make war with them."

"Tell me more," Walkara said, when Towats began to move away.

"You will be a great warrior and have many horses, Pan-a-Karry Quinker."

"Why do you call me Pan-a-Karry Quinker?" Walkara asked, but Towats left without answering. Almost before he knew it, Walkara found himself back in the dark tunnel, spinning and twisting. Then suddenly he didn't feel good anymore. His body wretched with nausea. He felt weak and thirsty. He was back in the snow cave. His spirit body and his old body had come together again.

Mustering all his strength, Walkara crawled out of the cave. If he could find the jerky he had thrown away, if he could get a drink of water, he believed he would feel better.

Chapter 6

Walkara felt better the next morning. Not only did he find the two pieces of jerky he had tossed away earlier, but as he began walking down the mountain he discovered a fat porcupine nibbling away at the bark in the top of a small fir tree. A sharp blow to the head with a pine bough and the prey was his.

He rolled the animal on its back, removed the entrails, and began removing the skin. His mouth started to water. Venison, elk and bison were the preferred meats of the Ute warrior, but there was nothing wrong with a fat rodent when one was truly hungry. Roasted porcupine was juicy and tender, similar in texture to the meat of the bighorn sheep.

After cleaning the animal Walkara stretched the carcass out on a clean rock while he gathered materials for making a fire. He fashioned a nest from dry, shredded sagebrush bark. Then he carved a spindle and baseboard from the same material. Using the loose string on his unstrung bow to make the spindle spin, he was soon engulfed in a puff of white smoke. Dropping the newly created spark into the bark nest, he began puffing it to life, carefully at first, not wanting to blow it out. But as the smoke became thicker and thicker he blew harder and harder, until the bundle burst into flame. Quickly he placed it under a pile of twigs and sticks.

Soon the little fire was warming his skin and his heart. The wind on top of the mountain had been cold. And the snow inside the cave had made his muscles and bones ache. Now that was all forgotten.

After using his knife to hack the limbs off a small pine tree Walkara shoved it up through the chest cavity of the porcupine, then rested each end of the tree on large flat rocks located on opposite sides of the fire. Soon he could smell the aroma of roasting meat. His mouth began to water even more.

A man who hadn't eaten a meal in two days wasn't about to wait until the entire porcupine was finished cooking. As soon as the carcass turned a golden brown and began dripping melted fat into the fire, he began cutting off small pieces of meat around the edges and stuffing them into his mouth. The more he ate the hungrier he became. It wasn't until the meat was about half gone that his appetite began to feel satisfied.

Stretching out on the ground beside the warm fire, Walkara felt better than he had felt in a long time. He could feel the youthful strength returning to his tired body. Good food, a warm fire, and the knowledge that he had talked to Towats lifted his spirits. Life was good. He felt happiness, an inner peace he had not noticed before. He was ready and eager to go on living, taking life one day at a time. A little meat was still left on the carcass when he fell into a deep, peaceful sleep.

The next morning Walkara felt strong, rested, confident, and ready to do something, but he wasn't sure what. He didn't want to return to his people. He had let them down. Some had died because of his carelessness. He owed a debt that he could not repay, at least not yet. But someday he would.

He remembered the tall warrior on the roan stallion, a Shoshone, possibly a chief, the man who was likely responsible for the death of his child bride.

56

Walkara looked northward towards the land of the Shoshones.

Walkara didn't have a horse, nor did he have companions to accompany him. But he had a strong body, a keen mind, his weapons, and the knowledge that he had spoken with the Great Spirit. Yes, he would go to the land of the Shoshones. He would go alone. He would get horses which, would help pay the debt he owed to his people. Maybe he would take some scalps, too.

Walkara did not hurry as he headed north out of the mountains. There were no promises to keep or deadlines to meet. In four or five moons, winter would come, but other than that there was nothing in his future he had to worry about.

As he walked along Walkara gathered the things he needed for weapons. He picked a wad of pitch from a pine tree that had been damaged by an elk polishing new antlers. He picked up feathers from birds of prey, magpies and ravens when he found them on the ground. When he killed a deer for meat, he saved some of the sinew, and he was constantly on the lookout for flint and obsidian rocks from which to strike off blanks and make arrow points.

When his bag was full with everything he needed, Walkara stopped one afternoon beside a thick patch of wild roses and began making arrows. After cutting and peeling the shafts with his knife and cutting a notch in both ends, he straightened them by heating them in the fire, then bending them to the desired straightness. Using a smooth rock he rubbed off the rough spots.

After shaping his arrow points by chipping off the edges with the tip of a deer horn, Walkara pushed them into the hot pitch he had applied to the larger ends of the shafts. After the pitch cooled and was holding the tip firmly in place he wrapped the rear end of the tip and the shaft with wet sinew to make sure the tip would not pop out.

He also used hot pitch and sinew to secure the split feathers to the rear end of the shaft, at the same time making sure plenty of sinew was wrapped around the shaft right in front of the notch to make sure the force of the forward thrust of the bow string would not split the arrow.

Walkara was proud of his workmanship, examining each arrow carefully as he set it aside to dry, wondering if that arrow might have the privilege of killing the Shoshone warrior who was riding the roan stallion. By the end of the day Walkara had crafted a dozen arrows, just like the ones father had taught him to make. He knew his father would have been pleased with the quality of the arrows.

As Walkara wandered northwards out of the foothills into the vast sagebrush and grassy flatlands, he came across an unusual trail, unlike any trail he had ever seen before. Actually, it wasn't one trail, but two, running side by side. It wasn't that he had never seen two trails side by side before. Around a well-used water hole it was not unusual to see many trails coming in somewhat parallel to each other. The unusual thing about these two trails was that the distance between them—the length of a bow—remained the same for miles in either direction. Even where the two trails passed through rocky areas or gullies, the distance between them remained the same.

Walkara sat down on a large rock and pondered the mystery of the parallel trails. Why would anyone want to make two trails when one would do? Walkara thought about it a long time, but could come up with no reasonable answer.

Walkara knew he was in Shoshone country, but that was about all. He had not been here before. He didn't know if he would find the enemy to the east, west or north, so he decided to follow the double trail. Perhaps it would lead him to an enemy camp.

Chapter 6

Following the trail made Walkara nervous. It was too much in the open, too far from forests and ledges, the kinds of hiding places a man on foot needed when traveling through enemy lands. Should mounted Shoshones come upon him, he would have a difficult time getting away from them. Still, his quiver was full of new arrows, and his legs had never felt stronger. He continued to follow the trail through the remainder of the day.

Just as the sun was going down Walkara spotted smoke drifting through some treetops just ahead of him. Quickly, he headed into the nearby brush, figuring he might have found an enemy camp. Wanting to get a good look at it before dark, he hurried forward through the brush to the top of a little hill.

Upon reaching a good vantage point he could hardly believe what he saw. The smoke he had seen was not coming from a tepee or a cook fire, but from a strange pile of evenly chopped trees. They were piled one on top of the other to form a rectangular structure with grass and sticks on top, apparently to keep the rain out. At one end was a vertical pile of river rocks from which came the smoke he had seen.

Walkara remembered his father telling him how some white men lived in log tepees. The young Indian concluded this must be a white man's tepee. White men weren't very smart. It would be very difficult to move the log tepee to a new hunting area.

Behind the log structure was a pole corral containing three horses. Walkara studied the terrain around the cabin, wondering how difficult it would be to steal the three horses without the white men discovering what was happening until it was too late. He guessed the white men would have the deadly fire sticks. But during the night they wouldn't be able to see him to shoot him.

Walkara wondered how many men might be in the log tepee, and if they had dogs. He didn't see any. It

59

would soon be dark. While stealing the horses looked easy, he was still very reluctant. He didn't know the white men. He didn't know how dangerous they were, or how smart they were. He didn't know why they built log tepees that couldn't be moved. He didn't know why they made trails that went side by side for miles. Maybe they had supernatural powers.

He finally decided he needed to know more about the white men before he tried to steal their horses. Maybe he should pay them a visit. It would be nice to see what was inside the log tepee.

It was almost dark when Walkara reached the front of the cabin. The door was open. There was no sign of white men or dogs. Cautiously, Walkara stepped up to the opening and peered inside.

He could see no people or dogs, but lots of things—a huge pile of deer skins and buffalo robes, and clusters of steel traps hanging from pegs in the walls. In the center of the room was a wooden platform balanced on four narrow poles. On it were boxes. Walkara stepped inside.

The first thing he noticed on the wooden platform was a pile of knives, the nicest he had ever seen, new and shiny, fifteen or twenty of them, more than two or three men would use in a lifetime. He took one and put it in his belt. Nobody needed that many knives.

Against the wall were about a dozen fire sticks. He figured he ought to take one of them too, but he didn't know how to make them work. His father had told him that they wouldn't fire unless you poured what looked like black dirt down the barrel.

As he looked around he could see lots of things he recognized—mirrors, beads, needles, hatchets, cooking pans. There were also lots of things he didn't recognize.

"Howdy, Injun," said a strange voice in a strange language. Walkara spun around to face the two white men who had just reached the open door. They were dressed in skins, like Indians in fall and winter. There was much hair on their faces. They had fire sticks in their hands, but they were not pointing them at Walkara.

"Shoshone?" asked the tallest of the two men, who was still smaller than the Indian they faced.

Walkara understood some Shoshone, but wasn't about to answer in the language of his enemies. He remained silent.

Gesturing in sign language the tall white man pointed at Walkara, then with two fingers made a walking motion across the back of his hand. Then he pointed questioningly in four different directions. Walkara understood. The white man wanted to know where he had come from.

Walkara pointed to the southwest, then, putting two fingers to straddle the edge of his hand, he made the motion of a man riding a horse. Then he tilted his head sideways on the back of his hand like a man sleeping four times to indicate it would take a man riding a horse four sleeps to ride from this place in a southwesterly direction to Walkara's home.

"Ute," the one white man said to the other, obviously pleased. The other man reached out before Walkara had time to stop him, and removed the new knife from Walkara's belt, returning it to the pile of knives on the table. Walkara wanted to leave, but the white men were blocking the door. They had smiles on their faces, but he did not trust them. He wanted to return to the safety of the woods.

The tall white man picked up the knife and handed it back to Walkara, motioning for him to keep it, a present. The tall stranger then picked up a metal box that had a round piece of wood plugging up a round hole in the top. After removing the wooden plug the man raised the box to his mouth and took a deep drink.

Then he handed the metal box to Walkara, who indicated that he wasn't thirsty.

The white man insisted that Walkara take a drink. Walkara didn't know why anyone would want him to drink when he wasn't thirsty. He knew the liquid in the container wasn't poison because the white man had taken the first drink. With hesitation Walkara took the metal box in his hands and raised the opening to his lips.

The liquid was light brown in color, like muddy runoff water in the spring. It had a strange smell and burned his lips, tongue and throat as he swallowed. He didn't like the taste. Walkara resisted the urge to cough and spit. His eyes began to water as he handed the container back to the white man, who drank a second time from the container before handing it to his friend, who after taking a drink handed it back to Walkara. By now he had a warm sensation in his belly and was feeling a growing thirst for more of the fiery liquid. The white men began to laugh as Walkara swallowed more the second time.

After the third drink the men put the metal box back on the table so they could teach Walkara about their trading business. Walkara couldn't believe how good he was feeling, and how thirsty he was for more of the strange water.

Piling Walkara's arms high with skins and furs they guided him towards the door, then back to the table, as if he had just entered the cabin bringing a large assortment of furs. As they removed the furs from Walkara's arms, one at a time, they replaced the furs with trade goods—a knife, a pan, a hatchet, a handful of iron arrowheads, and the metal box containing the strange water.

Walkara didn't have any trouble understanding what they were telling him. The white men wanted him and his people to come here to trade. They were telling

Chapter 6

him that with furs and hides his people could buy the white man's things.

Walkara pointed to the row of fire sticks against the wall, wondering how many furs it would take to get one of them. The tall man held one finger in the air, then pointed towards the horses behind the cabin, indicating he would accept one horse as payment for a fire stick.

Walkara was delighted at his discovery. With furs and horses he and his friends could buy anything in the world at this log tepee. The only problem was the location. The log tepee was in the land of the Shoshones. Traveling to and from this place could be dangerous. Still, the journey would be worth the risk because of all the wonderful things that could be purchased.

Pointing to a mat in one corner, the white men invited Walkara to spend the night with them, but the young man declined. Though the white men had given him a new knife and some of their strange water, he still felt uneasy around them. He wanted to run to the safety of the woods. But he knew he would be back, and when he returned he would bring many furs, and perhaps some horses too.

As Walkara started to leave, the tall man patted himself on the chest, saying, "Me Bridger, Jim Bridger."

Walkara decided to remember the stranger's name. Without telling the white men his own name he turned and disappeared into the darkness.

"I'll bet we see that Injun again," Bridger said to his companion, as they watched Walkara disappear into the night.

Chapter 7

It was almost a week later when Walkara found a Shoshone village. He was near the headwaters of the Green River near the Wind River Mountains.

He watched the camp for several days, studying the horse herd and trying to figure out the best way to get away with some of the best animals. There were twenty-four lodges in the village, and somewhere around 100 people, with the usual assortment of dogs.

Walkara remembered when he and Arrapeen had raided the Ute camp to avenge their father's death. It had somehow seemed easier then. Having someone with whom to discuss the plan of attack made the task easier. Now there was no one to confirm or disagree with a decision. Walkara concluded that raiding an enemy camp by oneself not only required more courage, but a lot more confidence in one's own decisions.

There were 67 horses in the herd, with four or five always tied up by the lodges at night. There was no sign of the roan stallion or the tall warrior. The village was still Shoshone, though, and therefore the enemy.

Except for the ones tied up in the village, the horses were grazing in a side canyon off the main valley. While the floor of the canyon was a long, winding, grassy meadow, the sides were steep and rugged. The twenty-four tepees were placed in a V across the opening of the canyon to prevent the horses from leaving their lush pasture.

Walkara's dilemma was whether or not to try to make off with one or two of the horses tied in the village, or try to drive off the entire herd, a much more difficult task, that if successful would make pursuit by the Shoshones more difficult. He knew he could never drive that many horses back to Ute lands all by himself, but if he could just drive them out of reach of the Shoshones so they could not pursue him, that would be the most important thing he could do to ensure his safe getaway.

It would be easier to sneak off in the night with one or two of the tethered horses, but in order to do that he would have to sneak into the enemy camp, risking discovery by dogs or Indians. Then if he made it safely away he would leave a trail that could be easily followed by his mounted enemies.

As Walkara watched the herd he took notice of which horses could be caught and ridden by the Shoshone herdsmen, and how they handled when ridden. He had to be sure that when he chose the horse he would ride it wasn't one that would start bucking, run away with him, or be too lazy or slow to outdistance the men who would surely come after him.

The next morning, shortly before daybreak, Walkara crept into the herd of grazing horses, having already determined that a tall bay would be the one he would ride. Slipping a rawhide noose in the animal's mouth, and pulling it tight, he scrambled onto the horse's back.

There was no time to lose. The camp would soon be awake. He had jerky in a pouch on his belt, and his weapons were strapped to his back. He hoped he was ready for the test of horsemanship and endurance he was about to face.

He eased his horse to the side of the herd furthest

from the tepees where the Shoshones were sleeping. With the line of tepees blocking the horses' exit from the little valley no guard had been posted. Walkara talked quietly to the horses as he eased them together. He didn't want the sleeping Indians to notice what was happening until it was too late. He urged his band of ponies into a trot towards the village, then a gallop.

His plan was simple: stampede the herd through the village barrier, hoping that the four tethered horses would break their lead ropes to join their galloping companions.

So far the plan was working perfectly. The sleeping Indians were still not aware of the herd approaching at full gallop.

Looking ahead, Walkara finally noticed movement among the tepees, what looked like a woman hurrying from one tepee to another. Within seconds the entire village would be aroused.

Walkara sounded his war cry—shrill, loud and long—urging the horses in front of him to run even faster. There was no turning back now.

The alarm had been sounded. Startled Shoshone braves stumbled from their tepees, some with blankets to wave at the approaching horses in an attempt to turn them back, others with weapons to kill those who would steal their horses.

It was too late for any organized attempt to turn back the stampeding horses. The fastest animals at the head of Walkara's band were already through the line of tepees, and with some already through, the rest were determined to follow. Walkara crouched low on the bay, his face buried in the black mane, hoping he would not be seen until it was too late. He noticed that two of the tethered animals had already broken free. He could not see the other two.

He felt the exhilaration of knowing his daring plan was working. Most of the horses were already through the barrier. Soon he would be through it too. Lifting his head, he sounded another war cry as he followed the last of the herd between the tepees.

Suddenly Walkara felt the sting of flying leather on his left shoulder. Before he could react, or even think about what was happening, he was jerked upright and off the back of his galloping horse. In that long moment between the time he left the horse's back and before he hit the hard ground, Walkara realized he had been lassoed with a rawhide rope.

For a brief moment he thought of that wonderful place he had seen from the tops of the mountains, the world of spirits where he had felt so happy. He hoped the fall from the horse would break his neck and send him immediately to that wonderful place, because he knew that should he survive the fall, the angry Shoshones would have little mercy.

Even before he hit the ground, Walkara was trying to slip off the rope so he would be free to run after the fleeing horses. But there was not enough time, and the more he tried to pull the rope free the tighter it seemed to be pulled around his shoulders. Even though he hit the ground running, the rope jerked him back, and before he could get free of it, three or four Shoshone braves had leaped upon him. The worst of his fears had been realized.

Almost before he had a chance to fight back, Walkara's hands were lashed tightly behind his back, his weapons and clothing were stripped from his body, and he was dragged across the ground towards a large pine tree. The rawhide rope that was secured to his tightly wrapped hands was tied to the trunk of the tree.

Without paying him any more attention, the Shoshone warriors left to catch their horses. Still, Walkara was not free to think about any kind of escape. He was surrounded by women and children, most of whom had sticks with which they began to beat him.

He thought of dropping to the ground and pulling his knees to his chest to better endure the beating. By appearing totally helpless, though, Walkara thought he would probably attract even more abuse. It seemed he was being thrashed with a hundred sticks.

The onslaught became so intense that his very breath was taken away. For a moment it seemed like he would be beaten to death. He sensed a desperate need to do something.

Mustering his strength, Walkara let out an angry roar with all his might, not unlike the sound of an injured lion. At the same time he curled back his lips, snapped his gleaming white teeth at the nearest squaw, and kicked the nearest child, a boy who had been beating mercilessly at his legs.

The surprised women and children drew back, forming a circle at a safe distance. For a moment, there was quiet. Walkara caught his breath. He was crouched like an animal, ready to snap or kick if the beatings resumed.

A middle-aged squaw, a stick in her hand, stepped forward. She looked Walkara straight in the eye to show she was not afraid of him. She stopped immediately in front of him. Those behind her remained silent. Without warning she spit in Walkara's face, and at the same time struck him in the genitals with her stick. In pain, Walkara growled back at her, but she did not retreat. The other women and children began to laugh at his helplessness, but the communal beating of the prisoner did not resume.

The woman who had struck him ordered the others to go about their business. There would be plenty of time for having fun with the prisoner later. As the women returned to their tepees to stoke up the morning cook fires, a group of the older boys maintained watch on the new prisoner.

Walkara would have liked a drink of water, but it

didn't even occur to him to ask his captors for any. He knew how his tribe would treat a Shoshone brave under similar circumstances, and he didn't expect any better treatment for himself. He also knew the greatest kindness he could hope for would be a quick death.

He knew what to expect from his captors. They would try to keep him alive as long as possible while inflicting as much pain as possible.

He wished he were already dead. Though he was hardened to the rigors of the trail, Walkara didn't know how he would stand up to the torture about to be inflicted. He knew the ultimate joy he could bring his captors would be to scream in agony as they abused him. The worst thing he could do would be to seem indifferent to their tortures, to appear insensitive to pain, to have peace in his mind and spirit as his body was being destroyed. He knew if he could do that his enemies would be frustrated in their attempts to hurt him.

It seemed a long time before the men returned. The sun was high in the sky, and their spirits seemed high too. They had recovered all the horses. They had captured the horse thief, though they were surprised that one boy had attempted such a daring raid and almost succeeded.

The men didn't seem to be in any hurry to eat their breakfast, but eventually they were finished and began gathering around their new captive. The women and children came too. No one wanted to miss the fun.

Walkara mustered all the strength and courage he could, trying desperately to withdraw from his body to his inner self. He didn't know if they would begin the torture by skinning him alive, removing his genitals, or gouging out his eyes. Whatever his punishment, he hoped he could bear it with dignity and what would appear to be outward indifference.

A short, broad man with a round badger face and

broken yellow teeth was the first to step forward. The man didn't look or act like a chief, so Walkara figured he was probably the man who had roped him, and therefore the man who had the privilege of being the first to get to torture the prisoner.

The squat man drew a knife from his belt. He rubbed his thumb against the blade to ensure its sharpness. Looking Walkara straight in the eye, the corners of the little man's mouth turned up in a menacing grin.

Walkara could feel his heart pounding. He could feel the sweat running down the small of his back. He felt sick. He wanted to run. He wanted to fight. He wanted to die. He wanted to scream for help, though he knew no one would come to his rescue. He wanted anything but to stand and take what was about to happen.

Two other men stepped to each side of him, taking him firmly by the upper arms. Walkara stared into the eyes of the man in front of him, who had now cocked his head to one side and was looking intently at Walkara's chest. The man reached forward with the blade and made an incision about an inch long above Walkara's left nipple. As the skin parted red blood welled to the edge and spilled over his chest in four fine, winding rivulets.

Walkara made no sound; in fact, he was surprised at how little pain he felt as his skin was cut. But he knew the worst was still to come. The short man made three more incisions, one directly above and parallel to the first one, and two connecting the cuts to form a near perfect square. Walkara remained silent as the short man roughly removed the inch of skin he had just isolated.

Walkara had heard how captives had sometimes been skinned to death by Shoshones, but doing it an inch at a time was something new to him. This way the torture could take days, even weeks.

When a second man stepped forward, knife in hand, to make a similar incision, Walkara decided it was time to try to do something. Sounding a loud war cry, he kicked forward with all his might, catching the warrior between the legs. The surrounding Indians howled with delight, while some bounced on the prisoner to hold him tighter. In spite of Walkara's frantic attempts to bite and kick, a second square of skin was removed, this time from the right breast.

Walkara stopped fighting them, realizing he had made a mistake. He would not panic again. He would never again give them the satisfaction of thinking they had frightened him, or of thinking that he could not bear their torture. Let them remove every inch of his skin, gouge out his eyes, and cut off his testicles. Whatever they did, they would not get another sound from him. No, he would not enter the world of spirits as a coward, or a man who could not bear pain.

Walkara stood straight, silently glaring at his captors, daring them to take another square of skin, a hundred more squares of skin. It didn't matter to him, because he was ready to enter the world of spirits a brave and noble warrior and there was nothing any of the Shoshones could do to change that.

Suddenly all the men left. It was as if they sensed Walkara's sudden mastery of the skinning game. So now it was time to try something else.

They gathered by one of the tepees where they engaged in heated discussion. In the meantime the women and children resumed hitting the prisoner with their sticks. The women, in particular, seemed to take pleasure in hitting Walkara's genitals, which were soon blue and swollen. He was helpless to drive them back.

After a while the men returned, ordering the women and children to stand back. One of the men was leading a white horse. Another man beckoned to Walkara, asking him if he would like to have the white horse. Walkara didn't have a full understanding of Shoshone, but he knew enough to know when he was being offered a horse. He didn't respond, however, knowing it was some kind of trick.   He knew they weren't going to free his hands and just let him ride away on the white horse.

In a few moments some of the men were helping Walkara onto the animal. His hands were still tied behind his back. In all the commotion the horse had become agitated and wanted to break and run, but two of the Shoshones held it firmly by the lead rope.

As soon as Walkara was seated on the horse's back, his two feet were hobbled together beneath the horse's belly. He was beginning to figure out what the Indians were up to. They were going to turn the horse loose with Walkara on its back. With his hands tied behind his back, they thought he would fall off, and when he did, the rope securing his feet together would hold him suspended beneath the horse. As the horse ran or bucked, its feet would strike his body, all the time stepping on his arms and head. The only way to avoid being struck by the hooves would be to fall off while the horse was standing still. But this half-wild horse would not stand still. Even if it wanted to, the Indians would make sure it didn't.

Mounted on the prancing white horse Walkara was led to the edge of the village. He was accompanied by 15 or 16 mounted warriors, eager to join in the fun when the white horse was turned loose.

Walkara was a good rider, but he knew it would be difficult to stay on a spirited horse with his hands tied behind his back, especially when the horse was first turned loose and would be accelerating quickly, possibly bucking.

Suddenly the horse was free. Just as one of the Indians was slapping a rope across its rump to get it moving, Walkara lurched forward on his stomach, cocking his head to one side, grabbing a mouthful of thick, white mane with his teeth.

As the spirited horse lunged forward, Walkara, with the help of his teeth and his knees, was able to keep his balance. Except for kicking up his heels a few times, the horse was running smoothly. It had not attempted to buck, as perhaps the Indians thought it would.

A band of galloping Shoshones was close behind, shouting threats to Walkara and his white horse. Not able to see very well where he was going, but trusting the horse was at least somewhat familiar with the area, Walkara dug his heels into the horse's sides, urging it to run faster and faster.

It appeared the Indians had given him a chance—though a slim one—to regain his freedom. Attempting a daring getaway on a speedy horse, even with one's hands and feet tied, was certainly preferable to being skinned to death an inch at a time.

Walkara was pleased the horse was responding to his heels. It raced with all its might across a sagebrush flat. The yells of the pursuing Indians were getting further and further back. A plan began to form in Walkara's mind whereby he might get away from his enemies. He urged the horse to run even faster, knowing that if he fell under the animal with his feet tied together the thundering hooves would certainly kill him.

A large wad of mane still between his clenched teeth, Walkara wondered if he could guide the horse by pulling the mane to the right or left. He tried, but his efforts seemed to have no effect on the horse. It seemed to know where it was going, and there was nothing Walkara could do to change that. All he could do was urge it to greater speeds by digging his heels harder against its ribs. He had no idea how he would stop the horse should that become his desired course of action.

After crossing the sagebrush flat the horse entered a grove of aspen trees, following a winding, dusty trail.

The trees became thicker, the trail more winding, making it more difficult for Walkara to maintain his balance.

As the horse dropped into a gully and began lunging up a steep hill, Walkara suddenly had an idea that he thought might greatly enhance his chances of escape. All along his fear had been that with his feet tied together a loss of balance would result in his hanging upside down under the horse, with its hind feet striking him in the head and back. Now that the horse was going up the steep hill, Walkara realized that if he let go with his teeth, instead of falling sideways and ending up suspended under the horse, he might be able to slip backwards over the rear end of the animal, in the process allowing it to step out from between his hobbled feet and leave him behind on the ground. There was a lot of good cover here where he could hide from his pursuers.

He decided to give it a try. Letting go with his teeth, he felt himself sliding back onto the rump. It was too late now to do anything but just let himself slide over the back of the horse. He felt the animal's hind legs catch on the rope between his ankles about the time his back hit the ground. Then the horse was free, galloping up the hill out of sight. Quickly Walkara rolled out of the trail into some thick ferns.

He could hear the thundering hooves of the approaching Indians. He could only hope that in the thick trees they hadn't seen him slip off the back of the horse.

With his feet hobbled together, and his hands tied behind his back, Walkara knew there was no way he could outrun his captors, even through the underbrush. His only chance was to hide from them. Rolling under the thickest patch of ferns, he held perfectly still, his face in the dead leaves covering the ground.

Not only could he hear the thundering hooves as the Shoshone warriors galloped by single file on the trail, but with his face to the ground he could feel each thumping hoofbeat. Walkara didn't need to look up to know they hadn't seen him. None of the horses stopped, or even slowed down.

Walkara knew it wouldn't be long before they saw the white horse was without a rider. As soon as they did they would reverse their direction and return along the trail, looking for their captive. Springing to his feet, Walkara hurried as fast as his hobbled feet would allow him, not up or down the trail, but away from the trail, laterally along the side of the hill into the thickest part of the woods.

There was about a foot of slack in the strip of rawhide that held his two ankles together, allowing Walkara to take quick, short steps. He tried to avoid bare soil where his feet would leave prints, walking as much as possible on rocks and leaves. He moved quietly, the low branches and undergrowth making little or no sound as they rubbed against his bare skin. Except for the lashings on his ankles and wrists he was naked.

While his ears listened intently for any sound of pursuit, Walkara's eyes were constantly scanning the country ahead of him, selecting the best course of travel and the best hiding places should his pursuers find his trail.

Occasionally, in the distance, he could hear the neigh of a horse or the cry of a warrior, but none came close, so Walkara continued his journey along the side of the hill, occasionally working in and out of a steep draw. Soon his ankles and wrists were sore from working against the restrictive, tough rawhide.

Finally, as Walkara was entering a draw that seemed deeper and more dense with foliage than the rest, he heard a welcome sound. Trickling water.

Not only would the water quench his burning thirst, but it would also allow him to free his hands and feet. The spring was little more than a trickle. Dropping to his knees, Walkara rolled onto his back, pushing his hands and wrists into the wet mud.

He lay still for a few minutes, enjoying the chill of the water and mud on his hot back. When he guessed the rawhide bindings were sufficiently damp, he began working his wrists back and forth, the slippery rawhide beginning to stretch until he was able to pull one hand free, then the other. A minute later Walkara's feet were free. He rolled over on his stomach and took a deep drink of cool water.

After daubing cool black mud over the two square wounds on his chest and lashing the rawhide lashings around his waist Walkara headed deeper into the woods. Traveling was easier now, allowing him to cover several miles in less than an hour.

By late afternoon Walkara's feet were sore, and knowing the Shoshones would search long and hard for him, he began looking for a place to hide. Coming into a pine forest with many of the trees having low-hanging branches, Walkara selected one that wasn't any larger or smaller than most of the others and crawled underneath. Next to the trunk, he scratched down through the pine needles into the soft black dirt, fashioning a little nest for himself. After curling up like a dog inside of it, he scratched dirt and pine needles around and over him, leaving only his face exposed. When he was finished he felt confident that an enemy rider could circle the tree a dozen times and not see him.

Walkara knew he was at least temporarily safe from his enemies. He was warm against the cool night air. To partially satisfy his hunger he chewed on a piece of rawhide for what little nourishment it might provide. When his jaws finally became tired, Walkara dozed into a restless sleep.

Chapter 8

Walkara stayed under his tree until the following evening, knowing the Shoshones would be looking for him. He would have liked to remain in his hiding place even longer, but his thirst was almost unbearable.

Less than a mile away, in a draw on a north-facing slope, he found not only a spring but one of the largest berry patches he had ever seen, acres of raspberries, huckleberries, curants, and thimbleberries. It was late summer and the berries were ripe. When darkness began to fall, Walkara was still stuffing his mouth with handfuls of moist, sweet berries. He continued until it was too dark to see what he was picking.

The night air was cold against his bare skin as he fashioned a new hiding place under the low-hanging branches of a pine tree. Covered with a warm blanket of dry needles, his thirst quenched and his belly full, Walkara fell into a deep sleep.

He slept a long time, because when he finally awakened the morning sun was sifting through the green pine needles above his head. Before awakening he was dreaming he was back in his Ute village, waking up to the smell of breakfast being cooked by his new bride. She sang as she cooked, a beautiful Shoshone love song. She was repeating the same part of the song again and again as if that were her favorite part.

As Walkara awakened from his dream, he sat up

suddenly with a jerk. He could still hear the love song. He shook his head from side to side and cleaned out his ears with a finger. He could still hear the song. It was real, not something in his imagination. He looked through the green-needled branches towards the berry patch.

At first he saw nothing, but as he continued to look in the direction of the music he finally saw movement. Something light brown in color was pushing through the bushes. Had he not been hearing the music he would have guessed a bear was feeding on the berries.

Walkara continued to watch in the direction of the singing, and eventually he saw a young Indian woman moving slowly through the bushes, picking berries she dropped into a leather pouch attached to a thong tied about her narrow waist. Her hands worked quickly as she moved among the bushes. She continued to hum her song. The woman was beautiful, her hair hanging neatly about her shoulders in Shoshone fashion. She had a smooth complexion and a healthy curve to her breast and hip.

Walkara's mind filled with questions. Was the woman alone? Had she walked to the berry patch, or had she ridden a horse? If so, where was the horse? Did she have a weapon under her dress? If so, should he try to take it away from her? Or should he just try to steal her horse when she had herback turned? Should he make his move now, or should he wait?

Walkara decided to wait and do nothing until he was absolutely sure the woman was alone, that no other berry pickers had come to the patch with her. She was moving slowly up the hill, so he figured if she had a horse it would be somewhere down the hill. He shifted his position several times to get a better look down the mountain, but still could see no horse. The woman continued to hum her song and pick berries.

As Walkara watched and waited, he scratched

quietly. The pine needles had made small puncture marks and scratches all over his body, causing his skin to itch. And he still had the two ugly wounds on his chest where the Shoshones had started to skin him. Though he had wiped away the pine needles, there was still a lot of dirt in the wounds. He longed to wash himself and dress in soft buckskins like the ones the woman was wearing.

He wondered how hard she would fight if he tried to take her buckskin dress. He would probably have to kill her to get her clothing. The thought repulsed him. The woman's song was medicine to his troubled soul. Watching her graceful movements, even at a distance, had somehow softened his feelings of loneliness and desperation. No, he would not harm this woman, not even to get the clothing he so desperately needed.

But he would steal her horse, if he could find it. Slowly, Walkara worked his way out of his nest, moving away from the woman, being careful to keep the tree between him and her so she could not see him. Carefully, he worked his way down the hill towards where he guessed her horse might be. He was very cautious, still not absolutely sure the woman was alone.

In time he saw a horse, a paint, tied to an aspen tree. There being no other horses near it, he was fairly certain the woman had come by herself to pick berries. Walkara was below the crest of the hill now, where the woman could not see him or the paint. He hurried towards the horse.

He wasn't very far from the animal when he heard the clatter of hooves on rocks in the draw just around the hill from him. Quickly, Walkara ducked under a bush. The noise could have been made by an elk or a deer, but he doubted it. The horse was looking in the direction of the noise too. Walkara waited.

He was sorry he had left the safety of his pine tree when he saw the mounted Shoshone warrior coming around the edge of the hill. It was the same thickset, round-faced Indian who had cut the first square of skin from Walkara's chest, the same one he thought had roped him and jerked him from his horse in the raid.

At least the man was alone. No more horses were coming around the edge of the hill. The man dismounted a short distance downhill from the paint. He looked around, apparently trying to find the woman. Walkara held perfectly still, not 40 feet away. When the man couldn't see the woman he tied his horse, a tall sorrel, to a tree, then walked up to the paint, looking at the ground, apparently looking for the woman's tracks. Walkara guessed this man might be the woman's husband.

Upon finding the footprints and determining the woman had headed up the hill, the man began to walk in the same direction. Walkara was delighted. Now he could steal two horses instead of one—as soon as the man was out of sight.

But there was something unusual about the way the man moved. He was not walking like a berry picker going to join a companion. In a half crouch, he would take a few steps, then stop and look for the woman. Then he would take a few more steps, making every effort to move quietly, avoiding dry leaves and twigs. Though the man had left his weapons tied to the saddle on his horse, he was stalking the woman, as a hunter would stalk a deer or an elk.

Walkara watched as the man moved slowly out of sight over the crest of the hill. When all was clear, Walkara jumped to his feet and hurried to the horses. First he untied the paint, then the man's horse.

He leaped upon the paint and turned it away from the berry patch, then hesitated. In his mind he could still hear the woman's song that had been so pleasant in his dreams. In his mind he could see the swells of her body beneath the soft buckskin, the beauty of her face, her neatly combed hair.

Walkara knew the woman and the man were Shoshones, his enemies. If they saw him, a new chase would begin. If caught, Walkara would be tortured and killed. The wise thing for him to do would be to leave as quietly and quickly as possible and put a lot more miles between him and the Shoshone camp.

But when Walkara thought of the squat Indian stalking the woman, his heart was suddenly filled with a bloodlust urge to rip the man's heart out with his bare hands. What amazed Walkara was that when the same man had cut a square of skin from him, he hadn't felt nearly so much hate and passion to kill.

Walkara didn't understand his feelings. His hands were wet with sweat. His muscles were quivering with excitement. His blood was surging through his body with a warmth he hadn't felt since the Shoshones had stripped away his clothing. While his mind was telling him to get as far away as possible from this band of Shoshones, something more powerful, from somewhere deep inside, was ordering him to defend and protect this beautiful woman.

He turned his horse away from the berry patch and urged it forward. The horse started walking, the sorrel following close behind. Walkara was looking over his shoulder, still fighting the battle between his passions and the cold reasoning that told him to go. He stopped the horse. He thought he heard something, possibly the scream of a woman.

He could withhold no longer. Leaping from the horse, he tossed the lead rope over a limb and began racing up the hill towards the spot where he had last seen the woman. He didn't think to grab the bow and arrows hanging from the saddle of the sorrel.

Around and through clumps of bushes Walkara raced up the hill. He heard the squeal of the woman and realized his instincts had been correct. She was being attacked.

When Walkara reached them, the man was crouched over the squaw, trying to suppress her kicking, biting and clawing as she tried to fight him off. Without a word, and without breaking stride, Walkara grabbed a stone about the size of a horse's hoof. Guessing the short, round-faced man probably had a thick skull, Walkara didn't hold back as he smashed the rock against the back of the man's head.

Without a fight the man collapsed on top of the struggling woman. Walkara grabbed the unconscious warrior by the ankle and dragged him off of her.

The woman was still on her back, pushing backwards, pulling her dress down over her legs. Walkara was amazed that she appeared just as afraid of him as she had been of the Indian he had just hit on the head.

That's when he realized he wasn't wearing any clothing other than a rawhide thong around his waist. Perhaps the frightened woman was afraid he too would try to assault her. Without hesitation Walkara pointed to the part of him that was still swollen and discolored from when the squaws and children had beaten it with their sticks, hoping to convey to her that he was in no condition to assault a woman.

At first she smiled, then began to laugh. Walkara didn't know what she thought was funny, but he was relieved that she no longer appeared to be threatened by him. He returned the smile, then dropped to his knees and began removing the buckskin shirt, leggings, moccasins and loincloth from the round-faced Indian who lay motionless on the ground. Quietly the woman watched, not offering to help. But she didn't seem to want to leave either.

Walkara was pleased to find a sharp knife in the man's belt, the same one that had been used to cut the skin from Walkara's chest. He slipped the knife in his belt. When he started to slip into the buckskin shirt the woman motioned for him to stop.

She walked up to him, closely inspecting the two wounds in his chest. With her fingers she carefully removed some dirt from the wounds, then motioned for Walkara to follow her to the spring where he had obtained water the night before. Apparently she wanted to wash his wounds, and he felt more than willing to let her do it, but first he had some unfinished business.

He bent over the round-faced Indian, still not sure if the man was dead or alive. Either way he had a nice scalp that would be worth taking home. After removing the knife from his belt, Walkara quickly cut a four-inch square from the top of the man's head, where the hair was thickest, and removed the scalp. Walkara tucked the knife and hair in his belt as he followed the woman to the spring.

Walkara seated himself on a smooth boulder while the woman obtained some wet green moss from the spring and began washing his wounds. He didn't mind the pain of cold water and moss rubbing against his torn flesh. In fact, he enjoyed the pain because it was the reason for this beautiful woman getting close to him, touching him with her hands, allowing him to look into her face as she worked.

"I am Susquenah," she said, "and the man you scalped is Nampbutts. We are from the same band." She spoke slowly, in her native Shoshone. Walkara understood.

"They call me Walkara," he said, looking her straight in the face. She returned the stare.

Suddenly Walkara was aware of the sound of breaking bushes, not very far away along the side of the hill. He looked over.

The naked Nampbutts was stumbling down the hill.

Blood from his scalp wound was oozing over his face and neck. He was heading for the horses.

Without a word Walkara jumped to his feet and raced towards the tethered animals, easily beating the still dazed Nampbutts. When the scalped Shoshone saw the young Ute standing between him and his horse, his only response was to continue down the hill towards the trail leading back to the Indian village.

The Shoshone brave showed no signs of aggression towards the young Ute, nor did he make any attempt to hide from the man who had scalped him. His only intention as he staggered down the hill seemed to be to just get home. Walkara let him pass. When Nampbutts was out of sight Walkara returned to the woman. But first he untied the two horses and led them up the hill to the spring. He wasn't about to leave two fine horses unattended with Nampbutts in the vicinity.

Susquenah was still seated on the rock beside the spring. Walkara wasn't sure what to say to her. It was time for him to leave. His life was in danger. Still, he lingered.

He remembered his medicine dream when he had journeyed to the world of spirits and met with Towats, how good he had felt, how he had not wanted to return. He felt the same way now, whenever he came near this strange woman. But she was not strange. Though he had first seen her less than an hour earlier, it was as if he had known her all his life, and perhaps longer. He didn't understand his feelings. Though he had loved Tah-mun, his young bride who had been killed by the Shoshones, the feelings he had had for her were nothing like what he now felt for this Shoshone woman. But there was no way he could express to her any of what he felt. He just looked at her, not even wondering if she had any of the same feelings towards him.

Earlier, Walkara had planned on taking both horses with him and leaving the woman to walk back to camp. He changed his mind, handing her the lead rope to her paint. She seemed surprised that the young Ute was going to let her keep her horse.

When Susquenah stepped around to the side of her horse to get on, Walkara offered to give her a leg up. There was a blanket on the horse, but no stirrups. Bending her knee, she kicked her left foot up behind her. Walkara took hold of the moccasined foot with both hands and pushed her onto the horse. Waves of passion surged through his body as he held onto the foot a little longer than necessary. He wanted so much to bend over and kiss the foot, but didn't. His whole body was hot. His heart was racing.

Chapter 9

Walkara should have been happy. He now had clothing, a knife, a good horse, a bow and arrows, and a fresh scalp in his belt. He could put as much distance as he wished between himself and the Shoshone camp. With the weapons he could obtain food. He was free to continue his search for the tall warrior on the roan stallion, or he could return home, if that is what he wished to do.

Yet with each step that took him further from the berry patch some of the warmth, some of the glow that had filled him, was gone. Each step his horse took carried him further from Susquenah. He could remember everything about her—the gentle calmness in her clear eyes, the way she combed her hair, her cautious smile, the strong hands that had cleaned his wounds, even the feel of her ankle and foot in his hands when he had helped her on the horse. He didn't think his hands would ever feel cold again.

Walkara didn't understand his feelings. He just felt he would never be content or happy with any other woman. It didn't matter that she was Shoshone. It didn't occur to him that she probably didn't feel the same way about him. It didn't occur to him that she might be someone else's squaw with children and a family.

He only knew what he felt, that from somewhere deep inside a primitive voice was telling him this woman was not only desirable, but important, that he needed her. The same feelings and instincts that had led him to the top of the mountains to find Towats were now telling him that the quest for Susquenah was the most important thing in his life.

Fear of the Shoshones and what they would do to him if they caught him was not important. If he died he would return to Towats. If he lived, he had to know more about Susquenah. He stopped the horse and turned it around.

Walkara felt a little crazy, returning to the Shoshone camp where he had almost been killed. He knew he must be careful. Traveling mostly at night, he found himself a secluded spot at the crest of a partly wooded hill nearly a mile from the Shoshone camp.

His plan was simple. After staking his horse out to graze on the back side of the hill, he intended to watch the camp until Susquenah left on the paint horse. Then, at a safe distance from the village, he would just run into her and see how things between him and her would develop from there.

It was nearly a week later when he saw the paint leave the camp, appearing to carry a female rider. Walkara took one last look at the camp before disappearing over the hill to catch his horse. Another horse was leaving camp, a black, and was going in the same direction the paint had gone. Walkara hurried to his horse, knowing he would have to be careful.

After making a wide circle of the camp, Walkara closed in on the trail left by the paint and the black. He was fairly certain the paint was carrying Susquenah because it was headed for the same hillside where he had first seen her a week earlier. The big question he had was who was riding the black. If they were going to the same place, why hadn't the two riders left camp together?

When Walkara found the paint it was tied to the

same tree where Susquenah had tied it a week earlier. The black was tied nearby. Walkara was on foot, having hidden his sorrel in an aspen grove a short distance away. Carefully, he began working his way up the hill to a brushy point from which he could see the main part of the berry patch and the spring where Susquenah had washed his wounds.

Upon reaching the point he spotted Susquenah seated on the boulder by the spring. She was washing her feet in the cold water. It occurred to Walkara that perhaps she longed to see him too. That would explain why she had come back to the exact spot where she had washed his wounds. He resisted the urge to hurry to her. There was still no sign of a second person in the berry patch, the one who had ridden the black horse. Walkara waited.

His patience was soon rewarded. He spotted a man creeping through the brush towards Susquenah. He was wearing leggings and a fur cap. There was something familiar about the way the man moved. He had a short, stocky build.

Walkara could hardly believe what he was seeing. Nampbutts was stalking Susquenah again, just like he had done a week earlier. The fur cap was undoubtedly a covering for the scab wound where he had been scalped.

Walkara had no idea why the same thing was happening again. He knew only that he would protect Susquenah a second time. He bent over, picked up a rock, and began to move towards Nampbutts.

This time Susquenah saw Nampbutts before he grabbed her. She turned to face him, ordering him to stay back. He responded by striking her in the face, sufficiently hard to knock her to the ground. Then he pounced upon her.

Walkara was not far behind. This time he brought the rock down on Nampbutts' head with all his might. Walkara felt the skull cave in from the force of the blow. This time Nampbutts was dead. Walkara pulled the body off of Susquenah, who appeared more surprised than the previous week.

"I am Nambutts' squaw," she offered. Walkara was confused.

"He liked to stalk me like an animal," she continued. "Then when he caught me he would beat me. That was his way."

"I killed him."

"Perhaps it was time for him to go."

"You did not love him?"

"He gave Washakie three trail-weary horses for me."

"Did you love Washakie?"

"I was one of many squaws, his favorite for one or two moons. That was all."

"What will you do now?"

"Become somebody else's squaw."

"Whose?"

"Perhaps Nampbutts' brother. I don't know."

Walkara paused. He wasn't sure what should be said next. He was feeling the same warmth as before. He felt like he had known this woman before, that she was not a stranger, that she belonged with him.

"Why did you come to the berry place again, to this spring?" he asked.

"I didn't think Nampbutts would follow," she said, avoiding his question. "His head was so sore. I just didn't think he would follow." She picked up her moccasins and returned to the boulder by the spring, where she resumed washing her feet.

"Why did you come here today?" Walkara repeated, following her to the boulder.

"I didn't think you would be here," she ventured, looking down at her feet.

"Then why did you come?"

"I wanted to come back to the place where you had

knocked down Nampbutts, where we had talked. I wanted to sit on the boulder where I had cleaned your wounds." She continued to look down at her feet.

"Why did you stay here?" she asked. "You knew the men from our village would be looking for you."

"I didn't stay here," he said. He told her how he had hidden on the hilltop near the village, waiting for her to leave on the paint, so he could follow her, so he could see her again.

She looked up at him. He looked at her. He knew how she felt, and she knew how he felt. And it was the same, but stronger now that both of them knew.

"Come with me," Walkara said.

"Where will we go?"

"I don't know."

"Your people, the Yutahs, won't like me."

"Your people, the Shoshones, will kill me."

"They will kill me too, if they learn I have willingly gone with you to become a Yutah."

"Too much talk," Walkara said, realizing she had spoken the truth. If her people thought she had willingly defected to the Utes, some would be eager to catch her and kill her if they could. Or, even worse, some would want to torture her for what they perceived as a lack of loyalty. Suddenly, Walkara thought of a way to avoid such a problem.

"You should return to your village," he said coolly. Susquenah looked into his expressionless face, not understanding the sudden change. She felt hurt, deceived. She wanted to flee, return to her village. She began to turn away.

Suddenly Walkara grabbed her by the arm, gently but firmly. As he spun her around he held a knife to her throat.

"I killed Nampbutts," he growled. "You are my prisoner, my slave. I take you with me."

90

Chapter 9

"You won't let me return to my village?" she asked.

"No. You must come with me."

"This is wonderful," she cried, flying into his open arms, where they embraced as if they had done it a hundred times before. Both had an overwhelming feeling of coming home. Walkara had never been happier. Susquenah had never been happier.

Chapter 10

Walkara and Susquenah did not return to the land of the Utes, nor did they stay in Shoshone country. Walkara remembered a lush, green valley just below the mountain where he had had the medicine dream with Towats in the world of spirits.

The valley was not near any main trails frequented by either Shoshone or Ute, so Walkara felt they would be left alone and undisturbed. There was plenty of grass for the horses, lots of game, especially deer and elk, and abundant timber and water.

With winter just around the corner, the first thing Walkara and Susquenah did was build their shelter, a roomy wickiup. First they tied three long lodgepole pine trees together before pushing them into an upright position, forming a tripod. Next, they leaned more poles up against the structure to give it additional strength and help cover the open spaces. Then they began piling on bark and brush in layers so the shelter would shed the rain and snow and keep out the cold winter winds. After that they leaned on more poles to hold everything in place. Across the doorway they hung two deer skins.

Then Walkara went hunting. Not only did they need meat for food, but skins and furs for warm bedding and clothing. While Walkara hunted, Susquenah kept busy drying meat on a tripod by the fire, fleshing and tanning skins, and sewing clothing and bedding. Both were looking forward to a long and enjoyable winter together, with warm bodies and full bellies.

As the days passed Walkara's hunting trips carried him further and further from the little valley. While he was successful in bringing home a gratifying number of deer and elk, he longed to kill some of the shaggy buffalo that roamed the plains to the east. Nothing kept one warmer on cold winter nights than a shaggy buffalo robe. He had seen buffalo in this area before and hoped that by extending his hunting excursions he might come upon some.

One fall morning, riding across a frosty meadow, he noticed a glassy stream in front of him. He was surprised his horse wanted to drink on such a cool morning. Over the distant mountains to the east, the sun was just coming up into a blue, cloudless sky. He loosened the reins to let the animal drink.

As he looked over the horse's neck into the crystal water he noticed what looked like glistening spots of yellow metal beneath the surface of the water. He backed away from the water and dismounted. His eyes had not deceived him. He retrieved a piece of yellow metal from the water. It was irregular in shape but smooth, about the size of a plump huckleberry.

Walkara was pleased. He knew the Spanish as well as the Mericats (Americans) would trade almost anything to get the yellow metal. Walkara spent the rest of the morning wading up and down the stream, occasionally finding another piece of the yellow metal. He found eight more pieces, the largest about the size of a bull elk dropping.

He was sure Jim Bridger would want the yellow metal. Now he would not have to find buffalo. He could buy the robes from Bridger. Perhaps a fire stick too. Perhaps some of the special water that burned the throat, then made one feel warm all over. Susquenah would be pleased. That afternoon he hurried back to camp to show her the yellow metal.

Because the trip to Bridger's and back would take three or four days, and because he was reluctant to leave Susquenah alone without his protection that long, he invited her to come with him. She welcomed the break from tanning skins and jerking meat.

It was in the middle of the second day when Walkara and Susquenah reached the two trails that traveled side by side, the distance between them never changing. Walkara explained to her how the trails were made by wheels attached to the sides of the huge land canoes used by white men to carry their belongings. She listened in awe. She had never been to this part of the country before, nor had she ever visited a trading post. She had seen white men before, trappers who had visited her village.

Walkara approached the trading post cautiously, not wanting to cross paths with any Shoshones coming to trade. He and Susquenah rode to the top of a nearby hill to get a good look at Bridger's place before riding in.

They were alarmed by what they saw from their hilltop vantage point. Nearly a dozen Indian ponies were tied to trees in front of the trading post. It appeared that all the Indians were inside trading. Walkara was about to suggest to Susquenah that they withdraw for several days until the Indians were gone, when one of the savages stepped outside.

He was a thick, soggy man with drooping jowls and an unmistakable slouch that Walkara recognized even at a distance. It was his brother, Grosspeen. Walkara looked at the tethered horses again, and recognized half of them. Utes, not Shoshones, were visiting Bridger's trading post. Walkara leaped upon his horse, and motioning for Susquenah to follow, galloped towards the cabin.

A minute later Walkara was exchanging slaps on the shoulder with not only Grosspeen, but Arrapeen as well, and five other Utes whom he knew. It was a joyous reunion. News of Bridger's eagerness to establish trade with the Utes had spread into Ute lands without Walkara's help, much faster than anyone, even Bridger, thought it would. Arrapeen and his men were trying to trade furs for fire sticks, and finding Bridger anything but generous.

When Walkara introduced Susquenah, his brothers nodded approvingly. All went inside, where the trading resumed in earnest.

As Walkara walked through the door he noticed something different, a white woman, the first he had ever seen. She was not pretty like Susquenah, but strong-looking. She wore a dirty gray dress that went to the floor. She had red hair that would show nicely hanging from a pole in front of a chief's lodge, a white face, and a mouth like a fish in that it kept opening and closing with incessant regularity as she chattered in a language none of the Indians could understand. But Bridger and his partner could understand, and they were glad she was speaking in English instead of Ute.

"See that fat savage by the door. Now watch him," she rattled on. "He's going to steal a knife, then cut someone's throat with it. You mark my words, he will. I don't know why you let these savages in here anyway. They'll steal from you, then when your back is turned they'll slit your throat just like they did poor Emmett's."

Emmett was the woman's husband. They had come west with a company from Independence, Missouri, hoping to get rich in Oregon. They had been separated from their company at South Pass. Crows had killed Emmett and taken the wife, Blanche, captive, thinking their chief would be pleased to receive a red-haired squaw. But after two days on the trail, listening to her incessant chatter and scolding, they just dropped her off at Bridger's, asking for nothing in return. They were glad to be rid or her.

With the wagon train already gone, winter coming on, and no more groups heading east, Bridger had no choice but to keep the woman, who had no money or valuables to pay her upkeep. It depressed him to think he might have to listen to that incessant chatter for the duration of the winter.

When they saw the Utes approaching Bridger had joked to his partner about hiring the savages to cut out the woman's tongue. His partner hadn't laughed, thinking it was a pretty good idea.

But now it was time to trade with the Utes. The problem was that the Utes wanted guns, but hadn't brought enough furs and hides to purchase guns, lead and powder. Bridger feared that if he sent the Utes away without guns they might not come back, and he very much wanted to get the Utes coming to his new trading post. If he lost money trading with them this first time, they would be angry when they returned and were forced to pay higher prices. Bridger wasn't sure what to do, so he opened a tin of Missouri white lightning and passed it around.

Arrapeen refused to be distracted by the firewater. He was standing over a pile of furs in the center of the floor demanding guns, powder and lead for all his men. Bridger insisted there were not enough furs to buy even two guns. Arrapeen began to pick up the furs like he was going to leave. Bridger urged him to drink from the tin. Arrapeen, not yet familiar with the taste of liquor, refused.

"These savages smell like smoke and bear grease," chattered Blanche. "You should insist they bathe before they come to trade." Bridger did his best to ignore the woman.

"Can you get more furs?" he asked in broken Ute.

Arrapeen insisted they had brought enough furs to buy every man a gun.

It was Walkara who finally broke the stalemate, spilling a handful of golden pebbles on the plank counter. For the first time since Walkara had entered the store the woman stopped talking. Bridger's jaw dropped. So did his partner's.

"Guns for everyone," Bridger bellowed, reaching for the gold. Walkara stopped him, indicating there needed to be a couple of buffalo robes thrown in, a tin of firewater, and some blue beads he had noticed a moment earlier. Bridger quickly agreed.

With the trading done, it was now time to relax. Bridger pulled a large, black kettle of simmering venison from the fire and motioned for his guests to help themselves. The Indians seated themselves in a circle around the pot and began to eat in earnest, pulling steaming chunks of meat from the kettle with their fingers.

Blanche began to chatter about their lack of manners, how someone ought to teach the savages about forks and spoons, saying grace, chewing with the mouths closed, and more.

Bridger winked at his partner, then started talking to Blanche.

"Sure wish I knew where the Utes get their gold," he said in English. "Bringing in fistfuls of it all the time. The Inca gold mines are somewhere near here. Spanish used to bring shiploads of it back to Spain. Now only the Utes know where it comes from, and they won't tell."

"Why not?" Blanche asked, taking the bait.

"Just won't," Bridger said. "They tell each other, and their squaws. Nobody else. If anyone ever found out where that mine was they would be a billionaire."

"Maybe they would tell a woman," Blanche suggested.

"Not a white woman, not if they wasn't married to her."

"Do they ever marry white women?" Blanche asked.

"Don't know, but if one did, that lady would be the richest woman ever to set foot in New York City. They'd take her to that mine for sure and she could fill a whole suitcase full of gold nuggets."

"Ask them if they ever marry white women," Blanche insisted.

"Do you really want me to?" Bridger asked, hardly able to keep from laughing.

"Do it," she insisted.

Bridger began to talk to Arrapeen in Ute. He asked the Indian if he was interested in buying a white woman. Arrapeen looked over his shoulder at Blanche, who smiled back at him. In Ute, Arrapeen told Bridger that even though she had a mouth like a fish she looked strong, like a woman who could do a lot of work. Yes, he would be interested in buying her, if the price was right.

"What did he say?" Blanche asked Bridger.

"Said his wife died about a year ago and that he has been very lonely. He's a Ute chief. Said his squaw's servants haven't known what to do since his squaw died. Would be nice for them to have someone to wait on again. Said he is going to the Inca mine again in the spring, and it would be nice to have a woman to go with him."

"Did he really say that?" Blanche asked, beginning to doubt what Bridger was saying.

"Of course," Bridger lied. "He's got to pay back Walkara for helping him buy the guns."

"Do you think he would marry me?" Blanche asked.

"I'll ask him," Bridger offered. His partner had already left the building, unable to keep a straight face.

"What'll you give me for her?" Bridger asked Arrapeen in Ute.

"The buckskin horse tied to the big tree," Arrapeen responded.

"It's a deal if you don't tell her about the horse. I don't want her to know she brought that high of a price."

Arrapeen nodded his consent. Blanche was beaming.

"I guess you are engaged," Bridger beamed in English. "Would you like me to perform the ceremony?" Then he said to Arrapeen in Ute, "Are you ready to receive the merchandise?" Blanche and Arrapeen both nodded their approval.

Taking them both by the hand, Bridger began a multi-language marriage ceremony. To Blanche he said, "Blanche, do you take Chief Arrapeen of the Ute nation to be your lawfully wedded husband, for better or for worse, in sickness and in health, till death do you part?"

"I do," Blanche said, without hesitation, taking a quick glance at one of the gold nuggets still resting on the plank counter.

Then in Ute, Bridger spoke to Arrapeen. "Arrapeen, do you agree to pay one buckskin horse for this woman whom I present to you as your personal property and slave to do with as you please?" Arrapeen nodded his approval.

Switching back to English, Bridger concluded. "With the authority invested in me as the head trader in these Rocky Mountains I hereby pronounce you, Blanche, and Chief Arrapeen, man and squaw."

"Is he going to kiss me?" Blanche asked as Arrapeen took her by the hand and pulled her outside.

"I don't know," Bridger whimpered before taking a giant swallow of whiskey and rolling onto the pile of furs, holding his sides.

A few minutes later Walkara and Susquenah left the trading post carrying a new rifle, buffalo robes and a tin of whiskey. Walkara was in a hurry to get back to his wickiup. He didn't trust or understand these strange white men. And he hoped Arrapeen hadn't made a mistake in buying the red-haired white woman.

Chapter 11

With the fire stick and buffalo robes Walkara and Susquenah were ready for winter. There was plenty of tall grass in the little valley and also on the hillsides above the valley, where the horses could paw through the snow for food even when the snow became deep.

And the snows did become deep, but Walkara and Susquenah didn't mind. For days they never went more than 100 feet from their comfortable wickiup. They spent hours just talking, learning each other's languages, sharing childhood experiences, looking into each other's faces, never seeming to tire of each other. Sometimes, facing one another from opposite sides of the fire, they would play the stick game, one day Walkara winning all their possessions, the next day Susquenah winning everything back.

Sometimes she would tease and he would chase her through the snow. When he caught her he would rub her face in the white powder—but never too much, never turning play into anger.

When Walkara's powerful body would become restless from lack of exercise he would wade off through the deep snow, taking long, powerful strides, carrying his new rifle in his hand. Sometimes he would bring home fresh meat, a deer or part of an elk, carrying the meat on his powerful shoulders. Exhausted, he would drop to the robes beside their fire, ready to spend more glorious days in the arms of Susquenah.

But as the winter became long, as the snow became crusty, as the days began to get warmer, Susquenah noticed that Walkara, more and more, would look at the distant mountains with a longing to go. Susquenah didn't deceive herself into thinking the good life with Walkara would last forever. She knew when the snow melted he would want to ride with other men. He would want to go on long hunts, steal horses, do battle with his enemies, and take scalps. She knew there would be many lonely nights wondering if he would ever return. That's why she liked the snow. In its own quiet way it kept Walkara home or close to home with her.

She knew most Indian women had never enjoyed a winter like the one she was having with Walkara. Trying not to think ahead she savored every day, knowing in the back of her mind that when the snow melted these happy times might be gone forever.

One evening as the snow was beginning to melt, Walkara and Susquenah had just eaten and were getting ready to crawl under their buffalo robes. Susquenah pulled Walkara's hand to her, gently pushing it under the folds of her deerskin dress. She let him feel a beginning swell in her abdomen. No, she was not getting fat. She was going to have a baby, his baby.

Walkara was delighted. His son would be a great warrior and horse thief. If the child was a girl she would be beautiful like her mother. As he took Susquenah in his arms, rolling together under the warm buffalo robes, she could hear water dripping in the branches of the wickiup. The snow would soon be gone. She began to cry.

When the snow melted Walkara wasn't as anxious to move on as Susquenah had supposed. He hunted. He fished. He made arrowheads and spearheads. He practiced shooting his fire stick. He was becoming a good shot, especially when it came to hitting rabbits. Rabbit skins stretched tight with green willow sticks were hanging in the top of the wickiup to cure in the smoke. When the skins were tanned Walkara stretched them out in front of him and begin cutting in circular fashion, starting at the outside and creating a two-inch-wide strip of skin and fur four to five feet long. Next he would twist the long strips of skin and fur, causing the skin to curl, leaving what looked like a long strand of soft fur about an inch in diameter. When Walkara had 40 or 50 lengths of rabbit fur he wove them into a soft, thick blanket, which he gave to Susquenah for their new baby.

He told her about the early summer fish festival on the shores of Utah Lake, where as many as 50 family bands gathered every summer to feast on spawning fish. This was the single event that unified many bands into what was known as the Ute tribe. There was horse racing, wrestling, courting, trading, dancing and many important meetings planning strategies for war and getting more horses.

Susquenah began to share Walkara's enthusiasm for the fish festival. They began to make preparations to go. Walkara had a special surprise for his brothers and friends at the festival. He still had the tin of Missouri white lightning he had purchased from Bridger the previous fall. Through the winter he had taken a sip or two to make sure it was still good, but most of it was still in the tin. He knew when he pulled the cork out at the fish festival he and his brothers and friends would have a wild time.

Susquenah wasn't nearly so enthusiastic. Her people had been getting firewater from Bridger and other traders for years and she knew what alcohol did to men. She, however, was pleased that Walkara was going to share his firewater with brothers and friends rather than drink it all by himself. She was pleased that he had the discipline to preserve his stock of firewater through the long winter. She had never known a man before that could do that. The men she had known would have consumed it all the first week. Walkara was different, she thought.

By the time Walkara and Susquenah arrived at the fish festival, most of the other bands were already there. Hundreds of brush and skin tepees were scattered across the lush grasslands. Everywhere, bands of horses were grazing. Groups of children were laughing and playing. Women gathered around cook fires, laughing as they shared stories about their husbands and children. Groups of men were gambling, trading, racing horses, or just swapping stories about their latest war exploits or horse-stealing endeavors.

Susquenah by now had a fair command of the Ute language, and found a place near the east side of the encampment in a circle of women who were making cradle boards and pieces of clothing for new babies they were expecting. Walkara found his brothers and opened the tin of white lightning.

Susquenah stayed with the other women while Walkara and his brothers guzzled every last drop of the firewater. Then they began to wrestle and gamble with reckless abandon—loud, boisterous, and quarrelsome. Some of the women, who hadn't seen the effects of liquor on their men before, were concerned and frightened. Those who had, like Susquenah, were sad.

Towards evening Susquenah, feeling uncomfortable with the growing baby inside her, decided to get away from the noise and confusion of the camp. She started walking eastward among the many grazing horses towards the snow-capped peaks. It was a beautiful summer evening, not hot. The setting sun was sending shafts of red and orange through a few scattered clouds west of Utah Lake. The grass was still green. Meadowlarks were warbling their evening songs. She wished Walkara was with her.

Suddenly two men stood up not five feet in front of her. At first she was frightened, then relieved when she recognized the faces. Then she was frightened again. The familiar faces were not Utes, but Shoshones, men she had grown up with from Washakie's band.

"We have come to rescue you," one of the men said. "Come with us." They started to turn, expecting her to follow.

"I can't," she pleaded. "I am Walkara's squaw now."

There was no further discussion. The men grabbed her by the arms and dragged her between them to a place where horses were tethered.

As they reached the horses they could hear the war cries of a dozen Shoshone warriors who had galloped into the open meadows to round up a herd of Ute ponies. The celebration came to an abrupt end as men raced to their weapons and horses and women scrambled to gather their children and find safety. Dogs barked, men shouted, children cried, women screamed.

The first group of Utes who managed to get armed and mounted galloped eastward to cut off the horse thieves. They were greeted by a second band of Shoshones determined to fight and take scalps. As the battle began the first band of Shoshones were free to drive its newly acquired herd of 70 Ute horses toward the big canyon to the east. The men who had picked up Susquenah joined this group. They had forced her onto a bay mare and were leading the horse at full gallop. Susquenah hung on tightly, fearing for the safety of her unborn child.

The Ute defenders were forced to retreat as the stolen horses disappeared up the canyon. When the Shoshone attackers saw the horse herd was safely into the canyon they suddenly abandoned the attack and retreated to join their companions with the horses. But before retreating several of the attackers were recognized, among them young chief Washakie and the tall warrior on the roan stallion. No one knew the name of the tall warrior, only that he had been seen frequently in raids against the Utes.

The raid was over with quickly. No one had been killed, though several women and children were still missing, probably hiding in the brush somewhere. Seventy horses had been stolen.

Walkara was sober now and was quickly organizing a retaliation raid against Washakie's band. While about half the men were going to ride with Walkara, the remaining ones were going to stay behind with Sowiette to protect the women and children and prevent further raids against the remaining horses.

Walkara instructed his men to bring plenty of weapons and dried meat, and be ready to ride at first light. As the men departed to get their things together, Walkara made arrangements for Susquenah to stay with Arrapeen's families while he was gone. Then he went looking for Susquenah. It didn't occur to him that something might have happened to her until he met a woman who said she had seen Susquenah walking eastward just before the attack.

Walkara's voice could be heard throughout the remainder of the night, calling for Susquenah. He did not find her, only the rabbit skin blanket which he tied around his neck. When morning came, he was the first one ready to head out in pursuit of the Washakie raiders, his rabbit skin cloat waving like a flag in the morning breeze.

Chapter 12

During the next cycle of the moon Walkara and his men raided, stole horses, killed and scalped. Though they had attacked numerous Shoshone encampments, in none of them did they find Susquenah, Washakie, or the tall warrior with the roan stallion.

In the course of the raids Walkara's band had become an ineffective raiding party. They were now too slow. They were driving too many stolen horses with them, and they had six prisoners as well, four women and two children. Walkara's men wanted to return home with their spoils. Walkara insisted they continue until Susquenah was found, but one morning, under the leadership of Arrapeen, the others headed for home, leaving Walkara a lone man to pursue his quest.

Not having found Susquenah in any of the Shoshone villages near Bridger's trading post, Walkara headed west towards the valleys of the big river that wound like a snake. He was leading two new horses with him, two tall blacks. He was still wearing the rabbit skin cloak.

Now that he was alone, a new plan began to formulate in his mind whereby he might get Susquenah back once he found her. That's why he was bringing the two black horses along.

His problem when he saw a Shoshone encampment was how to tell if Washakie and Susquenah were there.

If he saw the roan stallion that would be a good indication he had the right village, but if the roan stallion was not there it might still be the right village, but how could he tell from a distance?

Such was his predicament as he came upon the first Shoshone camp near the bank of the winding river. It was a large village with about 30 lodges and a big herd of horses grazing in the open meadows. It would be an easy matter to steal some of the horses, and he had to keep reminding himself that that was not his business this time.

He watched the village from a distant hilltop for several hours. He was too far away to recognize any of the faces. Susquenah could very well be among the women gathered around cook fires, or washing in the big river.

He guessed he was not known among the Shoshone bands this far west. He also guessed that news of the recent Ute raids on Shoshone camps near Bridger's trading post had not reached this far west. Having made these assumptions, he trotted his horses down the hill and towards the camp. He rode in the open, his weapons tied harmlessly at the side of his saddle. His head high, his back straight, Walkara rode directly into the Shoshone camp, ignoring the silent stares of men and women and the shouting of children.

Having spent the winter with Susquenah, he now spoke fairly decent Shoshone.

"Where's Washakie?" he asked a man. "I have horses for him." He was directed to a tepee near the river. Walkara was pleased he had finally found Washakie's village. If his new plan worked, perhaps Susquenah would be riding home with him tonight.

"Washakie," he called, reining the horses to a stop in front of the tepee he had been directed to. "I have horses for you."

A few seconds later the young Washakie emerged

from the tepee. He had the lean, strong face of a man immune to the hardships of trail and battle. At first he had a surprised look on his face, then a grin.

"A Yutah brings me horses?" he asked.

"I bring you these two beautiful blacks for the woman Susquenah," Walkara explained.

"Why do you want the woman?"

"She carries my child."

"How do you know she is here?"

"I heard she was."

"I will not sell Susquenah to a thieving Yutah."

"You do not want these horses?" Walkara asked.

"I think I will keep Susquenah and have the horses too," Washakie responded coldly.

Walkara knew he was in trouble. Armed Shoshones were gathering around him, some with bows and some with rifles. Forcing an escape would be suicide.

"I thought Washakie was a man of honor," Walkara said, not sure what he hoped to accomplish by the statement.

"A thieving Yutah cannot speak to Washakie of honor," Washakie said, anger in his voice. "Besides, there is no dishonor in scalping a Yutah and taking his horses."

"I also heard Washakie was a shrewd trader."

Washakie nodded.

"A shrewd trader would not ignore a fortune in horses for one lousy scalp," Walkara said.

"Explain yourself, horse thief," Washakie challenged.

"My people have many horses," Walkara said. "I would pay many more than two for the woman Susquenah."

"How many?" Washakie said, suddenly very attentive.

"I would pay ten horses for the woman," Walkara offered.

Paying ten horses for a woman was unheard of among the Shoshones and Utes. Washakie was grinning again.

"I would take 20 horses for the woman," he offered.

"It is a deal then," Walkara said. "Take the two blacks now. I will bring the other 18 later."

"There is one condition," Washakie said. "Don't bring me stolen Shoshone horses. I visit many villages and know what most of the horses look like. If you try to bring me the horses of my friends I will kill you, keep the woman, and return the horses to their rightful owners."

"I will not bring you stolen Shoshone horses," Walkara said, wondering how he would get 18 horses if he didn't steal them from Shoshones.

Washakie stepped forward to take the lead ropes to the two black horses. Walkara refused to hand the ropes over.

"I do not buy merchandise I cannot see. Show me the woman."

"Susquenah, come out," Washakie called towards the tepee he had just come out of.

Susquenah crawled through the opening. Except for a few bruises on the side of her face she looked fine. Walkara knew he should be leaving before conditions or circumstances changed. He had the agreement he wanted with Washakie. Still, he needed to talk with Susquenah. After handing the lead ropes to the two blacks to Washakie, he slipped from his horse and walked up to her.

"Are you all right?" he asked.

"Yes," she said.

"The baby?"

"Everything is fine."

"I'll be back for you. I made a deal with Washakie."

Chapter 12

"I know, I heard."

Sensing his time was running out, Walkara turned and leaped upon his horse. After nodding to Washakie, he spun the horse around and began galloping towards the edge of the camp.

Suddenly he was aware of a rider coming in from the left, swinging a rawhide rope over his head. Walkara urged his horse to greater speed, but he was too late. The rawhide loop floated over his head and was jerked tight before he could respond. With the loop around his neck, Walkara knew he was at the mercy of the other rider. Whether he would be allowed to bring his horse to an easy stop, or whether he would be jerked to the ground, he did not know.

Assuming the worst would happen, Walkara knew his only alternative was to act quicker than the man behind him. With one hand he jerked his horse into a sliding halt, immediately establishing some slack in the rope. With the other hand he grabbed the rope where it came away from his neck. Quickly gathering some slack, he looped two quick turns around the front of his saddle.

Quickly he spun his horse around and charged directly towards the man who held the other end of the rope. As Walkara charged by, his attacker was quickly wrapping his end of the rope around the front of his saddle, knowing the rope would soon be jerked taut by Walkara's horse.

The man's response was not quick enough. Walkara now had the advantage. When Walkara's horse hit the end of the rope, lunging forward with all its might, the other man's horse did not have its feet planted, not yet having figured out what was happening. As a result the man and his horse were jerked to the ground, the rope coming free as the man was forced to let go.

Walkara didn't stop, but continued galloping right up to the amazed, and impressed, Washakie.

"It will be difficult bringing you a fortune in horses if your people don't leave me alone," Walkara said as he pulled his puffing horse to a halt, at the same time removing the rawhide rope from his neck.

"Leave him alone," Washakie shouted to his people as Walkara turned his horse and, for the second time that day, galloped towards the open prairie. The rabbit skin cloak was flapping in the wind.

Chapter 13

When Walkara had made the offer to Washakie to buy Susquenah for 20 horses, in the back of his mind he had figured on stealing the horses from Shoshone villages. But now that Washakie had insisted none of the horses be stolen Shoshone ponies, Walkara wasn't sure where he would get so many horses. He knew his brothers and other Ute friends didn't have that many to give him.

He knew of the wild horses, mostly in the deserts to the west and south. The wild ones were not only difficult to catch, but more difficult to break. And they were smaller than the preferred Spanish or American horses.

The other tribes in Ute lands—the Pahvants, Piedes, Goshutes and Paiutes—were not rich in horses. In fact, most of the bands did not have any horses at all.

The Navajos to the south had horses, but a convenient trading relationship had developed with them, so the Utes did not steal their horses. Walkara knew that whatever he did, he would not get much support or help from his brothers. They could not understand why anyone would pay 20 horses for a woman, and would not help in any such foolish endeavor.

Walkara headed southwest alone, looking for wild horses. He passed through the valley of the Timpanogos River, where he spent a few days with Arrapeen. His brother still had the white woman, Blanche, but was trying to sell her. Before leaving on a hunting trip, Arrapeen had turned an entire elk over to her to jerk and smoke while he was gone. She had finished the job by the time he had returned, but she had used pine instead of cottonwood to make the smoke, and all the meat was ruined. Not even the dogs would eat it.

Arrapeen couldn't believe the stupidity of this white woman. Even the littlest of children knew better than to smoke meat with pine. And she still talked all the time. Arrapeen had tried to slap her every time she started talking, but his arm became weary as she continued her incessant chatter. He wanted to sell her, but so far no one had shown any interest.

When Walkara left for the west desert he had enough dried meat to last him for several months. He didn't intend to come back until he had enough horses to buy Susquenah's freedom.

He didn't have any trouble finding a band of the wild ones, but finding them and catching them were two different matters. After a week of chasing he had managed to catch only one scrawny mare. He was sure Washakie would not be happy with the mare.

As he wandered further west he realized chasing wild horses alone was a losing proposition. Three or four men working together could run the wild ones in relays, getting them weary enough to catch, but alone one only exhausted his riding horse, usually without even getting a chance to throw a rope.

At night Walkara could think only of Susquenah, held captive in the Shoshone camp, waiting to deliver his child. He hoped Washakie didn't treat her too roughly. He hoped she had enough to eat.

Late one afternoon a few days later, as Walkara was seated on a rocky point overlooking many miles of wasteland in his search for wild horses, he saw something very unusual. He saw what appeared to be two men engaged in a long and bitter battle. They were on foot, facing each other, trying to hit each other with long staffs or clubs. Other people formed a circle around the two combatants. They appeared to be women and children. Some were seated on the ground. No horses were to be seen anywhere.

Walkara got on his horse and rode closer to get a better look. He figured the people in front of him were either Piedes of Goshutes. It appeared the two who were fighting were in a leadership battle, or having a dispute over wives. Walkara did not fear for his safety. People too backward to own horses were no threat to a powerful Ute warrior.

Some of the women and children noticed Walkara's approach and moved cautiously away from him, but they did not run away as was customary when Goshutes saw Utes approaching. Perhaps their fear was softened by the fact that he was wearing the rabbit skin blanket. Normally, Utes did not wear rabbit, the customary dress of Goshutes and Piedes.

The only ones not to notice Walkara's approach were the two combatants. Apparently the battle had been going on for some time. Both were badly bruised, and both had blood flowing from many wounds. One appeared to have a broken arm, while the other was favoring a leg. Both glared at each other with red, determined eyes as they moved in a close circle, looking for an opening to strike another blow. Walkara guessed they were in a struggle to the death. One had part of an ear missing. The other had a bloody lip, exposing loose and broken teeth. Walkara wondered if either man would survive the contest. He admired their courage and determination. He did not intervene.

Finally, one of the men fell. The other delivered a series of sharp, powerful blows to the back of the fallen man's head, then fell on top of him. Neither man moved.

The circle of people included only women and children, no men. No one stepped forward to help either of the combatants. Instead, everyone turned towards Walkara, forming a circle around him. Some of the children held out their hands. They were begging for food. All of them looked half starved, some more than others, and this was summer, a time of abundance and plenty for most Indian bands.

In better days, Walkara might have turned and ridden away. Surely the children could catch grasshoppers if they were that hungry. The boys had sticks with which they could catch rabbits. Then he remembered he had not seen many rabbits the last few days.

Walkara opened his parfleche and tossed each person a piece of dried meat, first the children, then the women. All of them gobbled up the meat like hungry dogs. Walkara tossed them each a second piece.

It was getting dark. Walkara turned his horse and started towards a spring against the side of a distant hill where he intended to spend the night.

When he looked back the women and children were following him. He counted them. There were 14. His food supply wouldn't last long if he kept feeding these people, so he urged his horse into a gallop, soon leaving them behind.

When he arrived at the spring, Walkara staked his horse out to graze. After drinking deeply from the cool water and eating a piece of meat, he stretched out on the ground to sleep, using the meat parfleche as a pillow. He was very tired.

When Walkara awakened the next morning he sat up with a jerk. Fourteen pairs of eyes were looking at him. The women and children had followed him to the water hole, arriving sometime during the night. Quietly they had formed a circle around him, stretching out to sleep themselves.

Walkara tossed each of them another piece of

meat, then sat back against a rock, wondering if perhaps an opportunity might be presenting itself to him. He remembered his father telling him the Navajos bought slaves that they in turn sold to the Mexicans. The women and girls became house servants on the big haciendas. The boys went to work in the silver mines. Going to Mexico would probably be a dramatic improvement for these poor Goshutes, especially since their men were gone. Walkara assumed the two men who had been fighting had probably killed each other. At least they were unable to travel with their families.

These people seemed willing to follow Walkara. He wouldn't have to force them to go to the land of the Navajos with him. Maybe he could get enough horses to pay his debt to Washakie. He could try. This would be better than continuing his search for wild horses.

Walkara piled the smallest children on his horse and began leading it eastward. The women and older children followed. They had found a new provider and didn't question where he was taking them.

When Walkara arrived at Arrapeen's camp, leading his band of mostly naked Goshutes, Blanche took an immediate interest in the refugees. After making sure they all had plenty to eat, she insisted they all wash in the river. She showed the women how to comb their hair, and began fashioning crude moccasins for the barefoot children. She insisted that the women cover their breasts, not to keep themselves warm, but so the men could not see their nakedness. Walkara and Arrapeen, who were watching from a distance, were convinced this white woman was absolutely crazy.

Arrapeen asked Walkara if he wanted to buy Blanche. Walkara responded by saying a crazy woman was not worth even an old, poor horse. Arrapeen had to agree, especially if the woman talked all the time.

"But she could help you take the Goshutes to the Navajos," he reasoned. Walkara had to agree with that.

Having Blanche along to fuss over the women and children might make the trip a lot easier.

"Next time I go to Bridger's trading post I will get you a tin of firewater," Walkara offered.

"A deal," laughed Arrapeen. "I would have given her to you for nothing had you not offered the firewater."

"But let me warn you," Arrapeen continued. "If you tell her you bought her, she won't want to go. She is a stubborn woman. Tell her you are taking her to the white man's city of Santa Fe, that there are Indians there who know where the lost Inca gold mines are."

"Agreed," Walkara said as he walked towards Blanche to tell her about her new adventure. The next morning Walkara, Blanche and the 14 Goshutes began their journey to the land of the Navajos.

Chapter 14

Traveling with the Goshute women and children wasn't as difficult as Walkara thought it would be. Not only were the Goshutes already conditioned to the hardships of the trail, but they were easy to please when it came to eating. Walkara wasn't able to bring a lot of food with him, at least not enough to feed sixteen people every day for the duration of the long journey. As a result, every morning and evening he was off hunting, and no matter what he brought back to camp, the Goshutes seemed pleased. Sometimes he brought in only a badger or porcupine, but no one complained. If he got a deer or elk, everyone was delighted.

If he didn't bring back anything and nothing was left over from the previous day, the children seemed content with a few grasshoppers or grubs.

One evening Walkara killed a nice antelope, which he didn't clean until he had brought it back to camp over the front of his saddle. That evening his tiny clan consumed every ounce of flesh. The next morning one of the squaws borrowed Walkara's knife. She cut the antelope intestines into sections as long as her arm, giving one to each of the children to chew and suck on for the duration of the day.

On another occasion, about midday, the group came upon the foul-smelling carcass of a deer that had been decomposing in the sun for at least a week. It was

Walkara's intention to pass by the awful stench as quickly as possible, but the Goshutes had other plans. He watched with interest as one of the squaws, seemingly indifferent to the smell, ripped back the hide. At first Walkara was concerned his captives might get sick on the rotten meat, until he noticed they were not eating the decaying flesh, but the swarms of tiny, black-headed maggots.

Walkara was also pleased with the way Blanche was taking care of his slave band. She was thinner now than when she had first come to the Utes. The primitive life had not only made her thinner, but had hardened her muscles as well. She could walk all day without complaining, though she never seemed to stop talking. She made sure each of the children had a fair share of the food each night and morning, and seemed more concerned that the children slept comfortably than their own mothers did.

Walkara understood little of the Goshute language, and Blanche understood none, and she hadn't been with the Utes long enough to be very fluent in Walkara's language either. As a result there was little verbal communication, though Blanche never seemed to cease her chatter in English. It didn't seem to matter to her that no one understood what she was saying.

What amazed Walkara the most was that Blanche seemed happy. He had heard stories about two other white women, further to the east, who had been taken in by the Sioux and Crows. One of them had seemed to just wither up and die. The other had lost her mind. Not Blanche. The primitive life seemed to agree with her.

Sometimes in her broken Ute, around the fire at night, Blanche would try to get Walkara to tell her where he had found the gold nuggets. It was hard for her to accept the simple truth that he had found them lying in a streambed instead of in a mysterious Inca mine. Her understanding of the language was not sufficient to understand his directions on how to get to the stream. He reminded her that he thought the Navajos knew more about where to find gold than did his people. She seemed more interested in finding gold than returning to her own people.

The little group faced its first major obstacle after two days of losing elevation down a slick rock canyon. Before the group roared the biggest river in Ute lands, the one the white men called the Colorado. It being late summer, the river didn't appear as threatening as at other times. Not only was the water lower than in the spring, but with the weather hot, the water appeared more inviting. The river was brown, making it impossible to see below the surface. The water was too deep to wade, and too wide for a man to throw a stone across it.

Knowing his Goshute hostages did not know how to swim, Walkara had anticipated having to ferry them across the big river. He had brought a large buffalo hide with him, which he stretched out on the ground, hair side up. After cutting some green willows, he began threading them in and out of the stake holes around the edge of the buffalo robe. He was careful not to stretch the hide too tight inside his ring of willow sticks. Next he laid long poles across the robe, bending them downward into the robe and lashing them into place. The result was a big brown bowl with hair on the inside.

With the help of the women and children Walkara carried the boat upstream, to a point about a quarter of a mile above where he wanted to land on the opposite shore. The women and older children had paddles as they reluctantly crawled into the crude boat. Walkara tried to explain to them that they must paddle straight towards the opposite shore. He knew it was the tendency of people crossing the river for the first time to want to paddle upstream when they felt themselves being carried downstream. This was a waste of energy in a big river.

Walkara loaded half his people into the boat for the first crossing. Blanche was with those waiting for the second turn. The boat was floating now, and the women were holding onto willows growing along the shoreline, waiting for Walkara's order to let go and start paddling.

He secured one end of his long rope to the boat, then after getting on his horse, Walkara tied the other end to the saddle horn. After telling the women in the boat not to let go of the willows until all the slack was out of the rope, he plunged his horse into the river.

As soon as the horse was swimming and Walkara was sure it was headed for the opposite shore, he slipped off the back of the saddle, taking a firm hold on the horse's tail. When the slack was out of the rope, he waved for the women to let go of the willows and start paddling. He looked towards the opposite shore.

The rope grew tighter and tighter, causing the angle of the horse's swimming to point too much downstream. Something was wrong. Walkara looked back. The women in the boat were not paddling, but still hanging desperately onto the willows, afraid to let the boat be pulled into the river. There was nothing Walkara could do but wave to them to let go and follow him. They refused, overcome with fear of crossing the river.

It was Blanche who finally came to the rescue, running down to the boat, screaming at the women to let go and start paddling. When they refused, she picked up a stick and began beating at the hands that clung to the willows. Finally the women let go, and seeing themselves being pulled into the river, began to paddle furiously towards the opposite shore. With the tension out of the rope now, the horse was able to straighten out and head straight for the far bank. It wasn't long before the horse was scrambling up the bank and the Goshutes were piling out of the buffalo boat into knee-deep water.

Walkara got back on the horse, and after riding upstream a short distance, dragging the empty buffalo boat behind him in the water, he plunged back into the river, again slipping from the saddle as the horse began to swim.

With Blanche at the helm, the second crossing went smoothly. The women let go of the willows at just the right moment, and paddled hard enough and straight enough that the horse was hardly able to keep ahead of the round boat.

Upon crossing the river, Walkara and his wards were now in the land of the Navajos. They still had several days of travel to the nearest major village. None of the women seemed to be concerned when Walkara removed the willows from the buffalo hide in taking apart his boat. Since he was bringing only horses and no people on the return trip, he would not need the boat again. If any of the women were wondering about this, none said anything. Perhaps they thought Walkara would reassemble the boat on the return trip.

Walkara wasn't even sure the women and children knew they were his slaves. They had merely started following him, and he had started feeding them. As long as he provided them with food, they followed him without question. As for Blanche, he guessed she still thought he was taking her to Santa Fe, the nearest white settlement. He didn't tell her he had bought her by promising Arrapeen a tin of firewater. In fact, he guessed she still didn't know Arrapeen had bought her from Bridger for one horse.

Walkara avoided the thought that the women might feel deceived when they found out he was selling them to the Navajos. All he thought about was Susquenah, pregnant with his child and held hostage by the Shoshones. With 18 horses she would be his again. He had to get 18 horses.

Two days after crossing the river Walkara entered a

large Navajo village that looked just the way his father had described such villages. Still, Walkara was amazed at the differences. Instead of brush or skin tepees, the Navajos lived in mud houses. Instead of being surrounded by open meadows, they were surrounded by fields of the tall Indian grass that grew heads of grain on the stalks—the grain the white men called corn. Instead of skins, the Navajos wore beautifully designed blankets of many colors they had woven from the wool of sheep they herded in flocks. They had obtained the first breeding stock for their sheep herds from the Spanish.

The chief was an old man with many horses and half a dozen wives. Though his body was thin and his hair gray, his eyes shone with the cunning and brightness of an eagle. He very much wanted to trade for the women and children Walkara had brought to him, but he refused to pay more than 14 horses for 14 slaves. Most of the negotiations were carried on in sign language, neither understanding the other's language very well.

While Walkara thought 14 horses for 14 Goshutes was a fair trade, he told the chief that if he couldn't get 18 horses, he would have to move on to another village. He tried to tell the chief that under ordinary circumstances the 14 horses would be enough, but this trip he had to bring home 18 horses. He couldn't come home with fewer than that. The chief insisted that 14 horses was a fair and generous price, and he refused to give anymore.

The old man's women brought Walkara corn cakes and bowls of sheep soup while he and the chief crouched on the open ground, discussing their trade. The women had already fed the hungry Goshutes and Blanche.

Walkara had almost decided he would have to try to make his trade at another village when the old man asked if the white woman with the fiery red hair was for sale. Walkara had forgotten about Blanche. She might be worth more than one horse.

She did look good, much better than when he had first seen her at Bridger's trading post. The sun and wind had put color in her cheeks, and hard work had firmed up her body. She was a good worker, and though she talked a lot, she didn't complain much, at least not anymore. And she had flaming red hair. The old Navajo said he had never seen red hair on a woman before.

Walkara said he would not consider selling the white woman for less than five horses. When the old man asked why he wanted so much for the woman, Walkara rolled his eyes back and asked the old Navajo if he had ever slept with a red-haired white woman before. He knew that to demand that many horses for her he had to present Blanche as something out of the ordinary.

The old man asked if Blanche could spend a night with him before he decided whether or not to buy her. Walkara said under ordinary circumstances that would be fine, but he didn't have time this trip. If the old man didn't want her, Walkara said he would have to resume his journey to the next village. Walkara hadn't slept with Blanche either and couldn't take any chances of the old man being disappointed.

As Walkara got up to leave, the chief asked if Walkara would consider four horses for Blanche. Walkara finally had what he wanted. With the fourteen horses for the Goshutes, and now four for Blanche, he had his eighteen.

Five minutes later Walkara was walking among the Navajo horse herd with the old man, cutting out his 18. When both were satisfied, Walkara leaped upon his red pony and began driving his new herd northward towards the river.

He didn't say goodby to Blanche or the Goshutes. He tried to tell himself that he had saved the poor

Goshutes from certain starvation. He reasoned that with the Navajos Blanche would have a better chance of finding her gold mine, and that if she didn't, and wanted to return to her own people, from here she was not very far from Santa Fe. But even with this reasoning Walkara felt uneasy about going back to say goodby to the people he had sold like cattle, even if he kept telling himself it was in their own best interest. As he pushed his new horse herd northwards towards the big river Walkara did not look back.

Chapter 15

Driving 18 horses by oneself was not as easy as Walkara thought it would be, especially when he came to the Colorado River. The horses simply refused to be driven into the raging torrent, even though the weather was warm.

After repeated failures at driving the horses into the water, Walkara finally tied a lead rope to the number one horse in the herd's pecking order, a sorrel mare, and led her into the river. When both his horse and the mare were swimming, he slipped off the back of his riding horse, grabbed onto the tail with one hand but still holding the mare's lead rope with the other. Upon reaching the far shore he tied the mare to a tree in plain sight of the other horses across the river.

After swimming his riding horse back across, Walkara took the lead ropes to two more horses and brought them over just like he had done with the mare. And so the rest of the day went, with Walkara leading one or two horses at a time across the big river. Every two or three trips he would change riding horses. The swimming was very tiring for the horses. When he was down to the last four horses—none of them wanting to be left behind—they just followed him across the river. While annoyed with the delay, Walkara was grateful for the warm weather. Such a crossing would have been impossible in the winter.

Walkara knew he could have avoided the river crossing by taking the horses north on a route further to the east. But along that eastern route there would have been a much greater chance of running into hostile Shoshones, Crows, or even wandering bands of raiding Comanches. Plus the eastern route included several difficult mountain passes to go through. By crossing the river where he did Walkara would be able to head straight north through the heart of Ute-dominated territory, over a well-traveled and familiar trail. He would have little fear of a confrontation with Shoshones until crossing the valley of his birth.

As the days passed the horses fell into the pattern of travel and resisted less and less Walkara's efforts to keep them moving north. At night he would tie two horses in his camp, and send the rest north to graze. The next morning he would round them up as he resumed his journey. Between the Colorado River crossing and the Timpanogos River none of his horses were lost or stolen.

When Walkara reached the valley at the foot of Mt. Timpanogos, Arrapeen was gone on a hunting trip, but Sowiette, San Pitch, and Grosspeen were there. The brothers were eager to trade for some of Walkara's new horses, but Walkara was unwilling to do so. All were amazed that Walkara had obtained so many horses for just a handful of scrawny Goshute women and children. Even as Walkara headed north into Shoshone country the next day, Grosspeen and San Pitch headed west into the desert to see if they could catch some Goshutes to trade for fine Navajo horses.

There being a full moon, Walkara traveled at night now. He was in Shoshone country, and he doubted that Shoshone warriors not from Washakie's band would believe the Ute warrior was taking horses to Washakie. To avoid having to try to explain the situation to his

128

enemies, he traveled under cover of darkness, hiding the horses in wooded canyons during the day.

A week later he drove the eighteen horses into Washakie's camp. No one seemed more surprised to see Walkara than did the young chief, Washakie. Stepping from his tepee, he grinned broadly as the 18 horses trotted by. When Walkara dismounted the two embraced like old friends.

No sooner had they pulled away from each other than Susquenah emerged from a nearby tepee. When she saw Walkara, she ran to him. He was careful not to squeeze her huge belly too hard as he gathered her into his arms.

Susquenah looked wonderful. She felt wonderful. She smelled wonderful. It was so good to see her after all that had happened.

"Have they been kind to you?" he asked.

"Of course," she responded. "I grew up in this village. These people are my aunts, uncles, brothers and sisters. Washakie is my uncle, even though I was once his squaw."

"When is the baby coming?"

"Soon, I think. It is kicking hard. I think it's a boy, a strong young warrior like his father."

Walkara was eager to be on his way. He did not trust the Shoshones. Susquenah urged him to stay, to meet some of her relatives to share the evening meal with them. They could leave in the morning. Reluctantly, Walkara agreed to stay until morning.

After a supper of venison, fish and roasted camas bulbs, Walkara and Susquenah went for a walk. The land was beautiful with its sprawling grassy plains surrounded by mountains covered with pine and aspen trees. The big river that wound like a snake through these mountain valleys was clearer and cleaner than the Colorado.

Walkara told Susquenah about his frustrating

attempts to catch the wild ponies, then how he had stumbled onto the two Goshute men fighting to the death, and how the women and children had followed him after the fight. He told her how Blanche had taken charge of the children, and joined the march southward to the land of the Navajos. He described the tricky crossing of the Colorado River in the buffalo boat. Then he told her how he sold the 14 women and children, and Blanche, to the old Navajo chief for 18 horses.

"You sold 15 people into slavery so Washakie could have 18 more horses?" she asked, a critical tone in her voice that Walkara had never noticed before.

"Yes," he said, obviously proud of what he had done. He proceeded to tell her of the journey northward, following the difficult time he had getting the horses across the Colorado River. Susquenah remained unusually silent as he narrated the events surrounding the remainder of his journey.

"Is something wrong?" he asked upon finishing his story, finally noticing her silence.

"Because of me, all those people were sold into slavery," she said.

"I couldn't catch the wild horses."

"Those women and children were free. Now they are slaves."

"They would have starved to death in the desert," he argued.

"The desert is their home. They would not have starved."

Walkara realized that he and Susquenah had never had a serious argument before. He did not like it. He wished he could get Susquenah to forget the whole thing about the slaves, but he didn't know how. He did know she was deeply upset.

"I will not trade any more Goshutes to the Navajos," he offered.

Chapter 15

"What about the ones you just sold?" she asked,
her voice getting louder. "I wonder if any of the little
boys have died yet in the Spanish silver mines. I wonder
if the little girls like being forced to sleep with their
Spanish masters."

Walkara didn't know what to say. He loved Susquenah so much. He had traded the Goshutes and
Blanche into slavery for her. Now she was angry with
him.

"I can't get them back," he said.

"You could try," she scolded. Tears welled up in
her eyes.

"I won't do that," he said, beginning to feel angry.
He wasn't about to drive 18 horses all the way back to
the land of the Navajos. And even if he did, the women
and children would be scattered all over Mexico by now.
Even if he were able to find them, 18 horses would not
be enough to buy all of them back. But he wouldn't be
able to find the women and children anyway.

It was dark now, and Walkara and Susquenah
began making their way back to the camp. Neither
spoke. When they crawled under the warm buffalo
robes to sleep, Susquenah turned her back towards
Walkara, and when he tried to put his arm around her,
she pushed it away. All those nights on the trail he had
dreamed of this first night with Susquenah. He had
never imagined it would be anything like this. Perhaps
being close to having the baby made her this way. He
hoped she would like him better in the morning.

Things were not any better in the morning. Soon
after getting up Susquenah delivered an ultimatum. She
told Walkara that if he didn't bring the Goshute women
and children home and set them free, she would not
leave with him.

"I can't get them back," he said.

"Then I will not go with you," she responded.

Walkara had had enough. He walked over to

131

Washakie's tepee, called the young chief outside, and demanded the return of his 20 horses—the 18 he had just delivered, plus the two blacks.

"Why do you want them back?" the chief asked.

"I have decided to leave the woman here."

"We made a deal," Washakie said. "The horses are mine, and the woman is yours. I keep the horses."

"The woman doesn't want to go with me," Walkara explained.

"There are ways to persuade a squaw," Washakie said, offering Walkara his riding whip. Walkara turned and marched back to Susquenah.

"Get on the horse," he ordered.

"No," she said firmly. Walkara raised his hand as if he were going to strike her across the face. That's what his father and brothers would have done. Unflinchingly she stared into his face. He was aware the entire Shoshone band was watching to see if the Ute warrior was man enough to make his woman obey. He thought of grabbing Susquenah and throwing her over the horse's back like a bundle of deer hides, but that wouldn't do. She was carrying his child. He lowered his hand. He didn't want to take her if she didn't want to go.

"The Goshutes have already been sold as slaves," he said. "Whether you stay or go will make no difference to them."

"You could try to bring them back."

"It's too late. I can't do that."

"Then I can't go with you," she said, a tone of finality in her voice.

Walkara turned and leaped upon his horse. He jerked its head around and whipped the horse across the flank. As he galloped out of the village he could hear Washakie's laughter, and others joining in.

Seeing some grazing horses to his left he turned into them, causing them to gallop with him. He figured that if they wouldn't voluntarily give him his 20 horses back, he was entitled to steal as many as he could get away with. While still running, he got ropes on two of them, and two more continued to follow him as he galloped southward.

The further he got from the camp the angrier he became. Not only was he going to leave the Goshutes with the Navajos and Spanish, but he would catch another hundred Goshutes and trade them to the Navajos too. Susquenah would be sorry for what she had done.

Chapter 16

Upon returning to the valley of the Timpanogos River, later called Utah Valley by the white men, Walkara didn't waste any time persuading his brother Arrapeen to ride with him to get slaves for trading to the Navajos for horses. He told his brother how easy it was to feed the Goshutes, how they would eat insects and grubs, even maggots, if there was nothing better. He explained how they could be ferried across the mighty Colorado River in his buffalo hide boat, and how the old Navajo chief had given him one good horse for each of the women and children, and four for the white woman.

"How do you catch them?" Arrapeen asked,

Walkara held up a handful of dried meat. "People who are hungry will do anything for food. Feed them and they follow you," he said, as if catching Goshutes was the easiest thing in the world.

Two days later Walkara and his brother found their first band of prospective slaves, a group of nine including two men, three women and four children. The Goshutes were gathered around a small fire cooking a solitary rabbit they had just killed—not more than a bite or two each for nine people.

When the Goshutes saw the approaching Utes, their first inclination was to run and hide, but when they noticed Walkara holding out handfuls of dried meat, they hesitated.

"Food for you," Walkara said, using some of the Goshute words he had learned during his first trip to the Navajos. The Goshutes' former timidity evaporated and the Indians gathered around Walkara's horse, each receiving two pieces of dried meat which they wolfed down.

"Come with me," Walkara said slowly and deliberately in their language. He turned his horse to the east, motioning with his arm for the Indians to come with him. To Arrapeen's amazement the entire group of Goshutes began following Walkara.

But his success was short-lived. Walkara hadn't gone more than a hundred yards when one of the Goshute men stopped. The others didn't seem to notice until the little man barked an order at them. They seemed reluctant to cease following the man who had given them a good meal, but when the little man barked the order a second time, they all turned and started walking back the way they had come.

Walkara stopped his horse and looked at Arrapeen, not sure what to do now. Arrapeen, however, knew what he was going to do. He shot an arrow at the man who had ordered the people to stop following Walkara. The man tried to dodge the arrow, but wasn't quick enough to get entirely out of the way. The arrow glanced off his ribs, leaving a straight, clean slice about six inches long.

The Goshutes were bewildered, obviously wondering why the men who had just fed them were now shooting at them. They were all standing in the trail, looking first at Walkara and his brother, then at the man who had just been grazed by the arrow. No one seemed to know what to do next.

"Come," Walkara said, waving for them to follow him. When no one obeyed the command, Arrapeen reached towards his quiver for another arrow. As he did so the Goshutes suddenly knew what to do, scattering in all directions into the tall sagebrush. Walkara and Arrapeen galloped after them, uncoiling long, rawhide ropes as they charged through the brush.

By nightfall Walkara and Arrapeen had caught all three women and one little boy. They could find none of the others, and knew that during the cover of darkness the rest of the Indians would scatter far and wide, making it impossible to locate them the next day.

The next morning Walkara and his little band headed south in the general direction of the big river, constantly on the lookout for more Goshutes or Pahvants to lure with food or lasso with ropes. Arrapeen led the slaves, single file, a long rope extending from neck to neck.

A week later the string of slaves had increased to 15 and Walkara and his brother were headed straight for the big river, eager to see what the old Navajo chief would pay for a new crop of slaves. With Arrapeen to lend a hand the river crossing was uneventful. It being early fall the water was lower than it had been during Walkara's first crossing.

The old chief was delighted to see the new slaves arrive. He invited Walkara and Arrapeen into his hut to discuss business. The chief said that, except for five or six horses that weren't for sale, they could have their pick of the horses in the herd, one horse for each slave. Walkara and his brother quickly agreed that such a trade would be agreeable with them.

"But there is one more thing," the old man said in Navajo. "You must take back the white woman called Blanche."

"She is still here?" Walkara asked.

"Yes."

"But we do not wish to buy her back," Walkara protested.

"I do not wish to sell her. Just take her. A favor to an old man."

136

Chapter 16

Walkara and Arrapeen didn't understand why the old man wanted them to take Blanche. When pushed for an explanation, the chief called outside for someone to bring Blanche to the hut.

A minute later she crawled inside. Looking up and seeing Walkara and Arrapeen, she said, in English, "If it isn't the greasy bucks that sold me to the Navajos."

"What did she say?" Walkara asked the old chief.

"She wants to know why the great Yutah warriors sold her to the Navajos," he responded.

"Why do you want to give her back?" Arrapeen asked.

"I'll show you why," the old man said. Then to the woman, he said in Navajo, "Fix some corn cakes for me and my guests."

"Fix your own damn corn cakes, you worm dick savage," Blanche growled back. The old man's fist shot out and struck her in the side of the mouth. The blood began to flow.

"What did she say?" Arrapeen asked.

"She said she refuses to make corn cakes for the great Navajo chief," the old man responded.

A second time he told Blanche to make corn cakes.

"No, no, no," she growled back, glaring at him, refusing to look down or back down.

When the old man moved towards Blanche a second time, Walkara thought he was going to strike her again. Instead he just pushed her out of the hut, more gentle with her than he needed to be.

"Just take her," he said.

"I'd kill one of my women for talking to me like that," Arrapeen said, challenging the old man.

"She's a white woman," the chief responded calmly. "If I killed her and the white men in Santa Fe found out, there would be much blood spilled."

"How would they find out?" Arrapeen asked.

"When you have lived as long as I have you learn

137

that things like killing a white woman tend to get found out," the old man said wisely. "Just take her."

"I don't want her back," Arrapeen repeated.

"How far is it to Santa Fe?" Walkara asked.

"Five or six sleeps," the old man responded.

"Does she want to return to her own people?" Walkara asked.

"Of course," the old man said.

"Then I will take her," Walkara said.

"But why?" Arrapeen asked.

"White men are doing much trading near our lands. In five days she can teach me more of her language." Walkara didn't say what else was on his mind. Blanche had helped him with the first group of Goshutes. He had rewarded her by selling her to the Navajos. Susquenah had been right. He should not have sold her. Besides, he admired her spirit, the way she had challenged her master. A woman like that deserved to be free, to be with her own people, if that is what she wished. He would help her, and learn as much English as he could while they traveled together.

Walkara crawled outside the hut and found Blanche.

"Morning, we go Santa Fe," he said in broken English.

She just stared at him, her face full of distrust and hate.

"Morning, we go Santa Fe," he repeated.

"OK," she said cautiously.

The next morning, as Arrapeen headed north with the fifteen new horses, Walkara and Blanche rode east towards Santa Fe.

It didn't take long for Walkara to notice that Blanche had changed. The incessant talking had ceased. New scars on her face and arms were evidence of harsh treatment among the Navajos. But as she rode her horse, her back was straight and her chin up. None of the fire was gone from her eyes. On the contrary there was a sense of fierce independence that Walkara had not noticed earlier.

Walkara didn't know what Blanche would do when she returned to her own people, but he was convinced the year among the Utes and Navajos had made her a better woman.

Walkara was in strange country now, and moved forward cautiously. The old chief had warned him that the further east he went, the greater his chances of running into wandering bands of Apaches who would not hesitate to steal his horses, woman or scalp. Though the nights were cool, Walkara would not allow Blanche to have a fire after dark.

On the evening of the third day, as they were pushing against a cold east wind up a gentle mountain pass, Walkara and Blanche saw a log tepee, similar in appearance to the one Jim Bridger lived in. The brisk wind was sucking smoke from the chimney. Knowing it would be warm inside, Walkara and Blanche turned their horses towards the cabin. In a large corral behind the cabin, a half dozen horses stood quietly, their backs to the wind. One of them whinnied at the approaching riders.

A young, clean-shaven man appeared in the doorway. Wearing grey trousers and a red wool shirt, he was obviously pleased to see a woman approaching the cabin.

"Mind if we come in and warm up a bit?" Blanche asked, her voice friendly. The young man said she was welcome. Walkara tied the horses to a fence while Blanche hurried into the cabin.

When Walkara entered the cabin Blanche was telling the young man, who had introduced himself as Heber Smutts, how she had just spent an entire year with the Utes and Navajos, and was now returning to

Santa Fe. He was amazed, not only that she had survived the ordeal, but that she had come out looking so good.

Heber told her he was starting the first cattle ranch in this part of the country, that he had a herd of cattle arriving from Texas the next spring. As they talked, Walkara remained silent, sitting on the floor by the door. Blanche told the young man about the abusive treatment she had received from the Navajos.

Suddenly she stopped talking. Blanche was staring into the corner of the cabin in apparent disbelief.

"What is that?" she asked, looking at a copper tub, similar in shape to a small coffin.

"A bathtub, ma'am," Heber replied.

"Does it leak?" she asked.

"Doesn't get used enough to spring any leaks," Heber replied.

Blanche was silent, continuing to stare at the tub.

"Could heat up some water in a hurry," Heber offered.

"That wouldn't be too much trouble?" she asked, continuing to stare at the tub. "Haven't had a real bath in over a year."

Without another word Heber ran outside, returning a minute later with two large pails of water he placed on the cookstove. He opened the front of the stove and filled it with wood. A minute later the stove was rattling as the wood began to burn. Blanche and Heber continued to talk as the water became warm. Walkara remained motionless by the door.

When the water was hot, Heber dumped both pails into the copper tub he had pulled to the center of the room, then stepped back, as if waiting for Blanche to jump in. But she wasn't about to do that with Heber and Walkara in the room. A year with the Indians hadn't made her that uncivilized.

"If you'll excuse me, I'd like to bathe now,"

Blanche said. Heber hurried out the door, a reluctant Walkara following close behind. The door slammed behind them, and they could hear the bolt pushed firmly into the slot to prevent them from coming back inside.

Giving Walkara a big wink, Heber hurried around the side of the cabin. Curiously, Walkara followed. Carefully Heber removed a piece of chinking from between two of the logs. Bending over he looked through the opening. Walkara was amused and surprised. White men certainly did strange things. Walkara walked over to the corral to look at the horses. He was thinking about Susquenah, wondering if she had had her baby yet.

A minute later the young man was at his side, asking when he was taking Blanche to Santa Fe.

"Morning," Walkara responded.

"If you would like to be heading home, I would take her to Santa Fe for you," Heber offered. Walkara began to smell an opportunity.

"You want me leave her here?" he asked.

"That would be fine with me, just fine," Heber responded.

"Can't do that," Walkara said, paying close attention to a large white horse across the corral.

"White man will give Walkara horse when bring woman Santa Fe," he lied. Heber was quiet for a moment, taking the bait.

"Would you like that white horse?" Heber asked.

Walkara wanted to grin. This was too easy.

"Yes," Walkara grunted.

"It's yours if you leave the woman here," Heber said.

"Will you take her to Santa Fe?" Walkara asked.

"Yes, I will."

"I need saddle for horse," Walkara said, sensing he could have gotten more out of Heber. The young man jumped into the corral, caught the white horse,

141

threw an old saddle on its back, brought the horse outside, and handed the lead rope to Walkara.

"You must leave now," the young man urged.

Walkara accepted the lead rope, then leaped upon the back of his own horse. Nodding a thank you to the eager young man, Walkara turned his horse to the west and began his homeward journey, deciding he would visit the white man's village of Santa Fe another time.

"Yes, I will take her to Santa Fe," Heber said to himself. "Maybe in the spring." He hurried back to the place where he had removed the chinking from the cabin wall.

Chapter 17

Walkara caught up with Arrapeen just as he arrived home with the new horses. Before a week had passed they were again headed into the west desert after more Goshutes. They had discovered a new source of wealth and were determined to take full advantage of the Navajos' willingness to trade horses for slaves. The water in the big river would be low until the following spring. Many horses could be obtained.

Walkara and his brother became proficient at finding Goshute women and children and trailing them south to the Navajos, who prospered too as they traded the slaves south to the Mexicans for two or three times as much as they paid the Utes for them.

In early spring, when the big river became swollen with brown runoff waters from the distant mountains, Walkara and his brother drove a herd of horses north to trade with Jim Bridger. Not only were they able to obtain rifles, powder and lead, but also tepee canvas, rope, knives, iron pots, mirrors, brightly-colored fabric, beads and, of course, several tins of firewater.

While at the trading post Walkara received news that Susquenah ad had her baby, a little boy named Battee. Mother and child were doing fine. They were still with the Washakie band.

During the winter Walkara had taken two new squaws into his lodge, hoping that might help him forget Susquenah. It did, at least for a while, but when he heard that she had given him a son, he longed to see both of them. His chest still ached when he thought of Susquenah and the winter they had spent together.

But he told himself he didn't have time to see her now. He was an important chief. With the newfound prosperity, the family camp he and Arrapeen called home was becoming a large village with many lodges. Brothers and sisters, half-brothers and half-sisters, and other relatives and friends came from near and far to be part of the prosperous Walkara band. One day his mother and younger sister, Mountain Fawn, showed up to share his lodge.

As news of the new wealth in horses spread north, raids by Shoshones, who felt the Utes had too many horses, increased. As a result Walkara had to devote more of his time to retaliation raids against his red brothers to the north. Washakie had moved to the valleys surrounding the great lake, a three-day journey to the north and east of the salt lake.

In his raids against the Shoshones, Walkara was always careful to avoid raids against Washakie's village. He also avoided visiting the village, though on several occasions he watched it from the top of the big mountain west of the lake, wondering how Susquenah and the boy were doing. He wondered if she ever thought of him, if she knew he still wore the rabbit skin cloak he had made for their baby. He wondered if she knew he had become wealthy trading Goshute slaves to the Navajos. He figured she probably had heard about his new squaws, though he didn't know if she had found a new man yet.

The following summer Walkara and his men were so occupied building their horse herds by slave trading that they failed to bring in enough meat to get the band through the winter. The result was having to kill horses for food.

Determined not to let that happen again, Walkara moved his entire band towards buffalo country the following spring. His plan was to cross the Green River, and camp right in the middle of the best buffalo country. They planned to hunt and dry meat until they had enough for two winters. They had plenty of horses to carry the dried meat home.

As the band was camped on the west side of the river, waiting for the runoff from a spring storm to dissipate, children ran through camp one morning announcing the arrival of Wa-he-to-co, meaning "wooden leg." Also known as Peg Leg Smith, Thomas L. Smith was well known among the Utes, who had nursed him back to health after he had amputated his left foot following a skirmish with the Crows.

Peg Leg looked like he had had a hard winter. The white horse he was riding was little more than a shaggy bone pile, and it was blind in one eye. He had a few traps hanging over his saddle, but no furs. Peg Leg looked weary as he slipped from his horse in front of Walkara's tepee.

Walkara had heard much about the one-legged mountain man. Not only was the trapper a friend of the Utes, but he was supposed to be a very brave and courageous man. Walkara welcomed Peg Leg into his lodge.

Peg Leg ate like a hungry dog when Walkara offered him meat, but when the Ute chief pulled the cork out of a tin of firewater, the mountain man drank with the thirst of ten men. Fortunately the firewater was soon gone. Both men stretched out on skin beds, puffing slowly on stone pipes, discussing the prospects of the upcoming buffalo hunt. Peg Leg guessed his horse would probably die if he tried to chase buffalo with it. Not very much more was said before the mountain man was snoring loudly.

Walkara had just stepped outside to see how much

145

the river had dropped during the night when he saw Arrapeen galloping into camp, apparently with urgent news. Perhaps he had seen a herd of buffalo.

A band of Shoshones had crossed the river from the other side, not more than a mile downstream. The Ute camp was suddenly a hive of activity. Men were loading rifles and filling quivers with arrows. Boys and men were running into the meadow to catch and saddle the fastest horses. White, yellow, black and red war paint was being applied.

"Instead of hunting buffalo we're going to scalp Shoshones," Walkara shouted to Peg Leg as he entered the tepee to get his weapons.

"My old horse is blind in one eye," yawned Peg Leg. "He'd never make it. Think I'll just sleep through this one."

Walkara had heard too many stories about the trapper's bravery to let him go back to sleep.

"Get up! I'll give you a new horse," Walkara shouted. Peg Leg preferred to sleep, but Walkara would not let him. Finally the trapper rolled over and crawled outside. The Utes would soon be ready to attack. A boy handed Peg Leg the lead rope to one of Walkara's horses, a stocky paint.

"Is he broke?" Peg Leg demanded.

"Of course," Walkara responded. "The Navajos break all their horses."

"Have you ridden it?" Peg Leg asked. Walkara ignored the question. Peg Leg knew the horse probably had not been ridden since Walkara had bought it from the Navajos. He wasn't about to ride a horse he knew nothing about into battle, so he decided to try it out while the Utes were getting ready for battle.

The paint didn't jump around too much as Peg Leg threw his saddle on its back. He guessed it was broke, at least some. He climbed up to give it the final test.

The horse was prancing, but in the excitement of

everyone getting ready for battle, that was understandable. The paint reined all right as he turned it
towards the edge of camp. He couldn't make it walk.
The horse didn't seem to want to buck.

Once out of camp, Peg Leg loosened the reins to
see how the horse handled at a gallop. As he did so,
someone's gun went off. The horse spooked, lunging
into a dead run. Peg Leg jerked back on the reins, but
the animal refused to stop. He pulled harder, the horse
ran faster. It was running away with him.

He had been on runaway horses before, and knew
he would eventually get the paint stopped, if it didn't
run over a cliff or stumble on a rock. There was little
danger of these problems with lots of open meadow in
front of the horse.

The only problem, Peg Leg quickly realized, was
that the horse was running downstream, directly
towards the spot where Arrapeen said the Shoshones
were waiting to fight. Peg Leg had laid his rifle on the
ground by the tepee before getting on the horse. He did
not have a weapon. The rest of the Utes were not on
their horses. He was headed for the enemy camp all
alone and unarmed.

Behind him Peg Leg could hear the Utes shouting
at him to turn back. He tried to pull the horse's head
around, but was unsuccessful.

Reaching the top of a swell he could see 20 or 30
armed Shoshones not 200 yards in front of him. The
horse saw them too, but instead of being frightened, it
must have thought the Shoshone horses were friends,
because it continued running towards them.

Peg Leg's mind was racing. He didn't know what
to do. Ahead of him he could see the Shoshones milling
around, apparently unsure as to what to do about a
single attacking rider.

Remembering his trusty weapon in barroom
brawls, Peg Leg reached down with his left hand and

untied the rawhide lashing that held his wooden leg in place. If the Shoshones were going to get him, they would not do so without a fight. In the barrooms of California and Santa Fe he had smashed many a head with that wooden leg. He guessed that with the help of the leg now he could send a few Shoshones to the happy hunting ground before they got his scalp.

Switching the wooden leg to his right hand and holding it high in the air, Peg Leg loosened up on the reins and, kicking the horse with his stump and heel, urged it to greater speed. He roared his challenge to the waiting Shoshones. Peg Leg Smith was going to take on them all, single-handed.

The Shoshones continued to mingle in confusion. They had never seen such foolishness, or was it courage? They were being attacked by a man swinging his foot above his head. Perhaps this was not a man, but a devil. Perhaps what appeared to be a foot was some new kind of weapon.

One of the Shoshones decided he was going to have nothing to do with Peg Leg. The Indian kicked his horse into a gallop, towards the river. In confusion, the others followed. By the time Peg Leg reached them, the entire Shoshone band was halfway across the river. The paint stopped, rather than enter the water. Peg Leg shouted after the retreating Shoshones, calling them cowards, waving his leg at them.

Behind him Peg Leg could hear the approaching Utes. The battle had been won without firing a single shot, or shedding a drop of blood. Grinning, Peg Leg turned his horse around to greet Walkara, who ordered a celebration to honor the brave white man.

That night, amidst all the feasting, singing, dancing and drinking, Walkara called his people together to honor Peg Leg. Walkara described the events of the morning one more time, emphasizing the bravery of the white man who single-handedly attacked a Shoshone war party to defend his Ute friends.

At the conclusion of his speech, Walkara ordered all Ute maidens who were not yet someone's squaw to line up beside him.

Timidly, seven girls came forward, including his sister Mountain Faun, now 16 years old.

He then invited Peg Leg forward, offering the trapper his choice of as many Ute maidens as the white man wished to have. Peg Leg looked at Walkara, then at the girls, obviously pleased with his good luck. He certainly wasn't going to risk offending the young chief by turning down such a generous offer.

Peg Leg walked over to the girls, taking a good, serious look at each one. The camp was silent now, everyone watching, everyone wondering what the white man would do.

First he picked Mountain Fawn, then two others. Then he turned to make a speech.

"I was honored to fight for my friends, the Yutahs, today," he began soberly. "Offering me the hand of so many beautiful young women is a more than generous offer. Being a man of modest passions, I take only three."

"But you can keep the paint horse," he added.

Everyone cheered. The drums began to beat again. The dancing resumed. Peg Leg hurried off to Walkara's tepee, his three new brides following close behind.

Chapter 18

Peg Leg Smith and Walkara became great friends. They hunted and trapped together. Not wanting to leave his new wives unprotected when he was off on his frequent trapping and trading expeditions, Peg Leg set up his lodge with Walkara's band, now large because of the growing prosperity.

Later that summer Peg Leg helped Walkara move the entire band to the Sanpete Valley, about 70 miles to the southeast. Horse raids from the Shoshones had become too great of a nuisance. Walkara decided that by moving to the Sanpete, Shoshone raiding parties would have to penetrate much further into Ute territory, greatly increasing the risk of getting caught and killed while stealing horses. While the raids continued against the bands that remained in Utah Valley, those against Walkara and his herds seemed to come to a halt.

Walkara was now free to resume his slave-trading business, but Peg Leg had other ideas. He told Walkara about the land of the setting sun, next to the biggest of waters. The Spanish called the place California. There were more sleek, well-fed horses in California than in the entire world, Peg Leg said. He described millions of horses covering an endless sea of wild oat-carpeted hills. Three men could trap enough furs in one winter to buy hundreds of horses, he claimed.

His proposal to Walkara was simple. Contacting

his friends around Fort Bridger, Peg Leg would put together an outfit of furs which they would take to California and sell for gold. With the gold they would buy horses. Then, with Walkara's help, they would take the horses east, cross the Colorado River, and sell them in Santa Fe, where there was a big demand for fine horses. All would be rich. Peg Leg had never crossed the Colorado River before. Walkara could show the party where to cross, and guide them to Santa Fe.

It sounded like an excellent plan. Walkara, Arrapeen and San Pitch all agreed to go. While Peg Leg headed north to round up his furs, Walkara and his brothers went hunting. They wanted to bring in as much meat as possible for their families, because the trip with Peg Leg to California and Santa Fe might take as long as a hundred sleeps or more.

Two weeks later Peg Leg returned with nine trappers and a huge outfit of furs. One day later they were on their way south to California. Walkara was excited to see the new land he had only heard about. He was also eager to see the big water that stretched forever into the sunset.

After crossing the Mojave Desert, the fur trading party entered the land of California at a mountain pass named El Cajon. Immediately they began seeing huge herds of cattle and horses, more than Walkara and his brothers could count. In California, it seemed horses and cattle roamed wild, as did the buffalo on the great plains to the east. Had it not been for a cautionary word from Peg Leg, Walkara and his brothers would have ditched the furs and began rounding up a horse herd immediately. The Spanish ranches were few and far between. It appeared to Walkara that hundreds of horses could be rounded up without anyone ever missing them. There were that many. But Peg Leg insisted they follow through on the original plan of selling furs, then buying horses.

In a few days the trappers were in the Spanish village of Los Angeles. With the Spanish words he had learned from his mother, Walkara got along better than the others. He even served as interpreter when Peg Leg began selling the furs.

The trading was frustrating, because Peg Leg didn't receive nearly as much gold as he thought he would. When the furs were gone he spent half the gold buying a horse herd totalling only 60 animals. Everyone in the party was discouraged.

Peg Leg proposed a party to cheer them up. With the remainder of the gold they headed for the nearest cantina. Being Indians, Walkara and his brothers were not allowed inside. Peg Leg and his white trapper companions went in, leaving the Indians out in the street to sulk and watch over the tiny horse herd.

Peg Leg didn't come out for two days, and when he did the remainder of the gold was gone. All agreed, the trip was a failure. Sixty horses was not enough to bother taking to Santa Fe. Almost before Walkara realized what was happening, Peg Leg had sold the little herd and headed back into the cantina. Again, Walkara and his brothers were refused admittance.

This time Walkara didn't have any horses to keep him occupied. He brooded over the stupid Spanish. If he, a Ute chief, was not good enough to enter their stinking cantinas, why should he feel hesitant about helping himself to some of their horses? The Spanish were certainly not his friends.

Walkara and his brothers were almost ready to head out of town to find some horses, when a lot of noise began coming from the cantina. The drunk Peg Leg was roaring like an angry bear. Three Spaniards ran from the cantina, leaving the door open behind them. Walkara could hear men yelling, women screaming, the sound of breaking glass and furniture.

Two policemen, who ran inside to stop the disturbance, were soon rolling into the street, their noses bleeding. A few minutes later they returned with a man they called the alcalde, apparently the mayor of Los Angeles. His pretty wife was with him.

With an air of importance, his head high and back straight, the alcalde entered the cantina to put an end to all the fuss. The pretty senora followed.

A minute later the alcalde came rolling into the street. The senora did not follow. Soon her screams could be heard as Peg Leg tried to persuade her to marry him and come to the Rocky Mountains.

The alcalde charged inside, the two policemen close behind. Peg Leg met the attack by removing his wooden leg and proceeding to beat the alcalde senseless. Had the policemen not pulled him away, Peg Leg probably would have killed the man.

Peg Leg was thrown into jail for a length of time equal to how long it would take for the poor alcalde to mend, and no one doubted but what the healing process would take a long time.

Walkara had sat on his hands long enough. While he fully intended to postpone the return trip to Sanpete until Peg Leg was able to travel, he was not going to wait for his one-legged friend with nothing to do. Walkara and his brothers began gathering a horse herd of their own. They picked up a few here, and a few there, without anyone noticing what they were doing. There were so many horses no one seemed to miss the ones that had been taken. Every week or so Walkara or one of his brothers would ride into Los Angeles to see if Peg Leg was still in jail.

Peg Leg was in the jail for about ninety days, during which time Walkara and his brothers accumulated a herd of approximately five hundred horses. When Peg Leg found out he was furious, claiming that such actions would make them criminals in California and they would not be able to return. All of the party, trappers and Indians alike, laughed at Peg Leg, who had by official proclamation been banned from the city of Los Angeles for the remainder of his life.

When the police escort dropped Peg Leg off at the edge of town, without horse, saddle or rifle, with orders never to return, the one-legged trapper headed for the nearest ranch, where he and his trapper friends began gathering a herd of their own to accompany Walkara's back to the Rocky Mountains. When they joined forces at El Cajon Pass a week later the combined herd totaled over 600 horses.

Peg Leg and the trappers crossed the Colorado River where Walkara showed them it would be easy, taking their horses to Santa Fe to be sold for gold that was squandered on whiskey and women. Walkara and his brothers trailed their ponies to the Sanpete Valley.

Walkara now owned more horses than any Indian in the Rocky Mountains. By anyone's standards, he was a wealthy man, the wealthiest Indian of them all. He wondered if Susquenah would be impressed.

Chapter 19

It was a long winter, with deep snows, cold temperatures, and fierce north winds. But the wind was a blessing, blowing the snow off the hills in enough places that Walkara's horses could get to the frozen grass. The hard winter pushed more wild game than usual out of the mountains, making wild meat more plentiful. And when deer and elk could not be found, there was always a lame or old horse available for butchering. Walkara had enough horses to feed everyone. Life was good, or at least as good as could be expected during a hard winter.

Peg Leg was a frequent guest at Walkara's lodge. In addition to swapping stories, gambling and sipping whiskey, a plan for a great adventure began to develop. Both men had seen the rich valleys and hills of California, covered with countless horses. Both had little respect for the Spanish who owned them. Both knew that stealing California horses was as easy as rounding up one's own horses in the open meadows of the Sanpete. The blooded horses of California were taller, stronger and faster than the wiry Indian ponies of the mountains. As a result, the Spanish horses brought higher prices in Santa Fe, Fort Bridger and other points east and north.

It was no ordinary horse raid that Walkara and Peg Leg were planning. California was a big, rich land. Why not pull off a raid of major proportions, perhaps the grandest horse raid in the history of the known world?

With a little whiskey to fuel their imaginations, Walkara and Peg Leg began serious planning for a team of men, both white and Indian, to bring—not hundreds—but thousands of fine California horses to the Rocky Mountains. Together they would supply the American westward migration with all the horses it needed, and become fabulously wealthy in the process.

The team would consist of about 200 Indians—recruited and led by Walkara—and about 30 white trappers—recruited and led by Peg Leg. The trappers would go to California first, taking some of their trapping equipment with them. After passing through El Cajon Pass they would spread out, visiting the Spanish ranches as they worked their way towards the coast, asking about trapping opportunities in the land of the setting sun while secretly assessing the size and quality of the many horse herds.

While the white men were scouting California, Walkara and his men would go east onto the plains and kill many buffalo, then dry the meat and bring it home to stash at strategic locations all the way from Sanpete to El Cajon Pass. They figured the returning raiders would be in too big a hurry to hunt for food. The caches of dried buffalo meat would keep the raiders fed while bringing home the new horses.

Peg Leg headed east to assemble his band of trappers. Walkara sent Arrapeen north and San Pitch south, carrying the message that Walkara was looking for good men from all tribes to ride with him to California to steal thousands of fine horses. Shoshones, Crows, Navajos, Bannocks, Pahvants, Apaches, Flatheads and Blackfeet were welcome, provided tribal differences were forgotten. They would ride as red brothers and bring home many horses for the benefit of all tribes. It was a grand plan. Indians from different tribes had never ridden together like this before. They would meet in the Sanpete Valley as soon as the snow began to melt.

When Sowiette heard of the grand plan, he said red men from different tribes would not come because they would not trust each other, and would not trust Walkara. And if they did come, they could not ride and work together. The Apaches would fight with the Navajos. The Flatheads would fight with the Blackfeet. The Shoshones would fight with the Utes. The Crows would fight with everyone.

Walkara waited, wondering if Sowiette was right. Maybe it was not possible for red men from many different tribes to ride together. He would find out as soon as the snow began to melt.

As soon as the warm winds began melting the winter snow the first band of nine volunteers arrived. They came from the north, and were Shoshones. Walkara had anticipated they would want to ride with him. No one loved horses more than the thieving Shoshones. What concerned Walkara was that the leader of this first group of volunteers was a tall, thin warrior riding a roan stallion. Could he be the same warrior who had captured and killed Tah-mun, Walkara's child bride? Walkara was certain he was.

Fingering the trigger on his rifle, Walkara realized it would be an easy matter to raise the weapon and kill this enemy of many years. Nothing would give him more pleasure than taking this man's scalp. But Walkara hesitated. How could he ask other men to forget individual grudges and tribal differences, if he could not do it himself? Probably, many of the men coming together would remember former injuries, or crimes committed against them by other members of this new band of raiders.

"Do the Shoshones agree to obey me and my commands until after the stolen horses are divided?"

"We do," the tall warrior answered.

"What is your name?" Walkara asked him.

"Gray Wolf."

Again Walkara felt like forgetting the whole grand plan with Peg Leg and just killing Gray Wolf. He remembered the many unsuccessful days and weeks, wandering through Shoshone lands, searching for this Gray Wolf, determined to kill the wicked man. Now, finally, he could do it, easily.

Still, Walkara held back. At least for now, the grand plan was more important than his personal revenge. He would wait and kill Gray Wolf later.

Walkara's problems were just beginning. With the arrival of each new group of volunteers came new problems, many horse-related. With each new group, it seemed someone would recognize a horse that had been stolen from him, his brother, his father, his friend, and demand the return of the horse.

Walkara soon had a policy for handling such differences. Both parties were brought to Walkara, if they hadn't killed each other first. Walkara would hear both sides of the argument, then try to help the two parties reach an agreeable settlement. All understood that if a settlement could not be achieved both parties would have to leave. After leaving Sanpete they were free to fight and kill each other or return home, but they could not ride with Walkara to California as long as their differences remained unresolved. Some differences could not be resolved, like a Flathead recognizing the Blackfoot who had killed his father. Both men were sent away.

Finally Peg Leg showed up with his contingent of 30 trappers, a boisterous group eager to get to California, where they hoped to make the acquaintance of a few senoritas before gathering up all the horses. After settling on a rendezvous time in the hills north of El Cajon Pass, Peg Leg and his men headed south. A week

Chapter 19

later Walkara and his men headed east to get buffalo meat.

While hunting buffalo the men seemed to bury their differences and get along well. Buffalo hunting was fun and exciting. But when the hunting was over and it was time for the hard work of drying and hauling the meat to the cache locations, the fighting and bickering seemed to reach new heights. Walkara was continually solving and negotiating differences. He kept telling himself that for a thousand horses he could be as patient as the summer sun. And he really believed he might come home with a thousand horses. All the men understood how the horses would be divided up when it was all over. Walkara and Peg Leg would get half. The rest would be divided equally among the volunteers. Anyone who would not agree to that arrangement was invited to leave.

As the last cache was being prepared in some juniper trees before the party rode onto the big desert, Walkara became aware of a heated argument between two of the men working on the cache. He rode up to see what was the matter.

The big Navajo in charge of the cache had asked Gray Wolf to hand over his rawhide rope to be used in hoisting the bundle of meat and securing it in the tree. Gray Wolf had refused.

When Walkara, the mediator, arrived the Navajo explained that the rope was necessary to hoist the cache high in the tree to secure it against birds and other predators. Other men had volunteered their ropes at other caches. Now it was Gray Wolf's turn to volunteer his rope.

Gray Wolf said he was skilled with the rope, and would need it to steal and handle horses. The cache could be balanced in the tree without his rope, or green willows could be used to secure it.

Walkara's first inclination was to let Gray Wolf

keep his rope, but the incessant negotiations of the previous weeks were weighing heavy on him, and his patience was wearing out. He also knew he couldn't continue these endless settlements of differences among the men once they entered California. There would not be time. There had to be changes in how things were being done, and now might be a good time to make those changes.

"Give him the rope," he said to Gray Wolf.

The Shoshone seemed surprised that Walkara had decided so quickly on a course of action. He did not agree with Walkara's decision. Furthermore, he would lose face, giving his rope to the fat Navajo after refusing to do so earlier.

"Give him the rope," Walkara repeated, his voice mild, not forceful at all.

"No," Gray Wolf said, not noticing that Walkara's rifle was pointed at his chest.

Without a word, without hesitation, Walkara pulled the trigger. No one was more surprised than Gray Wolf when the rifle exploded. The heavy lead slug sent the Shoshone rolling backwards out of the saddle. For a moment he writhed in the dust, red blood gushing from his nose, mouth and chest. Then he was still.

Walkara grabbed the roan stallion's headstall with one hand. With the other he removed the rawhide rope from the saddle and tossed it to the Navajo. Then he called for all the men to gather around. He had something to say.

"I am no longer a tribal council," he began, when he thought everyone was close enough to hear. "The time for negotiations and much talk is past. We are now a raiding party. Anyone who does not do what I say will join Gray Wolf in the dust. Anyone who does not agree with that may leave now." Walkara looked at the men to see if anyone would leave. None did, not even the Shoshones.

Some of the men started to go back to their business. "Wait," Walkara said, "I have more to say. Today, if you do not like what I say you may go," he began. "Tomorrow, if you do not like what I say you may not go. You must do it anyway, or I will kill you and leave your bones for the birds to dump their dung on."

He could tell that some of the men did not understand what he was saying.

"We are now a raiding party," he continued, "and must stay together. When the Spanish discover what we are about they will catch us, if they can, and hang us from trees with ropes around our necks. We may have to fight for our lives. No one can leave. We ride together, we fight together, and if necessary we die together. After today, any man who tries to leave, I will kill. So if you want to leave, do so now."

Again Walkara looked around to see if anyone would leave. None did. He looked down at Gray Wolf. He remembered finding the body of Tah-mun. Walkara was glad he had killed Gray Wolf, and he hoped Gray Wolf had not died in vain, that the rest of the men would become a true raiding party now, more determined to steal horses than bicker with each other.

The next morning as Walkara and his men descended onto the desert the bickering had ended. For the first time Walkara felt confidence in his men. Finally, he was riding at the head of an army, bringing big trouble to the sleeping Californians.

Chapter 20

When Walkara and his men arrived at El Cajon Pass, Peg Leg was waiting for them. There had been a change of plans. Instead of sending all his trappers into California to check out the locations of the many horse herds and risk drawing attention to the sudden influx of American trappers, he had sent only one man, James Beckwourth, a black man. Peg Leg figured most of the Californians had never seen a black man before, so Beckwourth would be a curiosity. It wouldn't occur to them that an odd fellow like Beckwourth might be the lead man for an organized plot to steal half of California's horses.

Beckwourth was traveling with his trapping outfit, supposedly discouraged over the declining beaver trade and asking about sea otter trapping. He had been gone almost 30 days, and Peg Leg was patiently awaiting his return. Walkara and his men had brought plenty of dried buffalo meat, so the men made themselves comfortable, hoping Beckwourth would return soon.

They didn't have long to wait. Two days after Walkara's arrival from the east, Beckwourth arrived from the west. He brought with him glowing reports of huge ranches with vast herds of cattle and horses, with few cowboys to guard them.

He had traveled in a huge circle, first going southwest towards Mission Santa Ana, studying the various ranches along that route. The Spaniards had been kind to him, and generous with lodging and food. From Santa Ana he had headed up the coast on the road the Spanish called El Camino. The priests, or big hats, at the missions had kept him and his animals well fed. He continued to see many fine horse herds. He went all the way to a place called Mission San Luis Obispo before heading back inland again, across the Sierra Madre Mountains and back to El Cajon Pass.

Using a stick, Beckwourth drew a large map in the dirt, showing the rivers, the mountains, the missions and the ranches with the largest and finest horse herds. Walkara and Peg Leg, after asking many questions about each ranch, began dividing the men, whites and Indians, into groups, assigning each group to one or more of the large ranches. Beckwourth marked hillside locations near each ranch where he thought men could secretly observe ranch operations before attacking.

Walkara and Peg Leg gathered each group around the map, showing the men the best route to and from the target ranch and where to hide while surveying the ranch and waiting to attack. The men were given plenty of time to study and memorize the map. A leader was assigned to each group.

The overall plan was simple. The men had six days to get positioned in the hilltop hideouts above their assigned ranches and observe the targeted horse herds. On the evening of the sixth day, as darkness fell, just before the full moon came up in the east, they were to drive off as many horses as possible and travel with the greatest speed to El Cajon Pass. There they would join forces and push the combined herd onto the Mojave Desert. Hopefully they would be well into the desert before the surprised Spanish could organize a posse to follow. Peg Leg didn't think the Spanish would cross the Mojave.

The excitement was high as the men headed out the

next morning. Walkara led the groups with northerly assignments northwest towards San Luis Obispo. Peg Leg and Beckwourth led the rest towards Santa Ana.

While traveling, the men spread out, trying to avoid main trails. Six days gave them plenty of time to reach their assigned locations.

When the groups with Walkara had departed for their various assignments, Walkara still had ten men with him, to go to what Beckwourth said was the biggest ranch of all, located just east of Mission San Luis Obispo. Walkara arrived on the evening of the fifth day.

The next morning Walkara saw more beautiful horses than he had ever seen at one time in his life. Over a thousand horses grazed in the vast fields near the main hacienda. As evening drew near most of them were herded by ten cowboys into half a dozen large corrals.

Leaving a boy to bring their saddle horses to join them once the stampede began, Walkara and the eight men with him began sneaking through the tall grass towards the big corrals.

Never had Walkara seen such a big house or hacienda, not even in Los Angeles. There were other buildings too—a barn, servants' quarters, a stable, a cookhouse, a smokehouse, a grain shed, and a blacksmith's shop.

When darkness fell Walkara and his men were hiding in a draw less than a hundred yards from the nearest corral. They were waiting for some of the activity to cease. People were hurrying back and forth between various buildings. There seemed to be more activity than there should have been. The previous evening had been much quieter. Walkara didn't know what was happening.

Suddenly Walkara was alarmed. A dozen or so carriages were approaching from the direction of the mission. Numerous riders accompanied the carriages.

Chapter 20

At first he wondered if perhaps the Spanish had somehow found out about the attack and were making preparations to defend themselves against the Utes.

After thinking about it, Walkara realized that could not be the case. First, they would not be coming to defend against Indian attack in carriages. Second, they would not be bringing their women with them. Even in the fading light he could see that each carriage carried at least one finely dressed senora or senorita. Walkara and his men waited to see what was going to happen.

The carriages stopped in front of the big hacienda, the people getting out and going inside. Lamps glowed in all the windows of the hacienda. Apparently there was going to be some kind of celebration. Servants were hurrying from the cookhouse with trays of steaming food and bottles of wine.

One of the last guests to arrive was riding a large black carrying a silver inlaid saddle, the finest horse and saddle Walkara had ever seen. The carriages and saddle horses of the guests were tied to fences and hitching posts in front of the hacienda.

When Walkara's men wanted to know what they should do now, Walkara suggested a slight change in the attack plan. All agreed it was a good idea. They waited another half hour until the party was well underway, then began crawling towards the corrals.

Walkara became concerned when a curious dog began sniffing towards them, but a piece of dried buffalo meat quickly satisfied the dog's curiosity. While half of Walkara's men worked their way towards the big corrals, Walkara and the rest moved in among the saddle horses and carriages of the guests. Walkara untied the big stallion while his men untied other horses. They didn't bother with any of the sleek carriage horses because carriages couldn't go where they were going. Some of the men untied two or three saddle horses.

165

They worked quietly, several of the men leading saddled horses towards the corrals where the other men were already in position at the gates. When everyone had saddled horses to ride, the big corral gates were swung open.

The huge horse herds didn't need coaxing. The animals had already sensed the excitement of the evening. Perhaps they had smelled the Indians. As soon as the big gates swung open, every horse seemed to lunge simultaneously for the open country.

Walkara leaped upon the back of the powerful black and sounded his war cry, loud and long. The stallion reared, then plunged ahead into the darkness to join the thousand horses stampeding towards El Cajon Pass.

Not only did Walkara and his men have the longest distance to travel in reaching El Cajon Pass, but they also had the most horses to push, almost too many. Because they were such fine horses, Walkara was determined not to let any fall behind.

It was the afternoon of the fifth day when Walkara approached the pass. He could hear distant gunfire, but could see no horses. He found out the horses stolen by the other groups were already through the pass and beginning to cross the Mojave. Suddenly he saw Peg Leg approaching at full gallop, waving at Walkara to keep the horses moving.

When Peg Leg reached Walkara he said the rest of the horses were already headed east, and that he and about a hundred men were in a fight with a large Spanish posse on the west side of the pass. More Spaniards were arriving hourly. The fighting was getting fierce. He said he and his men would hold back the posse as long as possible, then join Walkara and the rest of the men and horses out on the Mojave, hopefully before they reached the Barstow springs.

Peg Leg was about to wheel his horse around and

head back to the fight, but Walkara had one more question.

"How many horses are there? How many did we get?"

"I don't know," Peg Leg yelled, grinning from ear to ear. "Thousands, many thousands, would be my best guess. We'll count them at Barstow." Wheeling his horse around and sounding a Ute war whoop, Peg Leg galloped back to his men.

An hour later Walkara's thousand horses were swallowed up by a herd four or five times as large. He wondered if anyone ever had seen so many horses together at one place at one time, a herd almost too large for a hundred men to drive, but drive it they did, trotting and galloping along the Mojave River, creating the largest man-caused dust cloud anyone had ever seen.

As far as Walkara could see, there was nothing but horses, and half of them belonged to him and Peg Leg. He wished Susquenah could see him now, could ride beside him and share with him this glorious victory. At least he hoped it was a victory. The Spanish were still determined to stop him. He hoped Peg Leg could hold them back.

The vast horse herd pushed towards the Barstow springs, across a 30-mile stretch of waterless desert. Much of the distance was covered at night. Walkara and his men kept the horses moving. There was no time for rest. Occasionally, where there was grass, they would let the horses graze as they walked.

As promised, Peg Leg and his weary men caught up with the herd just before reaching the springs. Peg Leg was worried. The posse had grown to several hundred men, and hadn't turned back at the edge of the Mojave.

The Spanish were well-mounted, well-armed, and determined to get their horses back, killing some trappers and Indians while doing so.

While the thirsty men and horses were filling their

bellies with cool water at the springs, Walkara came up with a new plan. Since Peg Leg and his men were exhausted from their forced march, they would move ahead with the horse herd across the desert. Walkara and a hundred men would remain behind at the springs to prevent the Spanish from getting water. The posse could not continue pursuit without water. Peg Leg was too tired to do anything but agree with the plan. He and his men moved west with the huge herd.

Walkara and his army began digging fortifications from behind which they could fight to keep the Spanish away from the water, but the more he thought about his plan the more unsure he became about how effective it might be. He didn't like the thought of allowing himself to be surrounded by a much larger Spanish force. The Spanish and their horses would be very thirsty, and determined to get to the water. The battle might be fierce. Many Indians might die. All might die without a path of retreat.

Walkara ordered his men to cease working on the fortification. He had a new plan. He and his companions rode into the thick willows below the springs, hiding themselves and their horses. Several scouts were sent to a nearby hill to watch for the Spanish.

Walkara's new plan was simple. He guessed that after crossing nearly 30 miles of desert without water, the Spanish would be tired and thirsty. Thinking Walkara, Peg Leg and all their men had gone ahead with the big herd, the Spanish would get off their horses to drink and fill their canteens. That's when Walkara and his men would attack. He emphasized to his men that the primary purpose of the attack was not to kill Spaniards, but to frighten their horses and drive them off. He told his men that if they were going to fire a gun they might as well try to kill a Spaniard while doing so, but the most important thing was to make noise and

168

scare off the horses.

Walkara and his men weren't in the willows more than several hours when the Spanish were seen approaching from the west. Making sure their rifles were loaded, Walkara and his men got on their horses.

They didn't have long to wait. When the Spaniards saw the water they allowed their thirsty horses to gallop to it. Walkara was glad for the noise of galloping hooves. Now there was no chance of the Spanish hearing his men or horses approaching through the willows.

As the Spanish reached the water, Walkara motioned for his men to stop. He didn't want to attack too soon. If the attack occurred before the Spanish horses had filled their bellies, it would be difficult to stampede them away from the life-giving water. Many would run back to drink, and could be caught again.

As Walkara had anticipated, the Spaniards jumped from their horses to drink and fill their canteens and water bottles. Some of the men jumped into the water. No guards were posted. Walkara waited. The horses were all drinking.

When some of the horses began to lift their heads, water dripping from happy mouths, Walkara sounded his war cry. A hundred screaming Indians charged from the willows. Many began firing rifles at the Spaniards. Many of the Spaniards had left their rifles in the scabbards on their saddles and ran to catch their horses, which by now were stampeding away from the screaming Indians. While several Spaniards caught their horses, most did not. Walkara and his men didn't stop to take scalps as they galloped past in pursuit of the stampeding saddle horses.

With their horses gone, the frustrated Spaniards had no choice but to finish filling their canteens and begin walking back to California.

When Walkara finally caught up with Peg Leg, the Ute chief was driving a herd of over a hundred saddled

Spanish horses. Not only would every man be made wealthy when the horses were divided up, but most of the men would have new Spanish saddles too.

As they continued to push the big herd across the desert, Walkara and Peg Leg tried to count the animals. They knew they had lost some while being chased by the Spanish, but they figured the ones that were lost included the lame and old horses that couldn't keep up. After repeated countings, they concluded that while they might have had as many as 6,000 horses when they came out of El Cajon Pass, only about three thousand remained. But that was enough. They guessed they had carried off the biggest horse raid in the history of the world, and that Walkara and Peg Leg, with fifteen hundred horses to divide, were two of the richest men on the continent.

"That black stallion you were riding today is the most beautiful animal I've ever seen," Peg Leg said as they rolled up in their blankets that night.

"Then he is yours. I give him to you," Walkara responded.

"Thanks, partner," Peg Leg yawned. "I guess I'm the happiest and tiredest man in the world tonight."

Walkara felt happy too. But he also felt lonely. He missed Susquenah. All the horses in the world could not take that loneliness away.

Chapter 21

Upon reaching the Sanpete Valley, Walkara and Peg Leg discovered their families had left with Sowiette for the annual fish festival near their former home in Utah Valley, about 60 miles to the northwest. Not wanting to miss the big celebration, Walkara, Peg Leg and their 200 men kept the big herd moving all the way to Utah Valley.

Some of the men from other tribes were eager to divide off their share of the herd and be on their way home, but finally all agreed to wait until Utah Valley to divide up the herd. They could do it while dancing, horse racing, and feasting on fish.

Dividing up the herd didn't take as long as Walkara had thought it would. After he and Peg Leg separated out their half, the men began taking turns riding into the herd and lassoing the animal of their choice, then removing it from the herd. This process lasted for four days until all the animals were taken. By Indian standards every man was now wealthy. In addition to the new wealth in horses, most men had a Spanish saddle too.

The men from faraway tribes were eager to be heading home with their new horses. Before they got away Walkara invited them to come back after the first snow settled in the mountain passes and they would go to California again, for more horses. Most said they

171

would be back. Some asked if they could bring brothers and friends. Walkara said he and Peg Leg would head for California as soon as they had 200 men to go with them. Those who came first would go, while those who came later would be left behind.

Walkara and Peg leg had discussed at some length how large their raiding party should be. The more men there were, the harder it would be to slip undetected into California. Too many men meant fewer horses for each man involved, but there had to be enough to steal and drive a large herd, plus offer a serious threat to any posse that might come after them. After much discussion they concluded 200 was just right.

With 200 men Walkara and Peg Leg led the most powerful fighting force in the Rocky Mountain region, more powerful than any one tribe. All the men were well-armed, and well-mounted. Sometimes Walkara wished he had not let any Shoshones in his army, thus making it possible to lead his men against the Shoshones in battle, but with men in his army representing nearly all mountain tribes, he knew there would be serious problems if he tried to pick on any single tribe. He concluded he would have to organize and lead a Ute-only band next time he decided to raid the Shoshones. He did notice, however, that with Shoshones riding with him that spring, there had been fewer raids by Shoshones on Ute herds.

When the fish festival started winding down, with the various Ute bands beginning to get their things together to leave, Walkara and Peg Leg sent their families back to Sanpete with most of the new horses. Walkara and Peg Leg headed north to Bridger's trading post, each taking fifty horses to trade for new rifles, powder, lead, steel traps, horseshoes, tepee canvas, whiskey, and anything else that suited their fancy. They had enough horses to buy just about anything in the world, they thought.

After the trading was done, Peg Leg hung around with Bridger for a few days while Walkara rode northwest looking for Washakie's camp and Susquenah. When he reached Washakie's favorite spot near the north end of the big lake, he saw no sign of him or his band. Walkara guessed they had probably headed east to hunt buffalo. He thought about going looking for them, but knowing Peg Leg was waiting for him, he decided he would have to wait until his next journey to Fort Bridger to look for Susquenah. Maybe by then the band would be back at the lake.

Walkara wondered how he might leave a message for Susquenah, something to let her know he had been there, that he was still thinking of her. The only thing he could think of was to hang his rabbit skin cloak high in a tree. Like a flag, it would be waving in the wind to greet her when she returned. But he didn't know when, if ever, she would return. If other Indians saw the banner first they would rip it down.

He treasured the rabbit skin cloak, which had become a token of the love he and Susquenah had shared that winter together. No, he would keep the cloak, but he would return. Perhaps by then her strong feelings against the slave business would be softened. Besides, he had not captured any new slaves since he and Peg Leg began planning the big California raid. Maybe she would want to come back to him now he wasn't actively slave trading. Perhaps he would give up the slave business altogether, it being much easier just to steal horses in California.

Walkara returned to Fort Bridger to pick up Peg Leg. As they returned to Sanpete they began plans for the next big horse raid. It would be bigger than the last. This time they would try for eight thousand horses. Their men were experienced now, better armed and better mounted. This time they would do better. They discussed how they would find new markets for the horses, having already sold Bridger more than he wanted. Peg Leg said he would take horses all the way to Missouri, if necessary, where good horses were said to bring as much as $150 where people were outfitting for the westward migration.

When spring arrived Walkara and Peg Leg were headed south, followed by an organized and disciplined army of Indians and trappers. Their pack horses carried plenty of dried buffalo and beef. Ahead of them they drove ten brood mares, which they intended to put at the head of the new herd to lead the horses home, thereby making the task of driving the herd much easier. The arrangement with the men was different than before, with ten percent of the new horses going to Peg Leg and Walkara, the rest being divided equally among the men. Expectations were high, each man planning on taking home 15 to 20 animals. Each man carried a new rifle with plenty of powder and lead. Any Spanish posse that wanted to make trouble for them had better look out.

Walkara and Peg Leg didn't notice anything different about California until after they had crossed El Cajon Pass. Whereas they had taken but a small fraction of the many horses they had seen the previous spring, now there were few horses to be seen, a few here and there, but no large herds.

They rode further towards the ocean, still seeing no large herds. Occasionally they saw bands of armed Spaniards, riding along roads and trails as if they were on patrol.

The search for large bands of horses continued without success. Finally, Walkara and Peg Leg divided their army into small groups, sending the men in all directions, looking for the horses they knew had to be somewhere. Their orders were that if they found a band of horses, they should hide out, then make their raid at a time that would enable them to be back at El Cajon

Pass in ten days. At the end of ten days they would join the stolen horses with the ten brood mares and head for home.

Walkara took three men with him and headed for the San Luis Obispo ranch where he had been so successful on the previous trip. He took his time, checking out as many ranches as possible along the way. The situation was the same everywhere: no large herds of horses. He began to feel uneasy. Something was wrong, very wrong. Still, he continued towards San Luis Obispo.

What Walkara did not know was that the Spanish governor, Echeandia, an amiable magistrate, had been replaced the previous summer by a young, aggressive warrior of a man named Manuel Victoria. In his inaugural address Victoria vowed the ranchos and haciendas would get the protection they needed. He said, "Those Americanos (including Indians) must be stopped before they sweep the coastal ranchos clean of animals, leaving only the saddled animal tied to the veranda.

"No longer will we tolerate such insults as are forced on our maidens, our workers, our government. I promise it will stop."

Immediately Victoria doubled the size of his mission garrisons by demanding that each rancho, mission, and hacienda provide not only guards, but food and equipment for them, from their own resources. The new guards patrolled the border areas, on constant lookout for tracks of incoming riders from the east.

Walkara didn't know his trail had been discovered even before he and his men had reached El Cajon Pass. The Californians already knew he was there, and the movement of his army had been carefully monitored up until he had scattered his men in all directions.

From their hilltop hideout above the vast San Luis Obispo rancho Walkara and his men finally found some horses. In a relatively small pasture in the middle of an open flat, about 30 horses were grazing peacefully. Though the herd was not large like many they had seen on the earlier visits to California, at least it was a herd, and it looked like it would be easy to steal. If they took it tonight, they could still make it to El Cajon Pass within the ten-day limit.

Still, Walkara was reluctant to leave his mountain hideout. Too many things had changed. More than the bands of armed guards, he was disturbed by the sudden disappearance of so many horses from the open valleys and hillsides. Though he couldn't put his finger on anything specific, he had the feeling that a force much bigger than a few bands of roving guards had been mustered against him and his men. He told the three men with him that they were going to return to El Cajon Pass without the 30 horses. He didn't want to try to steal them.

Two of the men didn't argue with Walkara, but the third one did, a bold young Apache named Red Duck. He hadn't come all the way to the Big Water to go home empty-handed. If Walkara didn't want the 30 horses, he would take them himself. Having no strong reason to dissuade the young man, Walkara told him to go ahead and try.

It wasn't quite dark as Walkara and his two companions watched Red Duck gallop across the open fields towards the pasture that held the horses. During the entire day, they hadn't seen anyone in the vicinity of the pasture.

Upon reaching the enclosure, Red Duck took down the gate and rode inside to round up the horses.

Suddenly Walkara was aware of about 25 mounted riders racing for the open gate. They had emerged from a deep ravine about half a mile to the north. Red Duck didn't see them until it was too late. He was trapped in the pasture. The pole fences were too high for his pony to jump. Half the Spaniards entered the pasture to catch Red Duck, while the other half, after closing the gate, scattered themselves around the outside to cut off his escape in the event he did get through the fence.

In a few minutes Red Duck was cornered, and one of the Spaniards threw a rope over his shoulders and jerked him to the ground. Walkara wanted to ride to the rescue, but challenging twenty-five with only three made a rescue attempt look foolish. It would be better to wait until dark. Maybe he could sneak into the Spanish camp and get Red Duck out that way.

But the Spanish had other plans for Red Duck. They knew exactly what they were going to do to him, and they didn't waste any time getting it done. Four long ropes were tied to him, one to each wrist and one to each ankle. Four spirited horses were roped and brought in close. Each of the long ropes already tied to Red Duck was tied to a separate horse by looping the rope around the horse's body in front of the hind legs with a slipknot so when the horse pulled against the rope the loop would become tighter around the horse's flanks, causing it to buck and kick.

As soon as the four ropes were in place, the spirited horses were let free. The Spaniards began waving their hats and shouting. The four horses stampeded, and as they did so the four ropes were jerked tight. The horses began to buck, ducking out in different directions. One broke free and raced back to the herd, dragging a bouncing arm at the end of its rope. A second horse broke free, dragging the other arm with it. The remaining two horses, unable to rip off the legs, finally came together, racing and bucking across the field, Red Duck's armless body bouncing and flipping each time it hit a bump or dip in the terrain.

The men left the pasture, looking down at the ground, finding Red Duck's incoming trail. Their companions soon joined them and all 25 began galloping straight towards Walkara's hiding place. He and his two companions leaped on their horses and headed towards El Cajon Pass, thankful for the approaching darkness.

All the way to the rendezvous point, Walkara was wondering what kind of difficulties the rest of the men had encountered. He wondered how many men had been ambushed and killed. He was sure Red Duck wasn't the only one.

Upon reaching El Cajon Pass Walkara was amazed to find all of his men. And they had horses with them. Not a large herd, only 225, but that was better than what had happened to Red Duck. At least they had something to take home. He told his men they would let California rest for a few years, get its guard down, then they would return unexpectedly and steal thousands of horses again.

The promise of more horses in a few years didn't lift the men's spirits. They had hoped for more horses now, but the Spaniards had outsmarted them. Discouraged and tired, the men drove their tiny herd towards the Mojave River. There was little talk, and no laughter, especially across the dry, 28-mile stretch to the Barstow springs.

Upon reaching the springs, the weary men dropped to the ground, fell on their bellies and began drinking, side by side with their thirsty horses. Suddenly the air was filled with the thundering of a hundred rifles. The ground seemed to shake with the noise. Bullets were kicking up water and sand. In panic, horses were trying to pull away as desperate men clung to lead ropes.

Resisting the natural instinct to jump to his feet, Walkara remained on his belly, holding tightly to his horse's lead rope, looking to the right, the left, then across the springs, trying to figure out what was happening. He realized he was experiencing a repeat of the attack he and his men had carried out against the

Spanish at this same place a year ago, except this time the tables were turned. The Spanish were the attackers.

There was another difference, too. Whereas the main objective of him and his men in the first assault had been to drive off horses, the objective of the Spanish now was to kill Indians and trappers.

Without any nearby cover for him and his men, Walkara knew the only reasonable course of action was to retreat into the open desert. The only nearby cover, the thick willows, was full of armed Spaniards bent on killing every Indian and trapper in sight.

Walkara leaped on his horse, ordering his men to retreat with him to the open desert. Many had lost their horses and were trying to follow him on foot. Some were riding double. Everywhere men and horses were falling to the ground. Many of the riderless horses had already found their way into the open desert.

A platoon of mounted Spaniards charged from the willows to cut off Walkara's retreat. He ordered his men to focus all their gunfire on the riders in front of them. The fighting was fierce, the Spaniards finally turning back towards the cover of the willows.

Walkara, Peg Leg and less than half of the men made it to the open desert. The Spanish did not follow them. Ninety braves and twenty-one white trappers were left behind, either dead or wounded, to be hacked apart by the vengeful Spaniards. The horse herd running ahead of Walkara and his men consisted of less than fifty animals. The raid that had been a disappointing failure a few minutes earlier was now a major disaster. Over a hundred friends, including some relatives, had been slaughtered by the Spanish. Ninety Indian families had lost the man who was supposed to bring in meat this coming winter.

As they continued eastward across the desert, trying to put as much distance as possible between them and the Spaniards before nightfall, Walkara tried to figure out what had happened. Because it had been so easy for Walkara and his men to steal 5,000 horses a year earlier, the Spanish had correctly concluded that Walkara and Peg Leg would try it again. The Spanish set a trap, and like fools, Walkara and Peg Leg had walked right into it.

Next time it would be different. Walkara vowed to himself that after some time had passed and the Spanish guard relaxed, perhaps in two or three years, he would find a new pass, north of El Cajon. He and his men would sneak in when least expected, and steal not only horses, but slaves as well. And they would take scalps and burn haciendas. The Spanish would pay dearly for what they had done this day.

"I think this was the worst day of my entire life," Peg Leg complained as they rolled up in their blankets that night. "I can tell you one thing. My horse-stealing days are over. I am going to become a trader, like Bridger."

Walkara didn't respond, but he remembered Peg Leg saying it was the happiest day of his life as they had rolled up in their blankets following the previous raid. Walkara also remembered how he had felt a year earlier, how he had longed to be with Susquenah. He felt the same way now. Whereas last time he had wanted to share his victory with her, now he only wanted to bury his face against her soft body and forget his dismal failure, if only for a few moments.

He needed her. He would find her this time, if he had to cover every foot of Shoshone country. He would ask her to come back. He would beg her to come back.

Chapter 22

After dividing up the 50 horses among the families of those who were lost in the Mojave Desert, Walkara headed north to Bear Lake to look for Washakie's band and Susquenah. Peg Leg rode with him. Many of the Utes blamed Peg Leg for their losses in California. Had it not been for the one-legged trapper, the Utes would never have gone to California in the first place.

Peg Leg was riding with Walkara to check out the land north of Bear Lake along the Bear River. Emigrants headed for Oregon had been passing through the area in increasing numbers, and Peg Leg thought he might be able to establish a profitable trading post. Washakie, the Shoshone who roamed the area, had been friendly to Peg Leg and whites in general. The situation appeared ideal, so Peg Leg wanted to check it out. He insisted his horse-stealing days were over.

As they proceeded northward, the two friends conversed in both their languages, English and Ute. During the years spent together both had become proficient in the other's language. When other Indians were around and they didn't want their conversation overheard or understood, they always talked in English.

It being winter, they were fairly certain they would find Washakie near home, camped in the thick cottonwoods along the river. Not only did the trees provide protection from the cold north wind and fuel for fires, but also feed for horses when the winter snows became too deep for the horses to paw down to grass. Horses could survive on the sweet inner bark of cottonwood limbs. The same limbs cut down by the braves for the horses to chew on made excellent firewood the following winter.

Washakie was camped in the cottonwoods like they thought he would be, and welcomed them into his camp. The chief had already heard about their unsuccessful raid to California, and he expressed his sympathy. Several of his Shoshone relatives and friends had been lost in the battle at the springs.

Washakie agreed to ride north with Peg Leg to show him where the wagon trail was, the one the Mericats used on their way to Oregon. The chief liked the idea of Peg Leg establishing a trading post. The Indians would benefit too. They wouldn't have to travel the long distance to Bridger's trading post anymore. He hoped Peg Leg's prices would be more reasonable. Peg Leg assured him they would be.

Before riding out, Washakie told Walkara where Susquenah was staying, with a sister in a tepee at the far end of the village. Walkara noticed that his heart began pounding in his chest when Washakie said she had not become anyone else's squaw. Walkara hurried to the tepee.

"Susquenah," he called. "You have a visitor."

The flap was pushed aside and Susquenah crawled outside and stood up. When she recognized her visitor she impulsively flew into his arms. He held her tight, neither of them saying anything. Walkara couldn't remember ever feeling better than he felt at this moment. It was so good to see her, to hold her, to feel her warmth and love. He hoped she still loved him.

"I'm glad you came," she said simply, when she finally pushed away. He did not want to let go. He felt like he could stand there and hold her all day.

"Come, walk with me," he said.

"First, there is someone you must meet," she said, turning back to the tepee. "Battee," she called. "Come outside."

The flap was pushed back again, and a little boy about three stepped outside, looking shyly up at Walkara.

"Walkara," Susquenah said. "Meet your son, Battee."

Walkara scooped the boy into his arms, gave him a firm squeeze, then held the boy out in front of him so they could both get a good look at each other.

"You are Walkara, the great warrior," the boy said.

"Your mother has taught you well," Walkara responded.

"Can I ride your horse?"

Walkara was impressed the boy could speak so well for one so young.

"Later, when it is warmer, after your mother and I go for a walk," he said, putting the boy down. Susquenah sent Battee back in the tepee.

After she grabbed a buffalo robe out of the tepee, Susquenah and Walkara began walking towards the river, wrapping the robe around both of their shoulders, forcing them to walk close to each other.

"I heard about the battle with the Spanish where many of your men were killed," she said.

"Yes, 90 braves and 21 trappers. It was a terrible defeat. There were no prisoners. The Spanish killed the wounded."

"I guess you won't be going back to California," she said.

He told her of his plan to avenge the deaths of his friends, how he would return to California in two or three years after they had let their guard down, how this next time he would take scalps and capture slaves, in addition to stealing their horses. He realized too late he probably shouldn't have mentioned his intention of taking more slaves.

"Do you ever wonder why the Spanish followed you into the desert and ambushed you?" she asked.

"Because we were trying to steal their horses, of course."

"If you weren't trying to steal their horses then all those men would not have died," she said.

"You do not think I should steal horses?" he asked. "All Indians steal horses. That is our way of life."

"Stealing horses causes much suffering. I don't like it," she said.

He and Susquenah walked in silence for a while.

"Will you and Battee come back with me?" he asked, figuring he might as well get to the purpose of his visit.

"I thought you would have found another squaw by now," she said, avoiding his question.

"I have," he said. "I have two."

"And you want me to be the third?" she asked.

"No, you would be the first."

"The other two might not like that."

"Then I would sell them to the Navajos," he said, realizing too late that he should not have made another reference to selling slaves.

"Does it bother you to sell someone into slavery?" she asked.

"No," he said, simply. "It's a good way to get horses."

"I don't like it," she said.

"If you don't like horse stealing and slave trading, how is a man supposed to get horses?" he asked, thinking he had her cornered.

"If you had ten mares," she responded, some enthusiasm in her voice, "and one stallion, you would get ten new horses every spring. A good hunter like you

184

could live very comfortably with ten horses to sell every year."

"Do you know what would happen if I tried to live that way?" he asked, trying to reason with her.

"No."

"One fine summer evening, while I was out hunting, your Shoshone cousins would gallop into our meadow and steal all my horses. And when I said I was going after them to take some scalps and steal their horses, you would tell me not to do it."

"Yes I would," she said.

"Where do you get these crazy ideas?" he asked. "Who do you talk to?"

"Myself," she said. "Without a man to gather wood, cook and make clothing for I have a lot of time to myself. Time to think. I think about the families of the ninety braves who were killed in the desert, how hard it is for them now the man is gone. If you had not taken those men to California that suffering would not be."

"You think that I, and other men like me, are the cause of all suffering in the world?"

"No. Winter winds make people cold. Children fall from horses and break bones. And sometimes people starve when the buffalo cannot be found. But without scalping, horse stealing and slave trading there would be much less suffering. Wouldn't it be wonderful, Walkara, if you didn't have to worry about someone stealing your horses or your children?"

"You seem to have all the answers," he said, beginning to feel angry, wondering why such a desirable woman had so many crazy ideas in her head.

"There's one answer I don't have," she said calmly.

"What is that?" he asked.

"I don't know how to get strong and powerful men like you to think as I do."

"Maybe you could figure that out if you came and lived with me," he suggested.

"I don't think I could," she said.

"You won't know unless you try."

"Let's try something else," she said. "When you agree to give up making war on other tribes, stealing horses, and trading slaves I will come and be your squaw again. How does that sound?"

Walkara turned and looked at Susquenah. She had never looked so beautiful, so desirable.

"When Washakie demanded 20 horses for you I thought the price was high," he said sadly.

"It was," she responded.

"The price you ask is much higher," he said.

"I know," she answered.

"I am Walkara. I cannot be what I am not."

"I am Susquenah. I cannot be the woman of a man who brings so much suffering to others." There were tears in her eyes.

"Words, words, words," Walkara cried. "How is it that mere words can keep two people who love each other apart?"

"I don't know," she said. "Maybe if you spent more time thinking and caring, and less time making war, stealing and slave trading, you could figure that one out. Let me know if you do."

"Then you will not come back with me?" he asked.

"No, I can't," she responded.

Walkara slipped out from under the buffalo robe, allowing its full weight to rest on Susquenah's shoulders.

"Is it all right if I take the boy for a ride on my horse before I leave?" he asked. Susquenah nodded her approval. He turned and hurried back to the tepee, leaving her to follow behind.

As soon as he had given the boy the ride, he went looking for Peg Leg. He did not say goodby to

Chapter 22

Susquenah. It was time to be heading for home. With the California borders closed off, it might be a good year for catching and selling slaves, and he didn't want to waste any more time with the woman who wanted him to give up fighting, horse stealing and slave trading. She might as well ask him to give up eating, breathing and drinking.

Chapter 23

Peg Leg kept his promise to give up horse stealing and become a trader. His three wives mourned the loss of brothers or half-brothers in the ambush at the springs. There being an abundance of new widows in the camp, Peg Leg compassionately added two more to his lodge, before beginning to pack up his things.

With everything he owned loaded on four travois, he mounted the black stallion and headed north to the Bear River country, his wives helping drive what remained of his formerly large horse herd.

The trapper's intention was to become rich selling horses and supplies to white men headed for Oregon. He promised Walkara and the Utes fair prices on guns, powder and firewater if they would bring him furs and horses once he was set up to do business.

Walkara liked the idea of trading with a friend, and promised to be Peg Leg's first customer. He also knew that Susquenah and Battee would not be far from the new trading post. He had decided never to visit her again. Still, the yearning for her, from somewhere deep inside, refused to go away. He hoped with time it would.

It would take time for Peg Leg to get his trading post set up. In the meantime Walkara went hunting, mostly for deer and elk in the nearby mountains. Sometimes in the sagebrush flats in the high mountain valleys he would chase his prey on horseback with bow and arrows. He took pride in his horsemanship and his marksmanship, having killed buffalo, deer, elk and one Crow Indian from the back of a galloping horse. He loved the feel of a good horse under him, and the excitement of racing after a fleeing deer or elk. It was only during moments like this that he didn't seem to notice the ache for Susquenah.

But as summer turned into fall, and fall into winter, Walkara grew increasingly restless. When he thought of Susquenah he became irritable. The love he had for her refused to die. Thoughts of her forced their way into his mind every time he entered his lodge and she wasn't there.

Walkara and his brothers discussed another slave roundup in the west desert, but slave trading had lost much of its glamour after the first big California horse raid. Slave trading was too much work for the amount of horses obtained. A group of men could spend all winter rounding up slaves and herding them to the Navajos, only to end up with 10 or 20 new horses. The same group of men executing a well-planned horse raid could end up with hundreds of horses. Of course, the risks were much greater.

There was no way anyone wanted to try another raid in California, at least not this year. Raids against the Shoshones were possible, but seldom netted very many animals.

Walkara began thinking about the land south of the Navajos in what the trappers called Old Mexico, the land where the Navajos traded their slaves for horses. Though Walkara had never been in the land south of the Navajos, he figured there were many horses there because the Navajos never seemed to have any trouble exchanging slaves for horses, even when the slave bands were large.

It would be exciting to explore a new land. It would

be exciting to execute a horse raid in a country where no one would be anticipating such a raid. Maybe he could get hundreds of animals, perhaps even thousands, like in the first California raid. Walkara announced he was riding to Old Mexico to steal horses.

To his surprise not very many men joined him. Memories of the Barstow ambush were still fresh. Still, he found fifteen young men who wanted to participate in the new adventure. The first thing he had them do was follow him into the west desert in search of Goshute women and children. With slaves to sell he hoped the Mexicans wouldn't wonder why he and his men were in their land visiting their ranches.

As the first winter snows swept over the mountains from the north, Walkara, his men, and a band of about 20 slaves headed south to the land of sunshine, where they hoped the unsuspecting Mexicans wouldn't be watching their horses too closely.

After crossing the Colorado River they spent several days with the Navajos, who were eager to trade Walkara out of his slaves. To keep peace and the door open for future trading, and so as not to draw any suspicions to him or his men, Walkara traded a few slaves with the Navajos, but held most for trading in the unexplored country to the south.

In efforts to soften his resolve against more trading, the Navajos sent young women to Walkara each night to share his bed. Though he gladly accepted the hospitality, he refused to engage in any more trading.

Old Mexico was different than California. Because the land was more barren, with less grass and less water, the distances between the ranches were much greater, and the herds of cattle and horses were more scattered. Walkara soon realized it would be very difficult to get a large herd of animals, but with only fifteen men to divide the spoils among he didn't need a huge herd to make the trip profitable.

Ten days later Walkara and his men were pushing nearly 400 horses north. A posse of angry Mexicans was less than a day's journey behind them and gaining. Walkara told his men that once they crossed the Colorado River the posse would give up the chase. He hoped he was right.

The formerly mild weather suddenly changed, a strong north wind blowing in cold air and a storm front from the north. With the wind in their faces the horses became more difficult to drive. The posse was getting closer and closer.

Snow was falling when Walkara's herd finally reached the Colorado River. The posse was about five miles back. There was plenty of time to cross the river and be out of sight up the north bank before the Mexicans saw them. With the snow falling, Walkara was more sure than ever the Mexicans would not follow. He guessed none of the men in the posse had ever crossed the Colorado River, even in summer. It appeared the Mexico horse raid had been a success.

Shouting their victory cries, Walkara and his men began pushing the horses towards the icy water. Hungry, tired and cold from the long journey into the north wind, the weary animals refused to enter the icy water. No amount of shouting, coaxing or whipping could change their minds. With the cold wind still blowing in their faces, the horses simply refused to plunge into the freezing waters.

Walkara was the first to look back over his shoulder. The posse couldn't be very far back. He pondered the alternatives as the men continued unsuccessfully to push the horses into the water. Knowing the posse outnumbered them two to one, Walkara didn't want to stand and fight. Neither did he want to abandon 400 fine horses he had worked so hard to obtain, now that they were so close to home territory. If the horses refused to cross the river there didn't seem to be any alternatives other than abandoning the animals or fighting the posse. The more the men continued to push the horses at the water, the more determined the animals seemed to be to avoid the river.

Suddenly Walkara had an idea. There wasn't much time. He shouted to the men to cut back about a hundred of the least desirable horses, the small and the old, and to do it quickly.

He shouted at them to hurry. The men had been with Walkara long enough to know better than to question his orders. They obeyed.

As soon as the new herd was separated from the main herd, Walkara selected five of his best men to help him push the new herd back the way they had come, towards the approaching posse. He ordered the remainder of the men to stay with the main herd, keeping the animals in the low country next to the river until he returned.

A minute later Walkara and his five companions were pushing the new herd back down the trail towards the approaching posse. With the wind at their tails, and believing they were going home, the formerly weary animals found new energy and raced forward at a full gallop, Walkara and his men galloping close behind.

They hadn't gone more than a few miles when they saw the bewildered posse ahead of them. It was larger than they had supposed, nearly fifty men. Nodding at his men to stay with him, Walkara pushed the galloping herd directly towards the posse which by now had stopped to try and figure out why the hundred horses were galloping towards them.

Walkara waved happily at the Mexicans as he and his men brought the galloping herd to a halt. As soon as the horses were stopped, Walkara, his rifle in his scabbard, rode up to the leader of the posse.

Walkara introduced himself as Pan-a-Karry

Quinker or Iron Twister, a Ute chief. He said he and his men had rebelled against the horse thief Walkara, and were attempting to return some of the stolen horses to their rightful owners. The Mexicans were listening. Walkara continued.

He said he had come to Mexico to trade slaves for horses, but Walkara had spoiled the trading expedition by stealing horses. He had rebelled against Walkara and in a fierce battle on the bank of the Rio Colorado was able to get back a hundred animals. Now he was returning the stolen horses because he didn't want the slave-trading business ruined. Where he lived there were many more slaves he hoped to bring to Mexico.

The Mexicans looked weary and cold. They were not accustomed to the rigors of the trail as Walkara and his men were. The hard pushing into the north wind had taken its toll on them too. They seemed eager to believe that the chase was over. This Iron Twister told them they would freeze to death if they tried to follow Walkara, who had already crossed the icy Rio Colorado.

Believing Walkara's story, the Mexicans seemed pleased that they could now turn around and head for home. They thanked him for bringing at least part of the herd back. They gave him and his men some dried beef. The Mexicans seemed even more pleased when Iron Twister told them he and his men were determined to hunt down and kill Walkara so he would not be able to ruin their slave-trading business in the future.

The Mexicans were ready to take their hundred horses and head for home, but Walkara was not through. It had been too easy. They had been too quick to believe his story. He had given them too many horses. Twenty would have been enough to satisfy this bunch of weary travelers.

Iron Twister said two of his men had been killed in the rebellion against Walkara. More would probably be killed as they continued to pursue Walkara. Didn't the Mexicans agree that he and his men deserved some kind of reward for their efforts to help the Mexicans?

The leader of the posse discussed Walkara's proposal with his men, after which he invited Walkara to cut back half the horses as a reward for what he had done.

The Indians and Mexicans cut the herd in two, the Mexicans driving their herd south while the Indians pushed their herd north. Walkara didn't look back.

The next day, with the north wind gone and the sun shining brightly in a blue desert sky, Walkara and his men pushed 350 Mexican horses across the Colorado River. If any of the men had doubted it earlier, they all agreed now that Walkara was the greatest horse thief anyone had ever heard about.

Chapter 24

News of Walkara's success and cunning in old Mexico spread among the Indian tribes of the Rocky Mountains. Many of the men who had ridden with him on the California raids returned to ride with him again. They brought friends with them. They believed that if they followed Walkara they would become rich in horses. And the Ute chief didn't disappoint them.

He resumed the raids to California, but the days when thousands of animals could be taken in a single night were gone. He found more frequent raids in which hundreds of horses were taken seemed to work best. In these new raids he was more brutal and aggressive, taking both scalps and slaves when the opportunity presented itself. His men had the fastest horses, the finest Spanish saddles, and the newest American rifles.

When they weren't off to California or Mexico, Walkara's men wandered the deserts of the Great Basin region, gathering slave children and women to trade to the Navajos and Mexicans for more horses. Walkara and his men supplied a steady stream of slaves to the Mexicans, and horses to Jim Bridger and Peg Leg Smith on the Bear River.

Every summer thousands of white men appeared miraculously out of the east, riding or walking beside huge land canoes behind weary teams of oxen and horses. The toil-hardened men drove their teams mercilessly as their women in peculiar bonnets and barefooted children trod the dust beside them. Their hunger for fresh horses at Fort Bridger and Bear River seemed endless.

Then, as suddenly as the new breed of white men had appeared from the land of the rising sun, they disappeared into the setting sun. The land of Oregon swallowed them up by the thousands. By fall each year all that was left were the tracks of the land canoes. The land was quiet and peaceful again, but everyone knew that when summer arrived a new crop of horse-hungry white men would come out of the east to make Bridger, Smith and Walkara even richer.

Then one summer a new breed of white men appeared. They called themselves Mormons. Walkara and his people called them Mormonees. Unlike other white men the Mormons did not disappear into the setting sun. Instead of turning north at Fort Bridger, the Mormons turned south, down Echo Canyon, eventually unhitching their wagons in ancient Ute tribal lands bordering the great salt lake. Immediately they began turning over the sacred earth with huge steel points pulled by horses and oxen. They planted seeds and diverted water from the streams to water the seeds. They began dragging trees out of mountains to build log tepees. It appeared the Mormons had come to stay.

Walkara had heard of the Mormons before. News of them and their battles with other white men had been carried along the Oregon Trail every summer and shared with the white men at Fort Bridger and on the Bear River. The Mormons had built a large and beautiful city beside the greatest of all rivers, and were constantly fighting with other white men because of their strange religious beliefs. They had a peculiar book that told the history of the many Indian tribes.

The Mormons were different from other white men who had come to the land of the Utes. Whereas the white trappers had talked about furs and wanted whiskey and women, the Mormons talked about God and wanted land.

Walkara knew too that an army of Mormons had marched west in the fight between the Mericats and the Mexicans, and that some of these Mormons had ended up guarding Cajon Pass to help stop Indian horse raids in California. For this alone, Mormons deserved to die.

Walkara stayed away from the Mormons, at least the first summer after their arrival. He didn't know what to do about them, so he avoided them, though he sent other Indians from time to time to trade a horse or a fur while finding out what the Mormons were up to.

On the one hand, for helping slow down the California horse business and for settling in Ute tribal lands without permission, the Mormons deserved to die. Walkara was furious that Chief Brigham of the Mormons had not come to Walkara or Sowiette to smoke the peace pipe and request permission to settle in Ute lands.

On the other hand, the land surrounding the great salt lake was a neutral place where people of all tribes could come to trade without fear of attack. No tribe lived there on a regular basis. This was the only place in the entire Rocky Mountain region where Indians felt safe from their enemies. Walkara was reluctant to turn this traditional peaceful valley into a war zone.

Walkara also remembered his medicine dream where he had gone to the world of spirits and been told by the Indian god Towats not to make war with the tribe of white men that would someday settle in his lands. He had always thought Towats was referring to the big hats or Spanish priests. Now he wasn't sure. The priests had not come, but the Mormons had. Did Towats want him to leave these people alone too?

From a business standpoint, Walkara could see the Mormons would want to buy horses from him, and once their farms were established they would be future sources from which he and his men could steal horses.

So Walkara waited, one day wanting to kill the Mormons, the next wanting to trade with them. He was moody as he waited, and he didn't know why.

Finally, the following March, in the year the white men called 1848, Sowiette convinced Walkara to join him in a visit to the place the Mormons called Great Salt Lake City and call on Chief Brigham. Walkara brought his men with him, mounted on their finest horses and armed with their newest American rifles. Hundreds of women and children followed the diplomatic party.

Upon arrival in Great Salt Lake City they learned Chief Brigham had not spent the winter in the valley, but had gone east in the fall to gather more of his people and guide them to this new home between the Utes and Shoshones.

Walkara was ready to turn around and return home, but not Sowiette, who wanted to negotiate peace with Chief Brigham's sub-chiefs. Walkara agreed to stay, and was soon disgusted with Sowiette, whom he concluded was soft like a woman.

Without waiting to stand toe to toe with their head chief Brigham, Sowiette was offering unconditional friendship and peace to the Mormons who swarmed like crickets from the east. To Sowiette it seemed unimportant that the Mormons had not first begged for permission to tear up Ute soil and build log tepees. When questioned by the friendly Mormons, the brooding Walkara ignored them, pretending he did not understand or speak English.

By the time Walkara and Sowiette headed south out of the new city, Walkara had pushed the memory of his medicine dream to the back of his mind and was making mental preparations for war against the Mormons. When Chief Brigham returned he would find only ashes and bones. The heat of anger dried up the words between Walkara and Sowiette on the homeward journey.

But Walkara was the only Ute filled with anger that day. Mormon food filled the bellies of everyone else. While the trading had not been good, the Mormons having little excess goods for trading, there had still been plenty to eat for all the visiting Utes. It wasn't that the Mormons had food to spare. The truth is they didn't. But from the first day in the valley it was Young's firm and unwavering policy that it was better to feed Indians than to fight them. He was determined, even in his absence, that no Indian left Great Salt Lake City hungry.

The band of Utes headed south past the great mountain Timpanogos, across the lush grasslands at its base, crossing the fish-filled streams. This was the land of Walkara's birth, a generous, beautiful land where countless generations of Utes had found shelter and food. It was only a matter of time until the Mormons would spread south and begin ripping up the face of this land too—unless someone stopped them.

Walkara was ready for war. All that remained was to convince Sowiette. While Walkara was off in California and Mexico stealing horses and trading slaves, it was Sowiette who stayed home and administered to the needs of the people. While Walkara, with his 200 followers, was undoubtedly the most powerful war chief the people had ever known, his older brother Sowiette was the administrative chief, and his go-ahead was necessary if the entire tribe was to make war on the Mormons.

Upon reaching the southern end of Utah Lake, the weary travelers began working their way up Spanish Fork Creek into the canyon of Walkara's birth, where they planned to spend the second night of their return journey. It was dark by the time the squaws had the tepees up and began cooking a feast of Mormon beef.

A cold March wind pushing relentlessly down the canyon soon drove all the Indians inside the tepees. Walkara felt the time was finally right to present his arguments for war to Sowiette. He asked Arrapeen, Grosspeen and another half brother Tobiah, to leave him alone with Sowiette.

For an hour the two Ute chiefs smoked silently, the younger and the older, heads bowed almost reverently towards the dying coals of the tepee cook fire. Outside, the wind continued to blow.

"There was a time when there were no white men," Walkara said, finally breaking the silence.

"It was not for us to know that day," Sowiette answered, quietly.

"Many Indians have been robbed of their lands by white men," Walkara said.

"It is true."

"Mormonees have come to take our lands."

"Mormonees have taken the not-wanted lands between what we call ours, and the lands of our enemies the Shoshones."

"Chief Brigham will bring armies of people to our lands until they are thick like grasshoppers. Those already here are just the beginning. Other Mormonees will come from California. You seem happy that this is so."

"I am not happy," Sowiette corrected.

"Are not white men your friends? Did you not offer them your hand in friendship when we were in their city?"

"Are not white men your friends too?" Sowiette asked. "You have ridden, eaten and slept with white men. Were they not your friends?"

"My white men friends wanted beaver and horses," Walkara said. "Your white men seek the very ground on which we squat. When your children are hungry, after the Mormonees have killed all the deer and elk, will the white men still be your friends?''

"I did not ask the Mormonees to come here," Sowiette replied. "But they are here. I did not ask Mormonees to be friends. They ask to be friends. They ask to live beside us in peace. It is best we live with them in peace."

"It is best that we take war to them," Walkara growled. "I see Mormonee scalps hanging from the belts of our warriors. Dead men cannot take our lands and starve our children. There are not too many Mormonees to kill. Later there will be. I count them as already dead."

"For every Mormonee we kill, ten more will come with guns to seek revenge," Sowiette responded deliberately. "Mormonees are countless, like locusts. To fight them is like trying to hold back the river with one's hands. It is better to fashion a canoe and ride with it."

"We must make war on the Mormonees," Walkara said with conviction, rising to his feet. "We must take their scalps and feed their flesh to the hawks of the mountains. We must steal their horses and slaughter their cattle. We must burn their wagons and log tepees to the ground. And when their Chief Brigham returns from the east Walkara will rip off his scalp, gouge out his eyes and eat his testicles."

"There will be no killing," Sowiette said just as deliberately, rising to his feet to face his younger brother. "We take no Mormonee scalps. Our people will live with them in peace and learn their ways."

"Sowiette talks soft, like a woman I once had," Walkara challenged. "War is for men, not women."

"My little brother has said enough," Sowiette growled.

"Perhaps my big brother is afraid of Mormonees," Walkara sneered, too angry to stop for any reason. "In his old age my brother has become a coward."

Without speaking, Sowiette bent over and picked up a rawhide whip lying across the back of his saddle. "How dare a dog call a man a coward," he howled, bringing the whip with all his might across Walkara's shoulders.

The adrenaline surging through his veins, Walkara was ready to kill his brother. His hand reached for the long knife in his belt. He stepped towards the angry Sowiette, then stopped.

He could see ahead, even with hot blood boiling in his veins. If he killed Sowiette, the brothers, including Arrapeen and San Pitch, would be obligated to avenge the death of a brother and respected chief. Walkara would be hunted by his own brothers. The Utes would be divided, fighting each other instead of the Mormons. Chiefs did not kill each other in private fights.

The gray-haired Sowiette was respected and loved. In killing him, Walkara would be the loser. He returned the knife to his belt as Sowiette raised the whip for a second blow. Walkara dropped his arms to his sides, offering no defense. Sowiette started to bring the whip forward, then stopped. Finally, he let it fall to the ground.

"Our people will not make war on the Mormonees," Sowiette said one last time as the defeated Walkara slowly turned and ducked out of the tepee.

Chapter 25

Humiliated, frustrated and angry, Walkara continued to brood. He loved his way of life—chasing buffalo, hunting deer and elk, and stealing horses. Especially stealing horses. The long trips to Mexico and California were full of adventure and profit. The hardships of the trail didn't matter. He loved trading, gambling, drinking white man's firewater, and the homecomings with his young and eager squaws. Though he wouldn't admit it to Susquenah, he even enjoyed catching and selling slaves. He liked the way he lived, and he sensed that thousands of Mormons moving into his valleys would somehow change the way he lived. Exactly how, he did not know. It was too hard to see the future.

In his frustration he called his men together and announced they were leaving on a major horse raid to Mexico. In the excitement of stealing Mexican horses and fleeing angry posses he would forget the Mormons, at least for a while. When he returned he could resume his worrying. Perhaps by then Sowiette would have a change of heart and ride with him against the Mormons. In a cloud of dust Walkara and his men headed for Mexico.

He led his men further east and south this time, in the area of a village named Chihuahua. He employed the time-proven technique of first scouting the country, then dividing his men into groups, then striking simultaneously the same night. Though the results couldn't be compared with the first California raid, he did end up with around 200 fine Spanish horses that he brought home to the Sanpete Valley. With 200 new horses to make him feel rich and successful, the Mormon problem didn't seem so serious. Owning a large number of new horses seemed to improve his feelings towards white men—the future buyers of his horses.

Not long after his arrival home, Walkara proposed to Sowiette that the two chiefs make another trip to Great Salk Lake City for a peace smoke with Chief Brigham and his captains. Pleased at his brother's change of heart, Sowiette readily agreed to go.

Several days later, with Walkara and his men driving the herd of new Spanish horses ahead of them, they left for Great Salt Lake City. Trailing were several hundred Indians, including warriors, women, children, and half a dozen dogs. Fifteen or sixteen buffalo hide tepees were brought along on horse-drawn travois. Going to the new Mormon city was an event none wanted to miss, especially this time. Walkara was finally going to meet Chief Brigham.

Five days later Sowiette and Walkara were invited into what the Mormons called the bowery, an outdoor meeting place where a brush-covered overhead pole structure protected those gathered from sun and rain. One of Chief Brigham's trusted captains, John Taylor, ushered the Indians in. A young man by the name of George Bean acted as interpreter.

This was the Mormons' first official meeting with Walkara. They didn't know he spoke fluent English, and Walkara wasn't about to let them find out, at least not on his first trip to Great Salt Lake City. He spoke only Ute while carefully listening to everything the Mormons said in English. He noticed that young Bean made quite a few translation errors, but Walkara didn't bother to correct the young man.

With Bean translating, Taylor invited Walkara and Sowiette to make themselves comfortable. He said Chief Brigham would be along any minute. Walkara guessed Brigham's tardiness was a subtle move on the part of the Mormon to establish some sort of superiority.

Walkara and Sowiette seated themselves on the ground in the designated area for the meeting and waited. Chief Brigham's captains tried to start a conversation with the two chiefs. While Sowiette seemed willing to converse, Walkara did not. He was a big chief, and would talk only with the Mormon big chief.

To Walkara's disgust, Sowiette didn't seem concerned with such formalities. It saddened Walkara to think his older brother was already well on his way to becoming a fort Indian, like those in the east who lived next to the American army forts, waiting for handouts.

Finally Chief Brigham arrived. While on the outside Walkara appeared indifferent to the arrival of the Mormon chief, inside he was eager to notice every detail, physical characteristics as well as the more subtle personality traits.

Chief Brigham was a stout bear of a man. He looked like he might be a powerful wrestler. In later years the head Mormon would become fat and walk with a cane, but now he was in his prime—healthy, strong, and confident almost to the point of arrogance. He was clean-shaven, and the hair on his head was combed back to expose a broad, high forehead. Though he was not quick to smile, his piercing blue eyes glowed with interest and warmth. Walkara couldn't help but like the man though no words had yet been exchanged.

Walkara was pleased that the Mormon chief knew enough of Indian protocol not to begin talking immediately, as most white men did when meeting with

Indian chiefs for peace smokes.

When Chief Brigham seated himself on the ground opposite Walkara, he did not speak. Taking this cue, his white captains ceased their chatter too.

Knowing that silence was not the way of white men, Walkara wondered how long the Mormon chief could remain silent. Many minutes passed. The Mormon chief seemed content to wait as long as Walkara wished before the talks began. Walkara was pleased, beginning to believe that this Brigham might indeed be a great man, and a worthy peer.

Walkara was the first to do something. He removed his stone smoking pipe from the buckskin pouch on his belt and began stuffing it full of tobacco, not with the sweet white man's tobacco, but with the stronger Indian tobacco. When he finished, one of his men seated behind him handed him a bundle of cedar bark containing embers from the morning cook fire. Carefully, using only his finger, Walkara nudged one of the embers into the bed he had formed for it in the bowl of the pipe. Gently, he sucked air through the pipe until the tobacco began to glow brightly.

After filling his lungs with the bitter smoke, Walkara passed the pipe to the white man on his right. Slowly, the pipe went around the circle. Upon inhaling the smoke, some of the white men coughed, much to Walkara's disgust, but not Chief Brigham.

Brigham was the first to speak after the pipe had gone around the circle twice. "We are pleased the two great Yutah chiefs have come to our city," he said. "After we talk we have much good food for our Yutah friends, and hope we can buy some of your fine horses."

Walkara was pleased with the words of Chief Brigham, but waited for Bean to voice the translation before answering.

"We wish to live with your people in peace,"

Sowiette began in Ute, allowing Bean to translate into English. "We want our children to grow up with yours as brothers." Brigham seemed pleased with Sowiette's words.

"If our people steal from your people," Walkara added, "tell me and I will stop them. We want peace." Sowiette looked over at Walkara, obviously pleased that his younger brother was finally accepting the Mormons.

The talks were proceeding favorably. Brigham decided to ask for an important concession.

"We ask our friends the Yutahs to stop stealing horses from the Spanish peoples to the south, and from the Shoshones," Brigham asked boldly, surprising both Walkara and Sowiette. The Mormon leader also asked that the Utes cease their slave trading. The two chiefs knew they could not agree to such requests. Their prosperity depended on a steady flow of slaves and stolen horses.

"Our people may love the Mormonees, but they hate the Spanish," Walkara said in an effort to buy time to think. He didn't want to just say no, which would put him and Sowiette on the defensive, forcing them to make excuses for their Spanish horse stealing. It would be better to make an equally impossible request of Chief Brigham, forcing him to say no too, thereby keeping the relationship balanced.

But what could he ask Chief Brigham? He couldn't ask the Mormons to pull out and move back to the land of the big river. That was a much bigger request than the one Brigham had made. He must request something less important.

"We will give the Mormonee chief our answer tomorrow," Walkara said, drawing a glance of surprise from Sowiette, who knew there was no way Walkara would ever consider giving up stealing horses from the Spanish or trading slaves.

"We will be staying in your city tonight," Walkara

said, beginning to lay the groundwork for his request. "When we visit our friends the Navajos or Blackfeet they show their friendship by sending us squaws to share our buffalo robes. I trust our friends the Mormonees will confirm their friendship by sending white squaws to warm our beds tonight."

Though there was no expression on Walkara's face, inside he was grinning. He already knew how protective white men were of their women, how some white men would rather die than see their women with red men. Walkara guessed Chief Brigham was this way too, and would have to refuse Walkara's request for a white woman. When Chief Brigham said no to loaning sleeping companions to Walkara and Sowiette, it would then be easy to say no to Brigham's request to stop stealing horses from the Spanish. On the other hand, if Chief Brigham surprised Walkara by sending a white squaw to his lodge, then it would be much more difficult for Walkara to say no to Brigham's request. But Walkara was counting on Brigham's refusal.

Chief Brigham stared at Walkara while the request was being translated. His face was expressionless, though underneath Walkara thought he could detect a slight grin or an urge to laugh. Brigham continued to stare at Walkara, looking neither to the right or left to discuss the matter with his captains.

Without asking, Brigham knew what he had to say. He also knew that Walkara was playing the negotiations game well, that in Walkara he had a worthy opponent.

"No, we cannot send our women to you. That is not our way," he said without looking away.

"And we cannot stop taking horses from the Spanish," Walkara said. "That is not our way." After Bean translated this last comment, there was silence for a brief minute.

"Then we might as well eat and trade," roared Brigham in a friendly voice, getting to his feet, nodding for Walkara to join him. The two men shook hands. Brigham liked Walkara. Walkara liked Brigham. Sowiette was already headed for the food table.

Walkara liked the Mormon food too, especially the bread, which was light and moist and covered with a yellow grease made from cows' milk and a sticky red honey filled with strawberries bigger than any wild ones he had ever seen. There were green onions, sweeter and larger than wild ones. The boiled beef was tasty like buffalo, but more mild and sprinkled with a black dirt the Mormons called pepper. But best of all was the sweet-tart, soft-crunchy dessert the Mormons called apple pie. Walkara thought he had never tasted anything as good in his entire life. No wonder so many Mormons were fat like horses left to themselves in tall grass. No wonder Indians lined up at the forts for free food.

He had heard Chief Brigham's policy was to feed rather than fight the Indians. Now he knew why. In Mormon food Brigham had a powerful weapon.

While Walkara couldn't have been more pleased with the food, he was very disappointed with the trading. The Mormons were stingy, shrewd traders. They appologized for being poor, but claimed they would someday be rich and more generous in their trading. Walkara didn't know whether to believe them or not.

Not only were the Mormons stingy with their trade items, but they refused to let Walkara and his men trade for whiskey and rifles. Walkra realized that Brigham was different than other white men who used whiskey to help make better bargains with Indians. Walkara traded only a portion of his horses to the Mormons, saving the remainder to drive north. Peg Leg was in Calirornia for the season, so he intended to go to Fort Bridger. His old friend Jim Bridger would give him all the rifles and whiskey he wanted.

As he left Great Salt Lake City, his belly full of

Mormon food, Walkara had an uneasy feeling. He wished Chief Brigham was not so clever. He wished the Mormon chief had chosen to fight the Utes with bullets instead of biscuits. Against force, Walkara's people would unite and drive out the Mormons. With Mormon food in their bellies his people would never unite against the Mormons.

Walkara would have liked to discuss the whole matter with Peg Leg, but with the trader off tasting the comforts of civilization, he would have to settle for a little advice from Bridger. The old trapper would probably have some ideas of his own on how to deal with the Mormons. The more Walkara thought about it, the more eager he became to hear what Jim Bridger had to say.

Chapter 26

The reception Walkara received at Fort Bridger was altogether different from the one he had received in Great Salt Lake City. With Jim Bridger, an old friend, none of the usual formalities were necessary, and whereas the Mormons had filled Indian bellies with good food, Bridger filled them with whiskey.

Even before Walkara and his men were dismounted Bridger's assistants were passing out bottles of a watered down version of Taos white lightning, flavored with brown sugar and chili powder, just the way the Indians liked it.

Walkara and his men gambled, wrestled, and raced horses with reckless abandon. And when Walkara finally collapsed into his buffalo robe to sleep, Bridger had arranged for a young Shoshone squaw to keep him warm.

The next morning the trading began in earnest. Earlier Walkara had supposed that with Peg Leg gone to California for the season, and therefore not offering trade competition for Bridger, Old Gabe's prices would be higher. But he was wrong. Bridger was more generous with his powder, lead, knives, rifles and whiskey than he had ever been before. Especially the whiskey. In addition to the old trapper's generosity, Walkara had never seen Jim Bridger so friendly and easy to trade with. Walkara wondered if perhaps the old trapper was concerned about the Mormons taking away his trade. But there was no danger of that as long as the Mormons refused to trade whiskey and rifles to the red men.

Whenever Walkara was sober enough to talk, either Ute or English, Bridger seemed to be around, encouraging Walkara in the future to bring all his horses to Fort Bridger, where he would get the best prices. Walkara promised he would, but that was not enough for Bridger.

"The Mormons are your enemies," Bridger would drawl in his easygoing way. "Jim Bridger is your friend."

"The Mormonees say they are friends too," Walkara responded.

"Friends, hell!" Bridger insisted. "Friends don't move in and take your land without asking. When all the Mormons get here you won't have a spot left to lift your loincloth and take a leak. You won't have a fish or beaver left in the streams, and who do you think will kill and eat all the deer and elk?"

"Mormonees," Walkara responded.

"Damn right, and they will tell you to stop taking horses from the Spanish."

"They already have."

"What do you do to people you catch stealing your horses?" Bridger asked.

"Kill them."

"What do you do to people who steal your land?"

Walkara hesitated. He knew what Bridger wanted him to say. But he felt foolish about how friendly he had been to the Mormons, who had taken his land without asking.

"Kill them too," he finally said.

"Good," Bridger responded triumphantly, reassuring Walkara that there would always be plenty of powder, lead and rifles at Fort Bridger. He said

Mormons were killing Indians.

Eventually Walkara ran out of horses to trade and Bridger's seemingly bottomless well of firewater finally dried up. Instead of going home, Walkara headed south, looking for his old friend Big Elk, chief of the Nampa Utes. In Big Elk Walkara found a sympathetic ear. The previous winter the Nampa Utes had fought with the Mericats near Taos, with the white men winning. While licking his wounds, Big Elk became more convinced than ever that all white men were his enemies, even the Mormons. Yes, he and his people would join Walkara in war against the Mormons.

Walkara was more sober than usual as he headed for home. Finally he had an ally against the Mormons. He also had a source of supplies, including guns and ammunition once the war began. Though he liked Chief Brigham, the simple truth was the Mormons would fill Ute lands if someone didn't stop them. Since Sowiette and Kanosh were already in the front of the line begging for handouts at the Mormon settlements, Walkara was the only leader strong enough to lead a serious attack on the Mormons.

Walkara remembered his medicine dream in which Towats had told him not to make war on the tribe of white men that would settle in his lands. He found himself wondering if the medicine dream had been real, or just a dream. Sending his men ahead on the homeward journey, Walkara turned towards the mountain where years earlier he had his visit with Towats. Perhaps he could talk to the Great Spirit a second time. Perhaps the Mormons were not the white people Walkara had been told to leave alone.

It being late winter the snow had not yet melted in the high mountains, so Walkara was not able to ride very far before the snow became too deep for horse travel.

After staking out his horse on a windswept, south-facing slope, Walkara continued on foot, occasionally able to walk on top of the crusty snow. The going was slow, preventing him from getting as high as he had been when he had his first medicine dream.

Finding a comfortable place under some leaning rocks where he would be out of the wind, Walkara built a small fire, then waited. Sometimes he called out to Towats, asking the Great Spirit to come to him, to tell him how to fight the Mormons, or that he should not fight the Mormons. Most of the time Walkara just waited, quietly listening for some kind of answer or sign from Towats. He neither ate nor drank. And he tried not to sleep, though occasionally he did—always a restless, troubled slumber. Mostly he just sat quietly, listening and waiting.

Walkara waited through the night, the next day, and a second night, all the time keeping his little fire going. Nothing happened. This time there was no medicine dream, only the cold silence of the mountains. Finally, late in the second day, he abandoned his lonely vigil and returned to his horse.

Rather than head straight for home, he rode to the little valley where he and Susquenah had spent the winter together. This year there was no snow, but the ground was frozen from the cold nights. The brush wickiup was still there. After covering over some of the holes created by time and weather, he crawled inside, built a fire, and rolled out his blanket on the exact spot where he and Susquenah had spent so many happy nights together.

During the night Walkara's thoughts were divided between memories of wonderful times with Susquenah and his failure to communicate with Towats. Could the Great Spirit be unhappy with him? Since Towats had not instructed him to the contrary, maybe it was all right to take war to the Mormons. By morning Walkara had concluded that if Towats wasn't going to stop him he would go ahead and drive out the Mormons.

When it was light he wandered over to the stream where he had found the gold nuggets. The gold could be used to buy guns and ammunition in time of war.

After building a fire near the edge of the stream, Walkara waded into the icy water to look for nuggets. He found three or four by the time his hands and feet became numb with the cold. Crawling out of the water, he crouched in front of the fire to warm his hands and feet. As soon as the feeling returned he hurried back into the stream to find more gold, having already decided he would plan his next gold-finding trip during the warmer summer months.

After crawling out of the water the second time, with two more nuggets, Walkara had the distinct feeling he was not alone.

He didn't look up right away, but remained motionless, his hands and feet stretched out towards the warm flames. His horse was munching on dry winter grass about 20 feet away. His loaded rifle was in a scabbard under the right stirrup. His hunting knife was in his belt.

Walkara hadn't seen anything out of the ordinary, and he couldn't remember hearing anything either. All he knew was that he had an uneasy feeling he was being watched from the steep, rocky hillside behind him. He didn't know if it was a man or a wild animal, only that someone or something was watching him. If it was an Indian, since he was in Shoshone country, it was probably an enemy.

He looked carefully at his horse to see if it had noticed anything on the hill. It continued to graze, seemingly without a care. Walkara's instincts had led him right often enough. He knew better than to ignore them.

Without looking back towards the hill, Walkara lunged forward towards his horse, half expecting to hear the crack of a rifle or the twang of a bow string. He was relieved to hear neither. Upon reaching the startled horse, he slipped his rifle from the scabbard and slipped around to the far side of the animal, positioning it between him and the rocky hillside. Extending the rifle over the seat of the saddle towards the hill, he began looking for whatever it was that had made him feel uneasy.

He saw a few pine trees, some bushes, and lots of big rocks, but nothing that could have made him feel like he was being watched. He studied the rocky hillside for a long time, but could see nothing out of the ordinary.

Finally, with rifle in hand, he decided to take a closer look. He moved cautiously along the stream towards the hillside. He slunk along like a cat, ready to dive for cover at the slightest sign of danger.

Approaching the hill, Walkara began to feel a little foolish, like his caution had been unwarranted. There was no sign of anything living on the hillside, nor in any other direction. He straightened up, relaxed, but continued walking towards the hill.

Moving along the base of the hill he came upon what appeared to be a well-traveled game trail working its way from the stream up into the rocks. The hunter in him told him to follow the trail, that it might lead him to game, or at least to a well-used feeding area. Since he had not yet seen anything to justify his uneasiness, he decided to follow the game trail.

He hadn't gone far when he realized something was wrong with the trail. Where it wound steeply upward between rocks, instead of the frozen soil being dug up by sharp hooves, as always happens on deer and elk trails, this one was packed smooth by a padded foot, like that of a bear, except there were no claw marks.

Walkara began to slink again, holding his rifle higher, more ready. The trail had been stamped smooth by human feet. People had been frequent users of the trail, apparently dropping down the hill to get water from the stream. He looked ahead and above, still seeing no sign of anyone. Cautiously he moved forward.

Eventually the trail led him to a steep rocky area near the top of the hill, just under a sheer granite cliff. As he looked ahead, it appeared the trail ended in a clump of thick bushes near the middle of the cliff base. It didn't appear the trail could go beyond the bushes, which were about 50 feet in front of Walkara. His rifle ready, he crept forward.

Upon reaching the bushes, the trail did not end, but continued through the thickest part towards what appeared to be a big crack in the cliff. Walkara stopped, realizing he was approaching some kind of cave or hiding place. It was possible someone or something had been up here watching him search for gold in the stream, but was now inside the cave. He looked down at his fire and grazing horse, cocked back the hammer on his rifle, then began moving cautiously forward towards the crack in the cliff.

As he walked closer, he could see the dark opening of a cave. It was barely large enough for one man to get through it on his knees. Walkara stopped beside the opening, wondering what to do now. He would be an easy target for any kind of weapon if he just dropped to his knees and crawled inside. Still, he couldn't be sure someone was in the cave. He had not seen or heard anything. He had only the feeling of being watched. Perhaps he had sensed the presence of a wild animal that had already gone over the top of the mountain. Perhaps he had not sensed anything real.

Walkara pondered several options. He could call into the cave, inviting anyone who might be there to step outside. A friend would come out. An enemy or a wild animal would remain silent.

Walkara began to feel a little foolish over his

extreme caution. He reminded himself again that he had not seen or heard anything. His feelings could be wrong. Anyway, if an enemy had been watching him and wanted to kill him, he would have been an easy target, warming his hands and feet at the fire. There would have been no need to lure him to the cave.

Tired of his indecision, Walkara dropped to his knees and crawled inside. The quick transition from the bright daylight to the darkness of the cave left him momentarily blind. Rolling back to a kneeling position, he waited for his eyes to adjust. To hurry the process, he closed his eyes for a moment. His right hand clung tightly to his rifle.

When he opened his eyes Walkara was so startled that he lurched backwards, nearly losing his balance and falling over backwards. Not five feet in front of him knelt a red man in buckskins, his arms folded peacefully across his chest.

After getting over the initial scare, Walkara realized that if the Indian had wanted to kill him he would already be dead. Settling to a kneeling position once again, Walkara let go of his rifle. Following the stranger's example, he folded his own arms across his chest.

For a minute or two no words were spoken as the two strangers looked into each other's faces. Walkara knew he was facing a strong man, a warrior. The man wore plain buckskins, without any ornamentation. His hair was cut shorter than was normal for a Ute or Shoshone. Perhaps he was Navajo or Apache.

Walkara remained silent, pondering an uneasy feeling in his chest and throat. He was not afraid, nor did he sense any danger. It was as though he was kneeling on sacred ground, facing some sort of holy man, though the man in front of him looked very ordinary.

The stranger was the first to speak, in a language Walkara did not understand but had a familiar sound.

Perhaps Apache.

"You speak Navajo?" Walkara asked in Navajo.

"Yes," the man said. "Pan-a-Karry Quinker, I speak Navajo."

Walkara was stunned. The man knew his secret name, the one Towats had given him in his medicine dream many years earlier.

"How did you know my name?" Walkara asked.

"The three ancient ones said you would come, if I waited long enough."

"Who are the three ancient ones?"

"The wise ones who do not die, the same men who told us how to find this sacred cave, and the other six too."

"This cave is sacred?"

"Yes. Our ancestors took much of the yellow metal from it. Some of the great ones hid here during the big war."

Walkara didn't know what the Indian was talking about. He had heard of seven hidden cities of gold where ancient ones used to live, but he had never heard of seven sacred caves containing the yellow metal white men called gold.

"I was getting the yellow metal from the stream," Walkara volunteered.

"There is much more here," the Indian replied, nodding towards the back of the cave. It was too dark for Walkara to see beyond the stranger.

"What is your name?" Walkara asked.

"I am Victorio. I am Apache."

"Why are you here?"

"The three ancient ones sent me. They said Pan-a-Karry Quinker would come."

"I have come," Walkara said reverently. "What do you want of me?"

"This cave is sacred," Victorio replied. "The yellow metal cannot be used to make war, or to trade

219

for weapons of war.''

Walkara was stunned. Not only did this stranger know his name, but also his purpose for coming to get gold.

"Did the ancient ones tell you I would come to get gold to fight Chief Brigham?''

"I do not know this Chief Brigham," Victorio replied. "I know only that you must not use this gold to make war. It can only be used for sacred purposes."

Walkara didn't ask what those sacred purposes were.

"I have given you the message. Now I go," Victorio said, beginning to crawl from the cave.

"Where will you go?" Walkara asked.

"Back to my people, my wives and little ones."

"Do you have food?"

"No."

"Come to my horse. I will give you some."

The two men crawled out of the cave and worked their way down the hill, neither speaking.

"Pan-a-Karry Quinker is a strange name for a Yutah," Victorio said as they reached the horse.

"That is only the name from a medicine dream," Walkara responded. "The people call me Walkara."

"The one who steals horses from the Spanish?" Victorio asked, sudden enthusiasm in his voice.

"Yes, I have taken horses from the Spanish, my enemies."

"Many thousands. Many say you are the greatest horse thief of them all. The Spanish would be very happy if I killed you and stole your horse."

"I hope you won't kill me, and there is no need to steal my horse because I give him to you."

"I cannot accept the horse of Walkara."

"You must. Your journey is much greater than mine."

Victorio leaped upon the horse's back as Walkara

untied the tether rope. The Apache gave only a brief nod of thanks before galloping across the meadow and disappearing into the woods.

Walkara returned to the cave, wondering about Victorio's strange message. Had Towats responded to his quest for a second medicine dream by sending Victorio? He remembered his first medicine dream and the caution against making war with white people in his lands. Now a strange Apache messenger told him the gold he had come to get was somehow sacred and he should not use it to make war. He wondered what the consequences would be if he went against the caution. Victorio hadn't said anything about what might happen to Walkara if he ignored the Apache's caution.

After crawling into the cave Walkara fashioned a torch from cedar bark and dried grass he found near one wall, apparently Victorio's former bed. After building a small fire of twigs, he ignited the torch and ventured further into the cave.

The first thing he noticed were strange writings on the wall, not pictures of things a man could understand, like etchings of people and animals, but strange meaningless marks, similar, he supposed, to those Peg Leg said white men used in their books.

Next he noticed a dusty pile of small rocks near the left side of the passageway. As he reached into the pile, his hand rubbing off the dust, he realized he was reaching into a pile of golden pebbles, similar in shape and smoothness to the smaller ones he had found in the stream.

His first thought was how excited Peg Leg and Bridger would be to see so much of the yellow metal in one place. The pile of nuggets contained more gold than one horse could carry. After scooping up a handful he retreated to the mouth of the cave, hurrying to get there before his torch burned out.

Upon reaching the cave opening Walkara dropped

to his haunches to examine the gold, but more to wonder what he would do with it if he couldn't use it to make war on the Mormons. Maybe Sowiette was right in his determination to have peace with Chief Brigham. Walkara still wanted to drive the Mormons from his lands, but how could he do it now that the gods themselves were insisting on peace. In some ways he felt relief as he headed down the trail towards the stream. Walkara would not be fighting the white men and Chief Brigham, at least not in the near future, he thought.

Chapter 27

Walkara was only a day into his homeward journey when he came upon a band of Shoshones camped in a cottonwood grove near a small stream. It was unusual to see Shoshones so far south in winter, but with an abundance of deer and elk wintering in the area, Walkara could understand why the Indians would want to camp here.

Though the camp was small, only four lodges, there was a good herd of 50 or 60 horses grazing in the nearby meadows. With no snow on the ground the horses were wintering well. Some even looked fat. Nearly all the mares were heavy with spring foals in their bellies.

Walkara was pleased with his good luck. After giving his horse to Victorio he had anticipated a long walk home. It would be easy to steal one of these horses, perhaps three or four. Then he wouldn't have to walk home. He watched the village from a distance, being careful not to reveal his presence.

He was concealed beneath a rocky overhang near the top of a hill. The ledge over his head, and the abundant brush around him, gave him plenty of protection, not only from watchful eyes, but from the elements as well.

Walkara was in no hurry to make a move. In fact, he enjoyed watching the little village. Several women were seated on a fallen log, pulling off long strips of meat from the hind quarter of an elk. They were carefully placing the strips on a willow rack for drying. Occasionally one of the women would throw a scrap of meat to one of three hungry dogs that were watching the women work. Nearby another woman was staking out the hide from probably the same elk for scraping and curing. She was having a hard time pounding the wooden pegs into the partly frozen ground. Four or five children were sliding across the ice in the nearby frozen streambed. The men were gone, probably off hunting, maybe on a horse raid in nearby Ute country.

Walkara realized that not only would it be easy to steal a horse or two, but with a little luck the entire herd could be driven off.

It wasn't until Walkara had left his vantage point and was working closer to the grazing horses that he noticed something unusual. A familiar voice. A woman was shouting to a child. Not only was the sound of her voice familiar, but so was the name of the child. "Battee," the voice called a second time.

Walkara moved to a small mound where he had a better look at the village. A woman was walking towards the children who were still playing on the ice. Though he couldn't see her face, Walkara knew by the way she moved that it was Susquenah. His son, Battee, was one of the children playing on the ice.

Walkara hurried forward, having forgotten the horses. His heart was pounding, his palms sweating. Memories of Susquenah filled his head. The memories he had tried so hard to push out of his mind and heart came gushing forth from somewhere deep inside with a force and power that made his knees weak and his head dizzy. He began running. "Susquenah," he called.

Suddenly, women were shouting and screaming, children were crying, and dogs were barking. The alarm had been sounded. Everyone thought the village was being attacked—except Susquenah, who had recognized the voice that had called to her. She was running towards Walkara, at the same time shouting to the other women that there was nothing to fear, that she knew the approaching warrior.

Walkara and Susquenah embraced, neither saying anything. In the village, the screaming and shouting stopped, though several of the dogs were still barking. Walkara did not say anything to Susquenah, nor did she speak to him. They just held each other close, for what seemed a long time.

When Walkara finally pushed Susquenah just far enough away to look at her face, he saw her eyes and cheeks were wet with tears. Her face was as beautiful as he remembered it, her eyes clear and alive and deep with feeling. She seemed as glad to see him as he was to see her. Could it be that she had missed him the way he missed her, that she loved him the way he loved her? It appeared so. It was absolutely crazy that they were not together.

After Susquenah's earlier rejections, Walkara didn't dare ask her again to come with him. His mind was racing, trying to think of a better way to get her to be his squaw again.

"How is our son?" he asked, the first to speak.

"Battee," she called towards the stream, "come here."

A boy in white buckskins, a thick mop of hair on his head, scrambled out of the creek bottom and began running towards them. He looked about ten years old. He appeared somewhat awkward, yet strong, as he ran to his father.

"My father, the greatest horse thief of them all," the boy said, excited, catching his breath as he came to a stop beside his father and mother. "Will you take me hunting?"

Walkara could not answer.

His son's words had triggered an emotion that was new to him. For an instant Walkara wondered if he was becoming soft like an old woman. He felt his eyes moisten.

"Will my father take me hunting?" the boy repeated. The wrenching feeling in Walkara's throat still prevented him from speaking. Yes, he wanted to take the boy hunting, almost as much as he wanted to sleep with Susquenah again.

"Yes, your father will take you hunting," Susquenah said, sensing Walkara's inability to speak. "Go catch two horses and get your weapons." The boy turned and raced towards one of the lodges.

"Battee needs a father," she said, watching the boy run. "A father to teach him to ride, to hunt, and to be a man."

Walkara wanted to ask her and the boy to come with him, but he remained silent.

"Do you still sell slaves and steal horses?" she asked.

"If I do are you still determined not to be my squaw?" he asked, regretting his words instantly, sensing he and Susquenah were heading into the same old argument that always ended in him leaving by himself.

"Maybe we shouldn't talk about that, not now," she said kindly. They turned, starting to walk arm in arm towards the frozen stream, neither speaking.

"Have you heard of the Mormonees?" he asked.

"Yes. They are the tribe of white people who live in log tepees by the great lake of salt."

"Their leader, Chief Brigham, told me the Mormonees do not sell slaves. They don't steal horses, either. He asked our people to stop doing those things."

"Is this Brigham a great man?" she asked.

"He is a strong man. His people obey him."

"It makes me feel good to know others, even if they are white people, believe as I do."

226

"Would you like to meet Chief Brigham and his people?" he asked.

"Yes."

"I will take you there. We can begin our journey tomorrow."

"I will go with you, Walkara," she said, turning towards him, looking into his face. "But I will not be your squaw."

"Not ever?" he asked, bewildered.

"I do not say not ever. If you wish we may talk about it again after we meet Chief Brigham."

"I do not understand, but I will still take you to the Mormonees."

"Good, we go tomorrow."

Battee came running up behind them, leading two horses. He was also carrying a bow and some arrows. Walkara, rifle in hand, leaped upon one of the horses, then reached out to hold the bow and arrows while the boy climbed upon the second horse.

"Woman," Walkara said, speaking to Susquenah. "The men in this family are going hunting."

"I'll cook some meat for you," she responded. "When will you be back?"

"After dark," Walkara said in mock gruffness, nodding to the boy to follow him as he urged his horse into a gallop.

Chapter 28

It was almost May by the time Walkara and his band rode out of Spanish Fork Canyon onto the sprawling grasslands of the valley of his birth. On his right the towering snow-capped Mt. Timpanogos reached to the heavens. On his left the sky blue waters of Utah Lake glistened like a jewel in the spring sun.

It was almost time for the annual fish festival. Upon leaving the Shoshone camp he had taken Susquenah and Battee with him to the Sanpete Valley. Their plan was to visit the Mormons and Chief Brigham in the new city by the sea of salt after the fish festival.

Walkara rode at the head of a caravan consisting of hundreds of Indians and as many horses. His son, Battee, rode at his side. Walkara had other children by his younger wives, but Battee was the first, and the oldest by several years.

Behind Walkara rode his well-equipped band of raiders, nearly a hundred strong. Behind them Piede slave boys herded a hundred horses to be traded. Last came the women and children, leading pack animals heavily loaded with furs and skins they hoped to trade at the fish festival.

Upon reaching the traditional camping place on the south side of the Timpanogos River just before it entered the lake, Walkara was stunned to see a swarm of Mormons putting the final touches on a log fortress, including a cannon above the main gate. It had been less than two years since the arrival of the Mormons and already they were spreading like hungry locusts.

Not about to camp by the new fort, Walkara guided his caravan to a more distant location. He remembered Jim Bridger's words, how the Mormons would take all the good land, and realized the old mountain man had been right.

Walkara learned that Bridger's claim that Mormons had been killing Indians was true too. But the Indians Brigham's men had killed at the base of Timpanogos belonged to a renegade band of Snakes and Timpany Utes. Walkara would have killed these Indians himself had the opportunity presented itself.

Walkara was disappointed, even offended, that Chief Brigham had established a settlement in the heart of Ute lands without first asking him. Walkara's men felt the same way, and there was considerable talk about attacking and tearing down the new Mormon settlement. Walkara made no effort to calm his men, and as darkness fell on their new camp, some of the last of Bridger's whiskey was brought out as the dances of war began.

Walkara was inside his lodge, sharing a quiet evening meal with Susquenah and Battee, when he received word that two of Chief Brigham's strong men, George Bean and Porter Rockwell, had been discovered entering the camp. Immediately Walkara left his lodge to investigate.

By the time Walkara had reached the center of the celebration, the younger Bean had been stripped of his weapons and his hands were tied behind his back. In the distance, at the edge of the firelight, stood Rockwell, a loaded revolver in each hand, apparently ready to gun down any Indian who tried to lay a hand on him or hurt Bean.

Walkara had heard of Rockwell, a strong man,

tireless to the rigors of the trail, a master with guns, who feared no man, either red or white, and had killed many, defending himself and his boss, Chief Brigham. Rockwell was a muscular, stern-looking man with the usual long hair and beard common among Mormons. Mericats, or non-Mormons, generally cut their hair short.

Walkara walked up to Bean and looked into his face. The young man looked back at him, not blinking or looking down. Bean showed no sign of fear, though his weapons were gone and his hands were tied behind his back. Walkara didn't say anything, waiting to see if Bean would change, perhaps realize the danger he was in, and panic.

The young man remained calm. Finally, Walkara asked him what he wanted.

"I bring Chief Walker a letter from Brigham Young. The Mormon leader wants peace with the Utes," Bean explained, his voice deliberate and firm.

"War is not good," Walkara said. "It makes women and children cry." He nodded for an Indian to cut Bean's hands free. As the young man rubbed the circulation back into his hands, Rockwell slipped his revolvers into his belt and walked up to join Bean and Walkara.

"We will meet with Chief Brigham to talk peace," Walkara said after Bean had read the letter. "Tell your chief he need not come here, that we will come to his city by the lake that is salt."

Walkara invited Bean and Rockwell to join him and Susquenah in his lodge. He asked them to explain to Susquenah why Mormons didn't steal horses and trade slaves, and about their sacred book that contained a history of the forefathers of the Utes. While Bean was explaining Mormon beliefs to Susquenah, Walkara and Rockwell shared a tin of trappers' whiskey.

The next morning after Bean and Rockwell left for

Great Salt Lake City, all the Indians went down to the fish festival to trade, gamble, race horses, feast on fish and have a good time. The Mormons came out of their new fort and joined in the festivities.

Walkara met Isaac Morley, the head Mormon, who invited the chief to join with him in observing a Mormon religious ritual at the edge of the river—the baptism of a man and woman. Walkara watched with interest as Morley baptized first the woman, then the man. They were in the middle of the river where the water was about waist deep. After saying a brief prayer with his right hand raised to the square, Morley pulled them under the cold water. The ritual was a symbolic washing away of sins. After the two people came out of the water and changed into dry clothes, Morley and others laid hands on their heads and said another prayer.

Walkara was impressed, wondering if perhaps his people might benefit from the Mormon religious beliefs too. He'd have to wait and see. Susquenah accompanied several of the white women back into the fort, where they said they were going to teach her to make white man's bread. Walkara hoped he hadn't made a mistake bringing her here. Though she spoke very little English, she seemed to be getting along almost too well with the Mormons. But there was nothing he could do about it now, so he and Battee went to see if they could win anything at the horse races.

Though the trading was good, with many furs, horses, slaves, blankets and other items changing hands, Walkara held back most of his horses for trading in the city by the salt lake.

It was nearly June when Walkara and his men headed north for the big smoke with Chief Brigham. Susquenah and Battee rode with Walkara, while the rest of the women and children followed about a day behind, travel for them being slower because they were expected to bring along the tepee covers and other camp items. The men, and the Piede boys driving the trade horses, were in the first band with Walkara.

Descending from the foothills called Point of the Mountain, Walkara's caravan didn't look like any ordinary band of Indians. Not only were the men well mounted on the finest Spanish horses and armed with the best American rifles money could buy, but they were decorated down to the last man with a vast array of jingling, ornamental loot from California and Mexico—including silver-studded saddles and bridles, large noisy spurs, colorful wool horse blankets, bracelets and rings of gold and silver, earrings and necklaces of turquoise, long Mexican bull whips, rawhide lassos and brightly colored neck scarves. Undoubtedly, to the Mormons Walkara's caravan looked more like a band of Spanish gypsies than native Americans.

Walkara rode right to the center of the new town, announcing he had arrived for the big smoke with Chief Brigham. He made the announcement in the Ute language. Though he knew English, he wasn't about to lose face by speaking Chief Brigham's language. Brigham would have to speak Ute if he wanted to engage in peace talks with the great Walkara.

Brigham and several of his captains came out to greet Walkara. They shook hands after the manner of white men, but it became apparent that the talks couldn't begin without an interpreter. The Mormons sent for Dimick Huntington, who was still in Provo. In the meantime the Utes were invited to make themselves comfortable in the lowlands to the west, by the river the Mormons called Jordan.

This was fine with Walkara. He wanted time to study the Mormon community before engaging in serious talks. He wanted to see how the Mormons lived, worked, ate and made things. He wanted to watch the steel points pulled behind cattle or horses to turn over the ground. He wanted to see how the Mormons planted their seeds in the soft earth, and how they watered the seeds by diverting water from nearby streams. He wanted to know if the men and boys were happy in a society that did not allow horse stealing.

He wondered if the people were really against trading in slaves as Chief Brigham said they were. He wanted to see their pigs, sheep, cattle, and the strange long-eared horses that were stronger than regular horses. He wanted to taste their bread, beef, and pie again, and the fresh things they grew in their gardens. He wanted to learn about their religion, especially their ancient book telling about his ancestors. And as much as anything he wanted to study their strengths and weaknesses in the event war did break out between the Utes and Mormons.

The Mormons gave him and his men a beef to eat while waiting for the big talk. Walkara was grateful for the meat, but he would have preferred whiskey.

Some of the men were eager to start the trading, but Walkara insisted they wait until after the big talk. If things went badly there would be no trading.

As they reached the Jordan River and began setting up their camp, the women and children arrived. Walkara soon realized he and his people were not the only guests in the city by the lake of salt.

The Mericats had discovered gold in the northern part of California the previous year. During the winter, news of the discovery had reached the east, and now thousands of Mericats were headed west to California, crossing the northern passes of the Sierra Nevada Mountains.

Walkara did not try to stop his men from trading with the California-bound Mericats who were desperate for fresh horses. Walkara's men were demanding and getting the most whiskey, gold and guns they had ever received for their Spanish horses.

The Mericats told Walkara they were just a few, the very first to leave for California, that thousands upon thousands of others would follow, that Walkara and his men would find a rich and endless market for all the Spanish horses they could possibly obtain.

Whereas earlier Walkara had felt pressured into making an unwilling peace with the Mormons, now he could finally see the wisdom of Sowiette's and Victorio's desires for living in harmony with the Mormons. With peace, Walkara and his people, along with the Mormons, could become rich trading with the goldseekers. Walkara realized how important peace could be, at least for the present while the Mericats were filling up California. Suddenly he became determined to make the big smoke as productive as possible.

As he studied the Mormons Walkara noticed that Chief Brigham had a council of twelve men, called apostles. These were his captains, men who led the church and the colonization.

To Walkara the quorum of apostles looked like a good way to organize and do business, so on the morning of the big smoke he kicked twelve of his best men out of their drunken slumber, telling them he had selected them to be his apostles. None of them seemed very excited about the new honor, especially Arrapeen, who was still very ill from too much whiskey the night before.

While most of the men didn't seem to care one way or the other about being made apostles because they knew in the end Walkara made all the decisions anyway, they did object to Walkara's method of initiation, especially Arrapeen.

After ordering his new quorum down to the edge of the Jordan River, Walkara announced he intended to baptize them all the same way Bishop Morley had done it to the man and woman at the fish festival.

Arrapeen flatly refused to have any part of the ritual, especially early in the morning in the cold river water. Walkara was in no mood to argue the matter, so without warning he threw his muscular arms around the surprised Arrapeen and began pushing his brother towards the water. In his weakened, drunken condition, Arrapeen was no match for his brother. Both men crashed into the chest-deep water. Walkara was the first to surface, standing upright, his right arm to the square, saying something about initiating Arrapeen into his official tribal council. Grabbing Arrapeen once again, he pushed him beneath the surface of the water.

Arrapeen came up sputtering and coughing, all the fight gone from him as he crawled out of the river. None of the others resisted. One by one each man waded into the water to be baptized into the new tribal council. Afterwards the newly washed leadership of Walkara's band returned quietly to camp to dress for the big smoke.

Even though it was summer, with the morning coolness quickly giving way to a scorching sun, Walkara crawled into a brown broadcloth suit Jim Bridger had given him. Next he put on an assortment of stolen Spanish jewelry, including four rings, three bracelets, a necklace and two earrings. Last he put on a beaver hat, the kind the Mericats wore in their eastern cities. He figured he would impress Chief Brigham with his knowledge of Mericat custom and dress.

Getting on his horse, leading his 12 newly washed apostles, Walkara headed for the bowery, the same place he had met with Chief Brigham the previous winter. Upon approaching the bowery Walkara was pleased that the Mormons esteemed the big smoke as an event of great importance. Hundreds of people had already gathered around the outside of the bowery to watch the proceedings. Uniformed policemen were lined up to manage the crowd. Walkara was flattered by the attention the Mormons were placing on the big smoke.

Walkara and his men dismounted and walked into the council area. Chief Brigham and his apostles were not there yet. Walkara was pleased the Mormons had not cluttered the council area with the wooden stools white men preferred sitting on. The only way to conduct a big smoke was to be seated on the ground.

Walkara motioned for his council to seat themselves on the hard-packed ground. Hundreds of people watched them as they waited patiently for Chief Brigham. They didn't have to wait long.

When the crowd parted to let Brigham and his captains into the bowery, Walkara noticed that only about half the quorum of Mormon apostles was present, and wondered if this might be reason for him to be offended. But Chief Brigham quickly handled the matter by apologizing for the missing apostles, who were either beyond the greatest of all rivers in the land of the Mericats or across the big water called the Atlantic Ocean.

The square-jawed, thick-chested Brigham looked the same as before, friendly and confident like a man who ruled the world. He wore a neatly pressed black broadcloth suit suitable for meeting with important dignitaries. In addition to Chief Brigham and his apostles, there was Bishop Isaac Morley from the new Provo settlement and Dimmick Huntington to translate.

In the awkward manner of white men not used to sitting on the ground, Brigham and his captains lowered themselves to the dirt floor, forming a semi-circle facing Walkara and his twelve captains.

Brigham again showed a proper understanding of Indian council procedure by allowing a good and contemplative quiet. Walkara was pleased. In time Brigham spoke.

"It makes Mormons happy to welcome to their

town the great Chief Walker and his people. We greet
you this day as friend and brother, and hope these good
feelings between our peoples will always continue.''

Though Walkara understood every word Chief
Brigham spoke, he waited until Huntington had finished the translation before showing any reaction or recep-
tivity to what had been said.

When Huntington finished, Walkara drew himself
erect to his full six feet. Using a Mericat match he lit his
carefully packed ceremonial pipe, drew it to a good
start, then gracefully stepped to the center of the circle.
There he turned his eyes upward to Towats in the
heavens. With outstretched arms, he offered his god the
first curling smoke from the pipe. Then he faced the
direction of the half-risen sun, and offered it again.
Slowly he dropped his arms, stepped back to the circle,
and as graceful as a mountain lion, dropped back to the
council squat.

Taking an immense drag on the pipe stem, Walkara
filled his lungs with the stinging, fragrant charge. Slowly, dramatically, he blew it outward from his lips, and
after the proper pause, passed the pipe to the first white
man on his right, Heber Kimball.

After Kimball sucked in an uneasy puff, the pipe
was passed to Brigham, who in turn smoked and handed
it on to the remaining white captains. Finally it reached
the newly baptized Arrapeen, then from him to each of
his companions until it finally returned to Walkara. The
hour for talk had arrived at last.

Walkara sensed no guile on the part of the
Mormons. They seemed intent on developing a
legitimate friendship with the Indians. They had been
friendly and courteous. The smoke had gone well so far.
Feeling warm and loquacious, Walkara rose to speak.

The words that came out sounded more like
Sowiette or Kanosh than Walkara. He said the
Mormons were truly like brothers, that they were

welcome in Ute lands. He continued for several minutes.

When Walkara sat down, Huntington did his best to interpret accurately. "Walkara accepts our friendship," he said to the brethren. "He no longer wants to fight us. He wants us to go to his land in the Sanpete Valley and make settlements. He will do what we want him to do."

Seeing Brigham's nod of approval, Walkara asked how many months it would be before the Mormons could come to the Sanpete Valley. Huntington translated.

"I have never killed a white man," Walkara continued. "I am always friendly with the Mormonees. I hear what they say and remember it. It is good to live like the Mormonees and their children. I do not care about the land, but I want the Mormonees to go and settle it."

Brigham Young's alert face softened as Walkara's words were translated, and he understood the extent of the chief's offer and its apparent good faith. The Mormon leader nodded his satisfaction to the elders beside him. A colony could now be established in the Sanpete Valley without opposition. Brigham nodded his gratitude to the stately war chief opposite him.

"We will need some of your men to pilot our wagons through to the Sanpete in the fall," Brigham said. "We will teach your children to read and write if they wish."

"You cannot come to our place now?" Walkara asked.

"In six moons we will send a company," Brigham responded.

Walkara began to feel uneasy, and he didn't know why. Perhaps he had given away too much too fast. Once the Mormons were settled, the land would never be the same again. They could not be driven out, not without a lot of bloodshed, if at all. Walkara tried to think of his medicine dream and the words of Victorio.

"It is not good to fight the Indians," Brigham was saying. "And tell your Indians not to steal anymore. We want to be friendly with you. We are poor now, but in a few years we will be rich. We will trade cattle for horses."

"This is good," Walkara responded.

"We will build a house for you," Brigham continued. "We will teach you and your people how to build your own houses."

"What is the nature of the land in Sanpete?" Heber Kimball asked. "Is it plow land? Is it covered with stones?"

"My land is good," Walkara answered. "No stones, but high timber. Plenty of high timber."

"We will raise grain for you," Brigham added, "until you learn to raise it for yourselves. We will trade you ammunition to hunt with until you can raise grain. We will bring you sheep, and teach your women how to make blankets. We want some of you to read the Book of Mormon, that you may know of your forefathers."

"I have a woman who would like to read your book. Will you teach her?" Walkara asked, thinking of Susquenah.

"Yes," Brigham replied enthusiastically. "Leave her here when you leave. Our people will bring her back to you when they come in the fall. By then she will be able to read to you from the book."

"That will be good," Walkara declared. "Yutahs want the Mormonees. Yutahs learn to read the book." He realized he was probably speaking too freely. He couldn't speak for Big Elk and others who probably still wanted to fight the Mormons.

"You must raise cattle," Brigham explained, "instead of depending on game."

"Much of the game is gone," Walkara said.

"You must raise cattle, sheep and hogs," Brigham

continued. "We will teach you so that in a few years you will have plenty."

"You want to trade cattle for horses now?" Walkara asked, noticing the interest his men had taken to the Mormon offer to trade.

"I will give you a bull, if you don't have one," Brigham offered.

"I have one."

"As to your land," Brigham continued, looking at the circle of Indians before him, "in six moons we will send men to look over the ground, probably in three or four moons."

"That is good," Walkara replied.

"We want to go where there is no snow," Brigham said.

"In Sanpete there is little or no snow. You will see."

"We would also like to put towns and houses in California. What do you know about California?"

"I have been to California," Walkara smiled, knowing probably no man alive east of the Sierra Nevadas knew California as well as he did.

"What kind of country is between your land and California?" Brigham asked.

"South of here not much grass. It is best about the Salt Mountain. From my lodge not a sleep."

"Tell us about that place."

"Beyond the mountains, plenty of streams," Walkara said, his hands suddenly alive and assisting. "From salt springs, over a mountain, lots of timber. Then next sleep, good land, plenty of timber, and good grass. All my land clear."

He swept his arms outward to the west and north, frowning derisively.

"I hate to have you stay on this land," he continued. "It is near my enemies. Timpany Yutahs killed my father. If you come on my land, my people will not steal your cattle, nor whip them. I want the Mormonee children to be with mine. I hate for you to be on this poor land."

"I am glad to hear you talk such peace," Brigham said. "I was worried about your feelings towards us."

"Indians all want peace," Walkara said. "It is not good to fight. It makes women and children cry. I told the Piedes to stop fighting and stealing, but they have no ears."

The anger Walkara once felt for Chief Brigham and his people was gone now. The talk had been good, and he had deliberately made it so.

There was a feeling of warmth and fellowship as Walkara slowly, silently opened his pouch and packed the pipe once more. The open-sided bowery darkened as clouds passed in front of the sun. Heber Kimball produced a sulphur match, lighted it on his boot, then held the flame while Walkara sucked the tobacco until it glowed warmly. Gracefully the chief started the pipe on its rounds by passing it first to Kimball. The tenseness was gone from the gathering, and both Indians and whites were talking in low tones one to another. Respectfully Walkara waited until Brigham had drawn on the pipe before speaking again.

"One day my brother Sowiette will come to this city," he said. "He wants Mormonees to settle among his people too."

"I want him to come," Brigham replied cheerfully. "I don't want to kill another Indian."

It was time now to talk trade.

"I want the Mormonees to give forty charges of powder for a heavy buckskin," Walkara said.

Brigham calmly shook his head. "Grant has given ten or twelve charges, Bridger up to twenty-five. Thirty are enough—as scarce as it is now."

"Little hides from ten to twelve? Then big, heavy ones up to thirty and forty?"

Brigham thought a moment, and looked at Huntington and Morley. "We should make most," he said, "by giving ten for small, fifteen for larger, thirty for good ones, and forty for big ones."

"Good." Walkara nodded his satisfaction, knowing the squaws would be bringing plenty of skins. Soon there would be lots of powder and balls.

"We ought to buy all your skins," Brigham added. "Do your people need hats?"

"They all want hats," Walkara answered.

"That is fine. When you are ready to leave, go in peace, Chief Walker. A good peace go with you. If we settle the land, we want peace, that our children can play together."

"It is good."

Everyone got up to leave. There was nothing more to say. The Mormons and Utes were as brothers. Walkara and his men returned to their camp to feast on another half an ox provided by the Mormons and to commence trading. To Walkara and Brigham Young, at least, it had been an eventful day.

The trading was good that day, as good as the Mormon food. By nightfall Walkara's people had much powder and lead, and many were wearing new hats.

It was nearly dark when Walkara found Susquenah. She had been conversing with some of the Mormon women most of the afternoon and evening. He invited her to walk with him. He said he had a surprise for her.

In the coolness of the evening they walked through the cottonwoods along the east bank of the Jordan River. He told her of Chief Brigham's invitation for her to stay and learn to read the sacred book that contained the history of the Ute forefathers. She was excited and honored to be selected as the first from her people to learn to read the white men's book.

"When you return with the Mormonees to Sanpete

in the fall you can read to me from the book," Walkara said, an unmistakable sadness in his voice.

"Yes," she said, "but why are you sad?"

"Today I invited the Mormonees to cover our lands with their farms and houses. Jim Bridger and Big Elk say the Mormonees will take the best land and kill all our game, causing our people to starve if they cannot beg for food at the Mormonee forts. Maybe I should have made war with them instead. The way we live will never be the same again."

"By making war many Indians would die, women and children too. And the Mormonees would not go away. You have done the right thing not making war," she said.

"Is Brigham right?" he asked. "Will I have to stop hunting and raise cattle, sheep and grain to feed my family?"

"Many things will change. Many changes will be good," she said.

"Maybe I won't be able to steal horses and trade slaves."

"Those will be some of the good changes." She stopped and turned to face him. When he faced her, she reached out and took one of his hands. "Maybe something else will change too."

Without saying anything, he waited for her to continue.

"Maybe you and I could have once again what we once shared," she said.

"That would make me happy," he responded.

"You don't look happy."

"What has happened with the Mormonees makes me sad."

"But the smoke was good. There will be peace. One should be happy."

"Walkara, the great warrior and horse thief, does

not wish to become a Mormon farmer," he said. "War with the Mormonees would bring much sadness to our people. Women and children would cry much. Peace with the Mormonees means Walkara must become a farmer. Don't talk to me of happiness."

"Then why did you make the peace?"

"There are some things a man must do that have nothing to do with happiness. I am . . ." he said, stopping before finishing. He looked away from her.

"You are what?"

Slowly he turned back to her. "The words of peace made me afraid, more afraid than I have felt since going into the village of the Timpany Yutahs after they killed my father."

"Peace shouldn't make one afraid," she said.

"This peace does," he explained. "What will our people do when our land is filled with Mormonees, when there is no game to eat, or horses to steal? Maybe our people will not want to be farmers like the Mormonees. Then what will we do? How will we live? Making war on the Mormonees would not frighten me so much as this strange peace."

"I believe the peace is good," she said, comfortingly. "As time passes I think you will believe it is good, too. Give the peace time to work."

"I told Chief Brigham I would."

"I will stay and learn to read the sacred book."

"Will you come back to Sanpete in the fall?"

"I will. But what will you do now?"

He let go of her hand and looked to the mountains to the east. "Tomorrow I go east. I will hunt buffalo, from horseback, with bow and arrow, the old way. Maybe I will steal some horses from the Shoshones. Until fall I will forget about the Mormonees."

"Will you take Battee with you?" she asked. He was surprised. As much as she seemed to like the Mormon ways, he thought she would want her son to go to the Mormon school too.

"Why do you want your son to hunt buffalo with me?"

"When a boy has a father who is a great hunter and a great man, he should be with him. Do you not agree?"

"I agree," he said. "Our boy will learn to chase buffalo on horseback. He will be waiting for you when you come to Sanpete in the fall."

"Thank you," she said, suddenly reaching up with her hands to his neck, pulling his face down and kissing him on the lips. He let her kiss him, but did not pull her to him, did not kiss her back.

"I will see you at Sanpete in the fall," he said, turning and walking away.

Chapter 29

Walkara didn't get away from Salt Lake City as quickly as he thought he would. Brigham Young invited him to stay around for the big celebration on the day the Mormons called July 24th, the second anniversary of the Mormon arrival in their city by the lake of salt. Brigham invited Walkara and his two hundred men, fully armed and mounted on their best horses, to ride in a procession the people would line up along State Street to watch. The Mormons called it a parade.

Thousands cheered as Walkara and his men rode in perfect lines, four abreast, their horses starting and stopping with drilled precision. Every Indian carried a new American rifle, a stolen Spanish saddle, and many wore large Mexican spurs.

Most were bare-chested in the July heat, including Walkara, who had packed away his broadcloth suit for cooler times. In addition to making him hot, the white man's suit made his skin itch.

His dress from head to foot consisted of a rawhide headband, colored with red and yellow vertical stripes, his medicine pouch attached to a silver necklace, a blue loincloth, white buckskin leggings, and American boots with large, jingling Mexican spurs. His muscular body glistened in the hot July son.

Riding by his side was his son Battee, on a short but lively paint mare. Walkara was riding the tall black stallion he had given to Peg Leg after the big California raid. On the white trader's way to California early that spring, he had left the magnificent animal for Walkara to care for in his absence.

As Walkara led his men down the parade route, the stallion was unusually calm. When Walkara had left Sanpete a few months earlier, the horse had been hard to handle, constantly laying his ears back at other male horses, sometimes reaching to bite or strike out with a front or rear hoof. And whenever the stallion came near a mare, he had to court her with his deep, chortling love talk. Walkara knew the stallion would be a nuisance on the trip, but he also knew the horse would win most of the races at the fish festival, and that it would impress Brigham Young and the Mormons. There was no finer animal in the entire Rocky Mountains.

But to the surprise of many, in the city by the lake of salt the magnificent black had become as calm and gentle as any of the old geldings. The sudden change in behavior was not the result of firm or consistent handling or training by Walkara, or anyone else.

Walkara discovered the Mormons in Great Salt Lake City were indeed impressed with the black. Not only Chief Brigham, but everyone else, seemed to appreciate the long hip, deep chest, and well muscled front and hind quarters. The thick bones in the legs indicated the horse would not break down under daily use, and the natural arch of the pencil neck added a remarkable touch of elegance. The Mormons knew a good horse when they saw one, and Walkara took full advantage of the situation.

Almost before Walkara's camp was set up, the Mormons began bringing their mares for the stallion to breed, as many as the black stud could service, three or four the first few days, but as the horse began to settle down, about two a day.

With each breeding Walkara received payment,

sometimes a big chunk of beef, a bar of lead, a hatchet, a knife, a hat, a bolt of cloth, a bar of soap, or even a gold coin.

To conserve the stallion's strength Walkara stopped riding it, giving it all the grain and grass it could eat. On the day of the parade, after several weeks of not riding the animal, Walkara was both surprised and pleased at how gentle the horse had become.

At the end of the parade route, Walkara and his people joined the Mormons in their holiday feast, consisting of all the good things the Mormons had to eat—boiled beef, roast chicken, bread with butter and honey, fresh vegetables, pies and cakes. Walkara and his men had to sneak in their own whiskey.

Susquenah spent much of her time with the Mormon women, rather than with her own people. It was unsettling to Walkara that she seemed so eager to learn the ways of the Mormons. Every once in a while she would wander over to Walkara, tell him something she had learned, then hurry back to her Mormon friends, where she seemed neither awkward nor out of place, though her command of the language was still not very good. She assured Walkara that she would return to him in the fall, after she had learned to read the book.

Walkara wondered what it would be like when she returned. Deep inside he knew being together again with Susquenah would never be like that first winter together. She had changed too much, and so had he. She had so many strange ideas in her beautiful head. He knew he would be better off forgetting this strange, wonderful woman, the mother of his oldest child, but he could not. Whatever she asked of him he would likely give her.

But now it was time to go. Between the Indians at the fish festival, the California goldseekers, and the Mormons he had done enough trading and selling to last a man a lifetime. He had all the material possessions a man could ever want—and more. His wives and slaves would be burdened carrying everything back to Sanpete.

With Walkara doing little but talking and trading, his muscles had become soft. His heart had become restless. Susquenah could stay and learn the ways of the Mormons, but his heart longed for excitement and adventure. He even missed the hardships of the trail. He was tired of eating fish and Mormon beef. His mouth watered for rich, red buffalo meat.

When the celebration was over, Walkara, Battee, and some of Walkara's men headed east for buffalo country. The rest of the men, along with the women and children, began preparations to return to Sanpete.

Walkara was pleased to have his oldest son riding by his side. The boy was enthusiastic and eager to finally be allowed to ride with the men. The boy filled Walkara's ears with endless questions about hunting, horse stealing, fighting enemies, and a hundred other subjects. Walkara did not tire of the boy's questions. He was teaching his son to be a man. He knew the boy would learn much on the trip, not just by having his questions answered, but by doing new things that required skill and courage.

The first challenge came at the Green River crossing. There had been several days of thundershowers to the north and the waters were higher than normal. The band of buffalo hunters had been riding along the foothills to the north of the regular trail, so when they reached the river they were at a place where Walkara hadn't crossed before. He was therefore unsure of the depth at the crossing.

Not wanting to ride several miles downstream to the usual crossing location, Walkara sought out a wide spot in the river, just above a rapid, and rode into the water.

The Green River was its usual color, a murky

brown, making it impossible to see the bottom. The shallowest places to cross were usually in the gentle ripples just above the roaring rapids. The water was sometimes shallow in the rapids too, but usually too swift for a horse to maintain its footing.

In the wide, calm spots between rapids the water was too deep, requiring a long, tiring swim. In the deep water riders had to slip off the backs of their horses and be pulled across by holding onto the horses' tails. While crossing in deep water, pack horses had to be unpacked and their loads ferried across in skin boats or rafts. By far the best method of crossing was to find a place shallow enough for the horses to wade, just above a rapid.

The place where Walkara entered the water was plenty wide, indicating the water was shallow. There were ripples all the way across too, indicating the rocks in the stream bottom were not far from the surface. Without a second thought Walkara urged his horse into the water, Battee not far behind, the rest of the men following single file. To their right, downstream, the river narrowed into a swift, thundering rapid.

When the tall black began to stumble, lunging forward and sideways to maintain its balance, Walkara began to think perhaps he had picked a poor place to cross, but since he was nearly halfway across the river, he continued to push ahead.

Looking at the steep bank on the opposite side of the river he knew what his problem was. The bank was strewn with hundreds of huge, jagged boulders, some as large as the log tepees the Mormons built. Over centuries the huge boulders had rolled into the river. The gentle ripples he had seen from shore were not made by little rocks, but big ones. The holes between rocks could be too deep for a horse to touch bottom.

Walkara looked back at his son. The boy was holding the saddle horn with one hand, the reins with the other. He looked frightened. Walkara wished he had ridden downstream to the usual crossing place. He hated to turn around in the treacherous rocks. Sometimes turning could be more risky than continuing ahead. It was nearly a hundred yards back to the bank where they had entered. Keeping the stallion's head pointed towards the opposite shore, he tapped its sides with his spurs.

The water became deeper, past the middle of the horse's shoulders. Walkara was wet to his knees. The current was swifter. The stallion stopped, planting its feet, pushing hard against the rushing current, trembling with uncertainty.

It suddenly occurred to Walkara that Battee's horse, the paint, was not as tall as the black, and would have a harder time holding its own in the deeper water. He looked back just as the paint turned and headed downstream, straight into the rapids. It had lost its footing and was swimming. Battee dropped the reins and grabbed the saddle horn with both hands.

"Hang on!" Walkara shouted. "Don't let go." He hoped the boy could hear him over the roar of the water. Horses were good swimmers, and eventually the paint would make it to one shore or the other. If the boy bailed out and was not a strong swimmer, he could drown. If he got in front of the horse's churning hooves, he could be trampled to death. The best thing to do was to just hang on and hope the horse didn't get rolled in the rapids.

Walkara was just turning his horse downstream to go after the boy when the stallion slipped forward into a deep hole. Suddenly the entire horse was underwater, and Walkara was up to his waist in brown water. He was still in the saddle. He could feel the powerful churning of the horse's legs beneath him. There were no rocks beneath its feet now, only water. He loosened the reins, allowing the horse to extend its nose towards the surface. He had seen men drown their swimming horses, pulling back on the reins, preventing the horses from getting their noses up for air.

In a few seconds the black's nose and face appeared above the surface of the choppy water, the flared nostrils blowing water and sucking air. Walkara could still feel the powerful churning of the legs beneath him, as the current began to carry him and the horse into the rapids.

Ahead of him he could see the boy's head bobbing above the white-capped waves. The paint appeared to be doing an adequate job of keeping itself upright. It was fortunate it had a little boy and not a heavy man on its back.

Suddenly Walkara could feel the black had regained its footing and was pushing into shallower water. The water level receded from Walkara's waist to his knees. The horse stopped, once again facing the opposite shore, bracing against the shallow but swift current. To Walkara the water ahead didn't look any shallower than that behind him. He wondered why the horse had stopped instead of plunging ahead for the safety of shore.

As the horse began to slip sideways into the rapid, Walkara realized what had happened. The horse had climbed onto a huge boulder. He was surrounded by deep, swift water, too deep to wade.

By the time Walkara had decided to turn the animal downstream and plunge into the rapids, it was too late. The powerful current pushed the horse sideways off the rock. The thrashing animal went over on its side as it was washed into the rapids. Losing his seat, Walkara pushed away from the horse, but he didn't push too hard. He knew the horse's thrashing hooves could kill him. He also knew the horse's tail was his lifeline to shore.

As soon as the horse was pointed downstream, its head and back above water, its feet churning underneath, Walkara reached out and grabbed the long black tail. He could feel the horse pulling him into the rapids. He stretched out on top of the rough water as best he could, knowing the powerful hind legs were striking out behind the horse almost the full length of the tail. Several feet underneath the water he could get struck by a hoof. On top, he was safe.

He was in the middle of the rapid now, the pointed waves capped with white froth. The waves were too high for him to see beyond them. He could only hope that Battee was all right. Even if the boy was in trouble, there was little Walkara could do now to help. He had lost all control of the powerful black. It would have to choose its own course to dry land. The noise of the crashing waves was deafening.

Gradually the water became calmer, quieter, and slower. The horse began plunging over submerged rocks towards the opposite shore, now only 30 or 40 yards away. Walkara continued to hang onto the tail until rocks began striking his knees. He let go and got his footing just in time to see the paint emerge from the water directly in front of him. Battee was still on its back. Walkara grinned his relief.

He looked back to see how the rest of the men were doing. Upon seeing Walkara and Battee getting into trouble, all of them had turned around and made it safely back to shore, where they had watched Battee and Walkara ride the rapids. They were waving their congratulations at Walkara and Battee for having made the run safely. Walkara waved back at them, then hurried through the shallow water towards shore to join his son.

Walkara half-expected the boy to be crying. It would be easy for a child, or anyone not used to the river, to become hysterical in that kind of a situation.

He was pleased that Battee was not crying. In fact, as Walkara stepped out of the water, the boy begged, "Please, can we do it again?" Walkara looked closely at the boy, not sure how to respond. Was the boy teasing? Did his son have an unusual sense of humor?

"Can we do it again?" the boy asked a second time. Walkara looked again, seeing the sincerity in the boy's face. No, he was not joking. Walkara wanted to believe his son had extraordinary courage, but finally decided it was just a matter of the boy being too young to appreciate the real danger of the situation.

"We'll do it again on the way back," Walkara promised.

"I can't wait to tell the other boys," Battee said. "I won't tell them I was afraid."

"I won't tell them either," Walkara said, mounting the black stallion standing quietly by his side. He waved for the men across the river to go downstream to the regular crossing before coming over. He and Battee rode downstream to meet them.

After the men had safely crossed the river Walkara led his band north and east towards the open prairies where the buffalo roamed in large numbers. Walkara had made the journey to buffalo country many times, but this time was different.

When they came to the two trails that disappeared into the land of the rising sun, the path the white men pulled their great, lumbering land canoes along, there was little grass and little wood for fires. The ground was dusty, barren, and littered in both directions, as far as the eye could see, not with trash, but with treasure.

There were stoves, the kind the white men cooked their bread in. There were wagon wheels, barrels, sacks of rain-moistened grain rotting in the sun. There were shovels, ploughs, axes, bars of lead, sewing machines, even boxes of tools. There were dead animals too. They hadn't been shot with arrows or bullets, but had been worked to death by the men going to find gold.

Walkara understood why valuable belongings had been left behind, and why the animals were dead. This new kind of Mericat wanted to get to the California gold so bad that nothing else seemed to matter. What Walkara didn't understand was how men could become that way. Why was gold so important to them?

He wondered what the Mericats would do if he told them of the place where he had found gold in the stream, and the cave where Victorio had shown him more gold. He decided he would never tell the white men of his gold place. If he did they would come and fill up his land like they were now filling up California. Having the Mormons was bad enough, if getting rich could be considered bad. The white men were making him rich beyond his fondest dreams, he thought.

Not finding buffalo in the usual places, Walkara and his men pushed on. Deer and elk were scarce too, at least along the wagon path. The Mericats had killed everything within a mile or two of the road. Walkara pushed further north.

In camp in the evenings, he fashioned himself and Battee bows and arrows, from serviceberry and wild rose stems. It was easy to kill buffalo with guns, but the old way with bow and arrows was better. Guns made noise and made the buffalo run faster, and sometimes they turned away from the sound of a gun. Guns were difficult to load while racing along on horseback. Pulling another arrow from the quiver was much easier. And when the hunt was over, if arrows had been used, there was never any question about who killed which animal. The arrows in the carcasses were certain identification.

The boy was not strong enough to pull a powerful bow, so Walkara made Battee a lighter one, with smaller, sharper arrows, telling the boy he would have to be content with chasing calves until his arms were strong enough to pull back a real bow.

One evening as the group rode up through some ledges to the edge of a sprawling plateau, the forward scout returned with news that a herd of deer was feeding only several hundred yards ahead of them, on the smooth, flat ground that was the beginning of the wide plateau. With no buffalo to chase the men had been getting restless. Walkara suggested they give the deer a run. There were nine deer in the herd, five bucks and four does.

Keeping out of sight, the men spread out along the edge of the plateau, Walkara and Battee on the far right. When everyone was in place, Walkara waved the signal and all riders charged onto the plateau, racing their horses towards the startled deer.

Too smart to head into the middle of the open plateau, and too timid to head straight back into the line of approaching riders, the deer headed off to the right, hoping to get around Walkara's end of the line and into the safety of the ledges.

Walkara notched an arrow on his bowstring and shouted for Battee to do the same. It appeared they had the advantage. The fleeing deer would not be able to beat them to the ledges. Barring unforeseen problems, they were likely to get some good, close range shooting.

The horses were racing full speed to cut off the deer. As the avenues of flight and pursuit narrowed to a collision course, the deer began to tire. But so did the horses, which had already run close to half a mile.

Not willing to be headed towards the open plateau where there was no cover, the deer continued on a collision course towards the ledges. Almost before they knew it, Walkara and Battee were running with the nine deer, right in the middle of them.

Walkara singled out the largest buck and began to maneuver his winded horse into position, on the right side of the deer, a little back so as not to head the animal off to the left. He was about 20 yards away from the buck, and getting closer. He had six spare arrows in his quiver. It was time to start shooting.

Chapter 29

Looking over at his son, racing on the paint not more than 40 yards away, Walkara decided to try to get a little closer to the deer. It would be more impressive to the boy if he shot the buck at close range. He touched his spurs to the sides of the big black, urging it to run even faster.

Walkara was getting closer, almost ready for the close shot, when he suddenly noticed they were nearing the edge of the plateau, where the ground dropped steeply to the valley below. If he continued on his present course and executed his shot, there would be no time to stop. He would go over the edge of the plateau with the deer. He didn't want the deer that badly. Releasing the tension in the bowstring, Walkara grabbed the horse's reins with his right hand and began pulling the stallion to a stop.

As the horse began to slow down, Walkara saw Battee's paint racing up beside him. The boy had apparently dropped his bow and arrow, because he was holding onto his reins with both hands, sawing desperately at the paint's mouth. The animal was running away with the boy, hard on the path of the deer, not about to stop, not for any reason.

Walkara's first reaction was to gallop alongside and grab the paint's headstall and jerk the horse to a halt. But there wasn't time. They were nearly to the edge of the plateau. He continued to pull his black in, hoping the paint would notice the other horse stopping and get the idea that it ought to do the same.

But the paint was watching the deer, not the black stallion. She continued to race at top speed, ignoring the little hands pulling desperately at the reins, finally disappearing over the edge of the plateau, close on the heels of the fleeing deer.

Walkara gave the stallion a little more rein, allowing it to speed up. He didn't want to let the boy out of his sight.

The deer headed straight down the edge of the plateau, leaping over and around boulders and clumps of brush, occasionally spraying loose rock and gravel into the air. Suddenly the closest deer stumbled, falling downhill, rolling over twice, nearly under the front feet of Battee's horse.

After two complete somersaults, the deer was again on its feet and running. The little paint never broke stride.

When the steep part of the hill leveled off into a plateau with fairly good footing, Battee was finally able to convince the paint it was time to stop. As the horse came to a jerking halt, Walkara was right beside the boy. Both were laughing as the deer disappeared from sight into a series of even steeper ledges.

"Were you afraid?" Walkara asked after they had caught their breaths.

"If I was will you send me home?" the boy responded.

Walkara started to laugh. The boy looked puzzled.

"Had I gone over the edge of the plateau the way you did, down through those ledges, I would have been frightened too," Walkara offered.

"You think so?" the boy asked.

"I know it would have been so," Walkara answered. "Everyone becomes frightened at times, even me. A warrior gets in many situations that bring fear. The important thing is not whether or not you are afraid, but what you do while you are afraid."

Walkara was surprised at his wise words. It felt good to be a father giving advice to a son, especially this son, the child of Susquenah, the woman he loved so much. In the boy he saw some of her, and some of himself. Being with the boy was almost as good as being with her, in some ways better. Walkara continued his lecture.

"When your horse started down through the

ledges, if you had tried to pull her head up, or turn her uphill, you would have increased the chances of her falling with you. Even though you were afraid, you did the right thing.

"When your horse began swimming into the rapids," Walkara continued, "had you started pulling hard on the reins to try to stop her or turn her around, the swift current would probably have rolled her over, and you would likely be dead now. It doesn't matter that you were afraid, only that you did the right things while being afraid. You can ride with me anytime."

"Should we go chase another deer?" the boy asked brightly.

"No," Walkara responded emphatically. "We'll find some buffalo. They run in straight lines, and they avoid ledges."

They turned their horses towards the steep incline of ledges leading back to the plateau where the rest of the men waited for them.

Chapter 30

The herds of buffalo could not be found. The endless stream of California-bound gold-seekers had chased and shot the shaggy prairie animals until they were gone from all the usual places. Walkara's men found a few stragglers, which they quickly ran down and killed if they caught up with them. But after everyone in the hunting party was fed there was little left over to dry, and most of that was eaten on the homeward journey. The extra horses that had been brought along to carry home heavy loads of dried meat did not carry loads of any kind on the homeward journey.

It was fall now, and as the unsuccessful hunters returned home, occasionally four or five men would head into the nearby hills to hunt for deer and elk. But even the numbers of these animals seemed to be down. Very few of the hunting parties brought back more than enough to just keep Walkara and his men in meat while they traveled.

What concerned Walkara was that in all the trading sessions with the Mormons, both at the fish festival and then in Salt Lake City, his people had neglected the critical responsibility of putting away food for the winter. Through it all he hadn't been worried, thinking the fall buffalo hunt would produce the necessary meat for the colder months. But the buffalo hadn't been there. He and his men were coming home empty-handed. There would be some deer and elk to kill in the mountains above the Sanpete, and if the snow became deep many of these animals would move down into the valley where they would be easy to hunt. But their numbers were limited, and there were a lot of families to feed.

Winter could come quickly to this land, blocking the mountain passes with snow. Walkara had no choice but to return home before finding the buffalo.

With the hunt unsuccessful he routed his homeward journey though Fort Bridger, figuring some of the unused pack animals could be traded for flour and beans and other food staples Bridger might have.

Whereas the old trader had been generous both with his whiskey and goodwill a year earlier, he was now cold and indifferent towards the Utes. Not only did Bridger seem upset that his plan to turn the Utes on the Mormons was a failure, but he no longer needed the fresh horses the Utes could bring him. With the hordes of forty-niners pushing west he had a new source of horses. He found the desperate goldseekers willing to trade two jaded horses for one fresh one. Bridger simply turned the worn-down animals out to pasture. In a few short weeks these animals, their bellies full and their strength restored, would find themselves on the other end of the two-for-one swap.

The goldseekers who could afford to buy horses, paid cash. Bridger was getting rich without having to buy California horses from the Utes.

When Walkara offered to trade horses for food, Bridger simply wasn't interested. He already had too many horses to feed through the winter. He said he would accept cash only for flour, beans, bacon, coffee and other food staples. And since Walkara and his men had little cash, they moved on, some bitter to see such a dramatic change in the once friendly and generous Bridger.

The homeward journey took longer than expected. Men were beginning to get ill with the dreaded white man's disease called measles. Walkara had heard how entire tribes along the Missouri River had been wiped out with another white man's disease called smallpox. Up until now, the white man's sicknesses had stayed away from the Rocky Mountains.

First came the high temperature, frequently causing the victim to become delirious. Then came the rash, sometimes so bad the entire body became scarlet. There was nothing to do but splash the victim with cold water and wait for the sickness to take its course.

Feeling an urgency to get home as quickly as possible, Walkara left groups of sick men behind, usually with one or two healthy men to care for them. They were to hurry home as soon as they were able. He guessed his people had picked up the sickness in Great Salt Lake City, either from the Mormons or the California-bound immigrants. His fear was that the women and children had caught the disease too, and were fighting the same battle back in Sanpete.

It was a cold, gray afternoon when Walkara finally reached the north end of the Sanpete Valley. A hard north wind pushed the horses' tails between their hind legs. Because the wind was at their backs, the horses moved easily, without coaxing.

A skiff of snow that had fallen earlier in the day was sifting like white man's flour through the tall yellow grass. Deeper snow covered the nearby hills. The leaves on the cottonwood trees along the river were already on the ground. It seemed more like winter than fall.

There weren't as many horses grazing across the sprawling grasslands as usual. It had not been a good year for horse stealing, plus more than the usual number of animals had been traded to the Mormons.

Even before he reached the first Ute village Walkara knew the measles had arrived ahead of him. On the open, snow-covered hillsides he began seeing lone people, sitting or lying on the ground, motionless and lonely, waiting to begin the long journey to the world of spirits.

Every winter some of the old people who had become mostly useless in village life were put out to die. Walkara had seen in the Mormon community how the old people were pampered and allowed to become burdens long beyond their useful years. He thought the Indian way was better. He didn't want to be a burden on his people when he could no longer hunt or steal horses.

But this year there were not only old people put out to die, but younger people as well, those dying of the dreaded measles. Some were wrapped in old buffalo robes, others in wool blankets. Some waved at him and his men as they rode by. Others just stared blankly.

It was a sad time for his people, a hard time. Even little Battee rode in silence. When they entered the first camp Walkara knew things would get worse. His people were already beginning to eat their horses. Everywhere horse flesh was hanging in the trees, high enough where the dogs could not reach the meat.

It was not uncommon to see a man butcher a horse near the end of winter, but to begin eating horsemeat now was a bad sign. If the winter became a severe one where deep snow prevented hunters from getting very far from camp, all the horses and dogs would be consumed. Even then some of the people might starve. And when spring came there would be no horses to carry the men to the best hunting grounds, or to California to steal more horses.

There was little talk as Walkara rode through the camps that were scattered along the Sevier River. Sometimes women wailed upon seeing his pack animals

263

were not laden with buffalo meat. There was little to talk about.

Walkara remembered Chief Brigham's promise to send Mormon settlers in the fall. There were no Mormons among his people, so he knew Susquenah had not come either. He wished he could just ride through the last camp and keep going to the warm lands of California, where no one had ever heard of measles, where there were plenty of horses to steal and game to eat. But this winter he would not be leaving for California, not with things as tough as they were at home.

His mother, Tishum Igh, was the first to come out to greet him when he reached his own camp. He slipped wearily from his horse. When she greeted the boy with a toothless smile and tried to embrace him, he pulled away from her feeble hold. Walkara did not scold the boy.

Walkara looked closely at his mother. Her hair was almost white. With her teeth gone, the weathered wrinkles in her face seemed deeper and more pronounced. She no longer stood straight and square like healthy people, but slouched forward, her shoulders rounded, as was common with the very old. She had a strong spark of life in her eyes, however.

As Walkara looked at his mother, he remembered her the way she had been, a hard worker, never one to complain, a good wife and mother. She had been a strong woman, especially during difficult times. But now it was time for her to go to the world of spirits. Her old body couldn't take much more. This would be her last winter. He feared this would be the last winter for many of his people.

After greeting his two wives and their five children, Walkara got back on his horse. He intended to visit the rest of the camps. He wanted to see how bad the sickness had become, and how much food there was for the winter. He wanted to encourage the men to hunt as hard as they were able before severe weather set in, making travel impossible.

As Walkara rode among the camps he saw men who were discouraged, women who cried, and children with sad faces. He remembered the previous summer at the fish festival and among the Mormons in their new city. The trading had been good. It seemed his people had become prosperous with plenty of guns, powder, saddles, blankets, cooking pots, knives, hats, and white man's cloth made from wool and cotton. It seemed his people had become rich.

But it wasn't any good to be rich if there was no food to eat, or if a third of the people were sick with measles. Walkara realized the white men had brought a false prosperity. Even with all the new things his people could buy, life seemed harder now than it had been before. Other than telling the men to go hunting, he didn't know what else to say to his people.

The next day Walkara went hunting, by himself. He wanted to be alone, to think about what was happening, to figure out in his mind what could be done to help his people. He needed to fight off the discouragement that seemed to loom over his head like a black rain cloud.

When he returned home two days later he had no new answers, but he carried a young doe over his shoulders. At least there would be meat for a few days.

As the women went to work skinning the deer and preparing an evening meal of venison stew flavored with camas bulbs and dried chokecherries, Walkara crawled to the back of his big tepee. With his back against one of his Spanish saddles, he silently watched his family go about their business. The women were busy with the meal, talking in quiet voices to each other. Two of the girls sat facing each other on a buffalo robe, playing the bone game. Outside he could hear the boys engaged in mock battle with Battee. The smallest child, a two-year-old girl, crawled on Walkara's lap and promptly went to sleep.

Listening to his wives make conversation with each other, he realized he hardly knew them. It was as if he were listening to strangers. He knew what it was like to eat and sleep with them, and to give them orders on those seldom occasions when he was home. He had no idea what they talked about when he was not around, what made them laugh, what they were afraid of, or if they had dreams of things they wanted to do.

He realized that after one trip to buffalo country he knew Battee better than any of his other children. Considered by many the greatest horse thief in the world, he didn't even know his own family.

Maybe it would be better to spend more time at home. He decided he would, if his family survived the coming winter and the measles. So far none of them were sick.

As he watched his mother toss the last few chunks of red meat into the stew, he noticed she had cut her left hand above the thumb. She didn't seem to notice that her blood was running onto the meat and into the black kettle. Walkara didn't say anything. When several pieces of meat fell on the ground beside the kettle, she didn't seem to notice that either.

At first Walkara thought his mother in her old age was getting careless, but suddenly he realized the problem was her eyes. She was losing her eyesight. Her teeth were already gone, and now her eyes were going too. It was time for her to go to the world of spirits.

He wondered if she would wander off into the night on her own, to begin her journey to the world of spirits, or if he would have to force her to do it. He didn't know which way it would be, only that the time to do it was rapidly approaching. It would be easiest and fastest when the nights were bitter cold. They were almost cold enough now. He wondered if she knew her time had come, and if she was ready to go.

After two days of hunting, with nothing more than a little dried meat and corn to eat, Walkara was eagerly anticipating the evening meal. The lodge was now full of the aroma of simmering venison. His mouth began to water.

As one of the women spread the wooden bowls on the ground by the fire in preparation for dishing out the stew, Walkara noticed his mother rummaging through a pack behind the tepee flap. She was looking for salt. Finally finding it she hurried back to the fire, intending to salt the stew before it was dispensed in the dishes.

Misjudging the distance between her feet and the simmering kettle, she accidentally bumped it as she dropped to her knees. The kettle tipped, spilling its contents onto the ashes and dirt. The other women gathered around to help salvage the meat and camas and as much of the juice as possible before it soaked into the ground. With food as scarce as it was there was no thought of throwing out the meal.

With ashes and dirt mixed in, the venison wasn't nearly as good as it would have been, but no one complained. In fact, there was little talk around the fire as everyone dutifully chewed and swallowed their dirty food. Not even the children complained.

Walkara watched his mother tear up the pieces of meat with her fingers before placing them in her toothless mouth. At least she didn't have the unpleasant sensation of teeth grinding on dirt, he thought.

Tishum Igh seemed to notice her son watching her. Almost shamefully, she looked down at her food. She thought she knew what her son, the chief, must be thinking, and she was afraid to look him in the face.

"Old woman," Walkara said, his voice gentle. "I think it is time for you to return to the world of spirits."

It had been quiet in the lodge before, but now there

was total silence. The women looked down at their food, not chewing. The children looked at their mothers. Tishum Igh stared into space. No one seemed surprised. Everyone knew this time would come. The only question had been when.

"My mother," Walkara said. "The time has come for you to go." Still, the women did nothing but look at their food. Tishum Igh made no response.

What Walkara was requesting was nothing new in a Ute lodge. This was the way of his people. When a man or woman became old, the day always came when they went off to die. Today was the day for his mother. It was for him as head man of the lodge to decide, and it was her job to pick up an old buffalo robe or blanket and disappear into the cold night, never to return. Upon finding her frozen body the next morning they would bury her.

"My mother it is time for you to go," Walkara said, repeating his request the third time.

"Katz," she said, emphatically. The word meant no.

"You must go," he said. "There will not be enough food for the children if you stay."

"I can care for the sick," she said. "I can scrape skins and pick berries."

"You have no teeth," he argued, "and soon your eyes will not let you see to scrape hides and pick berries."

"Katz," she said.

Walkara was beginning to feel angry. What he was doing was not easy. She was supposed to obey, and just disappear into the night, but she refused. It wasn't as if he was asking her to do something that had never been done before. When too old to be useful the aged were supposed to go off and die, without argument, without resistance. That was the way.

Tishum Igh had not moved. She still stared straight

268

ahead. She showed no sign of giving in, picking up a robe and disappearing into the frosty night.

Walkara got to his feet and stepped towards her. As he drew near she leaned away from him, raising her arm to the side of her face as if to defend herself against a blow from his fist. He had never struck his mother before. Why did she think he might now? He knew other old people had resisted this same thing before, and he had seen some of them driven away with stones and clubs. He would never treat his mother that way, and it hurt him to have her think he might. Still, she must obey.

Walkara leaned over and picked up his mother, at the same time grabbing a buffalo robe. She offered no resistance. As he stepped towards the door, she looked into his face. As he looked down at her, he could see tears in her eyes. She was silently pleading with him to let her stay. Without letting go of her, he bent over and stepped outside.

He was relieved that it was too dark to see her face anymore. Without speaking he carried her up the hill, away from the river. After going several hundred yards he placed her on the ground gently, her back against a log, and wrapped the robe around her.

"You must stay here," he said. "It is time for you to join my father." She said nothing as he turned and headed back to the tepee.

Walking back, Walkara looked up at the stars. He could feel the icy coldness of his own tears. His chest ached. He didn't understand the hurt and the tears. He had done the right thing. The food that his mother would eat was needed for the children.

Walkara didn't go directly to the lodge, but down by the river, where he relieved himself, waiting a few minutes for his cheeks to dry and the pain in his chest to go away.

When he finally returned to the lodge, the women

were tucking the children in for the night. No one said anything to him. He rolled up in his own robe and closed his eyes. He knew he wouldn't sleep, and hoped one of his women would join him under the warmth of his robe in an attempt to comfort him, but neither did. He spent the night alone, wondering what he might have done differently, and finding no answers.

The next morning, realizing his women still didn't want to speak to him, Walkara decided to ride among the camps again to see how many were down with the sickness.

As he stepped out of the lodge, he had to dodge to one side to avoid stepping on a furry mound. It was Tishum Igh, wrapped in her buffalo robe. During the night she had come down from the hill and rolled up in front of the doorway, like a dog. She was still very much alive. Without a word Walkara picked her up and carried her up the hill to the same place where he had left her the night before. He knew she would go quicker if he took away the buffalo robe, but he could not bring himself to do that.

"My mother, you must stay here," he said, before heading back down the hill to catch his horse.

Chapter 31

Walkara felt a growing melancholy as he rode from camp to camp. Everywhere he saw the victims of measles. Everywhere he saw people eating their horses and dogs. The only source of cheer was a bright sun in a clear blue sky. The snow from the recent storm was beginning to melt. But even the prospect of pleasant weather was dampened by thoughts of his mother sitting out on the hillside against her will, waiting to die.

Walkara felt more helpless than he had ever felt in his life. This late in the year there was little he could do about the food shortage. There was nothing to do about the measles. The further he rode the deeper his melancholy became. He silently offered a prayer to Towats. His people needed help.

A few minutes later as Walkara rode to the top of a gentle swell, his eye caught movement, far to the west, along the horizon. At first he thought he saw a string of white horses strung out single file. No, the objects he saw were larger than horses, but they were definitely white and they were moving.

He could hardly believe his eyes. Nearly fifty of the canvas-topped land canoes, used by white men to carry their belongings, were entering the Sanpete Valley. Chief Brigham had kept his promise. The Mormons had come to settle.

Urging his horse into a full gallop, Walkara raced

271

towards the wagons. Five minutes later he was riding beside the lead wagon, exchanging greetings with Bishop Isaac Morley, leader of the group of 224 settlers. Susquenah was riding on the wagon seat beside Morley. She had helped guide the wagons through the canyon. In Walkara's enthusiasm to tell Morley and his companions about their new home, for a moment at least the Ute chief forgot his earlier troubles.

That night the wagons formed a circle in the gray hills north of where most of the Indian camps were located. Some of the settlers didn't seem very happy. The Sanpete Valley didn't appear as lush as Utah Valley where the Timpanogos Utes lived. The settlers seemed better satisfied when Walkara assured them there was plenty of big timber in the hills, and lots of water for irrigation in the streams.

When Walkara told Morley about the outbreak of measles among his people, the bishop expressed genuine concern and promised to send the elders around to pray over the sick. That evening, as Morley and some of his men headed down the valley to visit the sick, Walkara rode with Susquenah to his lodge. She was eager to see Battee.

It was good to finally be alone with Susquenah. She looked so good, even in a white woman's dress. He liked her better in deer skins, but didn't say anything. She seemed happy, and looked healthy. The stay with the Mormons had been agreeable to her.

"Did you learn to read the Mormonee book?" he asked. "The one with the story of our ancestors

"Yes," she responded. "And I would like to read it to you."

"I would like that," he said.

"I believe the words of the book," she said. "Bishop Morley baptized me in a river. I am a Mormonee."

Walkara gave her a concerned look. "But you still

came," he said, fearing that her new religion might somehow prevent her from being his squaw again.

"I am still an Indian," she said, "and you are still the only man I have ever loved."

Walkara was surprised at her boldness. He felt his heart pound in his chest. He had feared he would never hear such words from Susquenah again. She still loved him.

"I will get a second lodge," he said. "We are already too crowded."

"I will want to worship with the Mormonees," she said. "I will want to read the book to you."

"That is fine."

"What about the slaves and the horse stealing?" she asked.

Walkara remained silent, remembering that it was at this point in earlier conversations that their efforts to get back together had always failed. He didn't want her to leave. At the same time, he knew that many horses would have to be eaten during the winter to keep the people from starvation. Come spring, the men would want to replenish the herds, and the best ways to do that were to trade slaves and steal. That was the way of his people. He couldn't think of any way to handle her question, so he changed the subject.

"Battee is a brave boy," he said. "He swam his horse through a rapid in the Sis-kee-dee River. He did not cry. Chasing big bucks, we galloped our horses down through some rocky ledges. He was very brave."

"He was ready to ride with his father and do brave things," Susquenah said. "But what about the slaves and horse stealing?"

"I love you as much as any man ever loved a woman," he said in earnest. "I don't understand how you can ask me to give up what I am."

"You don't need to make people your slaves," she said, her voice beginning to sound angry.

"If I agree to stop catching and selling slaves, will you look the other way if I bring home a few Spanish or Shoshone horses?" he asked, attempting to reach some sort of compromise.

"Yes," she said. "I'll agree to that." Walkara was surprised at the promptness of her response.

"Then you have come home to stay?" he asked.

"Yes," she said simply.

Walkara reached over and, taking her by the hand, pulled Susquenah from her horse, at the same time dismounting himself. He drew her gently to him, kissing her tenderly on the mouth. She slipped her arms around his neck, running her fingers through his hair. He began kissing her on the neck and shoulder, his hands running down her sides over the gentle swell of her hips. She tightened her hold on his neck, pulling him closer. They had been apart too long.

An hour later they reached his camp. It was dark. Battee ran out to greet his mother, telling her about his great adventure into buffalo country, crossing the Siskee-dee River, chasing the deer.

When they entered the lodge, Walkara announced to everyone that Susquenah had come home to stay. The other women didn't offer an enthusiastic welcome, knowing Walkara loved Susquenah more than he did them. They were polite, but cool, knowing they had no choice but to accept a new squaw. Susquenah continued to be cheerful, fully understanding how the other women felt.

"Where is Tishum Igh?" Susquenah asked as she began to put her things away.

"Up on the hill, waiting to die," Battee blurted out.

"You sent her away?" she asked Walkara.

"Night before last," he said. "She didn't want to go."

"I'm sorry," she said.

"Tomorrow I will find us a new lodge," he said, changing the subject. "It is too crowded in this one." Everyone agreed that would be a good thing to do.

The next morning, while the women began cutting and peeling new lodge poles, Walkara mounted his horse and set out to find a new tepee. He was leading a pack horse, and Battee accompanied him. If he couldn't find a lodge that could be purchased, Walkara intended to get enough buffalo skins to make one.

When he returned in mid afternoon, the pack horse was carrying the new lodge. Walkara had traded two horses for it. Although it was a little smaller than the old one, it would be a suitable second dwelling.

As the women and children went to work erecting the new tepee, Walkara stepped into the old lodge and gathered up some of the things that belonged to his mother—a comb, a spare pair of moccasins, a pouch containing blue beads, and a bone sewing needle. When he buried Tishum Igh, he intended to bury these possessions with her so she could take them along on her journey to the world of spirits.

Stepping out of the tepee, he headed up the hill to where he had carried his mother the previous morning. It was time to bury her, he thought.

Approaching the spot where he had placed Tishum Igh on the ground, he could see the buffalo robe—a motionless, furry lump. He could not see any part of his mother, not her face, not even a hand. She was totally covered by the robe.

Upon reaching the hide, he nudged it gently with his toe to make sure she was still there. Feeling the firmness of flesh against his toe, he dropped to his knees and pulled back the edge of the robe, fully expecting to find the cold, shriveled up body of what had once been his mother.

Instead he saw two black, fiery eyes glaring back at him—but only for an instant, because a leathery,

275

wrinkled hand jerked the edge of the hide back over her face.

Walkara stood up and took a step backwards. Tishum Igh had been out in the cold two freezing nights. She had not eaten in nearly two days. She should be dead. One more night would do the job. He would come back to bury her the next day.

He turned to leave, then stopped. Though he knew he was doing the right thing, he felt terrible, like he would die if he walked back to camp now, once again deserting the woman who gave him birth, who nursed him, who raised and loved him.

He turned back towards the furry mound, and once again dropped to his knees. He pulled back the edge of the hide, this time continuing to hold onto it so she couldn't pull it back over her face. This time her eyes were closed.

"Old woman," he said, "would you like a drink of water or something to eat?"

Her eyes opened and they began to fill with tears.

"Come back to camp with me," he said. "We have a new lodge. Susquenah has come to stay. We have fresh venison."

"I don't have the strength to walk," she whispered, her voice more frail than her eyes.

"Then I will carry you," he said, slipping his arms gently under her fragile body and picking her up.

"Old woman," he muttered as he started down the hill, "you may stay in my lodge as long as you wish. Walkara will never again put his mother out to die."

Chapter 32

If Walkara had had any doubts about the friendly intentions of the Mormons, they all disappeared upon the arrival of Bishop Morley. First the elders went among his people, saying prayers over the sick. Then came the Mormon women with their home remedies, hot tea and fresh biscuits. They had brought just enough food to get themselves through the winter. Still, they insisted on sharing with the hungry Utes.

A few days after the arrival of the Mormon settlers, one of Brigham Young's apostles, Parley Pratt, arrived with 50 men. Pratt was leading an exploration party towards the southern part of the territory to find additional settlement locations for the Mormons.

Pratt was moved to tears when he saw the plight of Walkara's people. Instantly he ordered his men to break out sacks of flour, sides of bacon, and other supplies needed for his journey south. Walkara followed Pratt from camp to camp as the energetic white man blessed the sick and gave freely of his supplies without any thought of being paid back. Walkara was moved by Pratt's concern for the Utes.

Upon reaching Arrapeen's camp, Walkara thought for a moment Pratt might change his mind about being so kind to the Utes. One of Arrapeen's daughters had just died from the measles, and burial preparations were underway. The child was dressed in her finest white deerskin clothing, and had been placed in an open pit when Pratt and Walkara arrived.

The Mormon apostle watched in amazement as a Paiute slave boy led the girl's favorite pony into the pit and held it there while Arrapeen shot it through the head so it could be buried with his daughter.

Pratt's amazement soon changed to horror. No sooner had the horse dropped to the ground than Arrapeen fired a second bullet into the boy who had led the horse into the pit. Before the boy even stopped his death spasms, Arrapeen stretched him out on the ground beside the girl, a companion to accompany her to the world of spirits, along with her horse and other belongings.

Stunned, but undaunted in his Christian duty, Pratt continued to share his supplies with the red men. A few days after his arrival among the Utes, Pratt resumed his journey south. Walkara's brother, Ammon, accompanied Pratt as guide.

After Pratt was gone, the winter storms swept down on the Sanpete Valley, burying Mormons and Indians in deep, white snow. Also buried was the grass that kept the oxen and horses alive. While the Indians cut down cottonwood limbs so their horses could chew off the sweet inner bark, the Mormons went to work shoveling snow off the grass so their animals could eat. This work was hard, and the progress slow, but it kept the animals alive.

In their continuing kindness the Mormons invited the Indian families who had sick among them to move their lodges closer to the Mormon camp, enabling the white women to do more for the sick.

Walkara liked Bishop Morley, a man who loved to roll up his sleeves and help people. He didn't just talk about it. And his people followed his example. Walkara had to admit, at least to himself, that with the help of the Mormons his people would survive the winter much better than they would without the Mormons.

Walkara spent an increasing amount of time at Morley's hastily built cabin. The kindly bishop always had time for Walkara. Morley told the chief about the Book of Mormon, which contained the religious history of the Utes and other Indians who in the book were called Lamanites.

The book told how, thousands of years earlier, Lamanite forefathers crossed the great oceans to the American continent. It told how the people built a great civilization, about their wars and conflicts, about great men who lived among them, and eventually how they divided into two warring groups, the one wiping out the other. It told how the Mormon god, Jesus Christ, visited the people in America after his crucifixion in the old world. The book was named after a great general and prophet, one of the last men to write in the sacred record.

Morley told Walkara how an angel had given the sacred record, inscribed on gold plates, to a young man in New York state named Joseph Smith. The young man had translated the records with the help of God so the Book of Mormon could be published. Smith then founded the Church of Jesus Christ of Latter-day Saints. The word "Mormon" was a nickname. Smith received vigorous persecution from other churches, which eventually led to the murder of Smith and the forced departure of his people from the east to the land of the Utes.

In addition to telling Walkara about the book, Morley read passages to the Ute chief. To Walkara, reading seemed a miracle. He was amazed that Susquenah had learned so quickly what appeared so difficult. He hoped someday he would learn to read too. He thought the ability to read probably had something to do with the successes and accomplishments of white men—Mormons and Mericats alike.

Morley also read from another sacred book called the Bible. He taught Walkara about Jesus Christ, the great one the Mormons called the redeemer and savior of the world. Morley told Walkara how Christ had taught his followers to love their enemies—and that it was wrong to steal horses, take scalps, and catch slaves. Upon hearing these doctrines, Walkara understood why Susquenah had embraced the Mormon faith so quickly. She had believed these things all along.

Morley told Walkara that Christ wanted those who believed in him to be baptized in water. When Walkara explained that he had already baptized himself and his men in the Jordan River in Great Salt Lake City, Morley tried to explain that only those with the authority or priesthood from God could perform such ordinances.

Much of the doctrine seemed sensible to Walkara, and that which didn't, he didn't argue about. He found it difficult to argue with people who were taking care of the sick and sharing their food.

In his visits to the Mormons, Walkara could see they were running out of food too, but still they continued to share with the Utes. Walkara was moved by these strange, kind white people. As the winter progressed, he wanted more and more to be like them, and he received much encouragement from Susquenah.

She told him that when he became a Mormon and accepted the gospel, she would want him to live like Jesus. Walkara would no longer kill, steal, or drink whiskey. He would lay down his rifle, and pick up a shovel. With work he would grow his own food. He would stay home and be a good father to his children, and a good husband to his wives. He would learn to read the sacred books, and he would pray every day. His life would be happy and peaceful. Everyone would love Walkara. He would be a great missionary.

The new life sounded good. Maybe Susquenah was right. With the coming of the Mormons and other white men the world around him was changing. Perhaps it was time that he change too. The Christian life sounded better to him every day.

One warm afternoon near the end of winter, after all the snow on the valley floor had melted, Morley finished reading Walkara a chapter out of the Bible. The bishop then invited the chief to offer a prayer.

Walkara admitted he had prayed to Towats on many occasions, but never to the Mormon god. He was hesitant to offer the prayer, not sure about communicating with the new Mormon god.

"He will hear your prayer and if you have faith he will answer it," Morley promised.

"Why would he answer my prayer?" Walkara asked.

"Knock and it shall be opened, ask and ye shall receive," Morley said, apparently quoting from one of the sacred books. "Try to pray, and I promise you your prayer will be answered."

"If I ask for a thousand Spanish horses, your god will give them to me?" Walkara asked.

"I've never heard of anyone asking for something like that before," Morley said. "He may not answer such a prayer, perhaps because it is too selfish. Try asking for something that will help others instead of yourself."

"That will be easy," Walkara said, lowering his head and closing his eyes in preparation to pray.

"God, bring us food," he prayed. "We are eating our best horses. We need them for hunting and for travel. Give my people and the Mormonees something to eat besides horse flesh, and please do it by tomorrow. Amen."

Walkara opened his eyes and looked up at Morley. "Was the prayer all right?"

"Usually we let the Lord pick his own timetable for performing miracles," Morley said. "Also, you might have given thanks as part of the prayer. Otherwise it was fine."

"I shouldn't have asked him to bring us food tomorrow?" Walkara asked.

"People aren't normally that specific in prayers," the bishop responded.

"Why not?" Walkara asked.

"Perhaps so they won't be disappointed if the prayer is not answered."

"You don't think the Lord will answer my prayer?" Walkara asked.

Morley hesitated, wondering why Indians couldn't understand simple concepts like prayer.

"Yes, I believe the Lord could send a lot of food tomorrow, enough so no more horses would have to be killed."

"Then why was it wrong to ask him to do it?" Walkara asked.

Morley was stumped. He didn't know what else to say. Deer and elk were gone from the nearby hills. Buffalo were hundreds of miles away. Deep snow still blocked the passes leading to the Utah and Salt Lake valleys where the rest of the Mormons lived. The prospect of new food becoming available the next day was highly unlikely, if not impossible.

"God might need more than one day to provide us with a new source of food," Morley suggested.

"You said God could do anything, that nothing is impossible to him."

"I said that," Morley confessed.

"Finding food for us so we don't have to kill anymore horses shouldn't be very hard for God," Walkara added, turning for the door. It seemed the man he looked up to most didn't have as much faith as he had supposed. Maybe this Mormon god wasn't as powerful as everyone said he was. He would find out the next day if this new god could answer his prayer. It would be good to have something besides horse meat in the cooking pots.

It was dark when Walkara arrived back at his own camp. From the way Susquenah raced out of the tepee to greet him, he knew something was wrong.

"Tishum Igh is gone," she cried. "As sick as she was she couldn't have gone far."

There was no moon. Walkara could hardly see the ground in front of his feet. Getting off his horse and turning it loose, he began walking in an ever-widening circle around the camp, looking for his mother. When he called her name there was no answer.

Tishum Igh had been one of the last to come down with the measles. Her temperature hadn't been as high, or the rash as bad, but she just didn't seem to have the strength to get well. The sickness seemed to linger in her, making her weaker and weaker. He was surprised she had found the strength to leave the camp.

He walked down by the river, then up the hill to the place where he had put her out to die the previous fall. He could not find her. Finally, he returned to the camp, telling his family they would resume the search in the morning.

At first light he headed back up the hill to the same spot where he had looked the night before. This time she was there, wrapped loosely in an old buffalo robe. Apparently she had been hiding from him the night before.

But she could not hide now. Her partially-covered body was still and cold. Tishum Igh had already begun her journey to the world of spirits.

Gently Walkara wrapped her snugly in the robe and carried her to the top of the hill. Even though he was rapidly accepting the doctrines of the Mormons, he intended to give his mother a proper Indian burial. On the crest of the hill he found a little clearing from which there was a beautiful view of the valley. He placed her on the ground, then returned to camp to gather up some of her belongings to be buried with her.

The rest of the family returned with Walkara to the top of the hill. While he and Battee scraped out a hole with the help of digging sticks, the women dressed Tishum Igh in a new deerskin dress. She was wrapped with her belongings in the buffalo robe, then placed in the bottom of the hole.

Walkara covered her with dirt and rocks. It was not a sad burial. It was finally time for her to go, and she had gone voluntarily, without being forced out of the lodge. Walkara felt good. He was glad he had brought her back the first time, when she was not ready to die.

Walkara did not place any kind of marker on the grave. Because it was customary to bury people with their most valuable possessions, some people would rob the graves. As a result, burial places were usually unmarked.

That afternoon Walkara rode back to Bishop Morley's. A half mile from the Mormon settlement, the Ute chief could tell something was wrong. He could see men striking at the ground with long sticks. He could hear people shouting and screaming. At first he thought the men were preparing some of the ground for planting, but that didn't explain why the people were so excited and making so much noise.

As Walkara continued to ride closer he began to laugh. He knew what had happened. His prayer had been answered. A new source of food was crawling out of the sun-warmed rocks. Unknowingly the Mormons had set up their winter camp beside a hibernating bed for rattlesnakes. The warming rays of the spring sun were bringing hundreds of rattlesnakes out of their winter resting places. The Mormons were killing them with shovels, hoes and long sticks and throwing the dead serpents in a huge pile.

"Throw them in a wagon and I will take them

around to my people," Walkara said to Morley.

"What do they want snakes for?" Morley asked.

"To eat," Walkara responded.

"But they're poisonous."

"The meat is delicious."

Morley called to a man to hitch up a wagon.

"Then I guess your prayer has been answered,"Morley grinned. Walkara nodded his agreement.

Chapter 33

On March 13, 1850, Walkara and Arrapeen waded into the icy creek at Manti and were baptized by Bishop Morley. Coming out of the water Walkara announced that he had given up horse stealing, scalping, capturing slaves and drinking whiskey. He was now a good Indian. He intended to live like Jesus. He said he intended to feed his family by farming. Bishop Morley would teach him how to do it. He said that in time he would even build log tepees or cabins for his families. He said he was starting reading lessons, so he too would be able to read the holy books. Walkara, the greatest horse thief the Utes had ever known, had laid down his weapons and turned his horses out to pasture.

The Mormons were delighted over the conversion of Walkara, or Walker as they called him. They guessed that once the chief had entered the waters of baptism others would follow. They were right. In the weeks following Walkara's conversion, dozens more were baptized—men, women and children. It appeared, at least to the Mormons, that the Utes and Mormons in the Sanpete Valley had taken a big step towards joining ranks to become a single God-fearing people with common goals, dreams and life-styles.

After his baptism Walkara fully expected to enter a new era of happiness and prosperity. Susquenah shared his optimism. He had never seen her happier.

Chapter 33

At first the only problem was Battee. When he wasn't in school learning to read, write and figure, he was helping his father clear farmland and dig irrigation ditches. He preferred Walkara's old life-style—swimming rivers, chasing deer and buffalo, stealing horses. The poor boy couldn't even get his father to take him hunting or fishing.

Walkara didn't admit it to Battee or anyone else, at least at first, but he didn't like clearing land and digging ditches either. He wondered why it was that a man tough enough to ride a horse to California in 20 days found it so difficult to spend two or three days on the business end of a Mormon shovel. At first he thought he might get used to the hard work. The blisters on his hands healed, and the soreness in his back and arms eventually went away. Still, he found little satisfaction in the endless ditch digging and land clearing.

Some of the Mormons liked to sing while they worked. Not Walkara. He could only wonder why he had given up the exciting life of stealing horses in California and raiding Shoshone villages for this. Instead of learning to like white man's work, he was learning to hate it. But he said nothing, thinking that perhaps with time his thinking would change.

There were other problems. Word of Walkara's conversion spread to the other Ute bands. The great war chief had laid down his weapons. Walkara was no longer a man to be feared. Indians who formerly walked softly and behaved mildly to avoid the great Walkara's wrath, now felt free to do as they pleased.

Walkara's half-brother, Antonguer, launched a brutal assault on the Mormons at Fort Utah. Members of Walkara's own band began stealing Mormon cattle right from under his nose at Manti. Patsowett had invaded Great Salt Lake City, stealing and killing cattle. Walkara's cousins, Unkerwenkent and Tishunah, went

287

to work stealing Mormon cattle and horses at many locations.

Brigham Young was surprised at the increase in hostile activity on the part of the Utes. He had thought that when Walkara was baptized into the fold, troubles between the Mormons and the Utes would cease, or at least decrease. The opposite was happening. Indians formerly controlled by the powerful Walkara now felt like they had been cut free. The waters of baptism had neutralized Walkara's power as a peacekeeper. The other Indians now felt free to go against the Mormons without fear of reprisals from Walkara.

Brigham Young didn't understand what had happened. Whenever Patsowett, Antonguer, Tishunah or Unkerwenkent launched some kind of raid against the Mormons, the Mormon chief sent a messenger to Walkara asking first for explanations, then for assistance in putting a stop to the new violence of red men against whites. The Mormon leader urged Walkara to use his influence to keep the peace.

"Why do you let your people do these things?" Young would ask in his letters. Walkara's response was always the same, that the only control he had ever had over the 50 or so bands of Utes was the fear some had of his ability to split heads with his battle axe. With baptism and trying to live the Christian life he had given up the inclination to split heads. The respect he once enjoyed was gone. Now the other Indians did as they pleased, content the once powerful Walkara was off in the woods praying or reading the Book of Mormon.

Walkara, through the interpreters and messengers, tried to explain things to Chief Brigham, but Young didn't seem to understand, because every time a new act of hostility occurred against the Mormons, the inevitable messenger was sent to Sanpete to ask Walkara why he was allowing his people to do such things.

The boredom of the constant ditch digging and the

frustration of not being able to keep fellow Utes in line began to wear on Walkara. The new life was supposed to be simple and happy. Instead it presented a combination of boring work and frustration. Every time a messenger arrived from Great Salt Lake City it was as if Chief Brigham were questioning Walkara's faithfulness.

One Sunday afternoon Walkara decided he could not remain silent any longer. He went to see Bishop Morley. They walked together along the stream while Walkara attempted to explain his frustration.

"Men are that they might have joy," Morley insisted, quoting from the Book of Mormon."

"I used to have joy riding my horse to California," Walkara said. "I found joy sneaking into a Shoshone camp and stealing their horses. I found joy in chasing deer and buffalo across the open prairies. I find no joy behind a plow or shovel."

Walkara continued. "There is no joy in watching bad Indians steal Mormon cattle, and not being able to punish them."

"Be patient," Morley advised. "Someday you will be happy to dig a ditch, and the bad Indians will be gone."

"Is it because I am doing something wrong that I am not happy now?" Walkara asked.

"Some things take time," Morley said, sounding wise.

"Some things take too much time," Walkara added in frustration.

They stopped beside the stream. Walkara pushed his loincloth aside to relieve himself. Morley had the same urge and began to unbutton his trousers.

"Why is it you are different?" Walkara asked when they were finished. At first Morley didn't know what Walkara was asking.

"The skin," Walkara explained. "It has been cut away."

Suddenly Morley knew what Walkara was talking about. The Indian wanted to know why the bishop was circumcised. Morley didn't have his Bible with him to read out of, so he just told Walkara how in the book of Genesis God commanded Abraham and the men with him to be circumcised as a token or sign of the covenant God had made with Abraham.

"Are all the Mormonees circumcised?" Walkara asked.

"I think so."

"Were Jesus, John the Baptist, and Paul? How about Nephi, Moroni and Mormon?"

"I'm sure they all were."

"Then why aren't the Yutahs?"

"I think baptism is enough."

"I feel like a secret is being kept from me and my people," Walkara complained. "Today I find out that every Mormonee and every prophet in the holy scriptures has been circumcised, and you tell me it is not important for me and my people to be circumcised too. Why not?"

"I don't know," Morley admitted.

"I don't like digging your ditches and clearing the land," Walkara said. "I don't like reading your books, and sitting for hours in your meetings. The baptism was supposed to change me, turn me into a Jesus, but inside I am still Walkara, Iron Twister, Hawk of the Mountains, the greatest horse thief of them all. I still have a deep thirst for whiskey. I am not a Jesus, no matter how hard I try. None of the other warriors are, either. What is wrong?"

"I don't know," Morley said. He had never had a convert to his religion talk like this before. He didn't know how to respond. The brutal honesty of his Indian friend was unsettling.

"If I be circumcised—you say it is a token of the covenant with God—would that make a difference?"

"I don't know."

"Maybe we should find out."

"Maybe we should."

The next Sunday Walkara called a special meeting for all the Ute men who had joined the Mormon Church. He didn't tell them why he called the meeting, only that it was mandatory that they attend. Also present were Susquenah and Peg Leg, who had come to the valley a few days earlier to buy some horses. Bishop Morley was there too.

When everyone was present, Walkara didn't waste any time with preliminaries like prayers and songs. He asked Susquenah to read from the book of Genesis where God told Abraham, not only to circumcise himself, but every man in his camp.

"Abraham, Isaac and Jacob were circumcised," Walkara said, when she had finished reading. "So were Jesus and John the Baptist, as well and Nephi and Moroni, and Joseph Smith and Brigham Young. All of us should have it done too. Any questions?"

"Sounds like a good idea," Arrapeen said. Every man nodded his agreement.

"But what does it mean, this circumcision?" Arrapeen asked. Others indicated they would like that question answered too.

Rather than attempt an explanation, Walkara asked Bishop Morley to open the front of his trousers and show them. The bishop refused. Walkara didn't under stand why. About this time Susquenah decided it was time for her to leave. Quietly she picked up her things and disappeared into her tepee.

Walkara then turned to Peg Leg, hoping his trapper friend would show the Utes what it meant to be circumcised. Happy to accommodate, Peg Leg unbuttoned his trousers and showed his surprised Ute friends what it meant to be circumcised.

"Who will be first?" Walkara asked, drawing a long skinning knife from his belt. There were no volunteers. On the contrary, several of the men were beginning to back away, apparently hoping for a convenient opportunity to get out of Walkara's sight as quickly as possible.

"Who will be first?" Walkara asked a second time. Still there were no takers.

"Perhaps you should set the example," Morley suggested, looking at Walkara. The men stopped backing up, thinking it might be interesting to watch.

"I got some whiskey to douse away the infection," Peg Leg offered, drawing a tin of firewater from inside his shirt. Grinning from ear to ear, the old trapper was the only one enjoying the proceedings.

"Arrapeen, why don't you be first?" Walkara said. "I will do the cutting."

"I agree with the bishop," Arrapeen responded. "You should be the example."

Arrapeen wasn't about to be first, and he didn't think Walkara wanted to do it either. In fact, for Arrapeen and the others, the idea of circumcision had been dropped on them pretty fast, and none of them was sure he wanted any part of it now that he knew what it meant.

What they didn't understand was that Walkara had been thinking about it all week, and was mentally prepared to go ahead regardless of what the others thought about it.

"I be first, then," Walkara said confidently. Pushing his loincloth to one side he pulled his foreskin forward, then with a quick sweeping motion of the skinning knife he sliced off the front half-inch or so of the foreskin. He was finished almost before anyone realized he had begun. As the blood began to flow Peg Leg doused his handkerchief in whiskey and handed it to Walkara, who quickly daubed the wound with the stinging whiskey.

Allowing his loincloth to fall back into place, covering his bleeding wound, Walkara motioned for Arrapeen to come forward. Walkara's brother hesitated. It was one thing to get baptized, quite another to be circumcised.

Walkara held the knife in front of his face, running his thumb slowly along the sharp edge of the blade.

Arrapeen realized this was probably one of those times when it would be better not to argue with Walkara. He stepped forward and pulled aside his loincloth. Pulling his foreskin forward, he held it unflinchingly as Walkara sliced downward with the skinning knife. Because the knife was razor-sharp and moved quickly, Arrapeen didn't notice any pain until the job was finished. He grabbed Peg Leg's whiskey-soaked handkerchief and wiped himself. Before a half hour had passed Walkara had circumcised 22 men and boys, including Battee, who saved the foreskins for Walkara by stretching them over the end of a peeled willow stick.

When he was finished Walkara held the willow stick high above his head, saying, "A sign and a token to Chief Brigham and to Jesus that Yutah warriors are good Mormonees."

"I'll say amen to that," Morley said.

"I'd like to see the official report on this you send to Salt Lake," Peg Leg said to Morley.

"There won't be any," the bishop replied.

"May the circumcision make us better Mormonees," Walkara shouted, holding the stick high above his head.

"I'll drink to that," Peg Leg said, taking a deep swallow from his tin of whiskey.

Chapter 34

Walkara and his fellow converts were too sore to help with the ditch digging and land clearing for several days. When they finally returned to work, they found the rite of circumcision didn't make the work any more enjoyable than it had been before. Spring had arrived in the Sanpete Valley, and Walkara longed to be on the trail again, astride a strong, eager horse. He longed to be on his way to hunt, steal horses, catch slaves, trade—anything but digging ditches and clearing land.

Quite unexpectedly the opportunity presented itself for him to get on a horse and leave. Several weeks earlier Bishop Morley had told Walkara about the great temple, or house of the Lord, that the Mormons were going to build in their new city by the lake of salt.

The temple would be the most majestic and inspiring structure any Indian and most white men had ever seen, Morley said. There would be stone pillars, taller than the tallest trees, reaching to heaven, windows of colored glass, and a great organ to play music such as could be heard only in the world of spirits.

On top of the highest pillar would be a life-size statue of the angel Moroni blowing a golden trumpet. Moroni would be made of gold too, real gold.

"Where will Chief Brigham get enough gold to do that?" Walkara asked.

"I don't know," Morley said, "only that when

Brigham Young says it will be so, it usually is. Maybe he will freight it in from the gold fields in California.''

"I know where there is enough gold to make a statue of a man," Walkara said.

Morley looked at him suspiciously, not saying anything. The bishop was reluctant to believe such an impossible claim.

Walkara removed the medicine pouch that was hanging around his neck and opened it. He picked out a gold nugget, one he had picked up in Victorio's cave. He handed it to the startled bishop.

Morley carefully inspected the nugget. It was smooth and heavy. He had no doubts about it being real.

"Where did you get this?" he asked.

"Not very far from here, in a cave, a three-day ride," Walkara responded.

"How much is there?"

"Plenty to make a statue of Moroni, and the trumpet too."

"Can I have this nugget?" Morley asked. "I want to send it to Brigham Young."

"Yes."

Walkara forgot about the conversation and the nugget, but Morley didn't. He immediately dispatched a letter by special messenger to Brigham Young. The nugget was enclosed with the letter.

Two weeks later Thomas Rhodes arrived in Manti. He had been in Salt Lake on business, delivering a shipment of gold from California, when Morley's letter arrived. Rhodes had come to Manti on special assignment from Brigham Young.

"President Young would like to know if you will make the whereabouts of the gold known to the church," Rhodes said to Walkara, not wasting any time getting down to business.

"I might," Walkara said, cautiously.

"What are the conditions?" Rhodes asked, his purpose intense. Walkara could feel the strength of the man.

"What do you mean when you say conditions?" Walkara asked.

"What must happen between us for you to agree to take me to the gold?" Rhodes asked. Here was a white man who didn't waste any time getting to the point. Walkara liked the directness of Rhodes.

"The Apache who showed me the gold said three ancient ones told him it could not be used to make war, that it was sacred gold to be used only for sacred purposes," Walkara said.

"If you show me where the gold is," Rhodes said, "I give you my word none of it will be used to make war, only to build the kingdom of God, and one statue on top of the new temple."

"You can't speak for Brigham Young."

"I will make sure he understands the conditions and agrees to them before I give him the gold."

"You make a lot of promises," Walkara said. "Many white men make promises they don't keep. How can I know you are different?"

Rhodes turned and walked away, thoughtfully rubbing his chin between his thumb and forefinger. Walkara seated himself cross-legged on the ground near the door of his lodge, patiently waiting for the white man to gather his thoughts.

Walkara remembered the Apache, Victorio, who had been told by the three ancient ones that Walkara would come to the cave. There had been something deeply mysterious, even spiritual, in the experience, like Walkara's medicine dream. He didn't know who the ancient ones were, only that they had known the new name given him by Towats. The whereabouts of the mine and the gold was not to be taken lightly, and not to be revealed to just anyone.

"We could become brothers," Rhodes said, suddenly turning around and facing the Indian. "We could become the kind of brothers who could trust each other with anything we had—our money, our wives, our horses, our very lives."

"That would be good," Walkara said. He liked the strong talk, the boldness of this man Rhodes.

"How could we become brothers?" Rhodes asked.

"A season ago I would have asked you to ride with me to California. We would steal Spanish horses. Then we would go east to kill buffalo and bring home much meat. A season on the trail would make us brothers."

"There is not enough time for that," Rhodes said.

Walkara wondered if he persisted in trying to live like white men if he would become like them, to the point where he would always be in a hurry too. Time always seemed very important to white men.

"Could I give you something of mine to put in your medicine pouch?" Rhodes asked. The request surprised Walkara. His medicine bundle contained only personal items, each with a special significance.

"I can't think of anything you might have that I would want in my medicine bundle," Walkara responded. "I can't think of anything you could give me that would make us brothers."

"What about this?" Rhodes asked, lifting up his right foot and pulling off his boot. Walkara watched with interest as the white man removed his stocking, then dropped to his left knee, the bare right foot on the ground in front of him.

Rhodes looked up at Walkara as he drew a knife from a sheath on his belt. Then, looking down at his foot he carefully placed the pointed end of the blade upon the joint of his second toe. Without any explanation or pause, he thrust downward with the blade, cutting off the end of the toe.

"Put this in your medicine bundle," Rhodes said,

picking up the end of the toe and handing it to Walkara. "Take this toe to remind you that in Thomas Rhodes you have a true friend, a man willing to sacrifice his own body to prove his friendship."

"I accept your gift and your friendship," Walkara said, impressed by the white man's actions. Walkara removed the medicine bundle from his neck and placed Rhodes' toe inside it. Placing the bundle around his neck once again, he looked back at Rhodes.

"What will you give me as an emblem of your friendship and loyalty?" Rhodes asked. At first Walkara thought of cutting off a toe too, but then he had a better idea. He ducked into his tepee, returning a minute later with the smooth willow stick, the one containing 23 partially dried rings of skin. He removed one of the rings of skin and handed it to Rhodes.

"I give you my foreskin," Walkara said, "the token of my covenant with God."

"I will carry it with me until the day I die," Rhodes said, removing a leather pouch from his pocket and carefully placing the foreskin inside of it.

"My brother, are there any other conditions before you take me to the gold?" Rhodes asked.

"I have concern about other white men you will take with you to get the gold," Walkara said. "I fear they will become greedy like the California goldseekers."

"No one else will come with me to the mine," Rhodes said. "No one else will know where it is, not even Brigham Young. I give you my word of honor."

Walkara looked at Rhodes. He liked this white man, and he felt that even though they had known each other only a short hour, this Thomas Rhodes could be trusted.

"I will take you to the gold in the morning," Walkara said.

"Good. What tools will we need to take along for digging?"

"No tools. Only strong leather bags to carry the gold."

The next morning Walkara and Thomas Rhodes headed for Victorio's gold mine. Rhodes hadn't slept. It wasn't the excitement of getting to go to the mine that had kept him awake, but the pain from the bloody stub that had once been the second toe on his right foot. Walkara hadn't slept much either, glad he was finally free of ditch digging and land clearing, at least for a while. It felt good getting on a horse again, to be heading out on another great adventure.

Chapter 35

Walkara never enjoyed a journey more than the one with Rhodes to the gold mine. While Rhodes told Walkara about the lawless gold camps of Northern California, Walkara returned tales of the magnificent Spanish haciendas in Southern California, and how much he enjoyed stealing the horses that roamed there.

Upon reaching the cave it didn't take them longer than just a few hours to load up enough gold to satisfy Thomas Rhodes. The yellow metal had already been mined by some ancient race of people, and stacked in leather pouches for someone to come and take, but that someone had never come. Much of the gold had spilled as the leather pouches had rotted and fallen apart. The gold was in the form of nuggets and dust, indicating the ore had probably been washed in the stream down the hill, then carried back to the cave.

They filled enough leather pouches to make a heavy load for one horse. Walkara reminded Rhodes of the warning he had received from the Apache, that the gold could not be used in making war, only for sacred purposes. Rhodes promised he would make that very clear to Brigham Young.

"This ought to give Brigham's new economy a healthy leg up," Rhodes said when they finally had the horse loaded. "It will provide enough gold plating for an entire stature of Moroni too."

Walkara would have liked to stay around a few days, explore the depths of the cave, and perhaps do some hunting, but as usual Rhodes was in a hurry. After traveling the first day of the homeward journey together, Rhodes announced he was going to head straight for Salt Lake, instead of going the long way through Sanpete. Walkara offered to accompany him to the Mormon city, but Rhodes insisted that was not necessary.

"Don't worry about the gold, and take good care of my toe," Rhodes said as he rode out of sight, leading the heavily loaded pack horse.

Walkara thought that perhaps he should feel uneasy watching the white man ride off with so much gold. But he didn't. He trusted Rhodes. The gold would be used for a good purpose, as the ancient ones intended. He wished he had asked Rhodes about the ancient ones. Perhaps there was something written about them in the sacred book. He decided he would ask Bishop Morley when he arrived home.

It occurred to Walkara that since he was now living the peaceful life, perhaps it would be all right to go back to the cave and get some gold for himself. He wouldn't be using it to make war. With a sack of gold to buy food and horses, he wouldn't have to work so hard digging ditches and clearing land. He decided that maybe he would go back in the fall. He would try the white man's hard work a while longer. Perhaps he would learn to like it. He didn't know how, but he had to keep trying.

As he entered the Sanpete Walkara was proud to see the face of the land changing. Fat cattle with calves at their sides were grazing in the foothills. In the valley, the first green blades of Mormon wheat were pushing up through the carefully leveled and tilled soil. Young fruit trees with pole fences around them were beginning to get leaves. Everywhere log cabins and barns were being erected. He had seen some miracles since meeting the

Mormons, but the biggest of all was the amount of work these religious people were able to accomplish.

Upon reaching the first group of farmers working in their new fields, he realized something was wrong. Each man had a rifle at his side. The men picked up their rifles as Walkara approached.

The chief was annoyed. Certainly by now they knew who he was, a fellow Mormon, their newest convert, and a very important one at that. The Mormons continued to hold their guns at readiness as Walkara approached. Walkara asked them what was wrong.

They said a Brother Baker from Salt Lake had been approached by several of Patsowett's men in the nearby canyon. The Indians demanded Baker give them some gunpowder. When he did, they loaded their rifles and killed him, along with an Indian boy who had been riding with him. Mormons everywhere were preparing for possible attack by the Utes. They asked Walkara which side he was on. The way they asked the question was not friendly.

"Where is Bishop Morley?" Walkara asked.

"In Manti," one of the men responded. Without another word, Walkara jerked his horse around and headed for Manti.

Upon reaching the new town he knew things were worse than he had supposed. Bishop Morley was not his usual friendly self. When Walkara asked him about the increasing conflicts between the Mormons and Utes, the sober bishop didn't attempt an explanation. He told Walkara to just hurry home to Susquenah, that she needed him. Walkara leaped back on his horse and raced home.

He could hear the wailing of his wives before the lodge was in sight. He spurred his horse harder. "Battee, Battee," the women cried as he leaped to the ground and rushed inside Susquenah's lodge.

Susquenah was on her knees, bending over what appeared to be the unconscious body of Battee. As Walkara's eyes adjusted to the subdued light, he realized the boy was not unconscious. He wasn't breathing. The boy was dead. There was an unmistakable bullet wound in his chest. Susquenah was washing and dressing the body of her only child in preparation for burial.

"Did Patsowett's braves kill him, along with the white man, Baker?" he asked, placing his hand gently on her shoulder. Susquenah nodded.

"Battee was going with Baker to Utah Valley to get a load of food," she sobbed. "They called our son a Shoshone snake before they killed him."

Walkara was torn between comforting Susquenah and burying his son, and grabbing his rifle and going after Patsowett. He decided to stay. After the boy was put to rest there would be time to go after Patsowett. There was no hurry. There was no place the renegade could hide where Walkara could not find him.

The next morning Walkara scraped out a grave for his son, in the same clearing where he had buried Tishum Igh a month earlier. It was a large grave, and took most of the morning for Walkara to get it just the way he wanted it. Then he returned to camp.

The boy was dressed in buckskin leggings and an elkskin shirt decorated with blue beads. He was wearing new moccasins and had an eagle feather in his hair. Battee looked properly dressed to begin his journey to the world of spirits.

Bishop Morley and several of the elders had arrived to help with the funeral. They brought shovels in the event Walkara needed help digging the grave.

Walkara climbed upon Battee's paint mare, the same one the boy had ridden across the river into buffalo country, the one he had chased the deer on. Walkara asked the women to hand him his son. Without letting go of the mare's reins, he cradled the body gently in his arms. Turning the mare up the hill he began riding towards the grave, the women, children and white men following close behind.

The other two wives sat on the edge of the grave and wailed as was the Ute custom, as Walkara and Susquenah placed Battee on a buffalo robe in the bottom of the hole. When they were finished they crawled out of the grave. Everyone gathered in a circle while Bishop Morley said a prayer.

He consecrated the grave as the final resting place for Battee, and said the boy would rise in the first resurrection. He said other things Mormons usually said when they buried their dead.

When the bishop was finished, one of the men who had come with him handed a shovel to Walkara, apparently expecting the chief to start covering his son with dirt. Walkara looked at the shovel, then at Morley, then at Susquenah.

Without a word, he dropped the shovel and walked over to the paint mare, which was tied to some oak brush.

"No," Susquenah cried, as he reached for the skinning knife in his belt. "We don't do that anymore." Ignoring her plea, Walkara's hand shot upward in a quick, slashing motion, severing the animal's jugular vein. Too late, the horse tried to jerk away, spraying red blood over the front of Walkara's shirt.

Morley and his companions stared in amazement as Walkara led the now subdued animal over to the edge of the grave. Blood was still spurting from the open wound. Holding the animal steady at the edge of the grave, Walkara stroked the side of its neck to keep it calm as its life ebbed away.

After a few moments the horse dropped to its knees. Walkara waited another moment or two, then gently rolled it into the grave. At first the horse offered some feeble resistance, then gave up altogether, resting its head on the ground beside the body of the boy. Walkara wished he had a few slave children to join his son and the horse, but since he didn't he crawled out of the hole and began throwing dirt on the two bodies while the others watched. The women resumed their wailing.

When they returned to the camp, Walkara entered the smaller lodge, the one he and Susquenah shared, and began getting his things together to go after Patsowett. It felt good to dust off his best rifle and clean the barrel. He checked his powder to make sure it was clean and dry. He made a few more balls.

He had sent the word out to his men the night before, that as soon as Battee was buried, they would go after Patsowett. He told them to wait for him where the trail entered the canyon. Some of his men had been lost to the measles, but he still had a formidable force. They still had the best rifles money could buy, Spanish saddles and good horses.

No persuasion was needed for the men to get ready to ride. They hated the ditch digging and land clearing as much as Walkara did. Riding after Patsowett was more to their liking, and over a hundred men were ready to ride as soon as Walkara gave the word.

As he got his things ready, Walkara occasionally looked over at Susquenah. She was sitting cross-legged on her buffalo robe, staring blankly at the tepee wall. She hadn't said anything since the boy was buried. She hadn't been wailing like the other women.

"I don't know when I will be back," he said, attempting to start a conversation with her. "When you hear I am coming home, you will know Patsowett is dead."

"Killing Patsowett will not bring our son back," she said.

"You do not want me to go?" Walkara asked,

surprised that she of all people would not want her son's death avenged. Perhaps she was concerned for her husband's safety.

"I do not want you to go back to your old ways," she said, choosing her words carefully. "I don't care about Patsowett. I care about you and what is happening to you. You shouldn't have killed the horse. It is like you are forgetting everything the Mormons have taught us."

"I have not forgotten anything," he responded. "I am not Jesus. I am not Bishop Morley. I am Walkara. I had to kill the horse. I have to go after Patsowett." She did not say another word as he picked up his things and headed out to his horse.

It took him only half an hour to reach the place where his men had gathered. They had seen him coming, and were mounted and ready to go when he arrived.

As he pulled his horse to a halt, one of the men tossed him a tin of whiskey. A week ago he would have passed. But today he took a deep drink. The burning sensation felt good in his throat.

Walkara looked over his men. He knew they would be armed and well mounted. He wanted to see what was in their faces. He saw no sadness. He saw no reluctance to go after Patsowett. The men appeared to be as eager as their horses to be on the trail again.

"If any man would rather go back and dig ditches he is free to go," Walkara shouted. The men jeered back at him. No one turned his horse towards home.

"Patsowett, prepare to die," Walkara shouted as he spurred his horse into a full gallop up the trail. Over a hundred warriors answered him with the Ute war cry as their horses plunged onto the trail behind their chief.

Chapter 36

By the time Walkara and his men reached Utah Valley, Patsowett had already been captured, not by Indians, but by Captain George D. Grant of the Mormon army called the Nauvoo Legion. Even as Walkara arrived they were holding a hasty trial, with Dimick Huntington as interpreter.

In the event the tribunal found Patsowett innocent, Walkara stayed close at hand to make sure Battee's murder was avenged. The trial was being held in a new barn, packed with Mormons. There was no room for Walkara to get inside, so he waited out front with his men surrounding the barn. They weren't taking any chances of Patsowett getting away.

Walkara and Arrapeen were leaning against the outside fence of a chicken coop when Patsowett was finally dragged, kicking and screaming, from the courtroom. Walkara knew without anybody saying anything that the tribunal had found Patsowett guilty. He was behaving like a cat who knew it was about to be thrown into a deep lake—kicking, scratching, screaming, biting. Two strong Mormons on each arm made sure the Indian would not escape his just fate.

Walkara and Arrapeen moved aside as Patsowett was brought over to the edge of the chicken coop. The prisoner continued to struggle. He knew they intended to kill him, and he was determined to fight as long as there was any strength left in him.

It was the intention of the Mormons to carry out the execution by firing squad, but the prisoner would not stand still long enough to be shot.

"Just turn him loose in the pasture and we'll all open fire when he starts running," one man suggested. Others cheered their approval.

Captain Grant, who was still in charge, said that shooting the man while running across a field was too sporting, too much like a turkey shoot. An execution by firing squad should be dignified, he said. The victim should face the riflemen, standing still, with or without a blindfold, taking his punishment like a man.

But Patsowett wouldn't cooperate. He wasn't about to stand still for his own execution. Finally, Grant asked if there were volunteers who would agree to hold Patsowett while he was executed. None of the Mormons volunteered for this duty, so Walkara and Arrapeen agreed to do it.

By this time Patsowett had mostly worn himself out, so Walkara and Arrapeen didn't figure he would be hard to hold. Besides, both were larger and stronger than Patsowett. Walkara took the right hand and Arrapeen the left, stretching the prisoner out between them, his back against the edge of the chicken coop. Everyone else backed away as the firing squad lined up about fifty feet back.

"You're only supposed to shoot the one in the middle," someone joked. Walkara didn't think the comment was very humorous. At fifty feet there was little chance of anyone missing the target.

Patsowett continued to struggle as Grant shouted, "Ready, aim, fire." Four rifles exploded, and four balls entered Patsowett's chest. He struggled for a few seconds longer, then went limp. Walkara and Arrapeen let him fall to the ground as both Mormons and Indians cheered.

What happened next came as no surprise to the Indians, but brought horrified looks from some of the white men, several of whom lost lunches.

Almost before Patsowett's body had stopped quivering, Walkara fell on the dead man's chest, made a quick incision just below the ribs, reached in the chest cavity and jerked out Patsowett's heart. Using his knife to slice it free, Walkara held the dripping heart high above his head as he let out his shrillest war cry.

Then, as nonchalantly as if he had just finished an ear of corn and was throwing the cob away, Walkara tossed the heart over the fence into the chicken yard. It rolled a few feet, gathering dirt, then came to a stop. Eight or ten big red chickens converged upon it, squawking their delight at having found something good to eat.

The Mormons for the most part were horrified, but to the Utes, Walkara's behavior was perfectly understandable, believing that a body without a heart could not make the journey to the world of spirits. In cutting out Patsowett's heart, Walkara had not only made a final end to the victim's mortal existence, but had stopped his immortal progression as well. The Indians grunted their approval. The Mormons didn't know what to think of such savagery.

With Patsowett out of the way and Battee's death avenged, Walkara had no intention of returning home. Antonguer, Unkerwenkent and Tishunah were still on the warpath. There was still hell to pay for the recent uprisings.

Walkara was beginning to think that what the Mormons really wanted from him was not an Indian Jesus or sandaled priest and doer of good, but an ally, a war chief, a strong man mounted on a powerful horse and armed with weapons of war. Once again he was

Walkara, the war chief, the greatest of them all.

He was now the relentless avenger against fellow tribesmen who had disturbed his attempt at the good life. Swiftly, and without mercy, he hunted down and put to death those natives guilty of killing Mormon cattle for food, stealing Mormon horses, or even those who voiced threats against the white usurpers of their ancestral lands.

He was the old Walkara once again, strong and arrogant. He avoided Susquenah, and lost interest in the peace council that had been arranged to take place in Manti with himself, Sowiette and Brigham Young. He had more important things to do, like go to the annual fish festival in Utah Valley. There was much gambling, horse racing, and trading to catch up on. Plus, he was thirsty for some good whiskey.

When Walkara and his men left Sanpete, plentifully stocked with goods and horses for trading, those that could followed. The measles had pretty much taken its course by now, though a few poor souls still lingered with fever and rashes. Those that couldn't make the journey were left behind to fend for themselves, or beg their sustenance from the Mormons.

On the journey to Utah Valley, Walkara became so ill that he could hardly stand up. But he wasn't about to let sickness slow his party down, so with the men helping him get on his horse, he continued the journey, weaving precariously back and forth in the saddle.

Upon reaching the Timpanogos River, Walkara fell to the ground, where he remained until his lodge was set up. For the next three days he neither ate nor drank as he fought a high fever and aching bowels. He was in a state of semi-consciousness, his concerned squaws eager to satisfy his every need, knowing that if the great chief died, some of them would have to accompany him to the world of spirits.

On the third day Walkara finally regained full consciousness, only to learn that the trade, games, feasting, and even the talks with Brigham Young had been going on without him. The Mormon chief, having not found enough Indians for peace talks in Sanpete, had come to Utah Valley too. The feeling of being slighted or left out was almost worse than the fever that had turned Walkara's mind to chaos.

Though he could not yet sit up, Walkara accepted a slab of roasted fish from Susquenah and sipped from a gourd of cold water. With the temperature gone Walkara would soon have his full strength back.

After eating, he attempted to stand, but fell weakly back to the earth. Susquenah and the other women rolled him back into his hairy bed. It wasn't until two days later that he could squat on his bed. That's when he asked to see Brigham Young, though he wasn't sure how badly the Mormon leader wanted to see him, now that he had traded his shovel and Book of Mormon for a rifle and battle axe.

Less than an hour later Arrapeen led Brigham Young into the lodge. The husky Mormon seated himself on the buffalo robe opposite Walkara. For a full minute the two chiefs stared into each other's eyes, attempting to sense the feelings in each other's souls. In the cheery blue eyes of Chief Brigham, Walkara could see no malice, no anger, no disappointment.

"The hostilities have ended," Young said. "There hasn't been any violence, not even a cow stolen in weeks. Thank you for helping." Walkara was pleased. It appeared Chief Brigham was not angry with him for his forceful peace-keeping tactics.

"I have a writing for you," Young said, pulling a white envelope from his coat pocket. "It is from Bishop Morley, about you and Arrapeen and Sowiette."

"What does the writing say?" Arrapeen asked.

"It is a recommend. It says you chiefs have been

good Latter-day Saints, that soon, if you continue to be good and serve the Lord, we will ordain you elders in the church.''

Walkara pondered what had been said. It would be something to be an elder, to be wise and mysterious, to go around blessing the sick to rise from their beds. It would be good to be an elder if he didn't have to live like one—digging ditches, clearing land, attending endless church meetings, reading holy books and praying all the time.

"I have been sick," Walkara said, changing the subject.

"I know," Young said. "We have been praying for you. Now you are getting better." Walkara thought how it was with Chief Brigham to turn every situation to his advantage.

"Did Thomas Rhodes deliver the gold?" Walkara asked.

"Yes, he did," Young responded, looking at Arrapeen, not sure anyone besides Walkara, Rhodes and himself knew what had happened. "When we build our new temple and you see a golden statue of Moroni on top, you will feel proud."

"It is good," Walkara responded.

"It is good there is no more fighting between our peoples," Young said.

"We will be at peace because I will kill those who are not," Walkara said.

"You must get well quickly," Young said, changing the subject again. "From Salt Lake City we have brought many things to trade."

"Guns, powder, horses?" Walkara asked. He wanted to mention whiskey too, but didn't. Bishop Morley had already made it clear the Mormons would not ever trade whiskey to the Indians.

"Mostly clothing," Young said. "And some things to eat."

When Young left, Walkara ate more fish. He felt better. While he was eating Susquenah asked if he would like her to read to him from the Book of Mormon. When he declined, she had nothing else to say.

From his bed Walkara knew the trading on the banks of the Timpanogos was going well. He knew the Mormons were not loose or generous when it came to business, but still the trading would be good. He yearned to be up and among his people. Through the night the drums throbbed as hundreds of bare feet thumped and beat on the ancient earth. He could hear the reed flutes, the gourd rattles, the wailing chants of the musicians, and vocalists chanting accounts of mighty deeds in the past. Through the night Walkara's strength continued to increase.

But while the Utes were celebrating, trading and dancing, a band of Shoshone raiders, under cover of darkness, worked their way down the canyon and onto the open flats where the Utes and Mormons were camped. Quietly they cut the tether ropes on a dozen animals, and rounded up another 50. When a Ute herd boy discovered what was happening and sounded the alarm it was too late. The horses were already stampeding towards the canyon.

A good portion of the stolen horses belonged to Walkara. The anger and humiliation of having his horses stolen right from under his nose added new strength to his disease-weakened body.

When morning came Walkara was able to stand and walk. He headed straight for Brigham Young's wagon, where he invited the Mormon chief to come with him, or at least send some men, to avenge the attack and try to recover some of the stolen horses. Some of the stolen animals belonged to Mormons.

To Walkara's surprise Chief Brigham wanted no part of the retaliatory raid. He said to attack the

Shoshones now would only encourage more hostilities. It was time to break the bitter chain of attack and retaliate, and attack again. Someone had to take the first step towards peace.

Not only did Young refuse to participate in the retaliation, but he also tried to persuade Walkara to do the same. He advised Walkara to stay out of Shoshone tribal lands, to peacefully go back to Sanpete to farm, hunt and fish. It was time to stop making war with neighboring tribes.

In tight-lipped anger, Walkara turned and strode away. His body was growing stronger by the minute. He had tried so hard to be a good Mormon, and now the words of Chief Brigham sounded like the words of a fool. There was no way he could let such a blatant act of horse thievery go unpunished. The Shoshones would pay dearly without the help of Brigham Young and the Mormons. Walkara advised his men he would be ready to ride after the Shoshones in the morning. By then he would be strong enough to ride.

"Don't go," Susquenah begged, as he began getting his things together for the raid. He didn't bother to answer her. Brigham Young couldn't talk him out of going after the thieving Shoshones, and neither could Susquenah.

"We are Mormons now, and the prophet has told you not to go," she continued. "We must obey the prophet."

"I go after my horses," Walkara finally replied. "Go back to Sanpete with the others. We will talk when I return."

"If you go now there will be no more talk," she said. "I will return to Salt Lake and you will never see me again."

"I am Walkara, not Bishop Morley. If you don't like that, then go." No more words were spoken.

Early the next morning a hundred mounted

warriors waited for Walkara at the edge of camp. The war chief had one last errand to attend to before departing. Riding up to Brigham Young's wagon, he called to the Mormon chief.

When Young pulled back the canvas flap and looked out, Walkara handed him a smooth willow staff containing twenty-two rings of dried skin.

"I present to you the foreskins of twenty-two Yutah warriors who tried to be good Mormonees," Walkara shouted, his voice ripe with emotion. "But we are still Yutah warriors. Baptism and circumcision cannot change that." Before Young could respond Walkara spurred his horse into a gallop towards his waiting war party.

Chapter 37

Walkara was angry as he and his men rode up Echo Canyon in pursuit of the Shoshone raiders. He was angry with Brigham Young for refusing to take part in the raid against the Shoshones. He was angry at Sowiette's seeming total submission to the Mormons. Lately, Walkara was thinking more and more how nice it would be to push the Mormons out of Ute lands. With Sowiette's help he could do it. It would be good to have things like they used to be, just Indians and wild animals. Let the white men go somewhere else. But he knew Sowiette would never join him against the Mormons. In fact, in such a war Sowiette would probably join forces with the Mormons.

He was also angry at Susquenah. Being a good Mormon was more important to her than being his squaw. He wondered what was wrong with her, what was wrong with him, that they could not live happily together. He was angry at himself for loving her so much, but he knew now he couldn't be what she wanted him to be. He would just have to try to forget her.

As these thoughts were racing though his head, causing his heart to pound and his body to perspire in the cool mountain air, Walkara noticed one of the scouts who had been sent ahead was coming back. By the way the man was spurring his horse, Walkara knew he was bringing important news.

The scout reported that a band of Shoshones consisting of six lodges was just a short distance up the canyon. It didn't appear to be the same group that had pulled off the raid in Utah Valley. The scout hadn't been able to identify any of the stolen horses, plus there were women and children with the group up ahead. Still, they were Shoshones. Walkara ordered the attack.

An hour later the six lodges were burned to the ground. Seven braves and four squaws were scalped and killed. Over a dozen horses were rounded up, along with three women and five children.

Walkara and Arrapeen were discussing whether to continue up the canyon or head for home with the new horses and hostages, when another scout returned from up the canyon. They could tell by the way he was spurring his horse that this scout carried some important news too.

The rider reported that another band of Shoshones had been spotted a few miles further up the canyon. In this band were eight lodges and nearly 40 horses, though none of the horses could be identified as the ones stolen in the recent raid in Utah Valley.

Walkara told Arrapeen to pick two or three men to help him take care of the slaves and horses just captured, while Walkara led the rest of the men up the canyon to attack the newly discovered camp.

"I've got a better idea," Arrapeen said arrogantly, emotion in his voice. "Why don't you pick a few men to stay behind with you to take care of the slaves and horses while I lead the men against the Shoshone camp?"

The comment caught Walkara by surprise. Arrapeen had never challenged his leadership before, at least not so blantantly. The fact that he had done it in front of the men had put Walkara in a corner. To ignore the challenge would be a sign of weakness.

Had any man other than his brother thrown down

317

such a challenge, it would have been a simple matter to raise his rifle and shoot the man out of the saddle.

Walkara looked at his brother. Arrapeen looked back. Neither intended to back down. Both understood that the only thing to do now was to fight. The winner would lead the men. The loser would stay with the prisoners. Walkara knew that even though he was getting stronger every day, his full strength had not yet returned. Arrapeen had picked a good time to fight.

Then the unexpected happened. "I'll stay with the prisoners," one of the men said. It was Ammon, their brother. "If the Snakes put up a fight, both of you will be needed." Looking around at the rest of the men, Walkara and Arrapeen could see in their faces that Ammon's suggestion was what the men wanted. Now was not the time for the two brothers to fight for control of the band.

"Then we ride together, my brother," Walkara shouted, turning his horse up the canyon. Arrapeen and the rest of the men joined him, except Ammon and a companion, who stayed to keep an eye on the prisoners and horses.

Although the second Shoshone encampment was larger than the first, the victory was easily accomplish-ed. The dozen or so warriors in the camp were no match against Walkara's hundred. Nine were killed outright, with three escaping into the brush. Eleven women and nine children were taken captive, along with 37 horses—more than had been lost in the Shoshone raid in Utah Valley.

Flush with victory, Walkara lined up the eleven women captives and began looking them over.

"I lost my Shoshone squaw just a few days ago," he told them. "Who would like to be the replacement? I live in a beautiful valley and have many horses. I am Walkara, the greatest horse thief of them all."

None of the women volunteered to be his squaw.

Chapter 37

They looked down at their feet without responding. Walkara's eyes settled on the youngest and prettiest of the group, a girl of about sixteen. She continued to look down as he walked up to her.

"I think I will make you my squaw," he said, placing his finger under her chin in an effort to get her to look up at him. She resisted his push.

He was about to take her face in his hands and force her to look at him when one of his men began to shout excitedly.

"Arrapeen is driving off the horses," the warrior yelled. Looking away from the girl, Walkara could see that Arrapeen and a dozen companions had rounded up all the horses and were beginning to drive them down the canyon. Some of Walkara's men were running after them.

Walkara ran over to a large rock and leaped upon it. From this vantage point he had a clear view of what was going on. Raising his rifle to his shoulder he took careful aim at Arrapeen's horse. He pulled the trigger. Two or three seconds following the report of the rifle, the horse went down. Some of Walkara's men cheered. Others raised rifles to their shoulders and began shooting the horses out from under Arrapeen's companions.

A few minutes later Walkara's men were rounding up the horses, at first on foot, but eventually all were mounted. Arrapeen and his followers had disappeared into the rocks.

Walkara climbed upon a tall sorrel and began herding the slaves down the canyon while most of the men were herding the closely gathered horse herd. No sooner had Walkara begun driving the slaves than the report of a rifle was heard from the rocks. His horse dropped to its knees, blood gushing from its nose and mouth. Walkara leaped away as the fatally injured

319

animal rolled on its side. More shots came from the rocks as Arrapeen's men shot the horses out from under Walkara's men. Walkara was furious as he headed for cover.

When no one was left riding a horse, Arrapeen's men charged down from the rocks, trying to catch horses with which to make their escape. Whenever Arrapeen or one of his men succeeded in mounting a horse, Walkara or one of his men shot the animal.

The Shoshone captives watched in amazement as the quarrelsome Utes battled each other, always careful not to shoot each other, but mercilessly gunning down each other's horses, until the battlefield was littered with nearly a hundred dead animals. Several of the men had flesh wounds in their legs, but none were seriously harmed. By the time all the horses were dead, most of the men were out of powder and balls.

"Should we now shoot each other?" Walkara asked Arrapeen when the last horse went down. He walked up to Arrapeen, and the two brothers stood facing each other. Walkara didn't feel like fighting. He was exhausted, and thought Arrapeen probably was too.

Walkara half-expected Arrapeen to lunge at him in an effort to finish the fight that he now wished had taken place before the raid. Instead of continuing the battle, Arrapeen began to laugh. Walkara didn't know why, only that hearing his brother laugh made him want to laugh too. Soon everyone was laughing, except the bewildered prisoners.

Arrapeen stepped up to Walkara and reached out, offering to shake his hand the way white men did. Walkara accepted the hand. The two walked among the dead horses, marveling at the foolish waste and destruction they had caused. A man was sent to fetch Ammon and the few horses that were with him. These animals could be loaded with the plunder from the two raids.

Chapter 37

There was nothing to do now but load the pack horses and head for home. Every man would be on foot, but at least they had some slaves to take home. That would allow them to save a little face.

Chapter 38

While marching through the Sanpete to his camp on the Sevier River, Walkara invited Mormons he knew to the upcoming victory dance to celebrate their success against the Shoshones. He went out of his way to make sure Bishop Morley got an invitation too. Never having been to a victory dance, most of the Mormons agreed to come, as much out of curiosity as anything.

The Mormons weren't prepared for what they saw. First, the men prisoners, after their heads were shaved, were forced to dance, carrying the scalps of their dead companions. The captive women and children were paraded in front of everyone too, as they were divided up among the victors, to be kept and used or sold as slaves.

Walkara received the young woman who had caught his fancy in Echo Canyon. Her name was Mary Long Grass. Her father had been a white trapper. Walkara told Morley the young woman was the replacement for Susquenah, who hadn't returned from the fish festival, but had probably gone on to Salt Lake to live with the Mormons. Walkara made the comment as if he didn't care that Susquenah had left him.

While the captives danced at gunpoint, one at a time the Ute braves told and retold the daring exploits associated with the two raids. Many words were used describing the bitter infighting between Walkara and

Arrapeen in which all the horses were killed. While not particularly proud of what had happened, they all knew they had made history by doing that which had never been done before.

The Mormons weren't sure what to think of the behavior of their newest converts. Not only had Walkara and Arrapeen been baptized, but circumcised as well. They had worked hard, digging ditches and clearing land. Their sick family members had been blessed by the elders. They had eaten Mormon food, and attended church meetings. Now they were torturing prisoners of war, and handing out captive women like prizes at a party.

The Mormons were discouraged when they finally returned to their cabins. They realized that to get an Indian into the waters of baptism was one thing, but to get the red man to turn his back on centuries of tradition and behave just like civilized white men, was something else.

After the Mormons went home the adult male prisoners were killed. Men were too hard to handle as slaves, and if allowed to go free, usually came back for revenge. There was no alternative but to kill them.

The dancing and story-telling continued until morning. What little whiskey had been found the night before was all gone now.

When morning came, while most of the red men retired to their tepees to get some sleep, Walkara headed up the hill where his son and mother were buried. He had some serious thinking to do. He felt very much alone. His brothers, Kanosh and Sowiette, were growing fat and content on Mormon beef. Everywhere, even in his own tribe, he could see the formerly proud Ute people becoming beggars, the result of Mormon generosity.

He tried to figure out why it was, with Mormons giving away so much food, that his people seemed poorer. He had fewer horses than he had had in a decade. There was less food in the camp than there had been in many years.

Without Mormon handouts many of his people would starve. Walkara tried hard to figure out what was happening to him and his people. There were many questions and very few answers. As for the Mormons, with his recent behavior he felt he was on the outside now. He had no intention of digging any more ditches, attending any more meetings, or having someone read to him from the Book of Mormon.

He would no longer try to be what he was not, even at the cost of losing Susquenah, the woman he loved more than any other, the only woman who had ever brought him true happiness. He guessed he would never see her again. This made him sad, but he had made his choice on how he would live, and there was no going back now.

He knew he had disappointed Bishop Morley and Brigham Young, but he could not be what he was not. Walkara was a Ute warrior, and that is what he would always be. He would never be a beggar. He would never be a farmer. He would never let someone who attempted to steal a Walkara horse go unpunished.

Walkara realized that for the first time in many years he was poor. While he still had many fine saddles, he had few horses to go under them. There was little ammunition, hardly any food, and few prospects of increasing food supplies by hunting in the nearby hills, where the game animals had been largely eliminated since the arrival of so many hungry Mormons. Yes, the Mormons shared their food with the Indians, but they also hunted game in the hills, leaving fewer wild animals for the Indians to eat.

Walkara realized the only hope for maintaining independence, at least for his own band, was to become prosperous and self-reliant so there would be no need to beg for Mormon food. He would help his people do that.

During the next few days, Walkara dispatched a group of men to California to steal horses. He sent another band deep into Shoshone country to see how many horses they could steal. Others he sent into the west desert to round up all the slaves they could find.

He began making plans to take what slaves were already in camp south to the Navajos. It would be a busy year, with the men gone much of the time, but with some luck his people would become prosperous once again, without help from the Mormons.

While among the Navajos selling his slaves, Walkara ran into a Mexican trader by the name of Pedro Leon, who promised to come to Sanpete the following spring to pay top prices for all the slaves the Utes could round up. No longer would Walkara have to make the long journey to the land of the Navajos to get rid of his slaves.

That winter the Utes increased their efforts to bring in new slaves. Their options for income had narrowed. The raid to California had failed. The Americans had taken control of California away from the Spanish, and had set plans in motion to stop the stealing of horses by Indians. One of the first things they did was establish a permanent post at El Cajon Pass, the only place where large numbers of stolen horses could be brought out of California. In 1850 and 1851, all major attempts to steal California horses failed.

Also, repeated meat hunting trips to the old buffalo hunting grounds became less productive every year due to the encroachment of white settlers and emigrants passing through. Every year it seemed the Ute hunting parties had to ride further, only to come home with less meat.

Slave trading was about the only profitable means of livelihood left, and Brigham Young said he was determined to stop that if he could. In the meantime the Utes intended to catch and sell all the slaves they could get their hands on.

By the time Pedro Leon entered the Sanpete, Walkara and his companions had rounded up nearly 150 slaves, all women and children. It was impossible for Bishop Morley and other Sanpete Mormons not to notice what was happening. As soon as Morley learned about the upcoming visit of Leon, he sent a messenger to Salt Lake to appraise Brigham Young about what was going on.

Leon brought many horses with him. Walkara fully expected to become rich in horseflesh once again. But it was not to be. No sooner had the trading begun than Brigham Young himself showed up, at the head of a heavily armed detachment of the Nauvoo Legion. Pedro Leon was arrested and rushed off to Provo to stand trial on charges of slave trafficking. The Mormons took possession of Leon's horses.

Not knowing what else to do, Walkara and Arrapeen, and most of the rest of their bands, including the slaves, followed the Mormons and Spaniards to Provo, hoping that somehow Leon would talk himself out of the predicament and still be able to buy the slaves.

Such was not the case. The Mormons made it clear to Leon there would be no slave trading in the Territory of Deseret. They agreed to let him go this time, providing he promised never to return to their territory. If he did, he would be arrested and imprisoned for a considerable length of time.

Upon his release by the court, without a word to Walkara or Arrapeen, Pedro Leon headed for home, driving his horses ahead of him. So hasty was his retreat that Walkara guessed this Spaniard would never be back.

"What do we do now?" Walkara asked Arrapeen.

"We have 150 slaves and not enough food to feed them another two weeks."

"Why don't we sell them to the Mormons?" Arrapeen asked.

"They're the ones stopping the slave business," Walkara responded. "They won't buy."

"They will from me," Arrapeen boasted.

"I'd like to see it," Walkara added.

"Then come with me. I'll show you."

Taking a nine-year-old Goshute slave boy by the hand, Arrapeen led him up to a group of Mormons. Several of Arrapeen's helpers herded another seven or eight children behind him.

"You want buy this boy?" Arrapeen asked brightly. The Mormons turned and looked at the boy.

"We don't buy slaves," a husky man replied.

"That's too bad," Arrapeen responded, "because if you don't want him, I don't either." Before the surprised Mormons had a chance to say anything more, Arrapeen grabbed the boy by the heels and swung his entire body in a high, sweeping arc. Then, with all his might, Arrapeen slammed the boy's body down on the hard ground, cracking the boy's skull and killing him instantly.

Tossing the body aside, Arrapeen walked over to where his men were keeping an eye on more of the slave children. Leading forward a seven-year-old girl, Arrapeen asked if there was anyone who wanted to buy her. This time there were many takers. Arrapeen received two horses and one good saddle before turning the girl over to her new owner. And so the afternoon went, the Mormons eventually buying nearly a hundred slave children and women.

While Walkara and Arrapeen were grateful they had figured out a way to get rid of the slaves, they made no pretense that such trading, against the will of Brigham Young, could continue.

For the first time in his life, Walkara didn't know where to turn. Without Mormon handouts his people would starve if they didn't find some way to get food and supplies. Other than horse stealing and trading, Walkara didn't see any other options—at least not until they returned to Sanpete.

Nearly 150 Yampa Utes had arrived from the lands further east. Their leader, Big Elk, had been killed by the Mormon gunfighter Bill Hickman. The band had come to join Walkara, who had had talks with Big Elk before his death. Their talk had been about joining forces to drive out the Mormons.

Suddenly the number of Walkara's followers nearly doubled. In terms of people to lead, he had more power now than he had ever had before in his life.

Walkara turned and headed back to Utah Valley. He knew he would not find allies in Kanosh and Sowiette. His objective was to get the Timpany Utes to join with him and the Nampa Utes in driving out the Mormons.

He and the men who rode with him were camped near Springville, a few miles outside Provo, just finishing talks with some Timpany Utes who wanted to join them, when a Ute boy came galloping up. The boy told them that at a nearby cabin a Mormon by the name of Ivie had just beaten two Ute braves with the barrel of a rifle, and was now clubbing a squaw to death.

What Walkara didn't know was that the two men and the squaw had approached Ivie's wife earlier, wanting to buy some flour with two big speckled trout. The two warriors waited outside the cabin while the squaw went in to make the trade.

When the squaw emerged from the cabin without the fish, and with only a small amount of flour, her husband was furious and began to beat her. Upon hearing the squaw's screams, Ivie crawled out of the hole he had been digging for a well and approached the

Indians, ordering the man to stop beating the squaw. Not about to be told how to treat his squaw by a nosy Mormon, the brave turned and swung his rifle, attempting to strike Ivie with the barrel.

The Mormon caught the cold steel in mid-air, and the two began to wrestle over possession of the rifle. Unfortunately for the Indian the firearm broke in two pieces, the Indian with the wooden stock, Ivie with the steel barrel. Ivie struck the Indian on the side of the head and killed him. The other Indian let an arrow fly into Ivie's side at close range. The wounded Mormon whirled and knocked this Indian senseless too. Then the squaw, seeing what had happened to her men, grabbed a club from the woodpile and went after Ivie, who then proceeded to club her senseless with the same rifle barrel.

Walkara rushed to the Ivie farm as soon as he heard what was happening. He saw the battered squaw weeping over her dead man. The other Indian had recovered. Ivie and his wife had already headed for town, knowing Walkara was camped nearby. The Mormons feared for their lives.

Quietly, Walkara looked over the situation. Then he looked at Arrapeen.

"Is it not time we drive the Mormonees from our lands?" he asked quietly. "Now the Yampa Yutahs and some of the Timpany band have joined us, perhaps we can succeed."

"I would rather die in battle against the Mormonees," Arrapeen responded, "than be a fat and lazy swine at the Mormonee trough, like Kanosh and Sowiette."

"Tonight we will enjoy the taste of stolen Mormonee beef," Walkara shouted. He pulled the battered woman up behind him. "We ride to Sanpete to prepare for war."

When Walkara announced it was time to break

camp and return to Sanpete to prepare for war, he said
he intended to collect some Mormon beef and horses on
the way. War had begun, the one the Mormons would
soon call the Walker War.

Chapter 39

Bishop Aaron Johnson of Springville, upon hearing about Ivie's battle with the three Indians, mustered the local militia. If hostilities broke out, Johnson intended to be ready.

By the time the militia was prepared for action the Indians had left Springville and were heading south towards Payson Canyon. While Walkara kept busy during the night recruiting Mormon cattle and horses to keep his warriors fed and mounted, Arrapeen announced he intended to attack the Mormon fort at Payson at dawn. They agreed to join forces in Payson Canyon, after the attack.

As Arrapeen and his men approached the fortress gate at first light, their rifles loaded and primed, the gate suddenly swung open. One of the sentries recognized Arrapeen and yelled to the Indians to come in for breakfast. Figuring the folks at Payson didn't know war had been declared, Arrapeen accepted the offer, and he and fifty men entered the fort without firing a shot. When the Indian bellies were full of bacon, hotcakes, eggs and coffee, Arrapeen thanked the Mormons for their kindness and got back on his horse. The rest of his men, silent and untalkative, followed him outside the gates. Near the edge of town, spotting an armed sentry, Arrapeen finally sounded his war cry. The Indians shot and killed Alexander Keele. As they raced to catch

Walkara the people at Payson knew the Walker War had begun.

The warriors fled up Payson Canyon, firing wildly at every Mormon within shooting distance. Arrapeen could tell by the tracks in front of him that Walkara was ahead of him with a sizeable herd of both cattle and horses.

After years of frustration Walkara knew now how he would fight the Mormons. After moving his band into the rugged mountains east of Manti, he began giving orders. His plan was patterned after the many successful hit-and-run surprise raids he had executed in California.

He had no intention of seeing his men shot like pigs in a pen, galloping around the Mormon forts, easy targets for both cannons and rifles.

Dividing his men into groups he launched simultaneous attacks on Manti, Springville, Pleasant Creek and Nephi. He quickly discovered his Mormon brethren were different than the Spanish landowners in California. The Mormons had a warning system as effective as Walkara's own grapevine and, more important, they had only to step into their walled cities and forts to be safe from anything Walkara and his men could throw at them. Mormon blood flowed, and horses and stock were taken in sizeable quantities, but otherwise the great raid proved mostly ineffective. The Mormons were not being driven from Ute lands.

In retaliation, the Mormons dispatched Colonel Peter Conover from Provo, with orders to penetrate Walkara's stronghold in Sanpete.

The village of Summit Creek, later Santaquin, was taken and occupied by Walkara, but the Mormons had already departed for safer ground in Payson. The only casualties were two of Conover's couriers, on the way home from Manti to seek orders from Brigham Young.

On July 23 one of Conover's scouting parties

engaged in open battle with twenty Utes only a few miles from Santaquin, and when the gun smoke cleared six of Walkara's men were dead and many more seriously wounded.

On August 10 warriors attacked a Mormon scouting party on Clover Creek. A Lieutenant Burns was wounded, and the horses and cattle were added to Walkara's booty. On August 17 four Mormon loggers at Parley's Park, high in a canyon east of Salt Lake City, felt the sting of one of Walkara's surprise attacks, with two Mormons killed. At Fillmore September 13, one of the town's guards died at his post from a well-placed shot from a hidden brave.

Four Mormons hauling wheat from Manti were shot and scalped on October 1. The next day eight Indians died, and others were captured in a bloody skirmish at Nephi. Two days later Walkara's men at Manti added two more Mormon scalps to their tally. And so the battle continued, with most of Walkara's victories the result of men straying, against counsel, from the safety of their forts.

While the killing and raiding didn't bring Walkara a resounding sense of victory, each separate attack sent a shudder of terror and apprehension through Mormon Zion. While Walkara was still an elder on the rolls of the priesthood, he had become the most infamous elder ever to wear a breechcloth. Children were frightened into good behavior by saying "Walkara will get you if you do not behave."

A tongue-in-cheek editorial in the Deseret News, the official Mormon newspaper, gave Walkara the credit for doing what Brigham Young had never been able to do. For years Young had been ordering, even begging, each community outside Salt Lake City to build fortifications against possible Indian attacks. In many communities the saints had been slothful, at least very slow, in following their prophet's counsel. But less

than a week following the outbreak of Walkara's war
every community was anxiously engaged in building and
strengthening fortifications. The Deseret News gave
Walkara credit for doing a better job motivating the
saints to build fortifications than President Young had
done. The editorial added that Walkara's war—rather
than exterminating the saints—was uniting them into a
common bond.

In all western history there is no greater oddity than
Brigham Young's tolerant and forgiving attitude toward
the aggressive Walkara. Had the Mormon leader
ordered the local militias to go after the Utes, the war
would have ended in less than 60 days. The most aggressive move on the part of the Mormon leader was to
send Conover to Sanpete, but upon arrival of the militia
in Ute homelands, a letter from Brigham arrived,
saying, "We wish it to be distinctly understood that no
retaliation be made, and no offense offered, but for all
to act entirely on the defensive until further orders. . ."

In none of his writings or speeches did Young show
the slightest contempt, disgust, or hate towards the
Indian that had the entire Mormon community hiding in
forts. From those bold enough to venture away from the
forts, scalps were being lifted almost daily. Still,
Brigham Young refused to fight back, even to the point
of angering some of his own trusted lieutenants.

Almost daily, herds of cattle and horses were arriving at Walkara's stronghold high in the mountains east
of Manti. Those driving in the cattle and horses often
had Mormon scalps hanging from their saddles. There
were plenty of guns, lots of ammunition, and plenty to
eat. The Utes waited anxiously for an enemy army to
move against their stronghold. None came.

To many of Walkara's people, it appeared they
were winning the war against the Mormons. But the
chief knew better. Yes, his men were stealing horses and
cattle, and taking scalps almost daily. But the Mormons

were still in their forts, stocked with plenty of food and water. The Mormon women were having babies faster than his men were taking scalps. Even with all the fighting, the Mormons showed no signs of wanting to leave. They seemed content to wait Walkara out, seeming to think that eventually he would tire of stealing their horses and taking their scalps.

It was as if the Mormon leaders didn't perceive Walkara as a real threat. All they had to do was wait, and eventually he would go away. The simple truth was that even though Walkara was taking scalps and stealing livestock, he was still losing the war. The Mormons believed they could whip Walkara with nothing more than time and patience. And Walkara realized that if the war continued on its present course they would be right.

Walkara brooded. He ate very little. He slept very little. His words were bitter, his patience short. Mostly he just wanted to be left alone to wander among the tall aspen trees, to ponder the future of this strange war, a war he would lose to an enemy that refused to fight him, if he couldn't come up with a better strategy.

One day it came. He raced back to camp and called an urgent meeting with Arrapeen, Ammon and San Pitch.

"I now know how we can deal a fatal blow to the Mormons," he said, an enthusiasm in his voice the others hadn't heard in many days.

"We will kill Chief Brigham," he said boldly.

"How will we do that?" Arrapeen asked. "He lives in the middle of their big city. We could never get to him."

"I can," Walkara said. "I will put on my white man's suit and go to their city. I will speak English. I will enter their city from the east. They will think I am a Mericat. I will be free to roam about. I will go to Chief Brigham's house and kill him."

"You will not be able to escape. They will kill you," Ammon said.

"Then you, my brothers, will have to continue the war. With Chief Brigham dead, many of the Mormons will want to leave, perhaps to California where there are no Indians to scalp them."

"Do you know where he lives?" San Pitch asked.

"I was a guest in his cabin the year before they baptized me. I still have my recommend," he added, pulling a wrinkled white envelope from his pocket.

The brothers looked at each other. To kill Chief Brigham would be a great victory, the one they had been looking for. It didn't matter that he was only one man. He was the greatest Mormon of them all.

"If we killed their chief maybe the Mormons would get angry enough to send their armies against us," Ammon said.

"If they would send their armies out of their forts, then we would have a chance to take some of the forts," Walkara responded. "We would have a chance to ambush their armies. Now all we can do is watch their armies in their forts. Anything is better than fighting a bear who refuses to come out of his den. Killing Chief Brigham will bring the bear out in the open where we can kill it."

"You may be right," Arrapeen said.

"If I am killed," Walkara added, "Arrapeen will be chief. I go tonight."

When his brothers were gone, Walkara handed his sharp skinning knife to Mary Long Grass and asked her to cut his hair short like that of the Mericats. She cut it shorter than Walkara had ever worn it before.

When she was finished, she mixed some white clay with water and rubbed some on his face, making the skin whiter, almost like that of a Mericat. Walkara slipped into a white shirt, broadcloth suit, and a silk hat. The disguise was complete. After putting a new

Spanish saddle on one of his horses, he disappeared into the night.

Three days later Walkara was hiding in the oak brush at the head of Emigration Canyon, wishing he had something better than a spirited Spanish horse to carry him into the city. Most of the Mormons had seen him at one time or another, usually mounted on a fine Spanish horse. He thought some men might recognize him from the way he sat his horse. A wagon would be better. Being on foot would leave him too helpless should he need to escape.

For the next day or so he watched wagons lumber by and wondered how he might get a ride without having to answer too many questions. Finally he decided he would approach the next wagon with a story of how Indians had stolen his horse, and that he needed a ride into the city to get another.

The next vehicle to come along was not a wagon, but a buggy. As he left the brush to walk towards it, he realized there was no man in the carriage, only a woman. That was strange in light of all the recent Indian hostilities. He guessed probably the greatest fear white women had was being stolen by Indians.
Even as he walked, he changed his story.

"Ma'am, don't you know the Utes are on the warpath?" he asked. "If they could catch a lone woman they would steal her. I'd be happy to give you protection, providing you give me a ride into town." He nodded towards his rifle to show her he was armed.

"I'll give you a ride into town if you give me one of them gold nuggets you carry in that medicine pouch under your shirt," she responded.

Walkara was stunned. How could this woman know he had a medicine pouch under his shirt? How did she know he usually had a gold nugget in the pouch? Her voice sounded strangely familiar, but he didn't recognize her face, what he could see of it underneath a yellow straw hat.

"Do you know me?" he asked, wondering if he might be better off running back into the oak brush and disappearing.

"How could I forget the man who sold me to the Navajos?"

"Blanche?" he asked, hardly able to believe it was really her, the woman Bridger had sold to Arrapeen. She removed the straw hat. It was Blanche.

"You did not stay with the rancher?" he asked.

"Only one winter, then on to Santa Fe."

"This is a nice carriage. These are fine horses. You have good clothes."

"So do you," she said. "Hardly recognized you without your breechcloth." They both laughed.

"Do you want a ride into town?" she asked.

"Yes," he said, wondering if he could trust the woman he had sold to the Navajos. He stepped into the carriage.

On the way to town she told him how she had made her fortune. Upon arriving in Santa Fe she had written to a New York book publisher, offering to write the story of her year with the Utes. The publisher sent her an advance. She wrote the story in six months. The book was an immediate success. The royalties started pouring in. She had married a few more times, but had finally decided she preferred living without a husband.

"White men are not any better than you and Arrapeen," she confessed with a loud laugh.

"I didn't know there was anything wrong with me and Arrapeen," Walkara said. "My three squaws never complain." She laughed again.

"Why are you dressed in those ridiculous clothes?" she asked.

"We are at war with the Mormonees," he explained. "If they catch me, they will probably kill me."

"Then, why in the world are you going to Salt Lake City?" she asked.

Walkara knew there was no way he could tell her the truth. He paused to think of something else to tell her.

"Some of us are sneaking into the city so we can steal a large herd of Mormonee horses," he finally said, hoping she would believe him.

"Never did like the Mormons," she said. "Think they are the only ones going to heaven. Can't understand why anybody would want to be a Mormon, anyway."

"I am a baptized Latter-day Saint," he said, "and so is Arrapeen. We got circumcised too. I have a recommend from Chief Brigham. It says I am an elder."

"I guess if Brigham Young is dumb enough to baptize a horse thief," she said, "he shouldn't feel too bad if the horse thief helps himself to Mormon horses."

"That's the way I see it too," Walkara added. They both laughed this time.

"Where do you want me to drop you off?" Blanche asked as they entered Great Salt Lake City.

"I want to see Chief Brigham's house," he answered, figuring there was no use wasting any time. "Could you take me there?"

"If you can tell me which way to go."

"I know the way," Walkara responded, pleased he had found a ride directly to the house of the greatest of all living Mormons. Perhaps tonight he could kill Chief Brigham.

A half an hour later Blanche dropped Walkara off at the corner of First East and South Temple, just a short distance from Young's house. Walkara jumped out of the carriage, shook hands with Blanche, and watched her disappear into the night.

A few minutes later Walkara found himself across the street from Brigham Young's house. He had seen no policemen or guards. Apparently the Mormons were not taking the war with Walkara very seriously. Tomorrow, if he succeeded, they would be more concerned.

Walkara hadn't waited more than half an hour when a carriage pulled up in front of the house. Walkara could tell by the stocky build and deliberate walk that the man getting out of the carriage was Brigham Young.

Walkara could hardly believe his good luck. First he was able to get a ride all the way to Chief Brigham's house. Now the Mormon leader was coming home. Walkara raised his rifle to his shoulder, but before he could squeeze off the shot, Chief Brigham disappeared into the home.

A few minutes later, a light went on in one of the main floor rooms. Walkara guessed the man had entered the room to do some business. Carefully, Walkara moved closer to the house. He still carried his rifle, and it was ready to fire. During the course of the evening he had checked the prime many times.

No sooner had Walkara reached the window where the light had just been turned on than another carriage pulled up in front of the house. Walkara dropped to the ground, behind some bushes, before anyone saw him. He waited as a group of men got out of the carriage and entered the home. Walkara knew something important was about to happen in Chief Brigham's home. He didn't know what it was, only that when a carriage full of important-looking men showed up at night, the business had to be important.

When the men were safely inside the home, Walkara worked his way back to the window. The curtains on the inside were not pulled together all the away, allowing Walkara to look inside. He could see all the men, and Chief Brigham too. He could also hear their voices. The thin glass let the sounds carry outside with little trouble.

Chapter 39

Walkara was pleased, but not surprised, when one
of the men said something to Young about Walkara and
Arrapeen. The man was talking about the recent battle
at Nephi, and how the Utes needed to be taught a hard
lesson, that it was time to muster the Nauvoo Legion
and attack the Ute fortress in the mountains east of
Manti.

Walkara listened carefully as the other men voiced
their support to what their leader, Daniel Wells, was
saying.

"Walkara is my friend," Young said.

"Is that why he's trying to scalp every Mormon he
can get his hands on?" Wells asked. There was anger in
his voice. He led the Mormon military, and felt his
hands had been tied long enough.

Young sat down in a big chair. Walkara tightened
his grip on his rifle. The big Mormon was an easy target.
Now would be a good time to shoot. Perhaps there
would never be a better time. Slowly, Walkara began to
bring the rifle to his shoulder.

"How many must die before we begin to give this
savage the beating he deserves?" Wells asked.

"Walkara is a fool," Young responded. "Only a
fool would fight the best friend he's got. If he goes
south the Mexicans will hang him. If he goes north the
Shoshones will scalp him. The only thing he can do is
stay right here with his friends. It is stupid for him to
make war. I am the best friend Walkara has."

Walkara raised the rifle to his shoulder. At this
range he could not miss. He looked over his shoulder to
see if anyone was around. He could see no one. He
looked back at Young.

"I will never make war on Walkara," Young was
saying. "Instead of sending troops against him, I will
send him food and clothing so he and his people will
have a comfortable winter."

"I don't mean to be disrespectful," Wells said, his

voice loud, "but this savage is killing Mormons. How can you ignore that?"

Suddenly Young stood up and walked over to the window. Quickly, Walkara ducked into the bushes. Young stopped in front of the glass, pointing outside.

"Someday a temple of the Lord will stand there," he said. "On top of the tallest pinnacle will be a statue of Moroni, made from pure gold taken from an ancient Nephite gold mine. The Utes believe the gold is sacred and should not be used to make war. In order to get the gold I had to swear before God and angels that I would not use it to make war, and now you want me to use that gold fighting the very Indian who gave it to us. I cannot and will not do that. Let him scalp another thousand Mormons, if he can. I will not lift a hand against Walkara. Instead of armies, I will send him food. And as your prophet and leader I command you to do the same."

Walkara lowered the rifle as Brigham Young turned and walked back to his chair. The big Mormon was still an easy target.

Walkara remembered the promise made by Thomas Rhodes that Brigham Young would not violate the sacred trust concerning the gold. With his own ears, Walkara was hearing Young's commitment to that sacred trust. This Mormon chief was a man of honor.

Walkara also knew that shooting Brigham Young would be a great victory for the Utes. Without Chief Brigham the Mormon resolve to stay in Ute lands might weaken. Without Chief Brigham perhaps the Mormons would go to California, leaving the land of the Utes as it once was.

But the things the Mormon chief had said about the gold and about being Walkara's friend were too strong. Walkara knew he could raise his rifle to his shoulder to kill an enemy. He had done that many times. But how could he raise his rifle to the shoulder and kill a man who insisted he was a friend? If he could not put his own mother out to die, how could he put a bullet in the big Mormon who insisted he was Walkara's best friend?

Walkara turned and walked away, his stride heavy, his spirit heavier. His war against the Mormons had failed, and it was his own fault. He didn't know what else to do. He had been defeated by Brigham Young, without the big Mormon even firing a shot.

As he left Salt Lake City that night, Walkara didn't care if anyone saw him or not. He walked right through the sentries without looking away. They didn't even bother to ask who he was. He would have told them the truth because it didn't matter anymore. Nothing mattered anymore.

Chapter 40

On November 28 Walkara sent his brother Ammon to Parowan with news that he no longer wanted to fight, that he would be willing to meet with Brigham Young in the spring to smoke the peace pipe if the Mormon chief so wished. The Walker War was over. The Mormons were now free to come out of their forts.

Rather than wait for the Mormons to demand the return of their cattle and horses, Walkara put together a herd of the stolen animals and headed south to the land of the Navajos. He wanted to get away from the Mormons and his problems with them. He took Mary Long Grass with him. He didn't know what would happen come spring, but with plenty of stolen horses and cattle to trade, he and his new squaw would enjoy a comfortable winter with the Navajos.

When spring arrived Brigham Young was ready to smoke the peace pipe with Walkara. While the direct attacks had stopped, there was still much uncertainty on the part of the Mormons. With the coming of warmer weather, they half-suspected Walkara would start the war again. Young felt it was important to meet with Walkara and try to work out a solid, lasting peace.

The neutral location the two chiefs agreed would be the best place to meet was Chicken Creek, south of Nephi.

Conducting peace negotiations with Walkara was

Chapter 40

no small matter for Brigham Young. His caravan consisted of 82 armed men, fourteen women, five children, and 34 wagons. His plan was to continue south on his annual visit to the southern settlements immediately following the negotiations. His bodyguards, Porter Rockwell, Amos Neff and George Bean, were riding in the twenty-fifth wagon.

The caravan passed through Nephi early one afternoon, then pushed ahead to make Chicken Creek by dark. Rockwell hurried ahead of the others, hoping to make the initial contact with Walkara and determine if it was safe for Young to enter the Indian camp.

It was still light when Rockwell drove the wagon filled with flour among the Ute lodges. Bean and Neff were following on horseback, driving 12 head of steers. Port warned some of the Indians who reached into the wagon for flour that it wasn't theirs yet.

It was a good sign to the white men when Walkara came out of his lodge to welcome the approaching wagon. Had the chief remained in the lodge, indicating a continuing belligerence towards the Mormons, Rockwell might have recommended that Young not enter the camp.

As it was, Walkara seemed pleased the Mormons had brought so much flour and beef, but he offered no warm greetings or handshakes—nor did he speak English with them, only Ute. Rockwell tossed the chief a bottle of watered-down whiskey, hoping it might warm him up a bit. Without so much as a grunt of thanks, Walkara jerked the cork out and guzzled half the contents of the bottle before removing it from his lips. Rockwell nodded for Neff to bring forward President Young.

The whiskey only made the chief more irritable. Rockwell realized he had made a mistake, but there was nothing to do now but forge ahead. A few minutes later

Young's carriage rolled into camp. It was almost dark now.

Young had brought Dimick Huntington as his interpreter, but Walkara—who was slurring his words by this time—was in no mood to listen. He demanded to know why the Mormons at Nephi were still building fortifications if all the Mormons wanted was peace. When Huntington tried to answer the question, Walkara cut him off, demanding to know why the Mormons continued to kill the deer and elk when Brigham Young had promised the deer and elk would be left for the Utes. When Huntington tried to offer an explanation, Walkara demanded to know why Ivie in Springville had not been punished for killing the Indian, the incident which had started the Walker War.

Walkara carried on in a drunken tirade for the next fifteen minutes. When he finally let Huntington get a word in, the interpreter said the Mormon chief wanted to be a brother to Walkara.

Then Walkara surprised his Mormon visitors by saying if Chief Brigham really wanted to be Walkara's brother, he would share his wives with him, at least for one night, as the Navajos did when he visited them.

"He wants a white woman, one of your wives," Huntington said to Young.

"Perhaps one of the sisters would volunteer," Bean suggested.

"Tell him Mormons do not loan or sell their women," Young said to Huntington, who translated the comment for Walkara. The chief responded by telling Huntington that a man with many wives, who would not share even one, was not a brother to him.

When that was translated, Brigham turned and started walking to his carriage. "I would rather see the war continue than see our women whores," he said. Walkara—as with everything said—understood before the translation was made. Young walked over and stepped up in his carriage, as if to leave.

Young might have faults, thought Walkara, but cowardice was not one of them. As Huntington was trying to translate the last comment, two warriors ran to Brigham's carriage and grabbed the horses. They intended to prevent Young from leaving.

"What's this about?" Young asked.

"They want peace," Rockwell said. "They need the food."

"What about the white woman?" Young asked.

"Offer him something else, so he doesn't lose face," Rockwell suggested. Young stepped out of the carriage and walked back to Walkara, asking the chief if the Utes needed anything besides beef and flour. Negotiations resumed in earnest. The matter of the white woman was not brought up again. Some of the flour was dispersed among the Indians.

By the time the talks were finished, Young had promised Walkara another wagonload of flour and six more beef cattle. Walkara agreed to stop the fighting and stop selling slave children to the Mexicans, a practice that was a growing concern to the Mormons.

Just when it appeared the negotiations might be finished, Walkara said he had one last request. He motioned for Young to accompany him to his lodge. Rockwell followed.

Walkara's second son, a boy of about eight, was stretched out on a buffalo robe, delirious with fever. He was pale and emaciated. It appeared he had been ill for some time. A squaw was wiping the boy's forehead with a damp cloth.

"Make boy well," Walkara said, speaking English for the first time.

Brigham was no doctor, but he knew exactly what to do. Reaching into his pocket, he pulled out a small bottle of consecrated oil, the kind Mormons used when blessing their sick. After gently anointing the boy's forehead with the oil and pronouncing a short prayer, Young called Huntington, Bean and Neff into the lodge. As the five Mormons laid their hands on the boy's head, Young commanded the evil spirits of every name and nature and all sickness to leave the boy. He commanded the boy to become whole again. He ended the blessing in the name of Jesus Christ. Walkara was impressed with Young's confidence in spiritual matters, and the forcefulness of his voice.

"Will the boy get well?" Walkara asked as Young got up to leave.

"Tonight we risked a continuation of war," Young said, "rather than compromise the chastity of our women. The Lord won't let such faithfulness go unrewarded. The boy will be fine."

The next morning the boy crawled out of the lodge and stood up. He was pale and weak, but the fever was gone.

"We brothers," Walkara said as Young climbed into his carriage. They agreed that when Young returned in a few weeks with more presents, they would smoke the peace pipe.

After the big smoke, at which Walkara's brother Kanosh was present, Walkara headed back to Sanpete. Brigham explained to Walkara that he could have any Mormon woman he wanted, provided she didn't belong to someone else and he could persuade her to be his squaw. Brigham had no problem with Walkara taking a white squaw if he found one willing to marry him.

As Walkara's band moved past the Mormon farms at Manti Walkara approached several white women, asking them to marry him. None were interested. Most were terrified, afraid the great chief might sweep them off their feet and carry them into the hills. Walkara concluded he didn't like the way the Mormons selected their wives.

Yes, Chief Brigham had said they were brothers,

but Walkara knew they were not really brothers, nor would they ever become such. After saying a final goodby to Bishop Morley and visiting the graves of Battee and Tishum Igh, Walkara and his band headed for Meadow Creek near Fillmore. The area was far enough south to have mild winters. The risk of being raided by Shoshones was minimal. At the big smoke, Brigham had given Walkara 40 acres of good land at Fillmore, but Walkara had no further intentions of becoming a farmer. He had tried that already, and it just wasn't in his blood to do that kind of work.

Instead he set up a conventional camp near Meadow Creek, where the Mormons hadn't yet claimed the land for farming. There was a good spring, game in the mountains, especially deer, and wild horses on the desert to the west.

Walkara spent many days thinking about the important events in his life. He couldn't help but wonder what he might have done differently. He remembered his first raid on the Timpany camp to avenge his father's death, and how he had taken his first scalp. Life was harsh in those days, but at least a man knew what he had to do.

He remembered his medicine dream, seeing Towats in flowing white robes, receiving a new name and being told not make war with a tribe of white men that would someday settle in Ute lands. He had tried hard to follow that counsel. The recent war was the only time he had acted in violation of the advice he had received from Towats.

He remembered the glory days of the California horse stealing, how he and his men had driven off 5,000 horses in one night. He remembered the many trips to the Navajos, and the buffalo hunts on the prairies to the east. He also remembered the many slaves he had owned and sold. Most of them he had treated well.

As much as anything he remembered Susquenah.

He had always loved her, and always would. She had found the Mormon religion easy to live. He had not. He remembered the many fine horses he had owned, especially the magnificent black he had given to Peg Leg. He missed the adventures. He longed for the simple life where a man knew what he had to do. He felt tired, more tired than he had ever felt after twenty days on the trail. He was being forced to give up his old ways and become like the white men, or Mormons. It had been easy for Susquenah to change, but Walkara did not want to do it, not anymore.

He had tried to make war against the Mormons, in violation of the warning from Towats. Nothing he could do seemed to influence the Mormons one way or another.

Walkara knew he couldn't lead a normal Indian life anymore. Even Susquenah had moved on to Salt Lake City, willing to never see him again.

It was as if his whole world, the one he loved so dearly, was being taken from him, and he could do nothing to stop it. Walkara was trapped. He could no longer live the wandering nomad life he loved so much. California was cut off to horse stealing. The Mormons had put a halt to slave trading. The deer and the elk in the mountains were mostly gone. The buffalo were no longer in the usual places. Walkara concluded it was time for him to leave, but where could he go? In the south the Mexicans would hang him. In the north, the Shoshones would scalp him.

He remembered the medicine dream of long ago, the beautiful place where he had gone to see Towats, how he had wanted to stay there. Maybe life would be better there. After giving Arrapeen instructions for his burial, Walkara crawled into his lodge, rolled up in a warm buffalo robe, became ill, and died. He was 46 years old. No one knew the cause of his death.

The next day the funeral procession began, winding

its way up the canyon into the snow-capped mountains at the head of Meadow Creek. In death, as in life, the greatest horse thief of them all was on a horse, but this time securely tied in the saddle. On other horses were the bodies of his squaws—not Mary Long Grass, for he had instructed Arrapeen to allow her to return to her people, the Shoshones. Two slave children accompanied the procession, as well as a small herd of fine horses.

When word of Walkara's death reached the nearby Mormon settlements, there was a scurrying for the safety of the forts. One of the chief's final requests, since he had been a member of the Mormon Church, was that several Mormons also be buried with him to accompany him to the world of spirits. None of his Mormon friends wanted this duty, and Mormon mothers were particularly watchful over their children for a few days.

Up the icy creek bed, up the face of the mountain, the funeral procession struggled, the wailing mourners with their gourd rattles keeping close, as well as the squaws with digging tools. The procession continued upward into the deep snow.

Walkara's last wish was to be buried higher than any Ute chief had ever been buried. So the procession continued upward until the snow was too deep and crusty for the caravan to go any further.

Arrapeen called a halt to the struggling column. The top of the mountain was but a short distance above them. In front of them was a convenient bald rock for a marker, which forever would be a marker to Walkara's memory. Pointing up the mountain like a jagged finger was a rock slide.

Arrapeen turned and faced the west, the eyes of the mourners turning with him. The vast valleys of Utah, still patchy with winter snow, stretched as far as the eye could see. From his last resting place Walkara would be able to see much of the land he loved so much.

Arrapeen grunted his satisfaction. With the January wind biting at them there was little time to lose. The squaws went to work, clearing out a massive hole in the rock slide. One by one they handed the rocks to each other as they excavated a pit large enough for three people.

When the hole was finished, Walkara was carefully removed from his horse and laid to rest, his head facing outward from the mountain toward the valley below, his cold, stiff hand clutching a last letter from Brigham Young. They covered him with his rabbit skin cloak, now ragged and torn.

The dead women were laid on both sides of him to serve and comfort him on the journey. Food, rifles, bows, steel-tipped arrows, and some of the ornaments he had looted and traded were all tenderly deposited with him for his future needs.

When the rocks were thickly and permanently placed upon the bodies, the squaws rocked up a circular enclosure on top of the grave. The whimpering and frightened Piede children, a boy and a girl, were placed inside. Over the top went freshly cut pine limbs, which were covered with heavy rocks to prevent the children from getting out.

There were no Mormons to toss in the grave, but fifteen horses were slaughtered and covered with rock. Everyone agreed the burial was a good one, worthy of a great Ute chief.

Arrapeen and the mourners began their long journey down the mountain, down Meadow Creek and back to the camp. Except for the crying of the Piede children and the howl of the winter wind, Walkara was left to the solitude of his final mountain retreat.

Epilogue

by Dan Storm

It was two years after Walkara's death that I happened to run into Susquenah. She was still living in Salt Lake City, and had not remarried. It was unusual for an attractive adult woman in the polygamous society of Salt Lake City to be single. I asked her why.

She didn't respond immediately to my question. I didn't know if it was a matter of her being reluctant to share part of her personal life with me, or if she just wasn't sure how to answer my question. I didn't push.

"I don't think I could ever love another man the way I loved Walkara," she responded after a considerable pause.

"Then why did you leave him?" I asked.

"I couldn't live the way he lived, and he couldn't change," she said.

"Did he try?"

"Oh yes, he did," she responded enthusiastically. Suddenly there were tears in her beautiful eyes. "If only for a few months, he tried so hard. He put away his rifle, dumped out his whiskey, turned his horses out to pasture, picked up a shovel and worked like a slave digging ditches. He went to meetings, and every day I read to him from the Book of Mormon. When he prayed for food the rattlesnakes came, and his people were fed."

"What happened?"

"He didn't like it," she said thoughtfully. "To him, stealing horses was better than being a farmer. Perhaps with time he could have changed, but when our son was killed, he had to do something. He returned to what he once was—a bold, daring Ute war chief, the man I fell in love with many years earlier."

She told me how the young Walkara had been taken captive in her Shoshone village, only to escape. She explained how they met, and how she dressed his wounds. She described falling in love with him, and spending that first winter together, just the two of them in a remote mountain valley. She told how she had been taken back to her people, and after that how she and Walkara could not seem to get back together, except during the brief period when he tried to be a Mormon.

There were tears in her eyes when she told me how he had put his mother out to die, only to give in and bring her back in the lodge.

Until talking to Susquenah, most of what I had learned about Walkara had come from the old trapper, Peg Leg, Bishop Morley, and other men. Listening to Susquenah, I saw another side to the great chief.

"Had I stayed with him," she continued, "I would have been buried with him at the head of Meadow Creek."

"I guess it's a good thing you left," I said.

"I'm not so sure," she said suddenly very serious. "I loved him, and sometimes I wish I had made the journey with him to his world of spirits. I still hope I can be with him again.

"After all," she continued, beginning to smile, "he is the greatest horse thief this part of the world has ever seen, and he loved me more than his horses."

I couldn't argue with that.

Lee Nelson Books by Mail

All mail-order books are personally autographed by Lee Nelson

The Storm Testament, 320 pages, $14.95.

Wanted by Missouri law for his revenge on mob leader Dick Boggs in 1839, 15-year-old Dan Storm flees to the Rocky Mountains with his friend, Ike, an escaped slave. Dan settles with the Ute Indians where he courts the beautiful Red Leaf. Ike becomes chief of a band of Gosiutes in Utah's west desert. All this takes place before the arrival of the Mormon pioneers.

The Storm Testament II, 293 pages, $14.95.

In 1845 a beautiful female journalist, disguised as a school teacher, sneaks into the Mormon city of Nauvoo to lure the polygamists out of hiding so the real story on Mormon polygamy can be published to the world. What Caroline Logan doesn't know is that her search for truth will lead her into love, blackmail, Indian raids, buffalo stampedes, and a deadly early winter storm on the Continental Divide in Wyoming.

The Storm Testament III, 268 pages, $14.95.

Inspired by business opportunities opened up by the completion of the transcontinental railroad in 1870, Sam Storm and his friend, Lance Claw, attempt to make a quick fortune dealing in firewater and stolen horses. A bizarre chain of events involves Sam and the woman he loves in one of the most ruthless schemes of the 19th Century.

The Storm Testament IV, 278pages, $14.95..

Porter Rockwell recruits Dan Storm in a daring effort to stop U.S. troops from invading Utah in 1857, while the doomed Fancher Company is heading south to Mountain Meadows. A startling chain of events leads Dan and Ike into the middle of the most controversial and explosive episode in Utah history, the Mountain Meadow Massacre.

The Storm Testament V, 335 pages, $14.95.

Gunning for U.S. marshals and establishing a sanctuary for pregnant plural wives, Ben Storm declares war on the anti-Mormon forces of the 1880s. The United States Government is determined to bring the Mormon Church to its knees, with polygamy as the central issue. Ben Storm fights back.

Rockwell, 443 pages, $14.95.

The true story of the timid farm boy from New York who became the greatest gunfighter in the history of the American West. He drank his whiskey straight, signed his name with an X, and rode the fastest horses, while defending the early Mormon prophets.

Walkara, 353 pages, $14.95.

The true story of the young savage from Spanish Fork Canyon who became the greatest horse thief in the history of the American West, the most notorious slave trader on the western half of a continent, the most wanted man in California, and the undisputed ruler over countless bands of Indians and a territory larger than the state of Texas, but his toughest challenge of all was to convince a beautiful Shoshone woman to become his squaw.

Cassidy, 501 pages, $16.95.

The story of the Mormon farm boy from Southern Utah who put together the longest string of successful bank and train robberies in the history of the American West. Unlike most cowboy outlaws of his day, Butch Cassidy defended the poor and oppressed, refused to shoot people, and shared his stolen wealth with those in need.

Storm Gold, 276 pages, $14.95.

In his quest for gold, Victorio Del Negro takes on the entire Ute Nation, and looses. A historical novel bringing to life the early Spanish history of the Rocky Mountain West, before the arrival of the Mormons.

The Moriah Confession, 182 pages, $14.95

In the heart of Utah's west desert wilderness they call the wind and the mountain Moriah. Ella Tanner went there to write about the senseless slaughter of hundreds of Goshute Indians. Emmett Hays went there to find a healing place for a deep personal loss. Fate brings them together in an unforgettable tale of love and temptation.

Favorite Stories, 105 pages, $9.95.

A compilation of Lee Nelson's favorite short stories, including Taming the Sasquatch, Abraham Webster's Last Chance, Stronger than Reason, and The Sure Thing.

Send orders to:

Council Press

P.O. Box 531

Springville, Utah 84663

VISA or Mastercard orders, call toll-free 1-888-433-5464

Include $1.50 per order for postage and handling.